T0312459

Maybe, Perhaps, Possibly

Joanna Glen's novels include *All My Mothers* and *The Other Half of Augusta Hope*, which was shortlisted for the Costa First Novel Award and the Authors' Club Best First Novel Award. She and her husband live in Brighton.

Also by Joanna Glen

The Other Half of Augusta Hope
All My Mothers

Maybe, Perhaps, Possibly

JOANNA GLEN

THE BOROUGH PRESS

The Borough Press
An imprint of HarperCollins*Publishers* Ltd
1 London Bridge Street
London SE1 9GF

www.harpercollins.co.uk

HarperCollins*Publishers*
Macken House,
39/40 Mayor Street Upper,
Dublin 1
D01 C9W8

First published by HarperCollins*Publishers* 2024
1

Copyright © Joanna Glen 2024

Joanna Glen asserts the moral right to
be identified as the author of this work

A catalogue record for this book is available from the British Library

Hardback ISBN: 978-0-00-860741-8
Trade Paperback ISBN: 978-0-00-860742-5

This novel is entirely a work of fiction.
The names, characters and incidents portrayed in it are
the work of the author's imagination. Any resemblance to
actual persons, living or dead, events or localities is
entirely coincidental.

'Puffin, The Little Hillyard' by Suzannah V. Evans
reprinted with permission from Suzannah V. Evans

Typeset in Minion by Palimpsest Book Production Ltd, Falkirk, Stirlingshire

Printed and Bound in the UK using 100% Renewable Electricity
at CPI Group (UK) Ltd

All rights reserved. No part of this publication may be
reproduced, stored in a retrieval system, or transmitted,
in any form or by any means, electronic, mechanical,
photocopying, recording or otherwise, without the prior
permission of the publishers.

MIX
Paper | Supporting
responsible forestry
FSC™ C007454

This book contains FSC™ certified paper and other controlled sources
to ensure responsible forest management.

For more information visit: www.harpercollins.co.uk/green

For Dad and Richard,
who taught me to love birds.

The world is full of magic things, patiently waiting for our senses to grow sharper.

W. B. Yeats

PUFFIN, THE LITTLE HILLYARD
Suzannah V. Evans
After Francis Ponge, 'La Barque'

Puffin pulls at her tether, shifts from foot to foot, foal-stubborn.

She's just a simple receptacle, a wooden spoon without a handle: but concave and contoured for a captain, she seems to have her own ideas, like a tilting hand signalling maybe–perhaps–possibly.

Mounted, she's docile, glides gently, is easily steered. If she rears up, it's for the greater good.

Left alone, she follows the current and drifts, like everything in the world, towards ruin. A blown wisp of straw.

2017

You can believe in the providence of God.

Free will.

Coincidence.

The mood-swings of nature.

Chance.

Circumstances.

Destiny.

Some of these, or none.

But you can't argue with what happens.

~

Meet Addie and Sol, before they meet each other.

Saturday 22nd April

Addie stares out of her bedroom window, watching the passenger boat shrinking into a grey blur of rain and sea, as her father and brother leave the island. She wonders what it would be like to come and go so freely. She's been here seven years, since she was fifteen, and she badly wants to leave, though this would mean betraying her mother.

'Life on the mainland would be overwhelming for you,' her mother tells her.

Addie wonders if she's ready to be overwhelmed.

Away they go, her father and brother, over the waves, under the leaden sky, rocking and rolling in the huge sea, which grows huger, grows darker, and over and under they go. *I'm over it*, thinks Addie, *and I'm also under it, under her, under the thumb, undervalued, undermined, overworked. Oversexed?* She laughs to herself, then feels like crying.

All she can see through the murk is a dark shape, which is the prayer island of Ora, joined to Rokesby by a strand of rocks. Beyond the crags of Ora lie the Farne Islands, and beyond them, the village of Seafields on the mainland, where her father and brother will get off the boat and disappear into their lives.

Addie sees herself unspooled, like thread, across the ocean, with Rokesby behind her and the future in front of her. Beside her sits her sewing machine on a scratched oak table, accompanied by a chaos of bobbins and a large pair of fabric scissors, blades open like jaws.

This morning, out swimming, Addie saw a shark. She thinks it was a Porbeagle, about two metres long. Her first thought was for Eureka. She dived to her den three times, heart racing with fear, and on the third attempt, she found her curled and safe, the tip of every tentacle safely tucked away.

Nobody knows about Eureka.

Nobody knows about Mac either.

Addie imagines herself like the set of antique Russian dolls she keeps on her bedside table. The good doll on the outside is painted with flowers: she saves un-nested fledglings and fish that flap too far up the beach; makes silk dresses and patchwork pinafores; cooks pretty suppers; arranges paintings on walls; lines pebbles along window sills; attends to the guests who've come here for the peace, smiling like it's a gift to serve them.

Underneath is her bad doll, her siren self, wild, dark-winged and unruly. Only Mac knows this one. Underneath the good doll and the bad doll, there's the sea doll, garlanded with strands of kelp, who loves the dolphins and the waves. Finally, there's the little doll who once loved too much, who shrank to the size of a kidney bean when her grandmother died and lies curled with her hands over her head, still weeping.

Addie's mother said, 'I've never heard of sharks round here,' before going back to her book, lying on the Indian daybed which Addie bid for in an online auction.

Addie's grandmother would have clutched her to her chest and begged her to stay out of the water and away from the shark, and, although Addie wouldn't have been able to comply, she would have felt the ferocity of her love.

The loss of her grandmother, when she was thirteen, has been the calamity of her life. Because when she was born, it was her grandmother who smiled into her eyes, who lifted her up and showed her the sea and the sand and the gulls on the air currents. Her mother left early in the mornings and came back late at night, bringing in the money because, as she said, someone had to. Her father, strangely, was never around at weekends.

Mirror neurons develop within seventy-two hours of a child being born, so Addie heard on the radio, and the face she mirrored was Grandma Flora's.

I love you; I love you back.

I know you; I know you back.

That's how it works.

Smile; smile.

Chatter; chatter.

Love; love.

That's how it didn't work with her mother, who only got into the swing of maternity six years later when her brother was born, blond and idyllic and male – a miniature version of their father, Peter Mimms. Addie watched her father singing into his tiny baby face, and her mother smoothing his cowlick curl, but when she nervously edged over to his crib and put out a hand to squeeze his warm shoulder, he started to whimper, and her mother said, 'Be gentler. He doesn't like that.'

'We'll call him Sydney!' said her mother. 'Where Uncle Ray's living.'

'I thought he lived in Adelaide,' said Addie.

Everything had moved: the furniture from her bedroom was now in the nursery, along with her mother's Winnie the Pooh bear and her father's flying aeroplane which used to hang from her ceiling lamp. And now Uncle Ray had moved too, from Adelaide, from where he used to send Addie postcards.

Addie pulls down the iron handle, and the window shoots inwards, designed this way on account of the wind. Her long auburn ringlets lash her face and fly up around her head.

Addie inherited her Lemming curls from her mother, Martha Lemming, who inherited them from her father, Frederick Lemming, who was an out-and-out sod. His wife, Flora Finch Lemming, was, on the other hand, a perfect angel. It's Grandpa Fred's fault that Grandma Flora is dead. Grandpa Fred is also dead, and that's his fault too. But – terrible to say this about another human being – nobody really minds about him.

The huge sky is framed by a pair of bedroom windows, and opposite them are four tall cupboards, with one door open, revealing rolls of material: netting and linens and velvets and silks. On the floor are Grandma Flora's baskets of fabric offcuts, arranged by colour – blues, reds, greens, darks and pales. Addie's been making patchwork dolphins for the guests, half-heartedly, boredom slowing her to a sludgy, resentful lethargy. She'd rather work on *the wedding dress* because making dresses is her gift, handed down to her by her grandmother.

If Addie could get off the island, she wouldn't go back to where she grew up. The Lemming house was in the tiny hamlet of Beal, overlooking the water and the causeway to Holy Island, but the nearest village was Braxham, half an hour away from Seafields where her father and Sydney are headed in the passenger boat.

The only thing Addie liked about Braxham was *Clara's Costumiers*, an old chapel jam-packed with satin evening dresses; and military jackets; and top hats and bowlers; and silk scarves and silk stockings arranged in slide-out wooden drawers; and fur stoles and mufflers; and curious objects with debatable uses – a whole world of miscellany and mystery in which she and her grandmother could lose themselves for hours.

'The world is full of mystery,' her grandmother used to say to her. 'As long as you know where to look.'

But her mother said, on the contrary, that all mysteries could be explained by the advance of science and the human intellect.

'Well then,' said her grandmother to her mother. 'Tell me what science and the human intellect have to say about love.'

'What good has love been to you?' said her mother.

Addie hated love when her grandmother died. Hated it! She pushed it deep inside her, far away from her heart, and it squeezed itself around the small bean doll in the dark, like amniotic fluid, now solidified to ice.

'Let me help you get a divorce,' Addie's mother used to say repeatedly to Grandma Flora.

'I made a promise,' Grandma Flora would reply.

To which her mother would say, 'It's OK to break a bad promise.' *Her mother said that.*

Addie has made a bad promise, and she wants to – *she has to* – break it.

· · ·

Sol sits in the driving seat, stationary, staring ahead. It's dark outside – and he too has been dark for three whole years, stuck in a hole, with nothing to hold onto, no one to help him out.

Peggy, he thinks, *I'll call you Peggy – as long as it's not bad manners to name a vehicle after a dead person.* He remembers childhood summers climbing down the cliff from Aunty Peggy's Cornish garden to go rock-pooling with a net, the thrill of what lay ahead filling his body with dopamine. He feels something similar now.

It's five o'clock in the morning: he's getting on the road early for what will be a long drive to his new life. He has a horrible feeling that his new life won't last, that some disaster will befall him. None of us knows the future, he tells himself, and perhaps this keeps us on the ball.

He looks in the rear-view mirror, puts his hand through his wavy dark hair and ingests the beauty of his new campervan, reconditioned, light blue and cream, with a split-screen bay window and a pop-top roof, a pull-out bed, teak locker-cupboards, a tiny fridge, a hob, a fold-away sink and brand-new curtains in a neutral seagull print.

His mother's curtains, still up at the vicarage, are not so tasteful: a riot of colour, toucans on stripes, kingfishers on branches and Frida Kahlo with parrots on her shoulders. Would his mother love or hate his campervan? Would she say it was *showy*? It is probably showy in a faux-modest kind of way, meaning it's not a Range Rover, but cost a fortune all the same. His father taught him, for biblical reasons, to be suspicious of shiny things.

Is the campervan an acceptable use of Aunty Peggy's money, money which had to be secreted into his bank account without his father or sisters knowing?

Sol takes a swig of water, and puts Lincoln into Maps, because why not? He plans to meander up the coast, diverting to the North Yorkshire Moors, on his way to Seafields, from where he'll take the boat to Ora and get away from his father and from Bee and from the horror of it all. In fact, from his sisters too, from his best friend, Tim, from the other teachers at the school where he's been covering a maternity leave, from old friends on his WhatsApp groups, who ping their newsy happinesses into his pocket. His sadnesses are not so newsy. He does not ping them into other people's pockets.

But today his happiness has doors and windows and an engine and a brown leather bench seat with cream piping where three people could sit companionably alongside each other, if there were two people he'd like to be taking with him. There aren't. This is always on his mind, whatever else he's thinking: the fact that he could have come this far without anyone to take with him.

Sol lives so deeply inside his mind that he's started to wonder what else he is other than his knowledge, his thoughts, his perceptions and ideas. This makes him feel strange and insubstantial. Half a man.

He takes his cereal bar and eats it, holding out his hand to catch the crumbs, before putting the key in the ignition.

Do not store up for yourselves treasures on earth, he thinks, involuntarily, guiltily, *where moth and rust destroy and where thieves break in and steal.*

But, and this is the point, *store up for yourselves treasures in heaven.*

Sol knows the Bible pretty much off by heart.

His father quizzed and tested him relentlessly through his childhood, and, like many children of unreasonable parents, he wanted to impress him, also relentlessly. Earthly treasure is one among hundreds of white lines that his father imposed on his life, each marking a precipice over which he might fall at any moment – *into the abyss.*

When Sol's father used to hold forth lengthily, his mother would stare out of the window, smirking slightly and fixing her eyes on the birds that came to the garden to feed on the seeds and nuts she provided in wire containers, or the suet balls attached to trees. When he'd finished, she'd take up her journal and silently add new bird entries beneath the day's date.

Goldfinch.

Nuthatch.

Green woodpecker.

This was a technique Sol learned from her, and as his father sermonised over the kitchen table, although he didn't dare smirk like his mother did, he too gazed at the birds in the garden, feeling himself flying away from his words, like a kite. But the thing was, however high and far he flew, his father was always there holding the end of the string. Until January of this year, when his father sent him a letter.

The letter.

When he finished reading it, he took a deep breath and cut the string.

He puts the windscreen wipers on full, as the spray shoots from his tyres.

'Mum,' he says, aloud. 'I'm going to the prayer house on Ora where you went before you got married.'

Tuesday 25th April

Here's Addie, three days later, down at Bird Beach, staring at the grey waves, whipped up by the wind, battered by the rain. This is the tail end of a storm which began just after her father and Sydney left. Before he got on the boat, her father told her mother that he loved her. Her mother looked as if she'd received a blow to her head.

Addie's been examining love closely for some time, and it's not to be trusted. Her mother and father love each other, but can't find a way to live in the same house. Her grandfather was supposed to love her grandmother, but he went about making bruises on her face and on her arms, and in the end he inadvertently killed her. Her brother doesn't love her, and as a result, she can't bring herself to love him. Is it that the age gap is too big? Did her mother want him too much? Were they always too different? Sydney went to school and had friends and played football. So was he too normal for her, or she too abnormal for him?

Her mother loves Sydney with all her heart, but Sydney doesn't love her enough to live with her or keep her surname. No, he recently changed his surname to Mimms, after his father, which made Addie consider changing hers to Finch, after her grandmother. Her mother took revenge on Sydney this Easter by calling him *Mimsy*, which means feeble. She also made him fudgy chocolate brownies which are his favourite. Pushing him away, reeling him in – this is the way of her love. She never bakes brownies for Addie. So does she love her? Addie doesn't think so. Or not enough. Or not as much as she loves Sydney.

Her mother likes to goad her father when he visits. She goads everyone she loves, which shows that love can be mean and unpredictable, which you wouldn't expect of it.

When her father arrived at Easter, her mother said to him, in the goading tone of voice, 'So what's going on with your *upcycling*?'

Her father said, 'I sold a couple of the chairlift chairs.'

Her mother said, laughing in a not very nice way, 'Not the cable cars?'

Then she stood up and kissed his cheek.

Her father is always looking for ways to make money, but he finds it hard to stick at things. Her mother likes to point this out.

Sydney is sixteen now, tall, fair and blue-eyed like their father, but he's dyed his blond hair black which makes him look ill. His face looked blank when he arrived, and all he wanted to do was play dark computer games, rather than spend time with his mother, who misses him so badly she sometimes weeps just thinking of his face.

The more you examine love, the less you understand it. You can say you don't want to get wrapped up in it at all, at the same time as knowing that it will always be after you. And if it isn't, that's worse.

Love doesn't seem to be after Addie.

And that, she tells herself, is exactly how she wants it.

On Easter Sunday, Addie's mother scattered some chocolate eggs around the garden in honour of Grandma Flora and/or the resurrection of Jesus and/or the arrival of spring. Then she went inside. Addie and Sydney half-heartedly picked them up and put them in

Grandma Flora's basket. Then Addie asked her father if she could perhaps come and stay with him and Sydney in Durham for a holiday, but her father said that her mother needed her too much here.

'Besides,' said her father. 'You've always loved Rokesby.'

(Is it easier perhaps to love a place than a person? It probably is.)

'I had to love Rokesby,' she replied. 'Someone had to stay.'

'It wasn't right for Sydney.'

'What if Rokesby isn't right for me?'

'I think it *is* right for you.'

'Surely I should be the judge of that.'

'Your mother came here for you,' said her father. 'To give you a new start. After all the bullying.'

'The bullying?' said Addie. 'I was at primary school!'

'Well, whatever,' said her father, which is how he likes to end conversations.

The water roars up Bird Beach, scattering shells in their thousands, stranding starfish, leaving tangles of jellyfish translucent and hopeless on the black rock. Addie wonders if Robert and Mac will be able to get the guests across in the passenger boat on Saturday. Mac is Robert the boatman's son, the same age as Addie, twenty-two now. When they bumped into each other unexpectedly in the harbour the week she arrived on the island, both of them teenagers, she felt curiosity like pain in her body, but wrapped up inside the pain was hope, longing, desire and other things that don't necessarily have names.

On the radio, this morning, Addie heard a woman saying that her body was an ally through which she experienced and expressed herself. She pricked up her ears. The woman said her body parts whispered to her. Addie's do too. Sometimes they shout and scream. The woman said *embodiment* was a conduit to wholeness. Addie stares out at the sea, enjoys the wind on her face, and she feels embodied, but not whole.

14

When she bumped into Mac for the second time, she had the strange pain again, and he said 'Hi' in a way that meant something else, and she said 'Hi' in the same way, and he said 'Shall we walk?' They walked, and wrapped up in the walking, as Mac took her hand, and she took his, was the hoping and the longing and the desiring and the other nameless things.

Addie stands on the beach, looking over at the harbour, where the guests will arrive on Saturday, as long as the weather calms. She must get back and sew, while she still has free time. There've been no guests for a couple of weeks to facilitate a *family Easter*. Her father fished; Sydney played computer games; her mother slept; Addie cooked and went on making the wedding dress. They were all escaping, she sees that now, in the fishing and the computer games and the sleeping and the sewing. Because love spends half the time trying to run away from itself.

Addie goes into The Retreat and heads upstairs to her bedroom, and as she sews, she thinks of Star's sister, who's paying the sort of money for this wedding dress that suggests she has very high hopes for love.

'We'd pay you to do it,' said Star when she was a guest at The Retreat.

'Pay me?' said Addie before saying no, nervously, and then yes, nervously.

She knows that she comes across as nervous.

It is one of the ways the people who knew her in Braxham would describe her, alongside *shy, self-contained, eccentric, stand-offish, weird*. Addie thinks these traits might be inevitable for people who are disappointed by other people. Perhaps the people who knew her in Braxham might add that she was precociously gifted at swimming and art and sewing, if they were feeling kind.

Addie's grandmother made haute couture dresses in Paris and London before she married Frederick Lemming and ended up doing sewing jobs for Clara at *Clara's Costumiers* in Braxham, not charging nearly enough to refashion wedding dresses, make christening robes from antique lace and ball gowns out of vintage silk and velvet.

Grandma Flora and Addie dreamed up mad designs for their own clothes on the kitchen table, matching outfits, accessorised from the bargain bin at *Clara's Costumiers*.

'Peas in a pod,' said Addie's father.

'Nutters,' said Addie's mother.

Addie began by helping her grandmother, and then off she went alone, from skirts to pinafores, from pinafores to dungarees, from dungarees to tricky dresses, and from tricky dresses to wedding gowns, this one for Star's sister with a fitted bodice and a skirt which bursts from a thick waistband like the layered petals of an upside-down tulip. Now she must make the silk bolero.

She gets up to stretch, and stares at the moody sky: so dark and turbulent, clouds hanging low over the harbour, just as it was when she arrived here for the first time. The whole way over, Addie's father and Sydney had sour expressions on their faces, which only soured further when they opened the door to their new home, a mouldering hotel (once a monastery) where mice had gnawed cables and made nests inside the foam innards of sofas.

Addie looks out beyond the harbour where *the bridge* would be if it wasn't so wild. The bridge is a raised stone road which passes over the rocks joining Rokesby to Ora, two islands which are in fact one land mass. The bridge is submerged under the wild grey waves today, but when the sea calms, it will reappear, and it will be like seeing the face of an old friend.

Not that she has an *old friend*, though she may have two newish ones, alongside Eureka, that is. Eureka, though not a human, is definitely a friend. Mac isn't.

If you pass the bridge to Ora on your left and keep following the contours of Rokesby, you come to the meadows with daisies and dandelions and buttercups and bits of old ruins in the long grass which are lethal for stubbing toes. Beyond is Penny Cove.

Maybe, Perhaps, Possibly

At the top of the island live three generations of Rokesby families, the Hulls and the Dempsters, bohemian and resilient, with free-ranging children and free-ranging animals – hens and pigs, and a llama which pops up in unexpected places. Like Grandpa Dempster, who's lost all his inhibitions. Addie's mother calls him Grandpa Dementia, which Addie hates. Everyone's a bit frightened of him, but she tries not to be, because the real him is still inside him trying to get out. Both families grow a range of vegetables in polytunnels which the islanders can buy from the trestle table shop. Addie falls between the generations of Hulls and Dempsters, and has found no friend among the Rokesby residents.

All along the top beaches are the lumbering seals, and beyond, at the top right of the island, is an estuary where the wading birds feed in their thousands. If you keep walking, you turn the corner to see the sea rushing up between the rocky breeding columns and thrusting itself in huge spraying fountains over one hundred feet in the air.

Addie likes to sit here on an orange blanket of *amsinckia intermedia* flowers, which people say were brought by mistake in poultry feed by an old lighthouse keeper. She watches the birds flying in on the wind for the breeding season – fulmars, razorbills, shags and puffins – and she feels the comfort of their return, as if they were family. Family like Grandma Flora.

If only she'd fly in too.

She won't.

She's irrevocably gone.

Opposite the crumbling lighthouse is Brother Andrew's white cubed chapel out on the promontory, and from there you're back where you started at The Retreat, Addie's home, or at least the place she lives. *Home* was Stone House in Beal, where she lived until she was fifteen, where the sea came up the lawn, where daffodils grew in circles around the apple trees, where Holy Island stood guard across the causeway.

17

The dark clouds burst and rain lashes, on the diagonal, whipping at the red stone walls of the hotel and battering its glass window panes.

. . .

Sol has left Lincoln and is now en route to Bridlington. He stops at a petrol station for a pee. After peeing, he takes out some cash from the cashpoint because the monk in Durham said that there was a tiny shop on Rokesby with basic supplies but no card facilities. If the weather is calm, Rokesby is joined to Ora, and you can get across.

Sol made all the arrangements with the monk in Durham because Brother Andrew, who lives in the hermitage on Ora, has no mobile phone or computer, only a landline for outgoing calls, which he was persuaded to accept for emergencies. He is called to seclusion, the monk explained, and will never leave the island – following in the footsteps of St Cuthbert of Lindisfarne, the Anglo-Saxon monk – although his calling includes a pastoral duty towards Rokesby inhabitants and the prayer retreat guests on Ora.

As Sol folds the slightly rubbery new notes into his wallet, he tells himself that this is a new start, a new start on the back of his father's letter, which brought on a kind of existential calamity. *Perhaps we need an existential calamity*, he thinks, *to change our lives.* He doesn't want to think about the letter.

In the car park, Sol sees a jay on a lamp post, its electric blue wing-patch lifting his spirits because every living creature is an epiphany. You can't grow up on the Norfolk Broads, as he did, and not think that the world is beautiful. It's really only the people in the world who are problematic, although they're supposed to be very good, so says the *Book of Genesis*. And plants and animals are merely good.

Plants and animals, good, and people *very good*?

Is that right?

These are the kinds of conversations Sol enjoyed with his mother, but which are not permitted with his father, who becomes stressed by the suggestion that the Bible is in any way puzzling or inconsistent or available for discussion.

Sol forces his father away, but his sister, Leah, bursts into his mind, Rachel not far behind – they're twins, and Rachel is always trying to catch up. He wonders when his sisters will notice that he's disappeared.

Leah, though only twenty-four, is already martyring herself for her twin babies and her older husband, Alan, who is shorter than she is, and balding, and rich. Rachel sees possible husbands around every corner, but the possible husbands don't see her. This, as she sees it, is the tragedy of her life.

When his mother got pregnant, Sol couldn't understand why he wasn't enough for her. He soon found out there were *two girl babies* coming to take his place. His mother said, 'You'll be able to play with them,' and, 'They'll probably love Lego.' But the two babies, when they mysteriously arrived, showed not the slightest aptitude for Lego, spending their entire time screaming and being sick. As they grew older, Leah and Rachel wrapped their arms around each other and put on fairy dresses and made up dance shows that enchanted their father.

They went on enchanting their father as they grew older and turned into the sort of women he would have liked his wife to be – domesticated and biddable.

'Your mother's spiritual gift is hospitality,' his father used to tell anyone who would listen, very happy for her to have been allocated this boring little gift, which didn't appeal to him at all.

Hospitality wasn't her gift, and in the end, she was freed from it because she found it hard to move about. The women from her prayer group came and cleaned the garden room (where for years they'd kept the badminton nets and the inflatable paddling pool), turning it into a downstairs bedroom. They'd each made her a cushion in a bird fabric – starlings and storks and swans – and these they scattered about, staring at each one intently, moving it to the left, to the right, until they were entirely satisfied with its position.

Sol's mother lay with her feet in his lap as he marked his students' books, and it was as if all that was peripheral had been sloughed off by her illness, and he felt a profound joy that has eluded him ever since.

Once she was ill, his father was always yelling upstairs to Leah and Rachel to see if they could rustle up a light lunch or a cup of tea or some cakes for his staff meeting. When one day Sol decided to bake some cupcakes with his mother's recipes to cheer her up, his father looked pained by such a failure in his masculinity.

Sol took his mother a cupcake in the garden room, but he found it later behind a vase with one bite-shaped hole in it because she'd lost her appetite and didn't have the heart to tell him. Looking at the indentations of her teeth in the icing made him think of her skull underneath her skin. He still doesn't want to think of her skull or her rib cage or her pelvic bones because bones don't make a person, and this is why he never visits her grave in his father's churchyard. He prefers to bake from her recipe books as a way of still smelling her.

Leah told him they should all pray daily that their father would fall in love again and find another wife, because it would be very lonely being a vicar on his own.

So that's what Sol did.

He's always tried to do what he's told.

It's nearly broken him.

Saturday 29th April

As Addie threads her needle with cream cotton, she wonders if love ever works for adults the way it worked for her and Grandma Flora. She hopes it might for Star's sister and whoever she's marrying, and she sews that hope fervently into her sleeve.

'Why didn't you marry Daddy?' Addie asked her mother soon after Sydney's birth.

'He never asked me,' she said.

'Where does Daddy go?' she asked every Saturday morning, week after week after week, until her mother, exasperated, said, 'We'll tell you when you're an adult.'

Addie wrote this on a piece of paper and asked her mother and father to sign it, and at her eighteenth birthday dinner in Rokesby, with her parents, when Sydney had opted to watch television instead, she took the note out over pudding.

Her father took a deep breath.

'I was married,' he said.

'You *are* married,' said her mother, her spoon paralysed in the air, dripping cream.

'My wife . . .' her father began.

His wife?

Did her father have a wife who was not her mother?

'My wife Pattie was involved in a terrible car accident,' said her father. 'She's in a persistent vegetative state – basically a coma.'

Addie couldn't get any words out of her mouth.

'I'm technically still married to her,' said her father. 'But as you will understand . . .'

He tapered off.

'Though Pattie probably doesn't know I'm there, I feel it's right to be with her at least part of the week,' said her father. 'I was always honest about this with Mum.'

'So no white wedding for me,' said her mother. 'I still dream about a wedding dress, with layers and layers of tulle, like a ballerina.'

Like a ballerina? How unlikely. Her father had a wife? How even more unlikely. How strange and cruel love could be. Addie started to clear the table, stiff with shock, and soon after that, everyone went to bed, the champagne for her eighteenth birthday toast remaining unopened on the sideboard.

So now she knew: it was impossible for her mother to marry her father in Brother Andrew's sugar-cube chapel at the end of the promontory, which had always seemed something that might benefit them as a family.

Her mother's life hasn't exactly gone to plan, Addie tells herself as she sews the wedding dress for Star's sister, and that's probably why she's so difficult. You'd imagine that *having* such a difficult parent would make you try everything not to *be* one, but maybe this is harder than it looks.

• • •

Sol drives along the rainy A1, finding himself hypnotised by the long straight grey road. He stops at a service station to refill his water, and his phone rings. It's his sister, Leah. Again.

'Will you please ring me back?' she says crossly on voicemail.

Sol will not ring her back.

Leah phoned him in January, the day after his father's letter arrived.

'God doesn't make mistakes, Solomon,' she said. 'You know that.'

'It wasn't God who made the mistake,' said Sol.

'We must honour our father,' said Leah.

He and Leah haven't spoken since, which is fine with Sol.

He's going to leave his phone in the campervan when he goes to Ora (a welcome requirement of the retreat) and if his sisters manage to get hold of Tim, he'll say that Sol's gone to the Greek Islands to meet women and drink ouzo (which is what he's told him, trying to act worldlier than he is), and they will be so horrified that they won't bother to try to find him anyhow.

He laughs aloud, and feels guilt rising up through his chest, as he holds his ham sandwich in his right hand, feeling for his mother's green feather in his pocket with his left. The barbs are clumped together from so much touching.

He will cover you with his feathers and under his wings you will find refuge.

His mother's favourite verse. When his mother was ill, Sol read Psalm 91 aloud, over and over, reminding God to rescue his mother and protect her and satisfy her with a long life, as was stipulated in the verses.

At the service station, Sol buys three small plastic water bottles, guiltily, because there's nowhere to fill his bottle and he has an irrational fear of being thirsty. He also buys a large red tin of assorted biscuits because it's on offer, and his mother used to buy those exact ones. Looking at the tin gives him an odd buzzing feeling inside.

As the girl at the till holds out the card machine, he holds out his debit card and notices a light coating of dark hair on her upper lip. He thinks of his gangly legs and his concave stomach. He always feels he should be bigger and more muscular, but he's never had sufficient interest in, or confidence for, the gym.

Twenty-six is too late to start going to the gym. Too late for other things he hasn't done – *two things in particular* – but he doesn't want to think about either of those right now.

The girl at the till has beautiful green eyes.

He'd like to tell her that.

But, for all sorts of reasons, he doesn't.

• • •

Addie's mother knocks on her bedroom door at the same time as poking her head around it – a habit which Addie finds infuriating.

'Are the dolphins done?' she says, without smiling.

'Nearly,' says Addie, putting down her sewing.

'So why are you working on that?' says her mother. 'If you haven't finished the dolphins?'

'Because,' says Addie, looking up, her shoulders aching, 'I'm getting paid for this.'

'The tyranny of money.'

Her mother likes to remind her that she's removed her from the trap of the capitalist system, whereby children are moulded into money-making adults, flogging back and forward to offices on commuter trains, saving for mortgages in substandard flats, sacrificing themselves to bring up children they will never see.

'I freed you,' she likes to say.

Addie's always been grateful that she was never forced to pass an exam or an interview in order to make her way in the world, but now she wonders how grateful she should be because she's *not* making her way in the world at all. She remains *out of the world* entirely, and is that really freedom or captivity? She wonders if she'll ever be brave enough to say this to her mother. She also wonders if there are other mothers who trap their children, perhaps in other ways.

Her mother again glares at the dress, as if she fears it might get up from Addie's lap and come towards her.

'That Star!' she says, with some disdain. 'I can't believe she's got you making her sister's dress.'

Addie, potentially, has a *friend and a purpose on the mainland*, and this, she sees, is a threat to her mother, who wants her here, in some illusion of togetherness, who wants The Retreat to function without the burden of her doing too much in the way of work, too much that she doesn't fancy doing.

There was another guest who liked Addie more than her mother, a birdwatcher from Alnwick called (amusingly) Robyn. Robyn the birdwatcher was quiet and knowledgeable and pessimistic about the future (her own and the world's). She had dyed green hair and her favourite birds tattooed up each arm.

'It wasn't worth the two thousand pounds,' she said before she left the island.

Addie tried to look apologetic at the same time as self-assured (a tricky combination), but she was horrified by the price: *two thousand pounds for a week*. Her mother told Addie, when she questioned her, that The Retreat was *reassuringly expensive*.

Robyn gave Addie her address and phone number when she left and said, gloomily, 'You know where I am.' She sends a Christmas card. Addie sends one back.

Her mother thinks Robyn is a drip, and not a threat to her in any way. But Star, with her startling blue eyes and her long silver plait, Star who travels the world, flying to and from her holiday cottage in Norfolk, which has its own private broad – she's quite a different matter. Star, the swimmer, who is, gloriously, a professional mermaid, though Addie had no idea such a job existed, who's won competitions and featured in aquarium shows and celebrity parties in Hollywood and blockbuster films such as *Underwater*.

When Star came to Rokesby, the first thing she said to Addie was, 'Are you OK?'

Addie said she was, but she couldn't stop thinking about the force of the question.

Star introduced Addie to monofin swimming, which seemed to irritate her mother. She told Addie that she was prodigiously talented, that she could use her considerable gifts by taking part in competitions. She could introduce her to the mermaiding world if only she'd leave the island.

Leave the island?

Addie memorised Star's phone number on the spot.

'Do you hear me?' said Star. 'Your life doesn't need to be contingent upon your mother.'

Bang!

Did her mother sense the betrayal?

And what a word!

A new word.

Contingent.

Addie took to it immediately, though it was probably too flashy for her to use. She's always been nervous around words, and she keeps conversations short.

Addie went only briefly to school. She arrived wearing socks embroidered with bees and a patchwork pinafore her grandmother had made from offcuts of old curtains, and once in the classroom, she started to lick the backs of her hands in order to console herself with the taste of salt. She'd taught herself to swim in the sea which lapped to the end of her childhood garden, deepening in the hours before and after high tide, and the water was her passion and consolation.

At breaktime, Dylan and Lorna cornered her in the playground and told her to lick her own face. The rest of the class watched, as Dylan said, 'Lick your left eye, Weirdo,' and Lorna, 'Now your right nostril.'

When her mother took her out of school two years later, Dylan and Lorna would regularly turn up at the Lemming house, putting notes through the door addressed to *Weirdo, Weirdo House*, unable to be fully happy, she realised, without someone to hate. She made a pledge with her grandmother not to hate back. Not even to hate her grandfather, but to try to understand him, which means she mustn't, on principle, hate her mother, even on the days that she's hateful, and hateable.

'But,' says Addie, to her mother, wondering if she will dare.

'But,' she says again.

'But what?'

'You didn't free *yourself* from the tyranny of money, Mum.'

'The Retreat is our enabler,' says her mother. 'And I cover everything you need.'

This is true.

'Can you please finish those dolphins?' says her mother.

'Do you think I really need to make them?' says Addie, hearing the tremors underneath her voice. 'Is it a bit ridiculous? Do you think the women throw them in the bin when they get home?'

'Rokesby is famous for its dolphins,' says her mother. 'You have such a way with them, and every little personal touch makes a difference.'

She will not be argued with. Addie knows this.

'We're such a great team,' says her mother.

Here's how their teamwork divides: Addie's mother takes charge of the computer, sighing and acting as if it's the hardest job on earth to send a few emails and update her occupancy spreadsheet. She provides *inspirational talks* on living your best life as well as ornithological lectures, and also life-coaching and yoga, should guests want it, payable by the hour. Addie does everything else: the cooking and the cleaning and the online shopping for provisions, and also the bird walks and the art and sewing classes, which are provided free of charge.

Her mother leaves the room. Addie stands up, and the floor seems unstable. She didn't know loneliness could make you dizzy, and she wonders if her body is whispering to her (like the woman on the radio said) that the time has come to leave the island. Actually do it.

She cannot find it in herself to make the dolphins.

She runs her hands along the selection of tails that Star has sent her. They hang on a railing to the right of the bedroom door: tubes that cover her legs from waist to ankle, with a monofin which extends from her feet, providing the propulsion needed for swimming. She has tails in neoprene (robust and practical); silicone and neoprene (itchy); silicone rubber (durable, heavy out of the water, but with a helpful buoyancy within); and her absolute favourite, a tail made of a mix of urethane and latex.

. . .

As Sol drives away from the service station, the rain rages against his windscreen so powerfully that his small wipers can't compete with it, and he drives more and more and more slowly because he can't see the road in front of him. Without taking his eyes off the road, he reaches towards the red biscuit tin with his left hand, and he pulls away the tape and levers up the lid. He wonders if he can tell which biscuit is which without looking.

Pink wafer – his mother's second favourite.

He doesn't much like them.

They taste of sawdust.

As he eats, specks of wafer fall into his shirt and nestle among the hairs on his chest. Sol remembers that he started growing chest hair at Cambridge, after growing hair almost everywhere else in the preceding years. His father had been warning him of bodily changes for as long as he could remember.

'Now you'll be going into *long trousers*,' he said the night before Sol's final year at prep school began, 'puberty could happen at any moment.'

Like some kind of hormonal earthquake, Sol wondered, enlarging your genitals to such an extent that they could no longer be accommodated inside your school shorts. He anxiously kept an eye on things down there every time he had a pee.

A couple of years after the *bodily changes* phase, his father moved on to *sexual arousal*, telling him that when boys saw girls' bodies, they couldn't help feeling aroused, but when girls saw boys' bodies, they didn't feel aroused at all. Sol didn't really blame girls for this, but it didn't seem an ideal situation. Girls, his father told him, felt aroused when they imagined making a lovely house to live in, with pretty flowers and cushions.

At Cambridge, everybody, whether boy or girl, was sexually aroused by absolutely everything, or at least that's how it looked to Sol. As he studied manically in the library, avoiding being sexually aroused, a fountain of dark hair grew between his nipples from a line snaking out of the top of his boxer shorts, making a kind of *palm tree* shape on his torso which remains to this day. He feels that ideally there should be more hair between the fronds, that it should be more evenly spread, like Pierce Brosnan's chest when he was James Bond.

He apologises to God for his strange and trivial train of thought, and wonders if women still like hairy chests these days, and then he apologises to God again. He stretches out his hand towards the red tin. *Hmm, bourbon*, he thinks, as he feels its double edges. His mother's favourite.

He remembers her laying out biscuits on the pale green plates at church, standing behind the trestle table at the back, next to the tea urn, every Sunday morning, looking through the stained-glass window, beyond the crucifixion, somewhere else.

Where else, he wonders now, as the rain continues to pelt the van. *Where was his mother looking?*

He wishes he was taking his mother with him back to Ora, a place she visited only once. She went there to decide whether or not to marry his father.

29

'Ora is a *thin place*,' she told Sol.

'A thin place?' he said.

'A place where there's no distance between earth and heaven,' said his mother. 'Where the veil is lifted and everything feels sacred and divine and full of glory. The sky, the rocks, the birds, even us. Everything's touched and we're touched, and nothing feels separate anymore. Not even God. Miss Turner's Island on Hickling Broad is a thin place too. Don't you feel it when we're over there?'

'I may do,' said Sol. 'I've never thought of it like that.'

'There's also a tiny peninsula in Eastern Crete I once went to after my mother died, and a little beach in the north of Mallorca, where you see the grace of God in the turquoise of the water. And there's Tromso in Norway, but I never visited. And now I never will.'

· · ·

Addie feels the long week of another group of guests stretching before her like a sentence. People are exhausting. She's never properly got used to them, that's the problem, aside from Grandma Flora, who she could be with every hour of every day and not feel tired. How does that happen? How do you find a person who doesn't make you feel tired?

Perhaps that's what true love is: not feeling tired with somebody. And perhaps it's also giving away a bit of your autonomy and liking life better without it. Grandma Flora had no choice but to look after her every day of the week at Stone House, but she didn't make it feel like a cost or a burden. Quite the opposite.

Addie's mother likes to tell the story of a tall man with a blond beard knocking on the door to ask if Stone House was a café, discovering that it wasn't but that Grandpa Fred had once tried his hand at carpentry, hence the unfinished wooden tables. The man with the blond beard said, so the story goes, 'I suppose a cup of tea's out of the question?' Grandma Flora said, 'Why don't you come on in?' So he came in. He was on his way to Holy Island, but he hadn't consulted the tide table. It was high tide and the causeway was submerged, and, as he'd hitch-hiked, he was stranded.

Her mother tells the story as if it's a bit of a joke, laughing as she says, 'He stayed for days and then weeks, and the result, Adelaide Mary, was you. Hahahaha.' It makes Addie's existence sound precarious, the unwanted result of a tide and unexpected sex.

Her mother hardly saw Addie. She had a full-time administrative job at the hospital, cleaned on Saturdays, cared for an old man two evenings a week, and studied at the library three or four, in order to improve herself. She did courses, read philosophers and self-helpers and planned to become a life-coach.

Addie admires her mother for what she sacrificed to keep the family afloat. She never followed her friends to university or jobs in exciting cities. No, she stuck at Stone House beside her mother. And for this, Addie's done her best to repay her since they've come here, but she's sure she doesn't love her like you should love a mother, and that's a good thing, she tells herself, because love makes you weak.

She stuffs the ninth dolphin wearily, and when it's finished, its arch is too flat and its black-threaded smile droops morosely. She stands it gloomily next to the eight OK ones. She has one more to make, but she badly wants to go swimming.

Once Star had got Addie into the monofin tail for the first time, they went looking for octopuses. They didn't find one, but when Star left, Addie researched online into the night, and the next day began to identify possible octopus dens – large rocks hidden in the kelp – with space beneath, diving daily, sometimes twice daily, losing herself between the ribboned forests, visiting, revisiting, until she finally saw the curled tip of a tentacle.

Eureka!

Addie mapped the area, getting to know the path through the misty forest: the transmogrifying shapes of the sand-eel shoals; the rainbow of multi-coloured sea slugs; the flexing starfish; the white plumose anemones, buried arms waving hair instead of hands; the dead man's finger coral spreading furry digits across the rock of Eureka's den; the diamond brittlestars like mermaid bracelets carelessly dropped at the entrance.

Addie went back again, and again, and again. Some days Eureka was in, and flexed an arm towards her in greeting, or in fear, or in rebuttal – she wasn't sure. Some days she was out hunting. But back Addie went, hiding in the kelp, reaching out to her, and then one day, Addie lifted a blade of slippery algae and she was looking into Eureka's bulbous, knowing cephalopod eyes.

Addie hovered in the water, as still as she could be, and there they were, creature to creature, tail and tentacles horizontal behind them, in a kind of quasi-symmetry, face to face. The moment made her quiver: she was no longer quite so alone in the world.

She needed to breathe, so she reversed slowly backwards and rose to the surface. When she came back, Eureka shot off, head forward, eight arms propelling her, and Addie followed, watching her bury herself back inside her den, her pale body darkening to match the stone. Eureka squeezed out her head and blinked her eyes at Addie, like an invitation to come and visit her there again.

When Addie doesn't see Eureka, she misses her gorgeous, impossible face.

No, not just her face, the whole package of her: her skirt and her beak and her pouchy head and her whirling arms.

• • •

Sol passes a brown road sign to SEAFRONT AND AMUSEMENTS, and he remembers going with his mother to The Amusements just outside Wroxham, only a fifteen-minute drive from the vicarage on the River Bure, entering through a metal gate beneath a flashing-red lit sign, proceeding to the helter-skelter and the merry-go-round and the dodgems and the two-pence and the ten-pence machines and that grabber that never grabbed the toy you wanted. After he'd spent his money, they'd walk through a clearing and land up improbably by the river, in a place no one knew about, where Tommie the bird warden used to live in a caravan, and this was the first place Sol saw a mandarin duck: red-billed, Mohican-crested, a white crescent above the eye, deep purple breast, ruddy flanks, orange *sails*. Sol stepped back in shock, marked by the duck's impossible beauty.

The riverbank stands in his mind like a dream, full of sunshine and colours, such that sometimes he wonders if it ever really existed.

As Sol passes a sign for *Seafields*, the name accompanied by a pair of abstract waterbirds, white and long-necked, he finds himself thinking of the pair of swans that used to drift outside the glass doors of the garden room at the vicarage, turning to face each other, curving their necks into the shape of a heart.

'Such a cliché, isn't it?' his mother once said. 'Yet somehow it only looks like a cliché in photos.'

'I find that strange,' said Sol.

'Maybe because life is to be lived, not recorded,' said his mother. 'Drink it up, Sol.'

'Drink what up?'

'Life. Live it fully. Love well,' she said.

He's still not sure how to do either of these things.

'If we don't have love inside us when we die,' his mother told him when she was dying, 'there's nothing left of us. Because that's what heaven is. A filtering out of anything that isn't love.'

He'd always wondered what heaven might be like, fearing that it might be an interminable church service with his father preaching from a gold lectern with his showy-off voice on.

'Feathers and wings, that's heaven. Soft as anything,' said his mother as her voice softened into the air.

She made a huge effort to reach into the pocket of her dressing gown and she held out her thin arm, and there was the green eider feather, diagonal across her dry palm.

'Keep this, Sol.'

'Where did it come from?'

'The island of Ora. Try to go there.'

Then she took out a folded piece of paper from her other pocket and gave it to him: it was her list of thin places.

The next day, something was different, and he knew that her love was leaving him. He could feel the change in the air temperature, and it was dusk, and the sun was falling out of the sky. He fell to his knees and prayed for a miracle. He'd been praying for miracles his whole life, but they never seemed to happen to him, only to his father and sisters, whose lives were log-jammed with the things.

He put his cheek against his mother's dead cheek and felt as if he was fusing to her, and perhaps this would be his miracle at last, going with her to the celestial city with the huge river and the trees bearing fruit every month. But then his father and his sisters came in, and his father told him to get up right away, and started issuing instructions about how he should be feeling and reacting, about how there was no need for crying because God would swallow up death forever.

In due course.

But not now, it seemed.

At his mother's funeral, Sol read from the first book of Corinthians, chapter thirteen, holding back his tears to please his father. He read that even if he could speak in tongues, even if he could fathom all mysteries, even if he could move mountains, or give everything he possessed to the poor, without love, he would be nothing.

Without love, he was nothing.

It was hard to love his sisters who bolted their bedroom door and didn't let him in, and it was hard to love his father because his father didn't seem to love him in any discernible way, which perhaps made his father nothing, thinking about it. Perhaps the person he could love lived somewhere else, far away, he wondered, he still wonders, which is why he must now, with no time to waste, go searching across the world.

To find love.

To become something again, instead of nothing.

Sol taps the brown leather of his bench seat, runs his finger over the cream piping, and he feels himself warming to the future that's already begun. His mother always wanted one of these campervans, but his father said they break down all the time, which is probably true. Still, it's so draining being sensible all the time. Presumably, if the van broke down, you could get it repaired, and maybe something interesting might happen to you while you waited. This is the kind of approach Sol's aiming for in his new life, an approach that would have appealed to his mother.

He wonders which new birds he'll see on Ora. Eiders, he hopes, the biggest of all ducks, the drakes with bright green neck feathers like the one in his pocket, and puffins, with their crazy bills.

He wonders if perhaps he'll be able to teach himself to swim on the little beach, where nobody will be watching. There have always been people watching. Not just swimming. Everything. Watching and commenting. Swimming is one of his *two things*. He should make a pledge to himself to get into the water every day of his fortnight on Ora. He should, but he's not sure he will.

He's driving into Seafields, which is grey and damp. He looks at his phone: it's ten past one. The passenger boat leaves at two thirty.

He parks in a large coach park with a big grass circle in the centre, and he strides through a gap in a hedge down into the village with his small rucksack empty on his back. He goes into the small shop and grabs things from the fridges and shelves, pays and walks back to the car park, with his rucksack full, guiltily carrying three plastic bags and a polystyrene box with two slices of chocolate cake in it.

He puts on his thick black anorak, ties his cagoule around his waist and his boots to the sides of his straining rucksack. Now stressed by the time, he tips his books out of his holdall – he'll have to do without those. He scrabbles around for his two favourites, shoving them into the right-hand pocket of his anorak. He puts his camera in the left-hand pocket. He bought it to record his nomadding journey in real photos, like the ones his mother used to stick in albums. He shoves all the food into the now empty holdall, and catches sight of his waterproof trousers. He can't think where to put them so he pulls them on.

He looks at his watch.

Two fifteen.

The boat leaves at two thirty.

He mustn't miss it.

He stares at his mother's old-fashioned grey suitcase. What if the campervan gets broken into? No, he'll have to take it with him, although he'll look a prat: the lining's made of pink silk, but it only shows through where there's a rip in the corner, so hopefully nobody will see. He puts his hand down his waterproof trousers and forces his phone out of the pocket of his jeans, and places it carefully into one of the van's little teak locker-cupboards above the sink, feeling as if he is hyper-ventilating at the thought of it staying here without him.

He shuts the locker door.

Opens it again.

Stares at the phone.

Shuts it again.

He runs.

• • •

Addie takes off her pinafore (a favourite of hers which she made out of worn pairs of jeans and a cut-up gingham tablecloth) and puts on her swimsuit and her big red anorak, selecting her best tail and heading downstairs.

'Are the dolphins finished?' says her mother.

Addie rushes through the front door, but her mother follows her.

'Please will you finish them?' she shouts after her. 'I can't relax until they're done.'

Addie turns: 'Just a quick swim and I will!'

'The swimming can wait,' says her mother crossly. 'The guests will be here this afternoon.'

Addie turns back. She runs up the three staircases to her bedroom, where she grabs the basket of reds. She lays her first piece of flaming orange on the cutting mat, holding down the quilting ruler and pushing the rotary cutter against it. Then she takes a piece of burning scarlet and does the same. As she cuts the third piece, she breathes deeply and tries again to understand her mother, see the good in her, as her principles oblige.

Her mother's relentlessness has made things happen, she can't deny this. She turned her greatest grief into her greatest opportunity – that's what she told Addie as they got off the ferry at Rokesby harbour, as the tractor with its enormous trailer dragged their whole life, packed in cardboard boxes and zip-up bags, into the mouldering hotel, her father and Sydney glowering at the dark sky.

As Addie cuts, she remembers those early hopeful days on the island, her mother, full of joy, telling her father that she would make the place beautiful, a boutique hotel. Addie threads her needle to sew the pieces together, and she hears her father's voice saying, 'I'm not sure people who like boutique hotels would come to Rokesby.' And her mother's voice saying, 'That's because there's no boutique hotel to come to.'

Then her father struck her mother in the heart.

'I'm not sure anyone in their right minds would come to this God-forsaken place,' he said because he was sad and he missed his friends and the pub and darts and watching Sydney score goals in his matches. 'There's *nothing here!*'

Her mother, trembling as if she'd seen a vision, replied: 'That's it. *Get away from it all on the island of Rokesby.*'

Her father said, 'What the hell are you talking about?'

And Addie felt tremors in the ground, like the anticipation of an earthquake.

She pulls the stuffing bag from her cupboard and starts to fill the little patchwork dolphin skin with her expert hands.

'A hotel for women!' her mother said.

The earthquake struck!

'Women?' said Addie's father. 'Just women? You mean no men at all?'

Her mother nodded.

'Where they can come and learn to be peaceful,' said her mother.

'Why can't men come?' said her father.

'Men don't want to learn anything,' said her mother. 'They think they know everything already.'

Her father shrunk and then grew and then exploded, but her mother kept poking at him like a fire, believing that she'd win him round because he loved her.

'And another thing,' said her mother, unwisely. 'Men have no interest in peace.'

Addie's father was a peaceful man, so this felt unfair to Addie. A little too peaceful, his mother would probably have said, uniquely gifted at doing very little. Her mother, on the other hand, never stopped working until the day she opened the hotel, when she realised that Addie was older now, conscientious, and capable with her hands. Her shyness, Addie sees now, is an advantage to her mother, who wants the guests' attention and admiration for herself.

There it is: a furious scarlet dolphin with an orange dorsal fin and a flaming tail. Addie threads the needle with black cotton to make the eyes and mouth, holding the creature up to examine its cross face and shark-like fin, too pointed, but so be it.

Once it was clear that the hotel was to be a retreat for women, her father lost all interest in the renovations, saying repeatedly, 'A women's retreat! Let's see how that goes, shall we?'

Addie lines up the ten dolphins ready for the ten new guests.

The women's retreat has gone very well, though Addie's father doesn't like to talk about this when he visits.

• • •

Sol races into the harbour with the wind blowing against the legs of his capacious waterproof trousers and flapping his hair around his face, and he feels tension buzzing between his eyes.

There are – he counts – ten women standing in the queue. They all have hair the same colour as Camilla Parker-Bowles, apart from one who has a grey short-back-and-sides, and another younger woman whose hair he can't see beneath her white bobble hat. The women are all looking at him, and he panics: has he accidentally booked onto a prayer retreat that's meant for middle-aged women? The monk definitely said he'd be the only person on Ora.

The rain has eased to drizzle, and Sol wants to take off his waterproof trousers, which are making him feel idiotic, but this seems inappropriate, even though he has his jeans on underneath. Would everyone feel that? Even confident men who date lots of women? Those kinds of men probably wouldn't be wearing water-proof trousers, he reminds himself.

Men like Carl Turlington.

Carl Turlington's big red captain-of-everything face comes into Sol's mind, trying to drown him in the school pool in *free swim time*. At some point, Sol mentioned this to his mother, begging her not to tell his father, and definitely not to tell any of the teachers as they believed in manning up and not being snitches. She did tell his father, but not the teachers.

'Love is what makes us big,' she said to Sol, 'not muscles or status or power.'

His father said, 'You're bigger than Carl Turlington.'

Sol said, 'I'm not bigger than Carl Turlington. He's built like a . . .'

He didn't say *brick shithouse*, because that would have sent his father crazy, and before he'd thought of an alternative, his father said: 'You're taller than him.'

And Sol said, 'He's taller than me.'

And his father said again, 'You're taller than him.'

There was never any point arguing with his father.

'Hit him back,' said Sol's father.

Sol said, 'What about turning the other cheek?'

And his father said, 'The New Testament wasn't written for bullies. Try the Old. An eye for an eye. A tooth for a tooth.'

And Sol said, 'Jesus repudiates that in Matthew 5, verse 38.'

His father sweated and said, 'There are times when we need the Old Testament.'

His father hated the fact that Sol was an introvert, and not an extrovert, an intellectual and not a sportsman, and most of all, that he couldn't swim. On holiday, when Sol didn't dare dive off the rocks with his sisters – a humiliation which still stings him now – it infuriated his father so intensely that he hardly spoke to him all fortnight.

In the end, Sol stopped telling his mother that Carl Turlington still tried to drown him in the pool or that he mocked him almost everywhere else because he knew how much his sadness hurt her. It was bad enough to cope with his own sadness, let alone hers as well. But even if he didn't talk to her, he knew he *could have* at any moment, and when she was gone, the blackness rolled in at night like sea fog, settling in his throat and in his nostrils, thicker and darker by the day.

Then *the letter* arrived, and the blackness started to appear in daylight, swooping on him when he was teaching in the classroom, or in the pub with Tim, chasing him outside to breathe air.

Sol let the blackness chase him to the teaching agency to withdraw his services and down the motorway to Brighton to make the exorbitant purchase of a blue and cream campervan, which he isn't anywhere near cool enough to own.

He's not cool enough, but he's *on the move.*

He will become a nomad.

He will grow a beard.

He will visit his mother's thin places.

He will start on Ora.

Then he will go to Tromso.

Don't stop me now!

(In the words of Queen, who he likes, because he doesn't have fashionable taste in music. There's a film coming out in the autumn, which will also be unfashionable.)

• • •

Addie takes the ten patchwork dolphins downstairs, attaching them to the driftwood key fobs, with the individualised luggage labels, as she does for every group of guests. She hears the echo of her solitary footsteps on the tiles. Then her mother's.

'It's just I get so tense before they arrive,' says her mother. 'I don't mean to exasperate you.'

This is how she wins her back, by being alternately unreasonable and reasonable, to confuse her into submission.

'What would I do without you, Ads?' says her mother, and she reaches out to hold her hand, which is odd.

Does her mother suspect something?

'Everyone leaves me,' says her mother. 'But not you.'

Her brother, Uncle Ray, off to Australia.

Grandma Flora and Grandpa Fred, dead in the front garden.

41

Grandpa Fred was at the wheel of his open-top Morris Minor, drunk, coming back from taking Grandma Flora out to dinner on Holy Island, as he did, grimly, every Saturday evening, when he skidded off the causeway en route back to Beal and both of them were flung from the car, the tide coming up and drowning them where they lay, unconscious.

Addie went into the garden of Stone House for her early-morning swim and her grandparents' swollen bodies floated up the lawn, with their clothes rippling around them, like giant human ragdolls. She looked up, and there was a man ambling down the lane eating a packet of crisps.

Addie remembers her mother kneeling beside her, pulling grass up from its roots with her hands and stuffing it into her mouth. She remembers throwing up on her own feet, and still not moving, and her father taking her inside and removing her shoes and socks so that he could wash them, which is what we have to do to stay sane, keep on doing the ordinary things. She remembers breathing her grandmother's herb garden into her broken heart – rosemary and basil and mint, shocking and medicinal – and she can still smell the heady sweetness of the jasmine on the side wall of the house, masses of white stars that chose to bloom on the very day that her grandmother washed in dead, as if the flowers knew. She put her head inside the clouds of petals, and inhaled, inhaled, inhaled. But even the smell she loved most in the world could not heal the crack running down the centre of her heart.

The crack is still there.

Perhaps it will always be there.

Perhaps by the time we die, our hearts are cracked all over.

She remembers saying to herself, I will never ever love anyone like I loved Grandma Flora. I will make sure of that. I will love only a little bit, or not at all. Because love lures us into thinking that we are fine, and then it leaves us, and when it does, we are unable to breathe. Because love, it turns out, was our oxygen.

'Some days I feel I can't breathe being away from Sydney,' says her mother.

'Would you feel that about me?' says Addie, shocking herself. 'If I wasn't here?'

Her mother says, 'Why would you say that?'

Then she adds, 'He's so beautiful. That face of his. I miss it so much.'

'I'm going swimming now,' says Addie.

'How can you stand the cold?' says her mother.

'My tail keeps me warm.'

'I don't know why you won't wear a wetsuit.'

'I want to feel like an animal.'

Her mother stares at her.

'Well,' she says. 'Well.'

As Addie walks, with her favourite tail over her arm and her bag with her mask and tube in hanging from her shoulder, she remembers the first time she and Mac went down to Bird Beach, when they both knew what they were going to do, and they both knew they wanted to by the way they squeezed each other's hands, over and over, as if they were passing messages through their skin, though what the message was, she's still trying to work out.

Is anybody out there, she might have been saying with her body.

Anybody *was* out there, it turned out, and the feel of him was good, and later not so good or very good depending on the angle of her thinking, but she wanted to feel him again, and then again, and again, his body and the air and the waves and her wildness, but not any more, because, as she walks, she sees that in all the times they've headed down to the cave at Bird Beach, in all the ways that being together has felt good, he's never really turned into somebody.

• • •

Sol watches two men approach. They're probably father and son: burly and weathered, prominent bearded chins and thick eyebrows and slightly unreliable eyes. Both boatmen, the way Sol's father wanted them both to be vicars. It's probably easier that way because dissonance feels like judgment in families.

'So, everyone for Rokesby?' says the younger man, who looks about Sol's age, and intimidating, as Sol often finds people his own age are – family friends, cousins, the enthusiastic teenagers who came to his father's noisy summer camps with frisbees and guitars.

'Ora,' says Sol, and it sounds like *oral*, which is the kind of word you avoid in the classroom.

'You're brave, mate,' says the younger bearded man.

Brave to stand in a queue with ten women, or brave to go to Ora, or both, or what?

Sol would like to call someone *mate* – and this is the kind of thing that might happen to him now he's bought a campervan.

'Let's get you on then,' says the younger bearded man. 'Anyone need help with their cases?'

The woman with the bobble hat says, 'Oh, go on then.'

The bobble on her hat is disproportionately enormous. Sol wonders why this is, as the young man drags her two holdalls onto the boat.

The older man offers safety advice over the loudspeaker, and then calls out: 'Mac, all good!'

It's such a burden being good, and Sol's quite had enough of it, if he's honest. He has a feeling that Mac isn't good, that Mac's had a lot of experience with women, you can just tell in the way he carries himself. *So cocksure*, thinks Sol, and then, *oh dear, what a word*.

It's the ultimate twenty-first century taboo – virginity – and it's the shameful *second* of Sol's *two things*. He can hardly bear thinking about it. He feels oddly estranged from his body. Sometimes he looks at it, long and hairy and stretched out in the bath, and he feels he has no relationship with it at all.

He'd lie to a doctor, no question, and to a future partner, no question either, although she'd obviously notice, wouldn't she? Because he wouldn't have a clue what he was doing. Although there must be a first time for everyone. Like there is, for example, for surgeons. No, that analogy feels all wrong. For hairdressers, more like, where the other person can experience the disaster as it's happening.

Stop right there, he tells himself. He heats up every time he thinks of his virginity, and dismisses the hypothesis of his *first time* as quickly as he can. He'd seemed so near to it, as well as so far away. And then.

He should have ignored his father and Ricko, the youth leader at church, and done it at sixteen behind the bike shed, without the pressure of adulthood and love. Do people have sex behind a bike shed? Or is it smoking that happens behind the bike shed? Where is this bike shed? Are there hundreds of couples smoking and having sex behind it? And why is he having such unsuitable thoughts when he's on his way to a prayer retreat?

They're off through the harbour, and the woman in the bobble hat catches Sol's eye. He wonders why bobble hats have bobbles on. Why do you need to understand things, that's what his father always asks him, why can't you just accept them? Sol's hand reaches for his pocket to google the answer, as he likes this sort of miscellany, which won him prizes in pub quizzes at Cambridge. He tries his other pocket. Only the green feather.

They are heading out of the mouth of the harbour, underneath the blessing of the Virgin Mary, who holds her stone hand above the boat, and Sol looks up at her, and he wonders if he'll be safe alone with no phone on an island in the middle of the sea. This is one of Sol's chief skills: thinking of things that could go wrong. He could write it as a hobby on his CV, not that he's going to have a CV anymore. His CV days are over, and this is a relief.

Now the sea is churning and his stomach too, and the blow heater is blowing, and Sol rushes up to the deck for air. The wind throws torrents of rain over him as he stands with his legs apart, scrunching his wet toes and moving up and down with the boat.

Slowly his sickness clears, and on they go, and ah look, isn't that a fulmar gliding, stiff-winged, low over the waves? And another, and another – yes, the boat's making its way through a whole flock of them, pelagic birds which land only to nest. Lovely uplifting word, *pelagic* – new on his word list. He loves words, matching them as precisely as he can to meaning, feeling the thrill and liberation of his eloquence.

The birds dive for fish, reappearing full-mouthed, and dive again. Sol feels his anxiety dissolving as the fulmars bear left and fly out of sight. The boat is rocking and rolling, his nausea dissipates, and tangles of seaweed float by, and look, there's his first puffin, flying in the direction of Ora, wings splayed, uplifted at each end, with a white feathered belly, fanned black tail, orange feet tucked in, and its wonderful technicolour dream beak, orangey-coral-red and blue and grey and white.

He hears his mother's voice.

Their pointlessly lovely bills.

He thinks of her lovely God, who loved her and him and everyone and everything. Her lovely God, who made puffin bills. He feels ecstatic, childlike, on top of the world, in the mood for miracles.

• • •

Addie dives into the water, making her way through the kelp forest, slaloming through the ribbony sea-trees, amongst harmless moon jellyfish, their short fragile tentacles drifting hazily from the sides of their bells. There are transparent combs here too, grape-sized and kiwi-sized, hanging weightless, reflecting wavelengths of light, changing colour. Addie reaches out her hand, and lifts one – it's both globby and crystalline. She needs to breathe. She lets it roll from her hand and heads towards the light.

She breathes and she dives again, powered by her tail towards

Eureka's soft coral-cloaked den, shells arranged like crazy paving, and here is Eureka, extending an arm towards Addie's outstretched hand.

Addie's heart is racing. She leaves her hand suspended, as Eureka continues to stretch her tentacle arm. And stretch it. And stretch it. And then she curls the end of it playfully around Addie's little finger.

There they stay.

Connected.

Addie needs to breathe again. Arms by her side, she flexes her monofin with such power and speed that she's flying through the water, and the dolphins appear, swimming with her, fully present, as animals are, as she is briefly, before her mind takes her back to the day that her mother saw her father climbing onto the passenger boat with Sydney. She remembers the dolphins swimming with the departing boat, leaping for joy, as her mother collapsed on the carpet and broke into pieces.

Addie flies with the arching dolphins but she can't keep up now that the present is shattering into the past and her mother is weeping, 'My boy! My little darling boy! I can't believe he kidnapped him.'

Addie, though only a young girl when her father and Sydney left, made grand plans for The Retreat as a way of sticking her mother back together again, as a way of helping her to love her like she loved Sydney.

'We'll make The Retreat wonderful,' she said to her mother, trying to be brave and helpful and lovable, and she took photographs to hang along the landings; she made patchwork quilt covers for the beds; she thought up themes for every bedroom; she bid for unusual ornaments and artefacts in online auctions, and they came over on the ferry.

Her mother said, 'Don't ever leave me, Addie, will you?'

'I won't,' said Addie because she had to. What choice did she have?

'Do you promise?' she said. 'Because if you ever left me, my life would be over.'

'I promise,' said Addie.

That was her bad promise.

She made it when she was fifteen years old.

She gets out at Bird Beach, and starts to walk back to The Retreat in the rain, and look, here's Grandpa Dempster, frail and tiny, with his hand down his trousers.

'I want to show you something,' says Grandpa Dempster, unzipping his fly.

She knows what he wants to show her, and she's seen it before.

'Go and see the orange flowers by the cliffs, Grandpa Dempster,' says Addie. 'They've just come out and they're lovely.'

She gets back to The Retreat, climbs into the shower and prepares for the new onslaught.

• • •

As Sol walks from the jetty, he sees a puffin – the puffin that flew with the boat? – on the grass.

He stops to watch it as it struts on its orange feet.

He feels.

Odd to say it.

Most out of character.

Bouncy.

He walks on, and he's singing an old hymn they often sang in assembly at school.

'For the beauty of the earth, for the beauty of the skies . . .'

The rain wets his hair and his cheeks, and falls loudly on the water.

'Hill and vale, and tree and flower, sun and moon and stars of light . . .'

His mother named him after the sunshine (Latin, *solis*); his father, after an ancient Jewish king (Solomon). Whenever his mother sat down, she turned and inclined towards the sun, like a sunflower. Her maiden name was Ray, and her first name was Clementine. It's the sunniest name he ever heard.

Look at the puffin's bill, and look at the huge herring gulls stretching their wings wide above him like angels. Look how promising the birds are, how big the horizon, how powerful the sea. For the first time since his mother died three years ago, he feels alive.

He stops and turns, and he watches the passenger boat making its way through the waves and the rain to Rokesby harbour, and he can see a large red stone house – monastery, abbey? – with a kind of glass pyramid at the centre of its roof.

. . .

In the shower, Addie remembers her mother collapsing with grief when Grandma Flora died, staying motionless in bed for several days before getting up and moving like a sloth around the house, groaning.

Addie's father became like one of the very good children at school, helpful, alert and energetic, thinking up multiple cheering activities to do with Addie and Sydney. He taught Addie carpentry: they sawed and hammered and nailed in the barn while tears ran down her cheeks like a fountain that never dried. Sometimes he let her steer the car around the drive that circled their land, and she changed gears when he told her to, and she parked by the sea where they drank hot chocolate from a thermos flask, the two of them, while Sydney was at school – and these are the only nice memories she has of those long slow weeks, the closest she ever felt to her father.

Addie's mother returned to her job at the hospital, working from dawn to dark, studying at the library in the evenings, but she looked bleaker and paler every day, and she took to screaming at her father when she got home: 'Why can't you earn some bloody money?'

She remembers the day her mother, still delirious with grief, rang the estate agent.

49

'I'd like to sell Stone House,' she said, that is the house that had been in the Lemming family since it was built, for generations.

Her mother couldn't stop crying as she packed their life into boxes.

'I can be heart-broken and excited at the same time,' she said to the bewildered Lemming relatives who came like vultures to predate on furniture, suspicious of her contradictions.

Addie thinks of possible approaches: Mum, I'm twenty-two, and I've lived on the island now for seven years, and I don't think that's good for me?

No.

I don't think it's good for me *any longer?*

Or how about: Though it's been the best possible place to live, I think it would be good for me to leave and try living *a normal adult life?*

No, no, no, her mother will collapse on the floor again and break to pieces, like she did when Grandma Flora died, like she did when her father and Sydney absconded. Addie can't risk leaving, can she, because she's not sure her mother can cope with another abandonment, and she's not sure either if she can run The Retreat without her. These are things neither her father nor Sydney ever felt obliged to consider.

Perhaps they could come back for a while.

They won't.

They'll say they aren't women.

Addie gets out of the shower, pulls on a pinafore and Grandma Flora's clumpy green boots, and goes downstairs. She heads for the pantry where she puts sprigs of thrift in her basket, before going into the sitting room which she prepared last night – tables dusted and sprayed, curtains tied back to reveal the garden and the tall white folly and the jagged shoreline and the sea beyond.

'Will it ever stop raining?' says her mother as she comes through the door, and when Addie looks at her, her face is set in that firm expression she always has, and she looks so strong that Addie can't believe she wouldn't manage on her own. She's strong, but she's weak; she's nice, but she's horrible; she reels Addie in, she pushes her away. She's all Addie has, when it comes down to it, and perhaps that's why she can't make herself leave.

Addie takes a magazine, slips it under a large spider, upturns a glass and puts it over it. Her mother sighs. Addie releases it through the glass doors. The spider cowers uncertainly in the rain, and she says, 'Oh poor thing,' taking it over the lawn to the woodshed.

Awful to be a spider, she thinks, *so unloved, yet so harmless.*

'Let's go up,' says Addie, as she comes back in, because this is their ritual when the guests are on their way, and she climbs the stairs with her mother, the first flight, then the second, then the third to their own private landing, and up to the glass observatory, a tiny pyramidal room which allows you to turn 360 degrees and see the whole of Rokesby, Ora out in front, and sea all around.

'Look,' says Addie. 'Someone's just arrived on Ora.'

· · ·

Sol stares at the neighbouring island of Rokesby. The glass pyramid in the roof of the big red building lights up and two people seem to bob and dance inside it like shadow puppets.

He watches them for some minutes, before turning around to survey his own wet island, Brother Andrew's hermitage out to the left, the prayer house in front, which he walks towards. The rain is getting stronger. He wonders if Brother Andrew will come and say hello, or if saying hello isn't what hermits do.

He opens the unlocked door, heads along the hall into a sort of common room, with a collection of second-hand sofas and armchairs and a big Formica table in the corner with odd chairs around it, and book-filled shelves behind, and a melamine chest of drawers with an old crate on top, full of pamphlets and magazines. It smells like the garden room at the vicarage, and he has a powerful memory of his mother's clogs clopping against the tiled floor.

He makes his way to the kitchen, which has a stainless-steel chest freezer and two large white fridges. He leaves his holdall of food here. Beyond it, he finds an empty stone room with lockers and a large room with chairs stacked in a row. Upstairs are the retreaters' rooms, one with a baddish painting of a puffin on the door, a row of beds behind it, another with a baddish cormorant, ditto, and here's his single room, with an eider duck, as promised.

He puts down his small rucksack and his large one and his mother's grey case, and he finds that he is kneeling to open it. He takes out his mother's perfume – *a floral mix*, so the white box says, *like an English garden, fragrant with jasmine and mint.*

He sprays, and breathes her in.

She's here again.

With him.

He kept her perfume when she died, and he sprayed it onto his pillow so that he could sleep. When it ran out, he bought another bottle, which he knows is strange behaviour for a grown man. He would never admit it to anyone.

• • •

As the passenger boat moors in the harbour, the rain eases to drizzle, and Addie puts down her basket and takes her rucksack off her back, scanning the guests' names on a clipboard as they disembark: well-coiffed blondes, one with an oblong-shaped mouth; a tall woman with short salt-and-pepper hair; another, younger, with a white bobble hat. Addie offers each of them a sprig of thrift.

'Terrible day,' says Mac, looking at Addie from beneath his thick dark eyebrows.

Addie wonders how she will tell him that she's not going down to Bird Beach with him again. That it, whatever it was, is over.

'We're very grateful to you for getting them over,' says her mother.

Addie shakes her head almost imperceptibly at Mac. Then she leads the guests towards the hotel, her mother walking beside them, examining each of them, head to toe, and answering their questions as if she is an expert on absolutely everything in the entire world.

As the guests come into the tiled hall of The Retreat, they exclaim at the sight of their numbered driftwood keys, with their patchwork dolphins attached, their names embroidered by Addie in silk thread on luggage labels.

'A gift we made for you,' says her mother.

. . .

On Sol's bedside table, there's a pile of books. The one on top is about St Cuthbert, the seventh-century hermit who lived on Inner Farne, confined to a tiny cell, which he never left. Underneath are maps of nesting sites, which he studies carefully, and bird guides, which he skims, and prayer books, which he glances through.

Sol walks onto the landing, and looks at Brother Andrew's hermitage through the window. The rain has stopped. He goes down to the kitchen, places two slices of bread in the toaster, waits for them to pop up, spreads them with butter and marmite and heads outside, pushing the front door open with his back, holding a piece of toast in each hand, and he sits on the picnic bench, which is wet.

To Addie, Sol is only a shape walking over the grass.

*To Sol, she's a dark silhouette against
the light of the pyramid room.*

*It's strange to think that we all appear
daily in the hinterlands of strangers.*

Nameless shapes passing each other by.

And that's usually where it ends.

And occasionally where it begins.

Think of the person you're closest to.

They too were once a shape.

Sunday 30th April

It's dark, not yet dawn, and Addie hasn't been able to sleep.

Her mother knocks and comes into her bedroom – simultaneously.

'Why are we both awake before dawn?' she says. 'Is something the matter?'

'I don't think so,' says Addie, although something is always the matter, and her mother has been particularly bleak since her father and Sydney left after Easter.

'You see, they all loved the dolphins,' says her mother. 'I was right.'

Oh yes, thinks Addie, wearily, *of course you were.*

She gets out of bed.

'Where are you going?'

'Swimming.'

'So early?'

Addie nods.

Her mother frowns.

Addie grabs her tail and the bag with her mask and snorkel and gloves inside, and tiptoes downstairs, creeping into the kitchen, where she takes the cakes for tea out of the freezer. She opens the front door to a breezy day. The storm is over, though another is forecast.

She makes her way through the rocks on Bird Beach and sits to watch the sun rise, wondering if the visitor on Ora is still asleep.

• • •

Sol wakes early, having dreamt of flying, and for a second, has no idea where he is. He lurches for his phone, staring mystified at the wooden stool which isn't his IKEA bedside table – where is he, and where's his phone?

Ah yes, Ora.

He looks at his watch – it's 6.40.

He gets up and opens the window: the sky is pink-gold, and the sea too. The air is pure and fresh and cold, and he is super-charged, super-oxygenated, raring to go, ready for he doesn't know what exactly. And there's a puffin – *the* puffin? – on the lawn. There it goes, nodding its way across the grass on its shining orange feet, back here for the breeding season to claim a nest, a nest being a disused rabbit burrow.

Puffins lay one egg a year, mating with the same life-partner, who they seem to find with ease. *Lucky buggers,* thinks Sol. Then he apologises to God: luck has never been permitted at the vicarage, nor swearing. He wonders how puffins choose a partner as they all look *exactly the same.* The pairs spend the six winter months at sea apart, but somehow identify their lover every spring, reuniting to breed, every single one a winner in love. Why is human love so hard, Sol wonders. And is it odd to wish you were a puffin rather than a man? Also, think how effortlessly puffins swim, essentially flying underwater.

Imagine the joy of it!

Sol imagines puffin sex is also nice and straightforward: a little dance, a little rubbing of beaks, a little uniting of cloacas, and hey presto, without the human angst, moral dilemmas, unwanted pregnancies, heartbreak.

He wraps his towel around his waist and walks to the shower, where he catches a glimpse of his concave stomach, his long arms and his unfortunate palm tree of chest hair. Yes, that's the other thing puffins don't have: body issues. Which is the nailed-on advantage of all looking exactly the same.

Think positively, Sol tells himself.

I can easily reach high shelves, for example, at the supermarket.

I can identify people in a crowd.

Breathe easily in a lift or on the tube.

I'm also very bendy.

Though useless at team sports, Sol came into his own in gymnastics, making spectacular crabs in the school gymnasium, arched right off the floor, aloft on his long legs and arms, able to rotate in large circles for the duration of the lesson, a skill which he still thinks was undervalued.

In the shower, he wonders if he can still do a crab. He hasn't tried for years. He gets out, lies down, arches up and crabs around the large bathroom, naked, feeling the muscles in his body stretching in a way that is not unpleasant, the air cool against his genitals, which feel a little unleashed without the protection of underwear, a little dangerous even. He collapses on his back, dresses, has a coffee and a bowl of cornflakes, feeling most unlike himself and slightly shocked, remembering his mother's breakfasts: challah bread, toasted with jam, and a big bowl piled with fruit, and frothy hot chocolate in striped mugs.

He sets off with his anorak and his wallet and his binoculars, seeing that *the bridge* to Rokesby has now been revealed. The bridge is a raised path over the rocks, low walls each side, the mudflats smattered with bulbous seaweed, like bubble wrap – it would burst if you jumped on it, which of course he won't.

It's years since he's jumped.

He wonders what it is that stops us jumping for the fun of it.

• • •

57

Addie sits staring at the rocky overhang where she and Mac used to throw themselves together, their rather frantic union giving her the sensation of waves crashing into each other and disappearing. She wonders if there's a way of having sex that doesn't make you disappear.

She sees a person making his way, yes, *his* – it's a man – towards her, and it must be the new visitor on Ora. She watches him as he walks. A tall man, very tall she thinks, with long legs and long arms, and he gets closer, tousled dark hair, and he's looking at her, she's sure he is. He's singing *Amazing Grace*.

Grandma Flora loved that hymn, the way it made joy and sorrow press hard on the heart, she used to say, squeezing something out of you, and into you, at the same time.

The man's voice comes to Addie on the wind and presses too. He's been through many dangers, toils and snares. It's a strong rich voice. Peaty. Like whisky. Grace has apparently brought him safe thus far, so he sings peatily, and grace will lead him home. She wonders where his home is, where he lives, what he does, why he's here.

He's stopped singing now, and he's coming closer, and why is she experiencing this uncharacteristic desire to speak?

She feels the vertigo which has become so persistent this week, the sky and the sea seeming to rotate around her. She thinks she'd like to tell the man that she's trapped here, that she's not happy, that she needs to get away.

She sees goodness in the man, purity even: the way he inclines his head skywards, inviting the wind onto his face, seeming to feel the joy of it as he walks. If she were anyone else, she thinks, a normal person, she could simply say hi and what brings you here?

But she can't, and she doesn't.

. . .

Sol sees a young woman through the lenses of his binoculars. Yes, it's definitely a woman. She's sitting on the rocks. He doesn't want to examine her in a way that might be threatening or inappropriate, so he lowers his binoculars and walks on, creasing his eyes to see her better. She has auburn ringlets, and she's wearing a huge red coat, and she seems to be holding a big thing, a bag, or a rug, no, perhaps a wetsuit, and something else slung over her shoulder. He can't take his eyes off those long auburn ringlets, which blow like streamers in the breeze. He's not sure he's ever known a girl with auburn ringlets.

Calm down, he reprimands himself, as his father used to say.

Don't act girlish, he also used to say.

Although he was young, Sol knew it should be girlish*ly*, and this is the way he tried to counter his father's disapproval. By knowing things.

Don't be clever-clever, his father used to say.

Sol liked being clever, though. He liked the classroom much more than the youth club. He liked gravity much more than levity. He liked study much more than games. He still hates games. At youth club, one was to play Twister, boys and girls together, touching each other permissibly, but only when suspended over the plastic sheet. Without the plastic sheet, certainly not. Sol, his bendiness notwithstanding, was not for Twister, so the girls were not for him despite his potentially aphrodisiac status as the vicar's son.

Sol tended to slip away when the others linked arms and jumped sweatily up and down with their eyes closed and their arms linked, buoyant with faith and hope and bosoms. He'd hover in the shadows of the graveyard until he could reasonably return to the vicarage to say yes, thank you, he'd had a great evening, and escape to bed.

He doesn't remember there ever being a youth club girl with long auburn curls. There's something about her flying ringlets and the big grey sky and the big grey sea and the circling birds above

59

him. Something rousing or spiritual or hopeful. Something *winged*.

He watches her sink her face into the palms of her hands before turning towards him.

. . .

It comes to Addie that she, even she, could wave, in a casual but friendly way, at the man. It interests her that she should want to do so.

. . .

A kittiwake lands on a rock in front of Sol, closely followed by a second, and there they are, the smallest of all gulls, soft-feathered and white with lemon yellow beaks and grey upper wings. They cross their bills and start gently to caress each other's heads and necks. A strange pain rises up Sol's throat from his heart, which might be desire, or longing, or hope, or despair. The kittiwakes fly away.

He looks at the young woman, feels he'd like to call out to her, but what exactly would he say?

He could walk over to where she's sitting, but even if he had the confidence to do so (and he doesn't), he can't see a path through the rocks. He hesitates, and wonders if he's seeing things. He really isn't. The young woman is raising her hand in a wave. His own arm rises in front of him, bent at the elbow, and his hand, seeming to act separately from his brain, moves from side to side in the air.

He is waving.

She is waving.

He is smiling.

She might be smiling – he can't tell from here.

She stops waving.

His arm falls.

He can feel heat rising up his thighs through his body to his cheeks.

She looks at her watch, rises to her feet and rushes away with the big thing and the other thing. Sol clears his throat and walks on, humming.

· · ·

Addie feels a tremor inside her belly. She waved at the man, and much more importantly, he waved back. There's no time for swimming now but *it doesn't matter*, and swimming never doesn't matter. She stoops and picks some yellow gorse flowers, and she heads, almost skipping (she doesn't skip) for her bedroom where she selects a turquoise pinafore she rarely wears and goes down to the kitchen.

She puts on her patchwork apron and places a red and white gingham cloth onto a tray, as her grandmother always did for her. She takes a bowl, sprinkling home-made granola on top of yoghurt, arranging coconut shavings over strips of alternating kiwi and mango and topping the arrangement off with the gorse flowers. She's humming, which is unusual. She arranges four more bowls in a similar fashion, carrying them on a tray into the dining room, where the ten women are seated, silently. She goes back to the kitchen for the next five bowls and returns, smiling, laying a bowl in front of each of them.

The ceiling chandelier which she imported from France – a tangle of iron branches with glass apples and pears – sheds bubbles over the table and over the guests' faces and hands as if they're all sitting underwater. The room shimmers and trembles, and the guests and the table and the red flowers at its centre seem to merge, as they never have before, their colours and edges seeping into each other. Addie wonders where the man has gone. She goes into the hall, sits at the Reception desk and stares out beyond the fountain. She opens the window and breathes in air.

· · ·

The window of the old monastery is opening.

Sol slows, tingling a little in the chest and arms.

He's sure it's her. He looks left, right, up, down, appearing to be looking for birds, for flowers, for insects, for something he's dropped, a contact lens perhaps (he doesn't wear them). She opens the window and smiles, so he smiles back, and then he walks on, feeling he might have a heart attack, or walk into something.

• • •

'What are you doing?' says Addie's mother.

'Nothing,' says Addie.

'Aren't you serving breakfast?'

'Yes I am.'

'No you're not. You're staring out of the window.'

'Oh,' says Addie.

'Are you feeling all right?'

'Yes,' says Addie. 'Thank you.'

Her mother glides into the dining room, wearing decorative yoga pants, humming birds flying over her faintly dimpled buttocks.

• • •

Perhaps she works here, thinks Sol, or lives here. Perhaps she was one of the shapes in the glass pyramid in the roof. People do live full-time on Rokesby, so the monk said, and that's a very strange thought. A wonderful thought, possibly, living outside the bounds of normal life, unburdened by conventional expectations. Yes, what a wonderful place to live.

'For the beauty of each hour, of the day and of the night,' he sings. That old school hymn again. He wonders why she had her head in her hands when he saw her on the rocks. What could possibly be wrong in a place as beautiful as this? Though remember *Eden* – snakes lurking, dodgy trees, universal doom. He sees a sign made of driftwood in the corner of the garden: *The Retreat*. Chickens cluck to the right of the vegetable garden, and there she is, crossing the lawn with a basket over her arm, like a character in a novel. He walks on, keeping his face straight ahead, but looking sideways, which strains the muscles in his right eye, and he goes on singing.

But look, she's coming back over the lawn, with her basket, and he decides to stop, not to walk on, and in order to calm his nerves, he keeps singing the old school hymn, which might be odd, but if he stops, he'll be standing in silence, which might be odder, and she's near now, near enough that he can see her freckled face and her green eyes and her wild ringlets and her smile, near enough that they are looking at each other, as he belts out *friends on earth*, turning down the volume on *friends above*.

'If heaven is above,' he finds that he is saying. 'It will depend on your theology.'

'I'm not sure I have one,' she says.

'Very wise,' he laughs.

'Oh, that's good,' she says.

• • •

Addie goes through the back door, wondering why she said, *Oh, that's good.*

What exactly is good? The fact that heaven's above? Or that she doesn't have a theology? Grandma Flora did. 'The whole world is full of his glory,' she used to say as she opened the window to the sea, letting the sun and the salt and the wind blow through as they sat at the old pine table, sewing, patchworking, drawing, painting, crocheting, embroidering, making lace with bobbins. This was all the education she had once she left primary school.

His singing has made her feel lighter.

Anyway.

She must get to the sitting room.

• • •

Sol walks on.

The old lighthouse is crumbling into the soft springy grass where the rabbits dig their warrens. He read last night that domesticated rabbits were introduced by a lighthouse keeper, and bred with the native species, and, as he walks towards the promontory, trying not to tread on the orange flowers, variegated rabbits, patched black and white and ginger, jump over his toes.

He could almost dance, and he hasn't danced since the school end-of-term ball in Upper Sixth when he was drunk, the only time he's ever been drunk, and he found he rather liked it, both the drinking and the dancing, or perhaps the combination.

He thinks briefly of the way he crabbed naked around the large bathroom this morning, with his muscles stretching and his balls unleashed. Most out of character, it was. Like dancing drunk. He feels a slight swelling in his groin. Now, he thinks, enough of that, this is supposed to be a retreat and you are supposed to be thinking retreaty things.

He feels for the green feather in his pocket as he arrives at a cubed white building, where goldfinches flutter and twitter in a bush beside him, the goldfinch being the bird (he reminds himself, trying to be a serious person again) which prefigured Christ's passion, plucking a thorn from his crown as he carried the cross and finding itself spattered with blood, so the story goes. His mother's story. Not his father's. His father says *story* in a funny voice. He favours parables. He likes a message or a moral, everything wrapped up, tidy-tidy, with no loose ends.

Sol opens the door to find himself inside a tiny chapel. He sits on a pew and stares through the glass wall, the non-stained transparent glass, which allows the water to be the artwork, the grey sea filling it, the sun having now disappeared, the dawn having over-promised. Sol stares at the grey water merging with the grey sky, the continuum making a kind of unsettling infinity, as his life has been, a drag, a dragging on, one day after the other, little punctuation.

And now this. And now *her*. An exclamation mark, a break in the tedium, or perhaps a colon – that's what he feels she might be. *A colon.*

:

A gate opening to something new, if that isn't too far-fetched, after such fleeting encounters.

A man appears from a side door in a black robe. He's small and wiry, his skin deep brown, his kind, grave face breaking easily into a smile. Sol smiles back.

'Brother Andrew?'

The man nods.

'Sol Blake,' he says, trying to look deep or respectable or holy or something he assumes he isn't – he's always seeing himself through other people's eyes, he doesn't know if other people do this.

'Can I help you with anything?' says Brother Andrew. 'Or would you rather be left in peace?'

'Oh, I think I'm OK,' says Sol, who doesn't want to offend him. 'I'm here to get away from . . . Well, honestly speaking, from my father. But there we are, that probably doesn't sound very charitable.'

'There's no obligation to sound charitable,' says Brother Andrew.

Sol nods.

'Don't be surprised if you have strange thoughts,' says Brother Andrew. 'It's quite normal when we leave behind our distractions and empty our mind.'

'Thank you,' says Sol awkwardly.

'So what brings you to Ora?' says Brother Andrew, smiling in a way that crinkles his eyes. 'Other than escaping your father?'

Sol feels bad: he's very good at feeling bad. He should never have mentioned his father.

He says: 'I'm not sure. I've never been able to work out what I think about God. Or perhaps what God thinks about me.'

'God isn't like an interview panel or an exam board,' says Brother Andrew. 'I didn't realise that for years. The secret, I think, if you want to know God, is this: be present and grateful. Say thank you. Whatever God brings into your life, don't resent it or reject it, but *welcome it with all you have.* Then you'll be able to be who you are where you are right now. Which is where God is too. With you.'

If he's to be who he is where he is right now, well, thinks Sol, he will have to be a man on an island who's become unusually preoccupied by a woman he doesn't know.

'You know, if you're walking, walk. If you're eating, eat. Then all of life's a prayer.'

And what about: if you're thinking obsessively about a woman you don't know, think obsessively about a woman you don't know? Is that a prayer? He wouldn't think so.

Sol smiles at Brother Andrew again, and finds himself putting up his right thumb, which is not something he does. Feeling embarrassed, he walks out of the chapel, back down the promontory, and turns right past the fissured columns which rise from the sea, with gulls, kittiwakes, fulmars, assembling, diving, landing, diving, landing. The waves explode between the columns in a tubular fountain, the spray reaching as far as Sol's face, and he feels himself lifting, as if on the cusp of something. But there's a voice behind him.

'Don't get stranded, Sol, will you!' says Brother Andrew. 'The bridge will be covered within the hour.'

Sol turns around and follows Brother Andrew, heading in the direction of the bridge, giving himself one more chance to go past the hotel place. *The Retreat.* Is there a way in which he could welcome the young woman with *all he has*, like Brother Andrew said? What exactly does he have, come to think of it.

All that I have I share with you.

When he studied the wedding vows, tense as anything, grinding his teeth at his predicament, he wondered if he had anything at all worth sharing.

. . .

As Addie walks bouncily into the sitting room, the women stare at her in silence. Her mother runs through today's activities. She says that patchworking is on offer with Addie at ten o'clock.

'A show of hands,' says her mother.

No hands show.

Life-coaching is available with her mother, for an additional charge, one to one, at any time. The young woman, her white bobble hat on her lap, puts up her hand, and Addie's mother smiles benignly and says she'll see her afterwards. She clarifies that lunch will be served at one o'clock in the dining room.

'The spa is open all day,' says her mother, 'and has a pool, jacuzzi, sauna and steam room. You can reach it through the doors beyond the toilets, and you've no doubt found the bath robes in your rooms. Towels are available at Reception. There's a lifeguard down there all day, and she can answer any questions you have.'

The lifeguard is Moira Hull, who left to get married and came back alone with a mongrel dog, after working in a spa in Scotland where Nicola Sturgeon once visited.

'I'll be giving an ornithology lecture at two o'clock,' says her mother. 'Followed by a birdwatching walk led by Addie.'

Addie dreads these walks. She's happy to point out the birds, but not to answer intrusive questions about her personal life. People can be very nosy at the beginning, before they realise that she doesn't have a personal life.

. . .

Sol slows his pace as he approaches the garden of The Retreat. The wind is swirling now, and with it gusts of rain, and the sky has turned blackish. He sees her: she's putting a bin bag into a plastic bin, a few yards away from the fence.

'Look at that sky!' he shouts over the fence to the back of her, his voice speaking without his permission as his arm waved of its own volition previously.

• • •

Addie feels his voice spreading over the surface of her skin.

'A storm's coming,' she says, holding her ringlets away from her face. 'The bridge will be covered soon! Be careful, won't you?'

As she says it, she rather likes the thought of him not being careful, of him being stranded here. After all, they have an empty room he could stay in, if her mother would break the women-only rule.

Her mother opens the back door, and Addie rushes inside. She goes to Reception and hands out towels to the blonde guests, and then she takes her binoculars from the hook behind the desk and puts them round her neck.

'I'm off to do some life-coaching with Lily Bairn,' says her mother.

Addie nods.

She heads for the bridge: it's now covered.

She wonders if the man got back to Ora.

• • •

Sol takes off his wet shoes and makes himself a cheese and pickle sandwich in the kitchen. He eats it at the common room window. Then he takes his binoculars and looks over at Rokesby. The rain is coming down in sheets, so he goes upstairs to his bedroom and picks up the book about St Cuthbert he started last night. But he can't concentrate.

• • •

After serving lunch, Addie escapes to her room. As the storm creaks and blasts, she looks up to see clouds of yellowing sea foam bouncing across the window panes. She gets up and looks out of the window. She can't see him anywhere.

. . .

Sol wakes with a jolt, the book on his face, the rain lashing the window.

He gets up and opens the window to hear the roar and the hiss of the waves as they rise and swell. The rain wets his face. He wonders whether Brother Andrew is back at the hermitage, or if he's totally alone on the island, cut off by the covered bridge. He wishes he had his phone.

He goes downstairs, fearing a power cut later in the dark, and he looks in three different drawers for candles and matches, which he finds. He takes the crate off the top of the chest of drawers. Ah! The removal of the crate reveals a phone that Sol hadn't noticed before, a landline, wonderful. His spirits lift. It has a label taped to it saying OUTGOING CALLS ONLY, presumably as retreaters wouldn't want the interruption of a phone ringing. He picks up the phone and hears the reassuring buzz of a dialling tone. He puts it down.

If the sea started to come over the island, he could call the young woman over at The Retreat, although what on earth could she possibly do to help?

He takes the crate to the sofa and picks a book about Grace Darling, the lighthouse keeper's daughter, who rescued survivors from the shipwrecked *Forfarshire* in 1838 just over there, when she was only twenty-six, the same age as he is. Then he gets up and stares at the enormous waves, struck by his own lack of courage.

He heads for the kitchen, returns to the common room with a cup of tea and the red tin of biscuits, thinking that perhaps he'll read about Grace Darling another time. The storm is roaring down the chimney and whistling through the windows. He takes the last bourbon, his mother's favourite, and remembers how she chose to die with only him beside her. Nobody else. He didn't even think of going to get his father or his sisters.

Now the bourbon section is empty, so he goes for a pink wafer, which makes his tongue feel dry, and the sea crashes against the rocks, and here he is on Ora, not having told a soul that he's here, sitting in a room full of furniture nobody else wanted, on a little dot of island in the middle of the ocean in the middle of a storm, eating his dead mother's second favourite biscuit.

· · ·

Addie lays out the cakes in the sitting room, lightning glaring, thunder rumbling, and she pulls on her waterproofs and heads for the mound, from where she looks over at Ora, where the light is still on. The storm rages around her. The bridge, she sees, is entirely submerged and waves are smashing over the harbour walls.

She pulls up her soaking cuff to see her watch. She's late for tea. She rushes back and into the sitting room.

'Oh my word!' says one of the blondes. 'You're totally soaked.'

'You'd better go and get changed,' says her mother, irritably.

Addie rushes upstairs, throws on some dungarees and returns. Her mother is holding court: the blondes have pulled their armchairs around her in a semi-circle.

'The best life is a life of happiness, so said Aristotle,' she says firmly.

Addie is struck by how unhappy she seems.

Lightning briefly illuminates the room.

'Addie and I built our life of happiness here on Rokesby,' says her mother, gesturing, tight-lipped, to Addie.

Did we, thinks Addie, as her mother shouts over the thunder: 'You just need to visualise your happy life, and imagine yourself into it like we did.'

Addie wants to say that she was a young girl and she did what

70

she was told, and she knows for sure not only that *she doesn't want her life to be contingent on her mother,* but also that she doesn't want it to be contingent on any other person. She wants to be free to imagine herself anywhere and anyhow she likes.

. . .

Sol takes his plate into the common room and plucks a book from the crate. It's more of a booklet, well-thumbed, underlined and highlighted in places. He puts it on the table behind his plate and cuts off a piece of pasty, sliding some baked beans onto his fork.

Questions For Your Retreat.

1 Why have you come here?

As Sol chews his pasty, he thinks he's come looking for his mother, who loved it here, who told him it was a thin place.

2 What do you expect God to do while you're here?

He thinks he'd like a version of the transfiguration from his childhood bible, except that beside the transfigured Jesus, instead of Moses and Elijah, would be his mother, briefly lent to him from heaven. If he could have one more afternoon with her, that would be enough. He'd like to ask her what he should do next in his life, and he'd like to hear her husky voice again, and her throaty laugh, feel her warm arm around his shoulder. He'd like to talk about his father's latest madness with her, though there again, perhaps not.

A shock of lightning dazzles the room, and he gets up and stares out at the sky, but there are no radiant figures transfiguring in the dark. Thunder shakes the prayer house, vibrating through his chest and leaving behind a wake of deep silence. He goes to the kitchen, returning to the table with a slice of chocolate cake, which he eats slowly, wiping his mouth.

The chocolate cake isn't that nice. Chocolate cake tends to be disappointing, he thinks, whereas coffee and carrot always deliver.

3 What exactly are you looking for?

71

Hard to answer, that one.

He wipes a baked bean off the pamphlet with his finger.

. . .

The guests gather for dinner: Addie has made parmesan and herb crusted salmon with asparagus and crushed new potatoes, followed by melt-in-the-middle chocolate pudding. She's done far too much cooking in her short life, and she doesn't especially enjoy it.

When she's cleared up dinner, she prepares the ensaimadas for breakfast, leaving the dough to prove. As the guests head into the sitting room for drinks, she says to her mother, 'It's a terrible night.'

'Every night's a terrible night now they've gone.'

'Do you mean that?'

'I sacrificed everything. My partner and my son.'

Addie feels anger rising in her, and she can't find a way to suppress it, because she doesn't think that's true. They left and she could have left with them, but she didn't want to. She wanted to be here.

'You seem very unhappy, in your *life of happiness.*'

Her mother scowls at her.

'We have a business to run,' she says.

'But it was your choice to come here, wasn't it? No one else's. Your dream.'

'If you don't work, you don't live.'

'I do a lot of the work,' says Addie.

'I've done nothing but work my whole life,' says her mother. 'Not that your father ever noticed.'

Addie slices the dough into rounds, which she rolls into long rope shapes, coiling them and leaving them to rise overnight. Then she goes out with her torch and binoculars into the storm, and finds herself up on the mound again, looking over to Ora.

. . .

Maybe, Perhaps, Possibly

As Sol stares through his bedroom window, the sky and the sea and the rain merge into a thick impenetrable blackness. It's followed him here.

He sees a light moving through the darkness on Rokesby. It rises up a slope, and down, then moves back towards The Retreat like a firefly. He remembers reading that in Japan they hold night-time festivals where people gather to watch clouds of fireflies, symbols of passionate love since the publication of the eighth-century poetry anthology, the *Man'yōshū*.

Passionate love, he thinks, the loveliest phrase, as well as the most terrifying. He can't imagine himself ever experiencing it, although other people seem not only to expect it, but to get it, one bout after another, like taking books out of the library. He thinks he'd only want to give himself once, to one person, bearing in mind the risk of it, the exposure, the vulnerability, the fear. But oh the glory of the thought.

The tiny light bounces forward towards The Retreat, in arcs, and is extinguished. It comes to him that he could call her. He really could, if he can find the number, and you never know, she might answer. Perhaps the number for The Retreat will be in the file inside the crate.

No.

Or in one of these pamphlets?

No. There are only adverts for fishing tackle and numbers for private charter boats and timetables for seal-watching trips. But look, here's a file of *Useful Information*, and here is the phone number.

He hesitates.

Then he dials.

• • •

As Addie crosses the drive, she can hear the phone ringing, so she pushes open the door and, uncharacteristically, races her mother to answer it.

Her mother stands beside her.

'Hello, The Retreat.'

'Oh,' says a man's voice. 'Is that you? I hoped it would be.'

'Yes,' says Addie, smiling, feeling her face warm, hoping her mother hasn't noticed.

Addie gestures to her mother that she should go back into the sitting room, which she does, as the voice, says, 'I thought I'd call and say hello. I found the number, you see. In a pamphlet thing.'

'Good,' says Addie. 'I'm glad.'

'I mean, with the weather so wild, it's just nice to hear another voice.'

'Yes,' says Addie, straining to find the words she wants to say, but no further words come.

'How long do these storms normally last?' he says.

'The forecast says it will blow itself out in the night,' says Addie.

'Good,' says the man. 'Perfect. Well, I'll see you around then.'

'Yes,' says Addie, wishing so much she could say something else.

'I imagine we may bump into each other again,' says the man.

'Yes,' says Addie.

'Bye then,' says the man.

'Bye.'

She is almost paralysed.

Her mother comes back out.

'Who was it?' she says.

'Just an enquiry,' says Addie.

'You normally pass those to me,' says her mother.

'You said you were having a terrible night,' says Addie, feeling emboldened. 'In fact you said every night here is a terrible night. So I thought maybe you weren't in the mood to take enquiries. And also, if it's so terrible, why do you stay?'

'It's our life, Addie.'

'But if it's terrible for you, you should do something else.'

'I just mean I'm lonely.'

'Mum,' says Addie, surprising herself. 'I feel like an employee. Not your child.'

'You're too old to feel like a child.'

'I didn't say *a* child. I said *your* child. I'm not sure when it changed.'

'Shall we turn in early?' says her mother.

Addie sometimes wonders if her mother is unable to hear the frequency of her voice, if it's the wrong pitch for her.

'I feel exhausted,' says her mother. 'The guests are all happy. You can pop down later and turn off the lights.'

Addie nods.

They climb up to the second landing.

'You see, motherhood just happened to me,' says her mother, perhaps to explain why Addie might not feel like her child. 'I was already the provider at Stone House. Because Grandpa Fred was so useless. At first, I was only providing for him and Grandma Flora. But then Dad came along. Then you. And after that, Sydney. Have you ever thought how that felt for me?'

They reach their landing on the third floor.

'I was a child,' says Addie.

'I was your age exactly when I had you. Twenty-two. With all my life ahead of me,' says her mother, staring down the corridor to the dark window over the dark sea.

She stares at the sea that she can't see, and Addie stares with her, at the sea that she can't see, and the life beyond it that she can't see either.

'And now I have *all my life* ahead of me,' says Addie.

Her mother opens the door and goes into her bedroom.

• • •

Sol lies awake in his creaky single bed feeling a total fool. Why on earth did he phone her and blather about hearing another voice?

What was he thinking? She sounded as if she couldn't wait for the conversation to end.

The blackness threatens to come in through the gap in the window, and he can only keep it at bay by thinking of *good things* he'd miss if he wasn't alive tomorrow or the next day or at any time in the future. This is a strategy he's employed for some time, but before he came to Ora, he was running out of good things to think of. He was in quite a bad way after reading his father's letter in January, and as the weeks passed, he only got worse.

But now he has several pressing reasons to want to be alive.

There's—

Well.

Don't be ridiculous.

Let's start somewhere else.

There's his campervan, number one.

(He hopes the van's OK in the coach park in Seafields. He hopes it hasn't been vandalised. He wonders what it would be like to live in a van long-term. He thinks he might miss having a flushing loo.)

Anyhow.

Where was he?

Reasons to be alive. This beautiful island, two. The seabirds he's going to see here, three. His nomadding tour of thin places, four. And then five – and truthfully not five but definitely *one*, who's he kidding – there's *her*, and he knows it's crazy that she should be a reason to want to be alive when he doesn't even know her name and she doesn't want to talk to him on the phone. But there's always the chance that they might meet again, might talk again, might even get to know each other while he's here.

Calm down, Sol, he tells himself.

But he doesn't especially calm down.

He's alert as anything, sleepless, anticipant.

Knowing someone is such a long process, isn't it?

One we probably never complete.

But it always begins small.

In the movement of Addie's hand, waving.

In the texture of Sol's voice, singing, then speaking.

*Covering random topics they will almost
certainly never return to: the theology of
heaven and the duration of storms.*

Those funny first conversations.

*The knowing that starts in the little squeezed
spaces between vowels and consonants.*

Monday 1st May

Unrested and not ready for the day, Addie races downstairs with her hair wilder than ever, her sleepless eyes burning. She would do anything for a swim but it's too late, she's overslept. She puts the ensaimadas in the oven. Then she grabs her binoculars and rushes into the strangely still morning, climbing up to the mound to get a better view of Ora and the bridge, thinking that she must stop this obsessive behaviour.

· · ·

Sol leaps out of bed and looks out of the window. Last night's storm is gone, and the blackness has gone, and the day is white-skied and bright.

He must update his bird list. Like his mother, he keeps a long-running list of birds he's seen, in date order, with semi-colons between each item. His other lists include favourite songs (with reasons why); a one-sentence summary about every book he's ever read (from the age of seven onwards); Bible verses that mean something to him; and poems; and meaningful quotes; interesting new words and phrases (recent additions – *haecceity, numinous, singularity, pelagic*); places he's visited, arranged chronologically.

The reedy island on Hickling Broad is on the list, a powerful memory of his childhood and the first of his mother's thin places, where Tommie the bird warden used to sit listing rare avian sightings in his hut or trying to record the low booms of bitterns from the hide. The island is named after one Miss Turner, a Victorian ornithologist, who owned a hut on the same spot. Tommie always seemed oddly unhurried for an adult man: when Sol was little, he showed him how to draw with pencils and charcoal, and let him use his watercolour paint set.

Sol's father dismissed his wife's notion of *thin places*, saying that he wasn't into all that Celtic nonsense. Or Catholic nonsense. Or something. But Sol is planning to visit them all, starting here.

'If the veil is very thin,' Sol said to his mother, gritting his teeth and trying to sound calm and brave. 'I suppose we might be able to sense each other, you and I?'

'When I'm no longer here?' said his mother.

'Maybe,' she said.

'I hope so,' she said.

'I'll miss you, Mum,' he said, and his voice split and split until it couldn't make any noise at all, and he had to mouth soundlessly to her pale face: 'I can't explain to you how much.'

'Will you keep going over to Miss Turner's Island when I'm gone?' she said. 'Go and look for bitterns with Tommie, won't you?'

'I will,' he mouthed. 'I will.'

'Yes,' said his mother. 'Yes. You will, won't you?'

She opened her mouth, as if she had something else to say, and he thought of a thousand questions he wanted to ask her, a thousand things he wanted to say to her, but his voice wasn't working.

His voice returned, but his hope didn't.

He didn't go to Miss Turner's Island when she was gone.

'Go to Ora, won't you?' said his mother, on another day. 'See the puffins' bills! They're so *pointlessly lovely*. And that seems to say everything about the loveliness of the God who made them. I watched them for hours when I was on Ora. And they spoke to me.'

'Spoke to you?'

She took his hand.

'And I suppose I didn't listen.'

'So,' said Sol. 'Are you saying you can hear the voice of God through something that *isn't* the voice of God. Like a puffin's bill?'

'The puffin's bill *is* the voice of God,' said his mother. 'And vice versa.'

He made her say it again, and then again.

'I looked at the puffins' bills and knew your father didn't bring me joy.'

'You knew that *before* you married him? Hadn't you gone to Ora to check the marriage was right?'

'I had. But I was too frightened to call it off. I was a total fool. It's so important to choose well, Sol. Don't learn from me.'

Enough.

It's his first full day on Ora.

He has a shower, and look, his chest hair isn't evenly spread *again*, and his legs aren't meaty *again*, and why do we have to think the same things every time we look in the mirror, couldn't we just think them once and be done with it, he wonders.

He lies on the floor and tries another crab, and again he enjoys the stretching of his muscles, and this time he feels more liberated, less afraid. He lets his body sink to the cold floor. He really is exceptionally good at crabs. He hasn't lost his knack at all.

He puts on shorts and walking boots and his thick fisherman's jumper, grabs his camera and the book on meditation, putting them in his capacious pockets, and he goes downstairs. As he sets off over the bridge he can see someone – and he's pretty sure it's her – up on the slope with a pair of binoculars.

· · ·

Addie watches the man coming over the bridge.

He walks slanting slightly forwards, and she thinks he might be singing again. He's wearing shorts, which make him look different, more vulnerable. She looks at her watch and rushes back to serve breakfast. She takes out the ensaimadas, which have been in slightly too long, and her mother tries one.

'They're very doughy,' she says, 'and really not very nice.'

Addie escapes to the dining room. The youngest guest comes in, Lily Bairn, her hair woven into a pair of loose plaits.

She says, 'I found the life-coaching very helpful yesterday.'

'Good,' says Addie, and when she speaks, she feels pain in her belly, and in her mouth, which won't shape itself normally.

'Your mother thinks I've got stuck on a track I don't want to be on.'

Addie nods and smiles at Lily.

'Have you ever felt that in your life?' says Lily.

'No,' says Addie.

. . .

As Sol walks, he thinks he must have sounded rather pathetic on the phone. Whenever he interacts with people, albeit briefly, he always finds his weaknesses too painful, and lives for a day or two afterwards in an agony of self-examination and self-recrimination. Why did I do that? Why did I say that?

This is what he's thinking when a tern dives into his head. He flaps it away, long arms flailing, and the tern divebombs him again, so he runs off at quite a pace. The tern is remarkably persistent, but Sol eventually outwits him by collapsing and lying still on the grass as if he's died. Please don't let her come past now, he prays, or thinks, or whatever is the difference between them, he's never been able to work it out. Which mechanism is it that allows God (whatever form God takes) to pick up the silent (or not-silent) thoughts of over seven billion people? He's pretty sure nobody knows the answer to that, although his father would no doubt claim to.

Sol slowly opens his eyes. The tern has gone. He takes a deep breath. Here he is, in the grass, with the wide sky above, and it's Monday morning, and he's not in the classroom. He closes his eyes again.

· · ·

Addie puts the doughy ensaimadas on a plate, but then she changes her mind and throws them all in the bin, leaving the kitchen and heading back to the mound – *again*, this is getting *absurd* – with her binoculars.

But look!

There he is.

He's lying in the grass, which is most unexpected.

She races down the mound towards him, and, when she's about, what, twenty feet away, she stops. He's lying in the grass breathing deeply, in and out, in and out, looking peaceful, rather than collapsed, with his eyes closed, and she doesn't think she should disturb him. But as she moves a little closer, he opens his eyes, and they're staring at each other.

She's close enough now to see the kindness in his dark eyes. She's close enough to notice his salty forearms with his blue wool sleeves pulled up to the elbows, and his bare legs with sand stuck to them, between the hairs.

She panics.

Because she's going to have to talk to him.

· · ·

As Sol looks up at the young woman, he remembers when he first saw the mandarin ducks as a small boy. In her pinafore, and her green boots, with her green eyes and her heart-shaped face and her red hair corkscrewing around her shoulders, what comes to him is how singular she is. *Singularity*, he remembers from his word list: the point of infinite density and infinitesimal volume, the point where space and time are infinitely distorted as they were at the beginning of the universe.

Space and time stretch and shrink and stretch and shrink, and so does she, she blurs and she clarifies, and she blurs and she clarifies, and now the lines around her body sharpen, and she is lovely, even lovelier than he could have imagined.

He can't think what to do, or how to react, to a loveliness such as this. He opens his mouth, but nothing comes out, until he finds that he is saying, 'Let me show you my party trick.'

He places his arms behind him, putting his backward-facing palms on the grass, stretching his liberated leg and arm muscles and raising himself up into a crab position, in which his whole body seems to fizz with life. As he's doing this, he can't think why he's doing it, but he's committed now. He starts to move sideways, and he hears her laugh. He keeps going in a perfect circle, before lowering himself onto his back and sitting up.

'Do you have any other party tricks?' she says.

'Just this one,' he says. 'Which is actually fine because I don't go to parties.'

She laughs again.

'I don't either,' she says.

Sol feels a strange burst of heat rising up his legs. She doesn't go to parties! This could be the most successful conversation with a girl he's ever had. Though shortish. So far. But who knows where it will lead?

'I apologise for phoning last night,' says Sol.

'Oh, please don't,' she says.

'It was quite out of character,' says Sol.

Then he can't think what he should say next, so he pauses and looks around him, but nothing springs to mind.

So he says, 'Do you like books?'

. . .

They're talking!

They're actually talking.

But Addie needs to get back.

And also, books?

'I think I have the potential to like books,' she says to him.

'Well, that's good,' he says.

'I didn't go to school after I was seven, so I never know which books to read.'

'I could help you with that.'

'Oh,' she says, and no more words come.

She looks at her watch. She's late for her mother's briefing, and she's never been late before, and she has no idea how her mother will react.

'I'm sorry,' she says. 'But I need to go.'

. . .

As she turns and walks away, Sol realises that he should have stood up, obviously. Who would stay sitting down to talk to someone who was standing up? Also, he knows he looks terrible in his beanie hat. He feels most peculiar, as if someone has taken him to pieces and put him back slightly wrongly. The recriminations start: why did I do that, and why did I say that?

There's a long feather on the ground, white with a dark tip, its fine barbs velvet-soft and perfect. Sol puts it in his pocket. Then he gets up and he walks on, and as he walks, he remembers the curls of her hair glinting as the sun caught them, and her face, which looked sad, inclined slightly downwards, and the peal of her laugh, and her tentative voice saying she had the potential to like books.

Could he give her a book? No, he left all his books on the floor of the campervan, and he brought only *Murder in the Cathedral* and *Blood Wedding*, which are his favourites, and covered in his notes, and with which he couldn't possibly part.

He passes the cove beyond the bridge as he sets out to explore the island. Oh no. *Swimming.* The first of his two things. Wasn't he going to swim every day here? He was, but he hasn't. But still. He really does have to conquer his demons.

Perhaps he'll conquer them later. Tomorrow, or the next day, or next year, when he will have a beard and the demons will take more notice.

• • •

Addie's late for the briefing. She goes inside, feeling faintly stunned. Her mother is sitting at the centre again, arrayed by the semi-circle of women, and she looks up and glares at her. Addie smiles at the thought of the man's long body bent over backwards, moving sideways like a crab, and her mother creases her brow and narrows her eyes at her.

Her mother says: 'If you want to pass an exam, you have to work hard. If you want to be happy, you have to work hard too, make an effort. It won't just happen.'

Addie wonders if this is right, if she hasn't tried hard enough.

• • •

Sol, now sitting by the crumbling lighthouse, having nearly completed his circuit of the island, takes the book on contemplation out of his anorak pocket. It tells him to be present without judging or evaluating, to let the life in front of him come inside him. He reads the same page about seven times, but all he can think of is what he must have looked like crabbing around the grass in his beanie hat.

'Concentrate!' he says aloud.

He closes his eyes and he opens his arms to the wind and tries to let the sea, the wind, the lighthouse, the rabbits and the rocky promontory come inside him, as the book recommends. He feels nothing, other than stupid. He opens his eyes and sees a feather beside him: black at each end, with a flash of golden-yellow in the middle and pale tips. Goldfinch, it must be. He puts it in his pocket with the other one.

He gets up, and he climbs down a steep path, so that he is walking along a narrow edge of wet sand, bordered by rocks which soon becomes sea, so he has to climb up a bank, and the bank is covered in primroses, which lift his spirits, and between which he makes his way upwards, coming upon two crumbling flinty abutments of what must have been an old arch. He finds himself taking a photograph, and another, and another, and he's drawn into a place that is now nowhere, and was once somewhere, and as he stands in that nowhere place, he has a sense of where exactly the walls once were, and he hears voices chanting over the tide.

The past is penetrating the present in a way that makes Sol stop quite still. Is the thin place thinning, he wonders, his heart racing. Male voices are singing: *The Lord's my Shepherd; I'll not want.* He stands inside the flinty arch stumps among the primroses. *My soul he doth restore again and me to walk doth make.* The voices are getting louder now, and Sol closes his eyes, and he remembers to be thankful to God, as Brother Andrew advised.

'Thank you God,' he says to the air and the sea, and that seems a good start, and he believes for a moment that his soul might yet be restored.

Yea, though I walk in death's dark vale, yet will I fear no ill.

He's been in the vale since his mother died with little hope of getting out, but it was she who told him to come here, and he's come, here he is, is she here too?

My head thou dost with oil anoint.

And again.

Maybe, Perhaps, Possibly

My head thou dost with oil anoint.

The voices are fading now, and though his head doesn't feel especially anointed, he looks around in case his mother is about, transfiguring, but she isn't. He turns towards the crumbling wall with a gap where there would once have been a door.

. . .

As Addie sits at the Reception desk, her head flicking repeatedly towards the window, the blondes come and ask for towels, before padding off down the corridor in flat white slippers, a line of oversized ducklings.

The one with the short peppery hair has gone birdwatching.

Perfect.

Peace.

The young one, Lily Bairn, has joined her mother in the library for another life-coaching session, and she wants to attend Addie's art class afterwards. Addie doesn't mind giving art classes: it's the sort of brief functional talking she can manage, and more focused on the doing than the saying. She likes to draw, and she likes to paint, and she likes what she's seen of Lily Bairn.

She walks into the glass room, humming, and she opens the sash window to air the room, noticing some movement over at the entrance to the old chapel, which is partly hidden by gorsy shrubs and a decaying wall. She wonders if the llama has got loose again. Or Grandpa Dempster. No, it won't be him. He's had a bad fall.

'Like Humpty Dumpty,' her mother said, laughing.

It bothered her.

. . .

Isn't that the young woman, Sol wonders. Yes, that's her, behind the glass, wearing a colourful dress, or would you call that a smock?

(What exactly is a smock? Girls' clothes, so confusing: skirts, dresses, smocks.)

He feels warmth puckering his skin as he watches her put daffodils in a vase, and now oranges, in a bowl. He thinks he might be trespassing in the hotel garden. Now she's taking a doll and holding it upside down. Is that quite strange? Putting the upturned doll into some kind of metal clamp? Is she an artist?

She looks up.

Her face is sad.

Her face is always sad.

She sees him, and she waves, so he waves back.

She disappears.

He walks to the window, which has been pulled up a little, so he puts the tern feather and the goldfinch feather on the inside sill. Then he dashes back, making a path through the primroses, between the now-silent stumps of arch, and he hurries away, his head still un-anointed, his mother still absent, retracing his steps down the slope, onto the shrinking sand, picking his way over the rocks, soaking his boots and his legs all the way up to his knees.

He feels a terrible wave of embarrassment, but he doesn't have the courage to go back and remove the feathers.

What on earth was he thinking?

• • •

Addie takes Lily out to the kitchen to fill up their jam jars with water, and then they come back and sit down at the table, with the doll in front of them, clamped upside down.

Addie looks out towards the old chapel, but the man seems to have gone. She shows Lily how to map out her page in squares, telling her to throw off anything she knows of dolls and to paint what she actually sees, not what she expects to see. This is why the doll is upside down, so that Lily won't try to make it look like a doll.

It's then that she sees two feathers that weren't here before. The breeze is moving them along the window sill.

As she watches them, Lily says, 'Your mother says we're all like trams.'

Lily stares at the doll and draws the curved line of her foot.

'Trams?' says Addie.

'We think there's only one track we can be on.'

'Did you find that helpful?' says Addie, trying to remain supportive of her mother, or if not supportive, definitely neutral. What she wants to say is, Don't listen to her.

'Well, yes,' says Lily. 'I was on this track with Magnus. Heading towards marriage and children. Then he said it was over. Completely out of the blue. And I just don't know how to get off and find a different track.'

'I'm really sorry,' says Addie, and she is, although she is also distracted by the feathers moving along the sill.

'I haven't been able to see another life, or to want another life, I suppose. Without Magnus.'

'Love is very powerful,' says Addie. 'Too powerful, I always think. For me anyhow.'

Lily doesn't seem to be listening, but Addie is listening to herself. If she met the man properly, would she be opening herself to the possibility of love, when she's not interested in love? Should she turn away now when what she feels is harmless curiosity and a bit of fun?

Love!

Don't be ridiculous, she tells herself, you've hardly spoken to each other.

'Or at least I can't think of another way to have children,' says Lily. 'I'm thirty-nine, you see. And I *have* to have a baby.'

Addie nods.

Perhaps there's another way to love, one she hasn't seen yet. She loved Grandma Flora like a child loves. Perhaps without the blood bond, love is lighter, more playful, less intense. Without the blood bond, presumably you can love one person, then move on and love another. Lily will find someone to love like she once loved Magnus. It happens all the time in normal life. Whereas she could never have moved on from Grandma Flora.

'So your mother told me not to act like a tram. To act more like a car.'

'I see,' says Addie, trying hard to see.

'Or like a Land Rover,' says Lily, looking radiant for a moment. 'That's my new motto. *Be more Land Rover.*'

Oh dear, thinks Addie, her mother seems to have stretched the vehicular imagery a little too far.

The tern feather blows onto the floor and makes its way over the wooden boards. Addie picks it up. Lily says, 'Oh isn't that lovely? You know what they say about white feathers?'

'What?' says Addie.

'That someone you've lost is looking over you.'

'Oh,' says Addie. 'I think it's just from a tern.'

'Or an angel,' says Lily.

'More likely a tern,' says Addie.

'Can I have it?' says Lily.

Oh dear, thinks Addie, because she's pretty sure she knows who it's from and she badly (ridiculously) wants it, but Lily has paid two thousand pounds to come here for the week, so it's quite hard, on an island full of feathers, to deny her a feather.

As Lily puts the feather in her pocket, she says, 'I mean, it's one thing being a car. With the choice of lots of roads. But a Land Rover can get off road and do what the hell it likes. So I need to think much more creatively about how I could have a baby.'

'I see,' says Addie. 'That foot is just right, by the way.'

'I take that feather as a sign,' says Lily. 'The way it moved towards me.'

Addie doesn't answer.

'I hope your mother pays you well,' says Lily Bairn. 'You never stop working.'

And that's when it comes to her.

She has never paid me a single penny.

Addie walks to the window sill and takes the second feather.

'Oh, what's that one?' says Lily.

'That'll be from a goldfinch.'

'I'm sure there's a meaning for gold feathers too,' says Lily. 'I'll look it up.'

She holds out her hand, and Addie gives her the feather.

• • •

Sol heads to buy fresh milk and bread and cheese and tomatoes from *the shop*, and he leaves the money as specified on the trestle table, checking and re-checking the amount and hoping it's OK for a non-resident to use the service. He's read that it is, but he's now doubting himself. This happens to him all the time. He used to stand at the front door of his flat after locking it, pushing against it with his shoulder, to be sure, and then pushing it again, and then sometimes, he unlocked it and re-locked it and ran for his life so that his uncertainty couldn't catch up with him.

What was she doing with the doll, and why does she always look so sad?

And why on earth did he leave the feathers?

As he sits on the grass eating a tomato and a hunk of cheese, he decides that she's an artist, a sad artist: still life with oranges, still life with daffodils, and still life with weird doll.

He'd like her to be an artist, but not a sad one, though artists make art from their melancholy, don't they? Is it even possible to be a happy artist?

He likes the colours she wears. He's always found it depressing the way so many women, and, to be fair, men, wear black.

He closes his eyes and he takes the young woman in her colourful smock to a riverbank, beside which he's parked his campervan. She's sitting painting at her easel, with a palette, and she's not sad, she's smiling, and there are crocuses on the ground, yellow and white and purple, and he lies back on the grass and closes his eyes and allows himself to imagine.

His mother once told him that it's hard to live a life we can't imagine, that our future starts inside our own mind. It would be hard, for example, to become a sailor if you didn't know there was a sea. So he will imagine himself onto the riverbank with her. It's spring and the blossom is out and she's happy.

He opens his eyes, and wonders if he's still in the dream, because he seems to be caught in a storm of butterflies. He reaches for his phone, which of course he doesn't have, so he takes his camera out of his pocket, only to find that he's run out of film. He will have to enjoy this moment without recording it – *life is to be lived and not recorded.*

The orange butterflies mass above his body, and he wonders if they're telling him something, or if, even, they've found their way to him from somewhere else, from the celestial city with the great river and the trees that bear fruit every month. Might these butterflies, he wonders, be the sort of miracle that happens in a thin place.

As he walks towards The Retreat, the butterflies flap into orange bunting along the top of hedges, and they blow and fall and rise, forming a sphere. A smaller sphere breaks away and thins into a line, and the line circles the sphere like the rings of Saturn, which are pieces of comets and asteroids and shattered moons – and if that wasn't true, you wouldn't believe it.

If butterflies weren't true, perhaps you wouldn't believe them either.

· · ·

Addie looks out of the sitting room window to see clouds of butterflies making shapes around the folly, ballooning and thinning, rising up like a fountain, billowing like laundry on the line. She heads for the garden as Lily Bairn climbs down the folly steps.

'Did you lay the butterflies on for us?'

'Of course!'

'I'm going for a walk,' says Lily Bairn.

'See you later,' says Addie, walking towards the flinty arch stumps of the old chapel, where she sees the imprint of his boots on the grass. She notices that he didn't tread on the primroses. Is he here researching a book, or is he a photographer, or a poet, or a historian, or a monk? No, a monk wouldn't look like that. And she doesn't want him to be a monk. She'll take poet. A poet who doesn't tread on primroses. A poet wouldn't, let's be honest. A poet sees the beauty of things, makes pain into transcendence and love. Could he do that with *her pain*?

But look, she takes her phone out of her pocket to photograph the butterflies as they change shape above her head. More are joining, more and more, making a huge orange sphere, like a planet.

Addie often tries to imagine the moment before the Big Bang, when *nothing* was about to explode into something or everything: the huge build-up of creativity and fertility and colour and breath and beauty. She tries to imagine a force so big and so extraordinary that it creates light and gravity and time and planets and icebergs and mountains and oceans and elephants and dolphins and butterflies and human beings with pink plaited brains, and octopi with eight arms and three hearts and blue blood.

What was that force, she wonders, which wanted all of this into being.

• • •

When Sol returns to Ora, he follows the nesting map from the stool by his bed, and he comes upon a pair of eiders preparing their nest, the male calling out *coo-roo-ah coo-roo-ah* as he worries at their chosen hollow, following the female's hissed instructions, removing unwanted objects, tidying mess, the female plucking her breast in motherly love, covering the nest with her own down.

He sits down, and he imagines his mother watching the eiders when she was a young woman here, right here. This is where she knew she didn't love his father, but where she decided she would marry him anyway.

What if she'd made the other decision? Then what would her life have been? The life that didn't happen. Around him swirls the ghost of the life she didn't live, the ghost of the life he didn't live either, the one where he didn't exist. The strange feeling comes, the feeling he sometimes has that he isn't real. He presses at his flesh, but even if the flesh is real, he may not be.

When his mother was ill, however fragile she felt, she was always wanting to go over to Miss Turner's Island to see a bittern. When his father was out, she'd wrap herself in coats and scarves, and she'd ask Sol to row her up to Hickling Broad, where Tommie the bird warden would give them cups of hot chocolate and slices of lemon cake.

Then one evening, finally, there it was, a bittern, stretching its neck upwards towards the early moon.

'*Botaurus stellaris,*' said Sol, and his mother took his hand.

The bittern formed and unformed itself in the camouflage of the reeds and still his mother held his hand, and she said, 'God comes to us, disguised as our life, Sol. Don't forget this.'

These words, though he didn't understand them, felt important, and he still doesn't understand them, and they still feel important. He wants his life to be worthy of his mother, to make up for all the years that were taken from her, all her dreams left unfulfilled.

He stares at the eiders, and he thinks: *God comes to us, disguised as our life.*

• • •

Addie goes inside to lay out the cakes.

'Where is everyone?' says her mother.

Addie shrugs: 'Tea isn't compulsory.'

'Can you check all the bedrooms? Remind them about tea.'

Addie climbs the stairs and knocks on Lily's door.

Lily answers.

Addie glances at the feathers on the side table.

'Sorry to disturb.'

'I'll come down. I can't resist your mother's cakes.'

My cakes, thinks Addie, but she mustn't be petty.

She tries the other doors, on both floors, but nobody is in, so she heads to the spa, where she bumps into the blondes coming up the stairs in a cloud of chlorine and body spray.

'I always say more lengths, more cake,' says the woman with the oblong mouth.

When Addie reaches the sitting room with the blondes, she sees her mother drawing her chair up close to Lily and taking her hand. *Perhaps I should sign up for some life-coaching,* she thinks to herself, *only I wouldn't have the money.* This turns out not to be a light and amusing thought.

Addie stares at her mother's hand, and she can't suppress her anger, but with her anger, there's a tiny flicker of hope, with which she is entirely unfamiliar.

She wonders what happens when anger meets hope.

. . .

Sol feels the green eider feather in his pocket.

He climbs to the highest ledges of the cliffs, tasting salt on the sea breeze as it blows over the clifftop, and here he sees his first ever fulmar egg, white and rough-textured, laid in a scrape of stone. He stares at the egg, and he feels the fragile wonder of it – an egg, who would ever have invented an egg? – like a current through his body. Yes, his body, his body! His body which feels as if it's waking up from a deep sleep, here on Ora, when all it's really done for years is carry around his brain. Is it the way he's stretched out his muscles with all his crabbing? Or is it something else?

He sits on a rock and watches the guillemots, and he's moved by their profound coincidence with the moment, and the wind blows his hair against his forehead and into his eyes, and he lets it, and he tries to allow himself to coincide with the present and the island, and as he does so, he feels a thought rumbling like thunder in his mind.

He'd thought, because of what his mother said, that it was the membrane between earth and heaven that might split in a thin place like Ora, allowing God, or heaven, to burst through, like the illustrations from his childhood Bible.

But in fact, is it something quite different that needs to split?

Might it be the membrane around *himself* that needs to split?

Might it already be splitting in fact?

And if so, who or what is about to come out?

．　．　．

Addie dribbles olive oil and pastes ginger over two large trays of cherry tomatoes, shaking cumin and turmeric, splashing lime, sprinkling salt.

Anger and hope seem to make courage. She didn't know that would be so.

As she twists the pepper grinder, her mother comes in.

'I have something important to ask you,' says Addie as she puts the first tray and then the second into the oven, setting an alarm on her phone.

Her mother says: 'Not now, not now. You've got dinner to make.'

'It needs to roast for fifteen minutes. I have plenty of time.'

'You've been acting quite strangely lately,' says her mother.

'Picture this like a life-coaching session,' says Addie.

Her mother says, 'What?'

'I've been thinking,' says Addie.

And here comes what courage is going to say.

'Shouldn't you have been paying me all these years? For working for you? Or are we sharing the profits? Because I've been working for you for seven years and I don't have any of my own money.'

'Money!' says her mother. 'You don't need money! I've always given you free board and lodging.'

'I came when I was fifteen,' says Addie. 'I think most parents would provide free board and lodging.'

'But you're twenty-two now,' says her mother.

'Yes,' says Addie, 'I'm twenty-two and I need to have my own life.'

'You have your own life,' says her mother.

'No,' says Addie. 'I'm mainly living yours.'

'What are you talking about?' says her mother.

'What I'm talking about is that I need to leave.'

'Leave?' says her mother.

And then louder, 'Leave?'

'And for that,' Addie carries on because she knows she mustn't stop. 'For that, I need some money. Even a small amount to get me started.'

'I gave up everything for you,' says her mother in a horrible taut whisper.

'I don't think that's quite true,' says Addie. 'I think you came because you wanted to come, which is perfectly reasonable. You might regret that now. But it doesn't feel fair to blame me.'

'You were being bullied!' says her mother.

'I was fifteen when we left and the bullying had been over for years,' says Addie. 'I think you came because you couldn't bear to live at Stone House without Grandma Flora. And I understand that because I couldn't bear it either. She brought me up.'

'*I* brought you up,' says Addie's mother.

'You worked every hour for all of us,' says Addie. 'And I'm grateful for that. But Grandma Flora brought me up.'

'How dare you?' says her mother.

Addie isn't going to stop now, not now that she has courage: 'I

97

think you wanted a new start. A different life. Something extraordinary. And there's a lot I've loved about Rokesby. But that doesn't mean I have to stay forever.'

Her mother breathes deeply.

'It's no crime to grow up,' says Addie. 'Or to want different things from you.'

'I've protected you,' says her mother. 'All your life all I've done is protect you. You were a very weird child. Did you know that?'

'I did,' says Addie.

'I took you out of school because you didn't fit in.'

'And I'm grateful,' says Addie. 'I hated school.'

'I thought we could do something special together.'

'And we *were* doing something special together,' says Addie. 'But then, we weren't.'

'That's not true,' says her mother.

'I think it is,' says Addie. 'You tell me what to do and I do it. And I don't want to live like this any more.'

'I won't have that.'

'And when two people see things differently, who judges?'

She hears her voice as if it's not her own, and now she's started, she can't stop.

'I think it's time for me to get off my track,' says Addie.

'Did Lily tell you I said that?' says her mother.

'She said she found it helpful.'

'The sessions are supposed to be confidential.'

'Surely her part, not yours?'

'What's got into you?'

'I would rather leave with your blessing,' says Addie. 'But if you won't give it to me, I'll have to leave anyway. So that I can work out who I am.'

'I won't give you my blessing,' says her mother. 'I can't see what kind of life you think you'd be able to make on your own. Without me. You know nothing of the world.'

'Precisely,' says Addie.

Her mother's face is hot and red.

'Is this how you repay me?' says her mother, and Addie watches rage spread over her face, as she turns around, picks up the large white china bowl of raw king prawns with both hands and holds it in front of her.

She looks at Addie, and Addie has no idea what is about to happen. She stands, and her mother stands, and between them there is only the large white china bowl with the prawns inside it. Her mother, staring at her intently, lets the bowl drop out of her hands. There's a terrible crash, which makes Addie's hands start shaking. She never knew courage would cause such havoc. Her mother stands totally still, her arms bent at the elbow, her hands sticking out into the air, holding nothing.

The bowl has smashed into hundreds of shards, and the prawns lie between them scattered, grey, helpless and dead.

Addie thinks, *at least there's chicken in the fridge.*

Then she thinks that something broke in her when her mother broke the bowl.

· · ·

Sol watches the waves lapping up the beach of the little cove on Ora, and he wonders if he should give the swimming a go. He'll regret it if he doesn't at least try once.

He goes to his room, pulls on his swimming shorts and makes his way down to the beach. He takes off his sweater and his trainers, and here goes. The water is a shock against his toes first, and then his balls, but he keeps walking, deeper and deeper, and as he lifts his right arm, curving it and drawing it over his head, he sees Carl Turlington's red face, and he sinks.

He's a boy again in free swim time. He tries the left arm, then the right, but he sinks, and sinks again, and sinks again. The shame of it. It's a mystery the way one person, *one child*, can incapacitate a person – that's one child that's still incapacitating an adult all these years later. Yet does Carl Turlington, no doubt out being big and important in the world, ever think of him? Does he even remember what he did to him? Probably not. He needs to let go of him: he's held on to him for far too long.

Sol goes back to the prayer house, has a hot shower, puts back on his jeans and his sweater and an extra sweater. He finds bags of charcoal in the shed, and firelighters in the porch, and once the barbecue's hot, he lays out the burgers, and the dark is falling fast, so he turns on the outside light.

He has a beer and another beer, and he eats a burger in a bap, and then another, and he walks around the island in the dark. His eyes are caught by The Retreat, its gold lights washing over the abstract sculptures and the fountain. She's in there somewhere, with her ringlets and her daffodils and her sadness.

He looks at his watch – it's eleven o'clock.

The swimming failure is gone now, and there are only the cries of birds calling across the air, and he throws his three beer bottles into the old bin – clank, clank, clank – and he checks the barbecue is out, then checks again, then fills a watering can from the outside tap and soaks it to death.

The clouds have blown away, and he sits and stares upwards at the open sky, and the stars pulse, and the island pulses, as tiny bird-beginnings substantiate beneath shells on cliff edges. Everything is waiting and on the cusp. He takes a final glance at the moon, stands up and walks inside.

• • •

After dinner, Addie sees her mother escape upstairs rather than join the guests. She puts the plates and bowls and knives and forks into the dishwasher and washes the pots and pans. When she goes into the sitting room, nobody is there.

She goes outside to lock up the chicken run, and she realises she didn't collect the eggs this morning. She's never forgotten before. She finds two white ones, which she picks up and puts in her pockets, one in the left and one in the right. She hurries to the bridge in the dark, and she walks over, and as she watches the prayer house, a light goes on in the upstairs bedroom. He's going to bed. She stands, staring, her fingers enjoying the smooth feel of the eggs' shells.

Now a small window, which is probably the bathroom, lights up. He'll be getting ready for bed. It feels rather odd, or perhaps rather intimate, to be here watching him. The light goes out. He doesn't take long in the bathroom, she thinks, so perhaps he showers in the mornings. He's back in the bedroom. The very bright light gives way to a duller light. Perhaps he's reading.

She stands and imagines him in his bed reading, and she wonders what, if anything, he's wearing, and she tells herself not to, and she wonders instead what book he's chosen, and she'd like him to choose a book for her to read, or, even better, to read to her.

Stop it, she tells herself, but standing here, just a few metres from his bedroom, she feels close to him, and a little bit less alone, and she wonders if she's used up all her courage because she doesn't seem able to knock on the door. She tiptoes to the table and leaves the white eggs between two of the greying wooden slats.

She returns to the bridge, crosses over and walks along the back of Bird Beach to The Retreat, where she hoovers the muddy carpets. She turns off all the downstairs lights, checks that the windows and doors are closed and the front door is locked, climbs the stairs, gets into her bed and closes her eyes.

She's afraid that the man will leave Ora, and she'll be left behind. Her only possible escape is by boat, and there's no way of going without being seen by Robert and Mac or by Johnnie who drives the ferry.

She looks out of the window.

The prayer house is dark now.
'Good night,' she says to him.

. . .

Something makes Sol get out of bed.
He looks over at The Retreat.
Only one light is on, upstairs.

Tuesday 2nd May

Addie wakes early to a thick veil of fog. She grabs a bikini and takes her favourite tail out into the grey silence of the near-dawn, heading to Penny Cove. The cold is painful and bracing as she flies through the kelp forest, and there's Eureka in her den. She reaches out one stretchy tentacle arm, then another, then another, retracting them one at a time.

Addie rises to breathe and dives back down, and as she does so, Eureka comes out of her den towards her, right up close, and she spreads her fleshy body across Addie's chest, extending her many arms up her neck and over her shoulders. Addie's skin tingles with her knobbles and bumps, with the squeeze of her suckers, and she's holding Eureka, or Eureka's holding her, and she stays perfectly still as Eureka nuzzles against her.

They're *embracing*.

Eureka nestles into her chest, staring into her eyes, and Addie loses herself in her gaze, as if there's no barrier between them, as if they are seeping into each other's flesh, but, oh no, she needs to breathe, she must separate, and she carefully massages Eureka's eight arms away from her skin, and she feels the gap of her, as

103

Eureka swooshes through the kelp, off to hunt, in clouds of ink, and as Addie zooms, gasping to the surface.

She dives back down as fast as she can, but Eureka has gone.

• • •

Sol gets up early, makes himself tea and toast and heads outside into the whitish day. A damp fog hovers over the island, and he can't see The Retreat. As he approaches the greying picnic table, he sees two white eggs. He puts down his mug and plate and picks them up. They look like mallard eggs, but what bird would possibly lay its eggs on a table? He must look at the records inside the prayer house and see if this has happened before, if it's some kind of specialised duck behaviour on Ora.

There's a figure in the mist. *It's my mother,* he thinks. *She's come for me, like she said she would.* The thin place has thinned. The butterflies were only the forerunners. Or, there again. Maybe it's the young woman.

If this could be either your mother or the young woman, who would you choose?

Where did that question come from?

He's always had the sense from his father that God was out to test him and find him lacking, but his mother said that it was the devil who tested Jesus in the desert.

You can have only one of them.

Who will you choose?

His answer comes.

He tells it to leave at once, this minute, immediately, now.

• • •

As Addie walks off the bridge, her hair wet, her body shivering with cold, or with the loss of Eureka's flesh, she sees a shape sitting at the table. She takes a deep breath and walks towards him.

• • •

And there she is. Sol's unbidden answer.

. . .

'I wanted to come and say hello,' says Addie. 'I wanted to ask you your name.'

'I'm Sol,' says the man, holding out his hand, which she shakes, awkwardly, and then drops. 'Sol Blake.'

'I like your name. I'm Addie. I haven't quite decided on my surname.'

The man looks surprised.

'These eggs appeared in the night,' he says. 'They look like mallard eggs. But what duck would lay eggs on a table? Have you seen this before?'

'Never,' she says, smiling. 'How mysterious.'

'Do you like mystery?'

'I love it. My grandmother loved it too. Anything off beam. Slightly odd. These are her boots.'

Addie gestures to her feet.

'She gave them to you?'

'She did. Well, kind of. I helped myself to them really. She's dead. The dead can't choose who to give things to.'

'I'm sorry.'

'I loved her more than anyone in the world.'

'Then I'm extra sorry.'

She feels his dark eyes on her, and she likes it.

'Have you ever lost someone you loved?'

'Yes. I think that's probably why I'm here. I never really grieved. I just kept going, but I'm trying to find a new path.'

'It's hard to get off our track, isn't it? But we're not trams.'

'Trans?'

'Trams,' says Addie, wondering why she's using her mother's bad metaphor at a moment like this. 'We shouldn't be trams. We should be cars. Not just cars. We should be Land Rovers. They can go off road, anywhere, can't they?'

'You seriously got off road. Before I came, I had no idea anyone lived here in the middle of the sea.'

'Well, it wasn't really my choice. My family came over when I was fifteen.'

'And they're all here, are they?'

'Only my mother. My father and brother left. The hotel's just for women.'

'I see.'

'Anyhow, I just wanted to see you again, that was all.'

'I see you've been swimming,' says Sol. 'Wasn't that dangerous in the fog?'

'It's not foggy underwater,' she says, laughing. 'And I was swimming with a friend.'

'Ah good.'

'Although she disappeared.'

He looks surprised, but she doesn't explain.

'Do you like swimming?' she says.

He hesitates, picking up one of the eggs and staring at it.

'Being honest, it's not high on my list.'

'That's sad.'

'Would you like to stay for breakfast? Mystery eggs and stale bread?'

'Sounds delicious, but I need to get back and serve the guests.'

'Maybe another time.'

Addie looks at her watch.

'Oh crap,' she says. 'I'm late for breakfast. Have a good day!'

'Yes, you too.'

'Sol,' she says.

'Addie,' he says.

'They're chicken eggs. I don't think ducks lay eggs on tables.'

He smiles awkwardly.

'I brought them over last night,' she says. 'But I think you'd gone to bed.'

. . .

If only she'd knocked last night. He would have invited her in, and he could have offered her a beer, or a cup of tea, or a stale marmite sandwich, or tinned tomato soup even. And then anything could have happened. They could, for example, have sat on the sofa together.

He feels his body tingling and stretching, and he also feels an idiot: of course ducks don't lay eggs on tables. Then he feels elated. She brought him chicken eggs.

She brought him chicken eggs!

He takes them inside, boils the kettle and places them carefully into the pan with the water. He waits five minutes, cracks open the shell of the first and plunges in his teaspoon, and the minerals and lipids and proteins of the deep yellow yolk taste golden and hopeful, like a possible *ontological renascence.*

He likes that phrase. Once he's finished the eggs, he adds *ontological renascence* to his list. He's whistling as he washes up the egg cups. Lovely eggs, lovely words, lovely her.

If he had a phone, he would possibly WhatsApp Tim, although Tim thinks he's in Greece, so he'd probably have to make her Greek, which wouldn't suit her at all. The person he'd most like to tell is his father. As revenge, he supposes. Something makes him want to read his father's letter again, to be furious and appalled by him again. He goes upstairs and opens his mother's grey suitcase, but before he's reached for the letter in the elasticated pocket, his eye is caught by his mother's perfume.

He hopes his mother doesn't know he chose Addie and not her this morning. Surely the dead can't see inside the thoughts of the living. He takes his mother's perfume out of its white box, and sprays it into the air. Then he takes her clogs out of their cloth bag and walks them around the wooden floor before returning them to the case.

. . .

Addie serves breakfast in a strange heightened state, her heart warmed by his name – *Sol Blake* – and his hair and his arms and his eyes, her spirit lifted by Eureka's embrace. Although there's a growing sense of alarm too. Where did Eureka go? And when will *Sol Blake* leave the island?

She makes her way around the bedrooms, dragging sheets and pillowcases off beds; bleaching toilets; pulling hair out of plugholes. She shines taps; she mops floors; she dusts shelves; she empties bins. There has to be a way to leave.

She goes downstairs, carrying the laundry bags over her shoulders, and she puts the bedding into the washing machines. She remakes the beds. She picks flowers. She prepares lunch. She has just under an hour, so she races back to Penny Cove, and throws herself in the water.

There's no sign of Eureka in her den.

. . .

Sol is out walking when he bumps into Brother Andrew.

'How are things going?' he asks.

Sol stutters as he tries to think of something holy to say.

'I saw this great sphere of orange butterflies with a ring around them like Saturn,' he says. 'Would that count as a miracle, do you think?'

'What's your definition of miracles?' says Brother Andrew.

'I guess something that doesn't happen normally, or naturally. You know, outside the order of things.'

'Are Saturn-shaped butterflies outside the order of things?' says Brother Andrew.

Sol hesitates.

'Well, never mind about the butterflies,' he says. 'Don't let me hold you up.'

'You remember me saying that people often have strange thoughts on retreat,' says Brother Andrew. 'Has this been your experience?'

'Well, I had this one awful thought.'

'Would it help you to say it aloud?'

'I don't think I can.'

'That's OK.'

'But in a way it might help.'

Sol prepares himself.

'I came here hoping to feel the presence of my mother, who's dead, you see,' he says. 'But instead of thinking about my mother, I've been entirely distracted by thoughts of a certain young woman. Almost obsessively so.'

Brother Andrew nods.

'And there was this moment when I felt as if God was asking me who I'd rather have if I could only have one of them: my mother or the young woman.'

'Yes?'

Sol wonders if he dares voice it.

'And for a second, before I had time to correct myself—'

Sol pauses.

'Yes?'

He takes a breath.

'I find this very hard to say. But I chose the young woman *over my mother*.'

Brother Andrew puts his hand on Sol's shoulder.

'Does that make me a terrible person?' says Sol.

'I don't think God was making you choose between your mother and the young woman. But I do think God sent the butterflies to you.'

'Oh,' says Sol. 'Were the butterflies my miracle?'

'What do you think?'

'I think', says Sol, allowing his thoughts to clarify, 'that I don't need a miracle. Because ordinary things are miraculous already.'

'I think you're right,' says Brother Andrew. 'Your life is just as ordinary as everyone else's. But it's also unique and miraculous because everything you experience is specifically addressed to you.'

Sol nods, though Brother Andrew's words don't especially make sense.

'Death is ordinary too,' says Brother Andrew. 'It happens to all of us. And it's also miraculous.'

'But mainly terrible,' says Sol.

'I think suffering is always part of the pattern,' says Brother Andrew. 'It's just we don't dare admit it to each other. Little deaths and resurrections, all the time, and then the big one.'

Part of the pattern?

'Easter?' says Sol.

'Which is a lesson in trust. Your mother showed you how to trust,' says Brother Andrew. 'By dying.'

'Trust?' says Sol.

'Trust, or surrender, which I suppose are other words for death,' says Brother Andrew. 'And every time we surrender, our life becomes bigger. Death must certainly be bigger than life I've always thought.'

'I don't fully understand what you're saying,' says Sol. 'But I have a strange feeling that I might cry. I do apologise. I haven't cried since I was very young, you see. My father didn't agree with it. I wasn't allowed to. So I kind of seized up.'

Brother Andrew puts his hand on his shoulder again.

His hand is very hot.

But Sol doesn't cry.

• • •

Maybe, Perhaps, Possibly

When Addie gets back to The Retreat, having failed to find Eureka, it's too late to shower. She serves lunch to the guests, but their voices sound tinny and far away, and she feels cold and shivery, and wonders if she has hypothermia.

• • •

Sol sits to watch the eiders. The first pair has been joined by a second. The first eider duck raises herself from her downy nest, and underneath her are her eggs, large, buff-coloured with a hint of olive green. As Sol counts the eggs (there are six), his ears tune to the voices of wind and sea, to the buzz of a lone bee, to the gurgling oohs of the nesting eiders. The sounds meld together and draw him inside them, as if he too is melding with them. The eider duck is lit by a shaft of sunlight as she waddles, illuminated, towards the sea and shrinks out of sight. Sol watches an ant move along a blade of grass, and both the ant and the blade of grass light up too. As he lights up with them. As everything does. For this one moment, rather than loving God, as his father requires, he loves *with* God, un-separate from God. He loves the world with God, and he loves his mother with God, and he and God and his mother and the world are all un-separate from each other, lit up.

• • •

Addie grabs her tail and sets off to Penny Cove. She dives down, and sees that Eureka is back in her den. She waits patiently, but Eureka doesn't offer an arm. Addie rises, breathes and comes back down, and Eureka is doing something strange. She's twisting and she's turning, and all eight of her arms are curling, and beneath her, Addie spots something emerging – tiny white capsules, floating up and being enclosed by her manic multiple arms.

She's laying her eggs.

That's it.

A male octopus must have come by some time ago.

111

This is the beginning of the end for Eureka, Addie knows this: she will string thousands of eggs together into a huge gelatinous structure and she will cover them and protect them with the whole of herself, choosing not to leave them for a moment to feed herself, bathing them repeatedly in her oxygen, until she has no more body and no more oxygen, sacrificing herself for the success of her children.

Addie races up to the surface to breathe, and dives back down, trying different angles to see her beneath her rock, but whichever way she approaches the den, Eureka won't look at her. She goes up again to breathe, and she flaps her tail to keep herself at the surface – and then it comes to her. Eureka knew, inside her, that the time had come, just like she knows, inside herself, in her body, her body being her ally and her messenger. Like the woman said on the radio.

She dives, and she holds out her hand, hoping for one final touch, but Eureka's touch is for her eggs now. It's over. Her life. Their friendship.

Everything ends, she thinks.

This is life's terrible secret.

She heads back to The Retreat, and curls up on her bed, and she looks up the meaning of sacrifice on her phone. *To give up something precious in order to gain or maintain something else.* Eureka will give up her life not to gain something but to gift life to her babies, even though ninety-nine per cent of them will die. Addie's not sure her mother ever gave up anything for her. Nor was she willing to sacrifice her island dream for her father and Sydney. Nor were they willing to sacrifice the life they wanted for her.

She wonders, therefore, if you can love and not sacrifice, and she wonders if sacrifice can ever become an unstoppable desire in human beings, as it has for Eureka, or if they're too selfish.

She hears a knock and the door opening.

'What's the matter?' says her mother's voice.

'Nothing,' says Addie.

Then she uncurls and sits up.

'I need to leave, Mum,' she says. 'We only get one life. You're always saying that to the guests. Would you sacrifice having me here to give me the chance of a life somewhere else?'

'Can we talk about this another time?' says her mother, standing by the door of Addie's sewing cupboard. 'I have a terrible stomach. I can't leave the bathroom. Was that chicken defrosted properly? I'm sure it was.'

When her mother says she's sure about something, it means she isn't – it's odd.

How have they moved so fast from sacrifice to defrosted chicken?

'I need to leave, Mum,' says Addie again.

'You can't leave, Ads,' says her mother, who having tried bowl-smashing fury is now opting for a different, calmer, more grown-up tack. 'We have a business to run, and I'm not feeling at all well.'

Her mother sits on the bed.

'You're going to have to stand in for me,' she says.

'I always do,' says Addie.

'Nonsense,' says her mother.

'When are we going to talk about my pay?' says Addie.

'Is this the right moment?' says her mother.

'It will never be the right moment,' says Addie.

• • •

When Sol's mother died, his sister Leah said that she could see her in heaven in a vision, and she was surrounded by doves. Rachel said she could too. Sol couldn't see the vision, and he was pretty sure his sisters couldn't either.

'Well, how could we think of crying when she's surrounded by doves?' said his father, speaking very slowly, breathing between words, calling out to his assistant, Margaret.

Sol's sisters went into the garden and Rachel found a white feather.

'This dropped from heaven,' said Leah.

'No it didn't,' said Sol. 'The swans are always out there. They shed their feathers all the time.'

'The feather dropped from heaven,' said his father in a stern voice, taking deep breaths between each word. 'We have no reason to be sad.'

Sol held in his tears.

No reason to be sad?

He didn't cry, not that afternoon or the next day. His body seized up so that he couldn't raise his hands above his head.

'Did anything happen?' said the physiotherapist.

Sol said that no, nothing had happened.

He never did cry about his mother's death, but as he makes his way back to the prayer house, he knows he will now, any minute. The crack begins in his chest as he climbs the stairs, and it splits into tributaries of cracks, and his rib cage is now shaking, as he lies back on his bed in the Eider Room on the island of Ora, his mother's thin place, the place where his own hard shell has been thinning and thinning day by day, and finally, finally, the tears come, surging as if a dam is breaking, and his carapace shatters, and shards of him fall invisibly around the bed.

Wednesday 3rd May

After breakfast, Addie takes her mother ginger tea, as she has requested.

'It's a beautiful day,' she tells her mother, 'and they all want to come on the picnic. They've finally tired of the spa.'

'I need more water,' says her mother.

Addie leaves the room, goes down to the kitchen and then back up three staircases with a large jug of iced water and a glass on a tray.

Her mother is either asleep or pretending to be. She looks at her lying with her eyes closed, and she feels something, but she's not sure what. She stares at the shape of her body under the duvet and her slightly flickering eyes, and then she turns and leaves.

. . .

As Sol wakes, he sees his mother's perfume bottle on the floor by the suitcase, its white box standing next to it. He takes his diary and, because his carapace has broken and he has emerged, changed, he writes determinedly: *Today I'm glad to be alive.* Then he stares at what he's written and feels tense.

He climbs out of bed, gets dressed, puts his diary and pencil in his pocket. Then he reaches down, picks up his mother's perfume box and throws it in the bin. He sprays his mother's perfume into the air and smells her. Then he takes the bottle determinedly to the women's bathroom and opens the mirrored cabinet, leaving it on the shelf with the half-used bottles of shampoo and bubble bath.

He looks in the hall cupboard for a rug or a deckchair and instead finds a child's bamboo fishing net. As he walks to the beach with his binoculars around his neck and the net over his shoulder, he remembers Aunty Peggy's house in Cornwall. He pokes about happily under rocks, examining shrimps and crabs, a starfish, sea anemones and pink feathery coral weed.

• • •

Addie bakes cheese sticks and scones and she ices a coffee cake, like a robot, and she makes smoked salmon sandwiches with cucumber, and tomato sandwiches with mozzarella, and she packs crisps and nuts and elderflower cordial and champagne.

She puts the picnic into rucksacks and baskets and takes them to the hall, where the women are waiting.

• • •

Sol is joined on the beach by a whole party of wading birds: turnstone, purple sandpiper, sanderlings and ringed plover, and several pairs of oystercatchers which are piping lustfully at each other and running about in a kind of dizzied frenzy of love. He sits leaning against a rock, and he takes out his diary and writes, apprehensively: *Something good is going to happen today.*

Then he feels terrified, and wants to cross it out because it's so much safer to assume that something bad is going to happen. It's hard to give up our ingrained ways of thinking, but he must. Perhaps, in order to ensure that something good will happen today, he will have to *make* it happen.

• • •

Addie leads the women towards the estuary, and after identifying different species of wading birds, they move on to a grassy finger which juts into the sea, overlooking the seal beaches. They lay out rugs, and Addie unpacks the picnic, watching her hands as if they don't belong to her. The guests compliment her on the flavoursome sandwich combinations, but she can't hear them, she's not here, she's somewhere else.

Lily Bairn stares at the sea. Addie stares at the sea too, and she wants to be in it, or over it, over there, to the left, on Ora, or to the right, on the mainland, not here. The blondes drink champagne, and Fran with the peppery short hair stands turning in circles, her binoculars to her eyes.

Then Addie sees him. He's watching the waders. She watches him watching the waders. Fran with the short hair watches him watching the waders. The blondes drink more champagne. Addie gets out the cheese sticks and the cheese scones, which the women demolish quickly, so she cuts the coffee cake and gives each of them a slice.

Sol Blake is walking towards them.

Look at him, so real and so here and so public.

It comes to her: Sol Blake will help her leave.

He stops.

'Lovely afternoon,' he says.

The women concur.

Addie has the strange feeling that she wants to run her hand along the skin of his forearms, she wants to rub the sand off his shins, feel his hairs, his flesh, his bones, and beyond to what's beneath. She's hot with the presence of him, which buzzes through the centre of her body, from the crown of her head through her stomach into her groin.

She needs to do something to resist. She looks around. She looks down. When she looks up, he's moved on, and there is only the back of him as he heads for the cliffs, and it's all she can do to stop herself running after him. A bank of purplish clouds rushes over the island, and the wind starts to blow up.

'Who was that?' says Lily. 'And would he like to impregnate me?'

Fran takes her binoculars off her eyes, and the blonde with the oblong mouth shrieks with laughter, then eats another slice of cake. Her laughter seems to burst the largest of the dark clouds, the wind blasting torrents of rain over the cliffs and down the back of their necks.

Addie tells the guests to go, to run, she'll meet them back at The Retreat, and they race off holding rucksacks and baskets over their heads, and Addie looks up, feels the deluge on her face, in her hair, and as she packs up the last bits of the picnic, she gives herself to the wind and the rain, feeling the wildness inside her, where she feels him, fizzing, where she feels her departure fizzing too.

As she walks, drenched, into the hall, there's no sign of the women, but the rucksacks and baskets are lying abandoned on the floor for her to clear up. She takes them into the kitchen, two at a time. She sits on the bench and puts her head in her hands, then allows her head to drop to the table. She can't possibly make the pastry for tonight's pies because she no longer has anything to do with pastry or pies.

She creeps upstairs with a jug of fresh water for her mother, and she stares at her closed, inanimate face, wondering what's inside her mother's mind, what her mother really thinks of her. She should go now, she knows she should, take her chance while Sol Blake is on Ora. Can she possibly leave with her mother ill and all the guests here? There'll never be a good moment.

Come on, she tells herself.

Come on.

She's never travelled before, so she can't think what to take with her. She puts things in her rucksack: her patchwork dungarees, her denim and gingham pinafore, her green boots, her toothbrush. She grabs her favourite tail, because she can't imagine not having it with her. She intends to be back, of course. She'll come and go. Like Sydney. She'll be a normal person.

Then she remembers the wedding dress and the half-made bolero jacket.

She stuffs them in too.

• • •

As Sol hurries towards the bridge to Ora, he feels a pressing sensation at each end of his spine, a current running from vertebra to vertebra, a tingling in the hands, a swelling pain in his groin, an odd ache inside his spirit, as if his spirit has been caged too long and wants out.

He heads into the power of the wind along the back of Bird Beach where he first saw her, and the rain hurls itself at him as he crosses the bridge, waves soaking his legs. When he gets to the prayer house, he drapes his wet clothes on hooks in the bathroom, and he puts on dry ones, and goes downstairs to make a cup of tea. As he sits at the Formica table, the storm lashes the walls, and he feels aroused and alive. He picks up a book from the melamine shelves and a postcard falls out. He thinks of writing to his father to tell him that he's met someone called Addie. No, perhaps he'll tell his father that he no longer needs to go seeking miracles because miracles are everywhere.

He remembers having this sensation as a little boy on the Broads. Was it a sensation, though, or an ability to see the miraculous quality in everything? He lost it somewhere, but it's come back . . .

He puts down the postcard. He will not write to his father.

He feels cold, so he heads to the bathroom, and in the shower, he has a powerful memory of being on the merry-go-round at The Amusements with his mother. He hasn't thought of this for years. He's a little boy wearing green shorts, and round they go, round and round. His mother's dark hair flies outwards as her

119

horse leaves the merry-go-round and flies away from him into the sky.

Sol gets out and gets dressed, and he sees that the bridge is now impassable. He grabs his binoculars. There's Brother Andrew, on the bridge heading for Rokesby. The water runs up to his waist, but he ploughs on, and the waves knock him over, but he pulls himself up, and he keeps going, and again he falls, he falls, and he looks so small and so frail, but he's got hold of a rock to steady himself, and he drags himself forward, and Sol can hardly watch, but Brother Andrew's determined and unbowed, and now he's caught by a wave, submerged, and might he drown, no, he's up now, and he's reaching the end of the bridge on his hands and knees, like Christ carrying his cross, he's made it, and he rises to his feet, and walks across the meadow heading north over the island.

· · ·

As Addie passes Bird Beach, she sees someone walking over the meadow, past the mound. She thinks it's Brother Andrew, soaked to the skin, and she wonders what emergency has brought him out in a storm. Perhaps the end is coming for Grandpa Dempster – that wouldn't be a moment too soon for the poor man – and perhaps he wanted consolation, or the last rites, or a holy hand to hold. Who wouldn't want to hold Brother Andrew's hand at the end? And is that a definition of holiness? A hand you'd want to die inside?

If Brother Andrew's made it over the bridge, it must be passable, she figures, and she will cross over. She feels sure that Sol Blake will help her, and this powers her forward, rucksack on her back, rain streaming down her face, binoculars around her neck, with her mask and snorkel, the wind blowing her tail sideways like a sail.

She passes the harbour, and waves are flying over the walls, and she turns back to check that nobody's behind her. But look, the sea is raging and the bridge is covered and there's no way she can get over.

So what next?

She'll swim to him.

Ora's so near.

It can't be too difficult.

She heads for Penny Cove, she takes off her binoculars and puts them into her rucksack, which she hides in a cave at the back of the beach, thinking, illogically, that she'll come back for it. She pulls on her tail and dives deep. There's Eureka, at the back of the den, hard to see now, with her strands of eggs layered like hanging foliage over her, hiding, until she blows her hatchlings into the sea and gives her body to the seals and the fish, being hunted as she has hunted, in the completed circle to which she will surrender. Addie has no choice other than surrender now, to trust that the sea will carry her.

She hovers beside the den, goes up to breathe, and finds herself upturned and thrown. She dives back to the calm safety of under-water, wishing she had gills instead of lungs and breath. She peers under the rock, and as Eureka blinks her horizontal dash-eyes at her, Addie knows that she will never see her again. She wonders if Eureka will dissolve into the sea and be nothing. She's scared now, not only for Eureka, but for herself.

She flips her tail madly and when she rises, the sea is wilder than she's known it, and as the waves pummel her, she fights, but the sea is too strong for her, and she's disoriented, upturned, dizzied, flailing, struggling, and her mask and snorkel are ripped off, and she flips her tail, and she conjures his dark eyes and his cheekbones and the contours of his face, and she curves her left arm to take herself forward, and tries her right, but though her tail is strong, her arms are no match for the force of the waves, and the sea is winning, and her arms are losing, and the water is pouring into

121

her mouth and up her nose, flipping her up, pinning her down, filling her lungs, and she's gasping and she's swallowing and she's choking.

. . .

Sol watches the sea from his bedroom window. There's a shape, a seal, a dolphin, whatever it is, being thrown about by the wind, and now it's gone – he moves his binoculars left to right, up and down – and there it is again. It could even be a person. He thinks of Brother Andrew struggling over the bridge. How brave he looked. How powerless. How oddly powerful.

'Fuck you,' he says, to someone, possibly his father, or Carl Turlington, or the old Sol who didn't dare jump off the rocks with his sisters, the old Sol who didn't swear. The word feels new and good on his lips: the fricative *f*, the short sharp *uck*. He runs downstairs and out of the door, and he heads for the bridge where the black sky has descended over the black rocks merging with the black sea, and he sees whatever it is being dragged towards the rocks beside the bridge, or where the bridge used to be, and it's pushed out again by the waves, and it's a person, he's sure it is. He feels impotent and pathetic, but he refuses to be impotent and pathetic, he's emerging, new and different, and now the rain comes in torrents, puncturing the waves, and the lightning cracks the sky, and the thunder roars.

He reaches for the rough edges of rocks as he wades towards the thing, and he catches sight of it, appearing and disappearing, and the whatever it is is being slammed against the rocks, and the thing – hold on a second – has human hair. And *the bleeding face of Addie.* Is he hallucinating? Having visions?

He struggles across the rocks, falling, getting up, and he holds out his hand, and a wave comes and knocks her past him, and he's feeling for her, reaching for her, now holding her hand, and now her other hand, and *what on earth is this tail?*

122

A huge wave throws them both against what feels like the low wall beneath the water, and they're knotted together, tail and legs. Sol manages to ram his leg against the wall, and he's bleeding too from his face and his palms, and she's got hold of the wall as well, with one hand, and now they have something to block them, as they slam against each other.

'Hold on!' he shouts.

The wave retreats and they scrabble sideways, falling over rocks and each other and landing in a heap in a rock pool, scraped and cut, and clawing their way out towards dryish land, where they collapse together on the grass.

Addie is half-woman half-fish, tangled in lengths of seaweed, like something Dalí would paint, or Picasso. The weeds twist between her sodden auburn ringlets, knotting around her wrists and her waist, hanging off the flukes of her tail. She lies on her back, and she flaps her tail, and she's gasping and she's coughing as she takes off her tail.

'Legs. What a relief,' says Sol.

She laughs and she coughs and she splutters up sea water, saying, 'I'm so sorry.'

'You know you're bleeding, don't you?' he says.

'You're bleeding too,' she says.

'I saw Brother Andrew, did you?'

'I think he must have been heading over to give Grandpa Dempster the last rites,' says Addie. 'He hasn't been well for a while.'

'He put himself at serious risk,' say Sol.

'He would do,' she says, and she lets him pull her up.

*Knowing a person proceeds, like learning a language,
in tiny units of discovery, in no particular order.*

*They've exchanged names, which strangely
(don't you find?) makes a difference, as well
as gifts – feathers and eggs.*

*Knowing each other might take a million years
at this pace, but the storm has thrown them
together (quite literally) in a way that their
diffidence would never have allowed.*

Thursday 4th May

When Addie wakes, Sol is sitting beside her on a small chair with a rug around his shoulders. She closes her eyes and opens them again, and he's still there. His presence fills her body with a deep and unfamiliar peace. The window frames are rattling and the rain comes in torrents down the panes.

'Have you been there all night?' she whispers.

He nods.

'Thank you,' she says. 'For rescuing me.'

'I think you actually rescued yourself,' says Sol, with a smile. 'I'm so relieved you've woken up. You've been completely out.'

• • •

Sol puts down a tray on the old chest of drawers.

'I've brought things which won't hurt your mouth' he says. 'So let's start with tepid tea.'

His checked pyjama top looks enormous with her body inside it, the sleeves rolled up to reveal her tiny freckled wrists. He wants to reach out and touch them, but he doesn't.

'I'd made up my mind to come over,' she says in a quiet voice.

Sol takes a plate of mashed banana off the tray and hands it to her.

125

She takes it.

'And when I saw the bridge was covered, I didn't really think. I just dived in.'

'Interesting decision,' says Sol.

'I was coming to ask you if you'd help me get away,' she says.

Sol tries to digest what she's saying. Get away for good? Is that what she means? And why would she come to him? His mind fills with questions, but when he looks at her, he knows she's too exhausted for answers. If she knew him, she'd see that she's chosen entirely the wrong person. In which case, he tells himself, he must become the right person, right now, without any preparation, when he's a man who prefers to be prepared.

'We'll make a plan,' he says, trying to sound confident. 'But for now, I think you should try to eat something.'

He rearranges the pillows, helps to prop her up, and as she eats, he finds that his body is cloaked in a strange new sensation that makes his skin tingle and upends the hairs on his arms. Perhaps the sensation that somebody is relying on him.

'If you wanted to tell your mother you're—'

'No!' says Addie, pausing and putting down the fork. 'No I can't. I mustn't. She can't know I'm here. Can she get hold of me?'

'No,' says Sol. 'The phone's only for outgoing calls.'

'That's good.'

Addie goes on eating the mashed banana.

'Won't she be really worried?' he says.

'Yes, she will be,' says Addie. 'And I know that seems cruel. But I can't tell her where I am yet. I'll work it out, but I need a couple of days without her to get my head straight.'

A couple of days.

Addie.

Here with me.

For *a couple of days*.

.   .   .

126

Addie notices that Sol smells of lemons, or possibly oranges.

'I wondered if you should have a hot bath,' he says. 'The bathroom's just here. It's pretty basic, but I've found some bubble bath. If that might interest you.'

'Yes,' she says, smiling. 'That definitely does interest me.'

And then she thinks that it's mainly him that interests her.

'The floor's freezing,' he says. 'Wait a second.'

He comes back with a pair of battered brown leather clogs, embroidered with cherries.

'I love them,' says Addie, and then she feels a little bristle of suspicion. 'Whose are they?'

'My mother's.'

'Then I love her.'

'I'll go and run the bath,' say Sol.

She waits for him to come back, puts on his mother's clogs and stands up, walking to the bathroom, wondering why he would have brought them with him. In the bath, her cuts sting but she feels giddy and weightless and hopeful, then afraid, then hopeful again.

'Keep blowing,' she says to the wind. 'I need a bit of time just to be here.'

She stays in the bath, washing off the blood with a flannel, adding hot water when it cools, soaking herself warm, thinking about the rucksack she left behind in Penny Cove, feeling anxious. It's odd to be here, naked, in the bath, with this man she doesn't know on the other side of the wall, in a kind of domestic intimacy she hadn't quite imagined when she threw herself in the sea. She gets out and dries herself, opening the mirrored cabinet door and spraying a little perfume onto her wrists and neck.

The smell of it! She stands on the spot, breathing in the jasmine-mint of her grandmother's herb garden, which she always carried in her skirts and on her hands, and as she breathes and breathes and breathes, she feels something for which she can't find a word, something that makes her tremble slightly, under the surface of her skin.

When she goes into the Puffin Room, he's remaking her bed. She loves to watch the way he enters things so fully, the way the actions he makes with his hands are so precise. She climbs back into the creaky single bed, still trembling.

'That smell' he says, and his face seems to pale. 'Is it—'

'I found it in the—'

'Oh yes. Yes, of course.'

'My mouth really hurts when I speak. It opens up the cuts.'

'I could read to you,' says Sol. 'You said you had the potential to like books. Or would that be awful?'

'It sounds lovely.'

'I brought my two favourite books. Both plays I read when I was a teenager and then taught as a teacher.'

'You're a teacher?'

He's clever, she thinks. He'll know long words like *contingent*.

'I was a teacher. Now I'm a nomad,' he says in what sounds a slightly tentative voice. 'I bought a campervan and I'm going on a tour of places that were special to my mother. Starting here. Then driving to Tromso. She said they were both *thin places*.'

'Thin places?'

'Places where there's no distance between earth and heaven. Where we get a sense of the divine.'

Addie inclines her head, not at all sure what he might mean, but curious.

'Like here,' he says. 'My mother came here before she got married.'

'Because?'

'Because she wanted to be sure she was right to marry my father.'

'And she was?'

'Well, in fact, she wasn't,' he says. 'But she went ahead anyway.'

'Oh,' says Addie.

'And also,' he says. 'My mother's dead. She died three years ago.'

'I'm so sorry,' she says, looking at the cherry clogs beside the bed.

'I loved her too much, I think,' he says.

'I understand.'

She watches him take a book out of his pocket.

'*Murder in the Cathedral*,' he says. 'I read it for the first time when my mother was dying. She died on Hallowe'en. My father was anti-Hallowe'en. He was lecturing the kids who knocked on the door, and she was dead in the garden room.'

• • •

Sol can't believe how honest he's being. He's never said this stuff to anyone before. He breathes in his mother's perfume, which, on Addie's skin, smells quite different, not at all like a pretty English garden, but wild, slightly alive, animalistic even, tenacious.

'How did you cope?' says Addie. 'When she died?'

'Autumn helped,' says Sol. 'The autumn leaves and the squelchy mud and the rain. The Norfolk Broads where I grew up. Have you ever been there?'

'We went there as a family,' says Addie. 'We tried having holidays after my grandmother died. We never had before. My dad thought it would help. But it didn't really. We were just sad somewhere else. Somewhere else a bit shitter, normally.'

'But don't tell me the Broads was shitter?' says Sol, smiling.

'Well, the houseboat leaked and Sydney and I argued. But I saw my first kingfisher. If I got up very early in the morning and crept along the bank, I'd often see him. We were moored in this little backwater—'

'Perfect spot,' says Sol. 'Kingfishers are always hungry after the night.'

'It felt like it should have been somewhere else. Australia. The rainforest. With humming birds. Or parrots. But not in rainy England. You know, it felt like the kingfisher had light inside it. And the rest of the world was black and white.'

'Do you know the poem?' says Sol. 'Gerard Manley Hopkins. *As*

Kingfishers Catch Fire. He was a Jesuit priest who struggled with doubt. But he saw a flash of divinity in the kingfisher. Who wouldn't?'

Addie is looking intently at him.

'My friend Star has a cottage with a private broad,' she says.

'That would be the perfect place to recuperate.'

'Star's the one who got me into the tails,' she says. 'She's a professional mermaid.'

'Is that a job?' he says, creasing his brow.

'Or I've got another friend called Robyn in Alnwick. She's a birdwatcher. Less bossy. But very gloomy.'

'Go to the Broads,' says Sol, and he loves the thought of her being there, in the place he knows so well. 'I can tell you my favourite haunts.'

'I like the thought of being by water,' says Addie.

'Should you call Star and see if you can stay with her?' says Sol.

'Will you start reading?' says Addie.

. . .

Addie hates speaking on the phone. She doesn't think she's brave enough to call Star yet. She closes her eyes, and allows herself to inhabit the words that he's reading, as the chorus of poor women is drawn ominously, rhythmically, through the seasons of the year, towards Canterbury Cathedral, in the sharpness of December.

'I can hear the year passing,' she says when he pauses. 'It sounds like a poem, not a play.'

'It's a play and a poem.'

He keeps reading, running through the shoots of spring to the heat of summer, as the women wait for yet another autumn.

'Is that a bit depressing?' says Addie.

'Depressing can be good when you're depressed,' says Sol. 'These words saved me when Mum died not because they cheered me up, but because they didn't. The last thing I wanted was to be cheered up. I was grieving. And this is a mistake people can make.'

'I didn't know how to grieve when my grandmother died.'

'I'm not sure anybody does.'

'Do you think you can grieve for alive people too?'

'Your mother?'

She nods.

'I think you can,' says Sol. 'Yes, maybe, for what they aren't able to be. Perhaps I'm grieving for my father—'

'Who's alive?'

'Alive, but we're not in touch anymore. Anyway, let's get back to the play.'

'What is it you like so much about it?'

'Its seriousness, maybe. I'm quite a serious person, if that's not off-putting.'

'It's not.'

'And the way Thomas, the Archbishop, is such a big man, whereas my father feels so tight and turned in on himself. He's a vicar, you see.'

'A vicar? Oh I see. My grandmother was religious, but never small,' says Addie.

'Thomas gives himself to the worst possible thing so freely. But anyhow, no spoilers!'

'I've never really felt free,' says Addie.

'Me neither,' says Sol. 'Until I came here.'

'I've set out with no idea what I'm doing or where I'm going,' says Addie.

'Me neither,' says Sol.

There's a pause which thickens the air, but Addie pushes through it.

'Do you write poems, Sol?' she says.

He hesitates.

'I did.'

'Keep reading.'

• • •

131

Sol feels his body wanting her. He's learned so little about his body in the course of so much learning. He knows a bit about his heart and his soul, and his heart and soul want her too. And his mind, his mind is utterly clear that he wants her, but he's no idea what to do with a body that wants as badly as this.

So he will read.

And read.

And read.

He will subjugate his wanting.

He will keep reading.

He will put all of himself into it.

He will be now and he will be here.

He goes on, his voice hoarse, through the pages, to Archbishop Thomas's demand that the cathedral doors should be open, making his own murder possible.

. . .

His voice, even when he's not singing, when he's reading, still sounds like stone breaking – soft beneath hard.

Haunting.

Deep.

And kind.

. . .

Sol hears the rain and the wind echoing over Ora as he reads the final chorus, the women praising God's glorious display in every creature on the earth, the calm and the storm, winter and spring, light and dark, life and death and in the renewal that surges from every death.

He remembers the ant and the grass blade and the ducks and the eggs, alight with existence, as he is alight now, Addie too, in the glow of the bedside lamp.

He reads on, and he has the strongest sensation of the present he's ever had.

He is electrified by it.

By the powerful sensation of.

Of what?

Of *this* play.

On *this* day.

In *this* room.

With *this* person.

Haecceity.

One of his new words.

That property or quality of a thing by virtue of which it is unique or describable as 'this'.

. . .

When Addie wakes, something is different. She looks around the room. Sol isn't here, but it isn't that. It's something else.

What is it?

The window frames aren't rattling, so the wind must have died down. She can hear no rain against the glass. She gets up and crosses the landing in Sol's mother's clogs and she clops to Sol's room from where she can see that the sea is calming, though the bridge, thank goodness, is still covered by water.

The sun is out.

Her mother is over there.

Without her.

She feels un-pegged, like Sydney's tent when it blew off the island in a gale.

. . .

The sound of the clogs on the floor makes Sol jump, rewinding him to the warm kitchen of the vicarage, or taking him out of the

133

vicarage finally, somewhere else. He goes to the sitting room to find the pamphlet in the box and brings it back upstairs.

'I think we need to get you a boat whenever it's safe to go,' says Sol.

He shows Addie the pamphlet.

'There's only this one running at this time of year,' she says, pointing to the bearded men.

'They brought me over.'

'We can't use them.'

'Because?'

'I know them.'

'And they'll tell your mother?'

She nods.

'Is there anyone else?'

She shakes her head.

'This is the problem,' she says. 'There's the Saturday ferry for supplies and stuff, but the ferryman knows me too.'

'We'll have to ask these guys not to say anything,' says Sol. 'Also. Don't panic or anything, but I think they're all out looking for you. Your mother and the women.'

Addie says, 'Oh no.'

And, 'I guess they would be.'

And, 'This was always going to happen.'

Sol says, 'Do you think you should call Star, or Robyn? And make a plan?'

'Let's get the boat sorted first.'

• • •

Addie asks for another cup of tea, and Sol has one too. When they finish, Sol puts the cups on the window sill, and Addie stares out of the window.

She says, 'I can't look at Rokesby. It makes me lose my nerve.'

She says, 'I have no money to charter the boat.'

'It's OK,' says Sol.

She takes a breath.

'You'd better call,' she says. 'But will you act like it's you who needs to get to the mainland? Don't mention me.'

'Of course.'

'But then I guess you'll have to come over with me. To make the story work. Would you mind? I know you've come here for your retreat and I've totally interrupted it. I'm sorry. I realise I haven't said that. You came to be here alone, and you've been so gracious. I mean, feel free to go straight back.'

What a horrible thought, him going straight back.

What a terrifying thought, leaving.

'Do you think I really dare?' she says.

'There's time to change your mind,' says Sol.

'I think it's the right decision,' she says. 'As well as the wrong one.'

'My mother used to say that things can be right and wrong at the same time,' says Sol. 'I don't know if that helps.'

'It does.'

'You could stay in my campervan until you get yourself sorted,' he says. 'I left it over at the coach park in Seafields.'

'I'd love that.'

• • •

When Sol calls, he's pretty sure he's speaking to the older bearded man, who names his price (which is exorbitant, but what of it?) and explains that his return journey would have to be tomorrow in view of their timings.

'Is it very expensive?' says Addie.

'No, it's fine,' he says. 'But I'll need to stay tonight. I've booked my return for midday tomorrow. I can find a guesthouse. Are there places?'

'Plenty,' says Addie. 'But equally you could—'

'We can work it out.'

'I'll find a way to pay you back.'

• • •

Addie clops across the deck of the boat, wearing Sol's pyjama bottoms and huge black anorak, holding her tail, and she looks over to Rokesby to see if there's any sign of her mother, wondering if she might take a risk and try the bridge.

She hates the way Mac's looking at her, the mockery in his eyes, the suppressed smile.

'Quick, quick,' says Sol to Mac.

'All right mate, calm down,' he replies.

• • •

Mate.

Sol thinks how much he dislikes being told to calm down – does anyone like being told to calm down?

'This is Mac,' says Addie.

Sol didn't like Mac the first time, but he likes him even less now. He turns to look back at the prayer house standing in the sun, and he remembers that he left the dirty tea cups on the window sill, which is something he never does. He always washes up before leaving the house. It was one of his father's rules.

'You look beaten up,' says Mac to Addie with a look on his face Sol doesn't like.

'I got swept against the rocks when I was swimming.'

'You must be mad.'

'Please don't tell my mother,' says Addie to Mac. 'Not a word, do you promise?'

Mac nods.

Sol wants to hate him, but hate has never been allowed.

• • •

136

Mac looks at Sol as if he's in some way superior to him, which enrages Addie, but she's not sure what she can do about it.

'What's with the clogs?' Mac says to her.

She doesn't answer.

It comes to her that Mac lives on the mainland, that he no longer has an arrival time and a departure time, that he might expect things of her over there. There will be no more *things*, though she hasn't told Mac, which isn't fair. Also, he looks like a wolf, she'd never noticed that before. Not a nice wolf, now she thinks about it, or now that she's met Sol.

She checks that she still knows Star's phone number in her head.

Robyn's always on Twitter, tweeting about birds, *as it were*.

She'll get in touch with one of them.

It'll be fine.

· · ·

Sol gets out his wallet to pay for the trip, wondering if Mac is going to wave away the money as a way of showing how well he knows Addie. But he accepts it, looking intently at Addie, and goes to join his father in the raised cockpit, closing the door behind him. Addie sits down. Sol sits opposite her, and he looks at his mother's clogs on her feet.

He smiles at her.

She smiles back.

'Are wolves ever nice?' she says.

Surprising question.

'My mother would say definitely yes,' says Sol. 'And so would St Francis of Assisi.'

Mac reappears, standing very close to her, and one of the clogs falls off Addie's left foot.

'Those clogs!' says Mac, and he starts laughing.

Sol would like to punch him, though he doesn't believe in punching. If he did, he could have punched Carl Turlington. He

137

pictures his fist crashing into Carl's mouth in the school pool, and his teeth crack and his gums bleed and the water turns red. Perhaps, if he'd punched him, he'd have learned to swim, and all sorts of things about his life would have been different. He imagines punching Mac too, which shocks him.

'So where are you going to stay?' says Mac to Addie.

'All sorted,' says Addie, rubbing her eyes.

Sol feels like vomiting, which wouldn't be ideal. He goes out onto the deck, and he fixes his eyes on a prominent rock on one of the Farne Islands, and he wonders if they could stay in the van together because it would feel horrible to be apart tonight. And, more importantly, very nice to be together.

The van, though, is extremely small, and, crucially, only has one bed. He feels his mind rushing ahead of him, and he doesn't have the will to stop it, and before he can stop it, his body joins his mind. How he'd love to hold her in his arms, so that he could soothe her and make her hurt less, if she'd like him to. He wonders if he could have that effect on another human being.

He tells himself that this is an inappropriate thought, and asks it to leave at once.

• • •

'Anything you need, you know where I am,' says Mac to Addie once they're moored, and he squeezes her hand, and she doesn't squeeze his back.

'I won't breathe a word,' says Mac, as she prepares to disembark, and she can see he wants to know where she's going.

Mac narrows his eyes and folds his arms, staring at Sol in a way that Addie sees is intended to be threatening. She hates the thought of Sol leaving her tomorrow. It makes her feel scared. She doesn't want Mac to find her. As they walk slowly through the harbour and up the hill, she sees Sol looking back every few steps until they turn the corner, and both the harbour and Mac are out of sight.

'Is there something going on between you and Mac?' says Sol.

'It's a long story,' she says. 'Or in fact quite a short one.'

'With an ending?' says Sol.

'Yes,' says Addie. 'Yes, with an ending.'

. . .

Sol leads Addie into the coach park through a gap in the hedge, wondering how recently her long or perhaps short story with Mac ended.

Addie says, 'Oh is that your van? It's beautiful!'

He slides opens the door, and there are his books scattered all over the floor. She sits on the sofa seat, stretches her arm to try the tap, peers inside the little fridge.

'It's like a Wendy house,' she says. 'I love it.'

Sol arranges the books along the shelf. As he does so, he notices that Addie is picking one book after another and looking carefully through each one.

. . .

'Look,' says Addie. 'It says your class name in it. Weren't you supposed to hand it back?'

'At A level you got your own so you could write in it.'

Words like *A level* are so alien to her.

'Why was it you didn't go to school?' he asks.

'I got bullied so my mother pulled me out and I never went back.'

She's always been grateful to her mother for this, but it cost her nothing. Grandma Flora looked after her.

'I got bullied too,' says Sol. 'A guy called Carl Turlington. My mother said I should try to love him. You know, love your enemies as yourself.'

'I've made it my philosophy not to hate my enemies,' says Addie. 'But loving them would be a step too far.'

139

Sol nods.

'I think that was asking too much of a child,' says Addie.

• • •

Sol parks at the supermarket with Addie beside him on the brown leather bench seat – finally he has someone beside him – and he wishes she hadn't said that his mother asked too much of him.

'I haven't been to a proper supermarket for seven years.'

'What?' says Sol. 'Surely you've been to the mainland?'

'We sometimes meet Dad and Sydney in Seafields in term-time, when they don't have the time to come over. There's a campsite we stay in, in a cabin.'

'And you don't leave Seafields?'

'We go for walks.'

'You've never been curious to go somewhere else?'

'Mum never wanted to. She said we had everything on Rokesby. Everything that mattered.'

'Did you feel that too?'

'I didn't have permission to question her.'

'My father's like that. A bit of a bully.'

'Oh I'm not sure she's a bully,' says Addie.

She hesitates.

'Unless she is.'

'My father's let me down,' says Sol. 'My whole life really. I've tried and I've tried, but at some point, you have to think enough is enough.'

'You've given up on him?'

'I think I have.'

'You don't intend to see him?'

'I don't.'

They go into the supermarket, her clogs clattering against the hard grey floor, and he watches the way she stops and stares and examines, pulling out a set of pencils, a magazine, a bunch of daffodils.

'Have whatever you like,' he says.

People look at her, this girl in man's pyjamas pulled up to the calf and cherry clogs and a huge black anorak, with a cut face and wild spiralling hair.

Sol chooses strawberries and apples and smoked salmon and bread and cornflakes and milk and mayonnaise and sausages and rolls, and he watches as Addie dizzies herself with jars of jam, selecting apricot and strawberry, and Nutella, and peanut butter, as she crackles the crisp packets, runs her hands over the tubes of biscuits, moves to the clothes section, to a white t-shirt with a yellow sun on the back, and a pair of cargo pants in khaki, and a crocheted red jumper and a big orange scarf, with tassels.

She says, 'Is it OK if I pay you back another time?'

She takes a packet of knickers, a pair of pyjamas, reduced to £5, three pairs of socks with fruit on, and she changes into her new clothes in the campervan while Sol goes for a walk around the car park.

Then they drive off, passing a sign for Zippo's Fair.

'Turn here!' says Addie. 'And let's park!'

The old organ music is playing, jaunty and jolly, and Addie pulls him onto the merry-go-round, and they ride on horses beside each other, up and down, up and down, and he tries to forget himself, not watch himself from above, not feel a prat, but rather be here, where he is, fully, and they're off the horses and they're swinging on the big wheel, and the sea is grey in the distance, and the Farne Islands are just visible, and Rokesby and Ora are invisible, and unbelievable, and Sol catches a glimpse, for a second, of a different future, before he dismisses it, telling her that he used to go on a merry-go-round with his mother when he was a small boy at The Amusements near his house – the memory came back to him in the shower yesterday. When they get off, he buys candy floss which they eat on a bench beside a bush where goldfinches chatter and squabble.

'My grandmother's surname was Finch,' says Addie. 'I've always thought I should be a Finch, not a Lemming.'

'Such pretty birds,' says Sol. 'But associated with suffering.'

'We could just sit here and eat candy floss forever,' says Addie. 'And die of malnutrition.'

'Yes, but at least we'd die together,' says Sol. 'I hated watching my mother die on her own. I prayed to God to let me go with her. I was worried she wouldn't find her way to the right place like she never could in hospitals. That she'd be stumbling down infinite corridors. On her own.'

• • •

As they park in the dark coach park in Seafields, Addie sees her mother changing shape inside her mind, turning into something crueller than she was when she left. She decides to stop thinking about her.

She sits on the padded sofa-seat, and Sol sits on the fridge box at the other side of the table, and she wishes the table wasn't between them. She wishes nothing was between them. She looks at his smile, his shadow of beard, his dark eyes, and a strange feeling rises up through her. She tells herself it's just his eyes. You can't love eyes, she tells herself. Except she can, in fact, love eyes.

Sol is making smoked salmon sandwiches. He cuts the crusts off and slices them into triangles. She stares at the back of his hands, the way the dark hairs grow from tiny follicles, and she wants to touch them. He pulls up his sleeves. He boils the kettle, fills a teapot and takes out two cups and saucers with roses on, which Addie suspects were his mother's.

She drinks her tea from the side of her mouth, avoiding the cuts, looking at his tanned forearms, dark hair running smoothly across them, and his surprisingly big hands, and the cups and saucers with roses on, and the hands and the cups turn out to be quite the unexpected combination.

You can love eyes and you can love forearms and you can love hands holding teacups, and she didn't know before today how much. What's the matter with you, she says to herself. But the thing that's the matter with her is a very nice thing.

. . .

As they eat sandwiches, Sol knows he needs to bring up the subject of the night, of where they might sleep, but he can't find the words.

He'd like to say, How would it be if we both slept here? Would you like that?

But it would be terribly embarrassing if she said no thank you, and then they were stuck inside this very small space together all night. Also, his mouth has never made sentences like that before. Also, why on earth would she like it?

What he actually says is: 'You see that seat you're sitting on, it turns into a double bed.'

Then he says, because it's all his mouth seems able to say, 'I can sleep here. On the bench seat. It seats three so it's quite long. It'll be fine. Totally fine. Sorry that I can't offer you more privacy.'

She nods.

'And then tomorrow you'll have the whole van to yourself,' he says with an awkward half-laugh. 'I'll be back on Ora with the birds.'

As he says it, a prickly feeling of unease runs over him because the words he's saying don't match anything he's feeling – and he wishes that he could turn himself inside out and that she could see the truth of him without words getting in the way.

He's never imagined that words might get in the way.

He's had total faith in them all his life.

. . .

Addie has abandoned her mother. She's broken her promise. She's left behind her rucksack, and the wedding dress and the bolero which Star trusted her to make. Which is another reason not to call Star. The thought of calling Robyn makes her feel tired. Star is definitely her best option for what happens next.

Sol doesn't make her feel tired.

She's just noticed.

'I never told you about my second favourite book,' says Sol. 'Do you know *Blood Wedding*?'

She shakes her head.

'Should she marry the man she's engaged to or the man she loves? That's the basic premise.'

He looks very serious, so serious that Addie wonders if he's sending some kind of message to her. Is he facing that same dilemma? Does he think he might love her? Is he engaged and making a pre-marriage visit to the island like his mother did? Is this a family tradition? And if so, surely he wouldn't make the same mistake as his mother did.

Choose me, she thinks, *choose me*.

I choose you, she thinks, *I choose you*.

Then she reminds herself that she doesn't want her life to be contingent on another person, but she can enjoy a love affair, can't she, without any sort of commitment. She can ride about in a campervan having fun. Would he like to have a love affair? Or is he just being kind to her?

'I mean, it's about doing the right thing or the true thing, isn't it?' says Sol.

Addie nods, trying to look like both the right thing and the true thing at the same time, and she wishes her face wasn't covered in cuts.

'My mother did what she saw as the right thing, not the true thing,' says Sol. 'She married my father though she knew she didn't love him.'

Addie tries to look less right and more true.

'She loved someone else?'

'Oh no,' says Sol. 'She just didn't love my father.'

'Did she tell you that?'

Sol nods: 'But she didn't tell my sisters. It was our secret.'

'What a burden for you.'

'No,' says Sol. 'It wasn't. I liked my sisters not knowing, and I didn't want my mother to love my father.'

• • •

'What must you think of me?' says Sol. 'It's just that my father didn't love me. He loved my sisters.'

Addie nods, frowning.

'Also,' he says. 'My mother really didn't burden me. Not at all.'

'Why don't you read to me?' says Addie. 'I love it when you read to me.'

He feels his face heat up. He reads and he reads and he reads, and the girls in the play wind red woollen thread, which is the thread of life, the colour of blood, and they sing of being born at four o'clock and being dead at ten, of the thread being obstructed by flint, by a knife, and he foresees a whole gamut of obstructions that might come between them.

'Keep going,' says Addie. 'Keep going.'

That's what he does.

Until he's hoarse.

Until the night is turning to morning.

Friday 5th May

As Addie stirs, her dreams recede and her body thrums and aches.

Here she is, *not on Rokesby.*

Here she is, *escaped.*

Here she is in a campervan on the *mainland.*

Sol's here and he's sleeping, or maybe he isn't, but if he is, she doesn't want to wake him. Will her mother find her?

She really should tell her mother she's not dead, but she's not sure how, and she's not sure when. She has to call Star. She has to avoid Mac. Her mind whirls. She can't see past the back of the bench seat, but Sol's over there, and sadly not here, and morning is coming, and with it, whatever will happen next.

When he finished reading in the early hours, his play-reading passionate face turned tense and drawn, and he folded down the bed and tucked in the sheet and unrolled the duvet and put her to bed as if he was her mother, and he squeezed himself onto the driver's seat away from her, saying nothing.

• • •

Sol has slept fitfully, if at all, worrying if his mother did burden him by telling him she didn't love his father, worrying if she should have told him to love Carl Turlington who bullied him every day, and also trying to find a way to fit his long legs onto the too-short seat in a way that might relieve the cramp in his calves.

Addie is as present as the air. He feels her, as if she's next to him, and his soul is stirred, and his body is stirred, or, more rightly, asphyxiated. He's not sure he'd survive being much closer without exploding, which would be embarrassing, and messy, as well as highly inconvenient.

There's also Addie's mother. There's also the long-or-short story with Mac. What if Mac tries to find her? Seafields is a very small place. What if she'd like Mac to find her, but isn't letting on? Is she awake? If so, would it be better to stay behind the barrier of the back of the seat and call out, in a confident voice: 'Good morning!' Or is that too formal? Would *hello* be better, or *did you sleep OK*? Or what's the etiquette around these things?

He's not used to sleeping in a campervan with a woman.

Or sleeping with anyone.

Anywhere.

• • •

Addie can hear that Sol's awake because he's making the seats creak.

'Good morning!'

Sol's voice is loud and sudden. He looks over the bench seat, like one of those faces Sydney used to draw on his exercise books, over a wall, with a big nose. Not that Sol has an especially big nose. No, it's a normal-sized nose, cheeks weathered by the wind and the beginnings of a beard and such dark sad eyes.

'Very formal,' she says.

He's up and dressed because he never got undressed, and he's out of the van so that she has privacy, but she doesn't want privacy, but he can't seem to see this, and she can't seem to say, so she dresses, and he comes back, and he makes toast and cups of tea,

147

and they sit with the door open and the air coming in, like children playing camps.

'You're going back at midday, aren't you?' she says, hoping that he might possibly change his mind and not go back.

He nods.

'My mother will come and ask you questions and you mustn't say. Not a word. If she says she saw us, say she didn't.'

'Couldn't we give her some kind of indication that you're OK?'

'I've been thinking about it all night,' says Addie. 'But she'll be angry and she'll try to force me back.'

'She can't physically put you on a boat back to Rokesby.'

'She's very forceful. She scares me sometimes.'

'That's why I've given up on my father.'

'Also, Sol, could you possibly get my rucksack? I left it in a cave at the back of Penny Cove. You'll see it if you go over there. It's got all my most favourite stuff in it, and a wedding dress I was making for someone. And my phone.'

'But will you be here when I come back?'

'When does the retreat end?'

'A week and a day. But I could come back sooner, if you need me to.'

Addie hesitates.

'Let me go and get some money from the cashpoint for you,' says Sol. 'While you think.'

'I'll pay you back,' says Addie, wondering how exactly she might do this.

.   .   .

As Sol walks, he feels he's been too pushy offering to come back sooner, but on the other hand, she said she needed the rucksack. At the cashpoint, he flicks his head around, hoping not to see Mac. He takes the maximum amount of money, knowing that he'd empty his bank account for her this morning if he had to, after years of saving and not spending. Is he turning into one of those people you hear about who get love-scammed on the internet, he wonders.

Is this what love feels like? Bank-emptyingly dangerous. He buys flapjacks from the baker. He's whistling. He'd rather make her some of his own flapjacks with his mother's recipe, but that will have to wait for another day.

Will there be another day?

He sits on a bench, putting the flapjacks beside him. Is there any chance she feels for him what he feels for her? He wonders if anyone *feels* desirable, or whether you can only imagine other people being desirable – I mean, nobody fancies himself, or herself, do they? Or maybe they do. Perhaps somewhere there's a niche group of people who fancy themselves. Looking at Instagram, he could well believe that to be true.

He feels the opposite, obviously.

He hates the thought of Mac finding her, climbing into his van, and who knows what might happen next? He's sure she'll look after the van, but perhaps he should tell her the circumstances under which he acquired it. Or perhaps he should tell her something else entirely. Perhaps he should tell her how he feels about her. Perhaps, if he told her, she'd ask him to stay with her, not to take the boat back to Ora at midday. Although thinking logically, all his stuff is over there. But anyhow. Solutions could be found.

He finds himself bursting through the door saying, 'Lorca says that the things you can't resist shouldn't be resisted.'

Addie looks up and smiles, and goes back to reading *Blood Wedding*. He'd expected more of a response to what he's always seen as a dangerous and subversive statement. Perhaps it's better to declare love in your own words. Or is he, as he suspects, quite easy to resist? He gives Addie the flapjacks, and she stops reading and suggests that they go for a walk over the hills.

They head out on a little footpath at the back of the car park. He thinks of holding her hand, but his hand won't move towards her, and they climb high, and red kites are playing on the wind currents, and they sit on the grass and watch them, and his spirits soar with them, and words he could say cluster at the bottom of his throat, forming possible sentences, but he can't find a way to get them up his throat and out of his mouth.

But never mind.

They're here on the hilltop together, and this is joy. He'd forgotten what it felt like. It feels like wind on your face and wings and sunshine. They talk about why he came on the retreat to Ora. He asks her how she survived all those years on a tiny island, and she says that she gave up on humans when she was quite small and put her faith in nature instead. He talks about his rowing boat and the river and the birds and the Broads.

She talks about the power of swimming and the pleasure of making things, particularly difficult things, like lace, which involves anything up to fifty pairs of bobbins, which he finds surprising, and she again mentions the wedding dress which she left in her rucksack, and he asks her if she could start a wedding dress business in her new life, and she hesitates and blushes and says that this is an excellent idea.

She asks him what it's like to be a teacher and whether teenagers aren't terrifying, and he says they can be, and she says that people in general are terrifying to her, and he laughs, and they head home and eat mediocre flapjacks.

'I need to get going,' says Sol, wondering if he really does need to get going.

She nods. He wishes she'd ask him to stay, but she doesn't.

'Also,' he says, reaching up to the little teak cupboard, 'I want you to have my phone. Here it is, and here's the charger. And here's the code. I can call you from the landline at the prayer house, but remember I can't take incoming calls, which isn't ideal. If I took my phone with me, you could call me. But then you wouldn't have a phone.'

150

'True,' she says, smiling, and she puts the phone in the little teak cupboard.

'Also,' he says. 'FYI.'

Why did he say that? He hates it when people say that.

'Addie,' he begins. 'I've only just bought this van. My aunt left my mother some money in her will, and as she wasn't going to need it, she gave it to me secretly, and none to my sisters. And I could never make myself spend it. Until now. So it's very precious to me.'

He's been verbose, and he also thinks he sounded a bit wet, the way he said precious.

'I'll take good care of it,' says Addie. 'Don't worry.'

'Thank you,' says Sol. 'And your rucksack?'

'Yes.'

'How will I get it to you?'

'Call me,' says Addie. 'And we can make a plan.'

'Good,' says Sol. 'Keep my anorak.'

Not a great last line, he thinks, as he climbs out of the campervan. He must say something else. He takes the van keys out of his pocket and hands them to her, and he wants to hug her, but she's inside the van, and he's standing on the tarmac, and he can't exactly get back in when he's just got out.

'Thank you, Sol,' she says. 'I'll always be grateful.'

'Well,' he says, 'See you soon!'

A possibly worse last line, and as he says it, he has a strange and terrible feeling that he will not in fact see her soon, a feeling that, after this moment, he may never see her again. But he dismisses it. He knows he's a pessimist, and the thought is too terrible to countenance.

He starts walking, just as a coach driver drives in. Sol walks towards the gap in the hedge, and finds himself doing a humorous little leap, two feet in the air, soles together, as he passes through.

(Why why why why why?)

· · ·

Sol's jaunty sauté reminds Addie of *Toad of Toad Hall* or the old *Morecambe and Wise* shows Grandma Flora used to watch. So unlike him too. Such a serious man doing such an unserious thing. Again. Just for her. Like the crab in the grass. She hopes he doesn't do leaps and crabs for anyone else. Is it odd to hope that?

Will she wait here for him to come back? Or will she call Star? Or will she call Robyn? She holds the van keys in her cut hand, and she remembers driving her father around the drive after Grandma Flora died. She remembers the two of them sitting on the stone wall and him saying he wished cars had never been invented, and her wondering why, and her father biting his nails until his fingers bled.

She finds herself climbing into the driver's seat of the van and putting the key in the ignition. She could perhaps try circling the grass, to see if she can remember how to drive. No, she mustn't. She said she'd look after his van, and she will. She takes the keys, gets out and climbs back in through the pull-back sliding side door, opening the fridge and eating a strawberry. She opens the teak cupboard and stares at his phone. She should only use it for emergencies because it's his and she mustn't snoop. Except she wants to.

What next, she thinks. She climbs out and walks around the coach park. The coach driver waves at her. She decides not to wave back. Sol will be on the boat with Mac, and what might they say to each other? And will her mother be waiting for him on Ora with questions?

She walks along the side of the main road, and cars race past, dangerously close, dangerously fast, but she can see a garage ahead. She feels Sol's money in her pocket – such unfamiliar things, money and cars and garages. With trembling hands and a stuttering voice, she buys a Cornetto from the garage shop, feeling the thrilling novelty of it, seeing the man staring at her cut face and hands.

She goes back into the coach park through the main entrance, eating the chocolatey pencil point with her hurting mouth, and she sees a poster for Zippo's Fair, the same fair they went to yesterday, which is moving here for the weekend.

· · ·

Sol goes out onto the deck, remembering his first trip only six days ago, and he watches the fulmars, and remembers the word *pelagic*, and Pelagius who rejected the notion of divine grace, believing it to lead to moral laxity, and he thinks of his own moral laxity. He's made a promise to Addie, a promise to lie, and to lie in a way that will hurt her mother, and he therefore knows how badly he, for that and many reasons, needs divine grace.

I've finally fallen in love, he thinks, as the boat takes him further and further away from her. Has he? Can this be true? Can one fall in love so quickly? Nothing else would make him skip through a hole in a hedge, would it? Nothing else would make him give up his very pricey black anorak.

I wish you could meet her, he says to his mother.

But look, here's Mac.

'Where is she?' says Mac, and Sol knows he's in love with her too, and how might something like this be solved? In *Blood Wedding*, two men are in love with the same woman and both end up dead, and that kind of makes sense to him looking at Mac's punchable face.

'I said where is she?' says Mac.

'I've no idea,' says Sol.

'Lying git,' says Mac.

Sol walks onto the deck and heads for the bow. And it comes to him that Addie could drive the van somewhere else, and he hopes she does, so that Mac won't find her, so that he can go to the fair with her again.

· · ·

Addie watches the coach driver climb into his coach and drive away. The coach park is quite empty now. A crow lands by the hedge and puts its head inside a cardboard chip packet. It squawks as it hops towards the van, where it stops and looks at her.

She opens the teak cupboard, and she takes out Sol's phone. She puts in the code.

Ping ping ping.

Sol's phone is coming to life.

B: Are you OK Sol? x

B: Where are you Sol? x

B: Please call. I can explain. x

B: Just tell me you're OK. x

B?

He didn't say anything about anyone called B. Does he do leaps and crabs for B? Does he buy her flapjacks? She reads the messages again and again and again. Is that why he slept behind the bench seat? Didn't hold her in his arms? Because of B?

She wants to delve into every corner of his phone and his life, but she restrains herself, because she can't bear to know, and she puts the phone on the shelf above the sink for a moment, so that she can catch her breath, and then a police car drives in and parks beside her, and a policewoman gets out and says that Addie needs to move her van because the coach park is now closed – did she not see the sign?

'The fair's coming,' she says. 'The first lorries will be arriving soon. So if you could vacate please.'

'Yes,' says Addie, thinking, please don't watch me try to start the van.

The policewoman climbs back into her car and leaves.

If Sol could receive calls, she'd phone him and ask what she should do.

A ping.

Will it be Sol?

No, he'll still be on the boat, or just arriving, and anyway, she has his phone.

It's B.

B: Tim says you aren't in the country anymore. Where ARE you, Sol? x

Addie pauses.

She takes a breath and, without thinking what she's doing, she calls.

When B answers, she has a tight clipped voice.

'Sol?' says B. 'Sol?'

Addie can't think what to do, or what to say, so she says nothing.

B says, 'Sol, where *are* you? Tim says you're in Greece? I'm so glad you've called. Why aren't you speaking?'

Pause.

'I so need to see you, Sol.'

Pause.

'This is quite ridiculous. Can you speak to me?'

Addie doesn't speak.

'I can explain, Sol,' says B. 'I can explain everything.'

Addie ends the call without finding out the everything that B would like to explain.

She climbs over the bench seat and puts the keys in the ignition.

• • •

Sol walks across the grass to the prayer house, planning to phone Addie the second he gets there because he badly wants to hear her voice, and he badly wants to plan his return to her. But here's Addie's mother approaching: she has the same heart-shaped face as Addie, and the same auburn ringlets.

He must lie. His mother told him never to lie. She felt passionately about it.

Never lie Sol because lies are like ivy. They grow and they mark.

Addie's mother says, 'We've lost my daughter.'

155

Sol nods.

'It's most unlike her,' she says, looking away, holding herself together.

'I'm sorry to hear that,' says Sol, and he is sorry.

That's true.

That's not lying.

But it feels brutal.

'I saw you come back on the boat today,' says Addie's mother, taking a step towards him, so that she is very close.

'Yes, I had to charter a boat. Both ways.'

'Because?'

'A personal matter,' says Sol, trying his best to stay calm and measured and truthful. 'Now solved.'

Addie's mother is staring at his face intently.

He says, 'Well, do have a good look around.'

'I already have. I found two teacups on the window sill.'

'Two teacups?'

'For one person?' she says.

'One person who clearly didn't wash up,' says Sol, emitting a strange fake laugh, thinking that perhaps his father was right about washing up before leaving.

'She was everything to me,' says the mother, clenching her jaw.

Then: 'She *is* everything to me.'

Sol can't believe that this woman doesn't love Addie.

There must be something he can say.

'I'm sure she'll come back. Sometimes we need a bit of space. That'll be what it is.'

'You seem to be sleeping in two beds,' she says.

'Two beds?'

'You seem to be sleeping in two different rooms.'

'Ah yes. Trying to find a comfortable bed,' says Sol, laughing hollowly, or even slightly manically. 'Like *The Three Bears*.'

Why on earth did he say that?

'So she didn't come over?' says Addie's mother, looking at his scabbed hands.

'I don't think the bridge was passable,' says Sol.

Addie's mother turns to leave, and as she walks away, it starts to rain.

Sol puts on the kettle, avoiding the cuts on his fingers, wondering if her mother believed him, wondering if he should run after her and put her out of her misery. He must phone Addie and say she simply has to call her and say she's alive. It's inhuman not to, whatever the circumstances.

He'll think of the right words over a cup of tea.

• • •

Addie starts the van. Puts it into first gear. Leapfrogs forward. Now she moves into second gear. She stalls. Presses the foot brake. Pulls up the hand brake. And starts again. She's moving. She has to get out. The fair is coming.

She heads towards the exit of the car park, and she turns into the narrow lane. Seized with fear, she drives upwards, realising with some horror that she's heading towards the main road. She waits and waits and waits, not daring to risk a turn. The car behind hoots. A small queue forms. She indicates. Pushes into first gear. She turns left because left is much easier than right, and judders into second gear.

Just keep in a straight line, she tells herself.

Where am I going?

Third gear. Fourth. Very slow.

She keeps on, thinking that she should never have done this, but she had to, she had no choice, but as soon as she can find a place to stop and park, she will, and she can turn and make her way back to Seafields, and she can stay in some other car park, and he'll come back with the rucksack, and she'll be waiting, and she finds that she is muttering *I am so sorry Sol, I am sorry*, as she drives, *I am so so sorry*, and her cut hands rub against the steering wheel, and her heart is racing, and her stomach is churning because a car has overtaken her and another, and another, and it's started to rain, and it's raining hard, and Sol bought this van a week ago, and she can't find the thingie for the windscreen wipers, and she can't see, she can't see, she can't see, and she dreads the next junction, or roundabout, or traffic lights, or traffic jam, and she still can't find how to work the wipers, and she dare not look down while she's moving, and she can't see ahead of her, and there's a red lorry in the rear-view mirror hazy with the rain, and, oh help, she still can't find the wiper thingie, and oh no, oh shit, shit, shit, there she goes, slam-bang into the car in front, with a deafening, bone-shaking crunch, and she's screaming at the shock of it, when a massive crash sends her flying forwards, sends books and pans flying too, and it's the lorry behind, it must be the lorry, and something is smashing into her left cheek, and her mouth fills with blood, and her leg twists, and everything cracks and splinters, and her body is thrust forwards, leaving her crushed leg behind, as she hurtles towards the windscreen.

• • •

Sol prepares to tell Addie that her mother came to see him, that she's desperately worried, that she simply has to call her. He phones her on his own mobile number, but she doesn't answer. The phone is dead, as in silent, as in *nothing*. He calls repeatedly, with hope, then without hope. He calls again and again through the night.

If the phone's dead, is she dead? Did a coach driver come into the coach park and murder her? This is the problem with his imagination. He should never have left her, alone, in a coach park.

He calls and he calls and he calls.

Sol feels, like we all feel, the hellish limits of his own eyeline, beyond which anything might happen.

This is why fear will always accompany the kind of knowing that's possibly becoming love.

But then.

Saturday 6th May

Addie's inside a huge kaleidoscope, she knows she is, though she can't quite find the limits of herself: a circle of jasper turns one way on the outside, and inside it, a circle of sapphire turns the other; inside the sapphire, a circle of agate, then emerald, then onyx, ruby, topaz, pearl, each turning in opposing directions; and at the centre a diamond rose, which she takes in the palm of her hand, where it sits still, perfectly still, perfectly still.

· · ·

Sol heads for the hermitage as the sun rises, with a terrible fear at the centre of him, a terrible fear which is the shape of Addie with nothing inside it. Until he finds her, until she's in front of him and he can touch her, until she exists again, then he can't function.

So here goes. His next lie. Brother Andrew opens the door.

'My father's died,' he tells Brother Andrew. 'Is there some kind of speedboat that could get me to Seafields fast?'

'I have a phone to make emergency calls,' he says, disappearing into another room, talking urgently and coming back. He puts his arm around Sol's shoulder.

'What was it?'

'A heart attack.'

It's so easy to lie once you get started.

'The boat will be here within the hour.'

'What do I owe you?'

'Nothing.'

Sol's vision feels oddly blurred. He can't see right. He can't think right.

'I think you were sorting through some issues with your father,' says Brother Andrew.

Sol nods.

'Don't be too hard on yourself, will you?'

'Thank you,' says Sol.

'Trust death,' says Brother Andrew. 'Then resurrection will take care of itself.'

Sol nods, feeling awkward.

'The young woman you mentioned,' says Brother Andrew. 'Did you meet her here?'

'Oh no!' says Sol because he mustn't give her away. 'Not at all! She was someone I knew from my school. A colleague. I'm a teacher, you see.'

He's talking very fast and his cheeks are warm, and his fear is expanding and filling the Addie-shaped space inside of him.

'I must get going,' he says.

Back at the prayer house, he calls Addie, completely pointlessly.

Nothing.

Where is she?

He puts on his old cagoule because he gave Addie his black anorak, and he dashes out of the prayer house and sits behind the rocks (hiding from her mother, hiding from everyone) with his big rucksack and his little rucksack and his holdall and his mother's suitcase, and the rain batters his non-waterproof (as it turns out) cagoule, soaking his blue jumper, and he apologises to his not-dead father, and hopes that by saying he's dead, he hasn't caused him

161

to die, and he begs God to keep Addie safe, to make his worst thoughts not true, and he says he's so sorry for his multiple lies, and he tells his mother she was right, that lies are like ivy, the way they grow.

He sees the boat racing over the water.

Addie's rucksack!

The *one thing* she asked for.

He didn't get it, and now it's too late – the boat is mooring at the jetty to rush him to his dead father who isn't dead. To Addie, who may be, who, if she isn't dead, is almost certainly gone. Without his phone.

The bald man at the helm says he's so sorry for Sol's loss and he'll be as fast as he can. The boat thumps over the water and Sol jams his mouth shut to try to stop himself throwing up.

• • •

Addie is swimming with dolphins in a silver sea, the water running off her body like mercury, and now she's washed up on the shore, grasping for some sense of where she is or who she is, and nearly knowing, until she doesn't, and she's being upturned by two men with beards, Mac and his father, and put in a large metal clamp, her head close to the ground, her hair falling on the sand, mercury dripping from every strand in sticky globules.

• • •

Sol buys a bunch of white tulips from the florist, which is a way of holding on to the belief that she's still alive, though he can feel no sense of her here. The tulips are under his armpit, his rucksacks on his front and his back, his holdall and suitcase crashing against his legs.

He hates to fail people, and now he's failed Addie, and he'll have to tell her straight away that he doesn't have her rucksack, with her favourite things and the wedding dress and her phone in it, although if he were to tell her, it would mean she was still alive.

I've been so worried!

That's what he'll say, if she's alive, and he'll climb into the van, and he'll put on the kettle and they'll drink tea, and he'll tell her that he didn't give her away, that he lied for her. But he must also tell her that her mother is beside herself.

Oh the joy of drinking tea with her, the joy even of telling her he forgot her rucksack because it would mean she existed – how he took her existence for granted. Why on earth did he leave her? If he finds her, he will never let her out of his sight.

There's a buzz of noise as he reaches the coach park. He blinks. The coach park is no longer a coach park, and his campervan is no longer here because here has become something else altogether, as here can, if you let it out of your sight. *Here* is packed with lorries and caravans and striped awnings and generators and men with biceps and women holding babies and dogs barking. Everywhere there are people building, hammering, folding, unfolding, shouting, laughing. Radios are blaring; the merry-go-round is partly built; the house of horrors is being assembled; and so is the rollercoaster.

Sol puts down his luggage. The bridge of his nose buzzes, his temples throb and the cuts on his palms hurt as he's seized with his own absurdity, his own smallness and weakness amongst the burly masculinity of the fair.

Might his van be there, cordoned off amongst the brouhaha of machines and generators and radio and shouting? He takes a tentative step. A bearded man wearing a white vest says, 'No entry mate.'

'I left my van! Have you seen a campervan? Blue and cream?'

He wishes he'd said white, not cream.

He wishes his voice wasn't so posh.

'The place was cleared before we came,' says the man.

'But—'

'It probably got towed away, mate. There was a big sign.'

'Thank you,' says Sol.

He walks away and sees a bench by the bus stop. He drops the tulips on the bench, puts his luggage down and looks helplessly around him as if the van might re-materialise from the tarmac on the road. He must check every car park in Seafields. Perhaps it was towed away, or perhaps Addie drove it somewhere else, but he can't get hold of her because she's not answering his phone.

He picks up his tulips and his luggage and sets off down the lane to the harbour car park, which is full. The van's not there.

'Do you know where the coaches are parking today?' he says to a man leading a group of red-capped children.

'Head away from the harbour and keep walking,' says the man.

Sol walks, with some difficulty, the wind blowing his luggage out at strange angles. When he arrives at the coach park, there's a row of coaches, side by side, looking out to sea, but there's no sign of any campervan. He knocks on the window of a coach and asks the driver if he could leave his luggage with him for, say, half an hour, an hour. The driver says yes. He leaves everything, except his small rucksack which he carries on his back, but he still has no idea what to do as he walks back towards the harbour.

• • •

Addie is somewhere light and bright, she's not sure where, she's not at all sure where, but her hand is feeling for something solid, and whatever it is feels cold and hard and shiny, and she opens her eyes and the ceiling is white, and she can't open her mouth. No, her teeth are stuck together.

• • •

Sol has an hour. In an hour the coach driver may leave with all his possessions. He wishes he could climb back into his carapace in reverse-metamorphosis and be the old Sol who would never

164

ever have found himself in this kind of a mess. He wishes the fairground too would reverse-metamorphose and be a coach park again. He wishes the hands on his watch would reverse, that time would flow backwards.

Didn't Addie say we aren't trams? She's wrong. We *are* trams, and we are stuck in time's groove and we can't get out, except that he did on Ora, when he heard the monks singing from the past, and when the ant was on the grass blade and the sunlight was on the duck, and he was out of time altogether.

But he isn't now. He's stuck in one weary step, then another.

He pushes the door into a guest house called Harbourside, and the humourless woman at the desk says that she can give him their one single room, which is a little poky, but the only one she has left – it's the breeding season on the islands, and it's busy, and can he pay up front? He pays and rushes back to the coach park for his luggage. The driver is listening to the radio.

There's a diversion on the A1 following an incident yesterday involving multiple vehicles. It won't be Addie. Or his van. It will all be fine.

'Thanks, mate,' says Sol. He finally says mate, but it doesn't matter now, and he wonders if the coach driver has any idea what kind of mania is bubbling under the surface of his ordinary words. Perhaps the coach driver is bubbling too, underneath, Sol wonders. You wouldn't know. Perhaps everyone's bubbling.

Sol's shaking as he walks, struggling with his luggage and the tulips under his armpit, wishing he could find out more about what happened on the A1 yesterday. Is the blackness coming for him again? He thinks it is. A white tulip head falls off at his feet next to a bench. He stops. He doesn't need the tulips. He opens his armpit and lets them drop onto the bench, and there they sit as if someone has died.

Has she died?

Of course she hasn't died.

165

Sol is shown to his small single room on the first floor with side views of the harbour through a narrow window. He phones his mobile from the phone on his bedside table, although he knows it's pointless. He's lost Addie, and he's lost his phone, and he has no van, and he can't go to Tromso, or grow a beard, or be a nomad.

He feels a horrible sense of his own pitifulness as he sits in the tiny window seat, eating a packet of crushed crisps which he found in his pocket, and he cranes his neck to see the boat turning into the harbour beneath the stone Virgin Mary. There it is, mooring. The phone rings, which makes him jump.

'What time would you like breakfast tomorrow?' says the voice.

'Eight thirty,' he says, relieved to have found a question he can answer.

The boat has moored and the passengers are dispersing.

And there's Mac.

He opens the narrow window to let in the air and the sky and the sounds of life. There are the women, the blondes and the one with short hair and the one with the hat with the enormous bobble, and they're embracing each other, kissing each other's cheeks. A week ago, he thinks, he was waiting for the boat in that very same harbour. It seems such a long time ago. A week ago, he had his van, and inside his van were the infinite possibilities of his new life. Mac walks towards the women, and says something, and they gesticulate and nod their heads.

With his hands shaking, Sol dials the number of the vicarage, and as the phone rings, his heart races and his mouth dries. He hears his father's familiar shouty voice on the answerphone, so loud he holds the receiver away from his ear.

Sol opens his mouth to leave a message, but he can't speak. The blackness lurks outside the window. He puts the phone down. He opens the leather file on the bedside table and calls a taxi to Chathill station, from where he can apparently (says the taxi man) catch a train to Newcastle, and from Newcastle to King's Cross. He'll go to Tim's flat in Aldgate, the thought of which comes back to him from another world. The world he lived in before he came to Ora. When he was a different person. *Only one week ago.* How quickly life can change, as well as how slowly.

The humourless woman at Reception says she can't give his money back. Sol shrugs. The taxi arrives, he puts his luggage in the boot and his mother's grey case on the seat next to him, and he stares at the little rip where the pink silk lining shows through. He has a strange clenched feeling in his heart, as he stares out of the window, praying that by some miracle she'll walk by.

As the taxi driver starts the car, Sol takes his father's letter out of the elasticated silk pocket, the letter which arrived six months to the day after he received Bee's diamond ring in a jiffy bag because his decision to end his ordination training was a decision, Bee said, to *end their engagement.* She wanted to marry a vicar, she said, and she'd made that quite clear to him.

Six months later, *the letter* fell on the doormat in Aldgate.

He looks at the letter in his hand.

He feels carsick.

A letter with his father's handwriting on. Sol's father had never written to him before. He remembers the strange sensation of dread he felt as he opened the envelope in his poky bedroom with the too-short blinds at the window.

His father wrote of the need for Sol to believe the best in people, to seek God's perspective in difficult times, to believe in God's unwavering goodness above his own wavering emotions, and, crescendoing to his main purpose, he readied himself to describe the circumstances in which he'd reacquainted himself with Bee.

Reacquainted himself with Bee? Sol's ex-fiancée, Bee? Why would his father need to reacquaint himself with Bee?

In an appropriate pastoral context, with others present.

His father described in carefully edited paragraphs the ways in which both he and Bee had committed their way to the Lord, trusting that he would act, and that he had acted, the net result of God's acting being that *he and Bee were engaged and getting married.*

Sol, horrified at a number of levels, didn't reply to his father's letter. He still hasn't. Why would he? He hasn't spoken to his father or to Bee since. No, he left his old life behind and he bought a campervan and set off on his nomadding tour, starting, and as it turns out, ending, right here.

He puts the letter back in the elasticated silk pocket.

Where is she where is she where is she?

Her absence is too much to bear.

The taxi is driving up through narrow streets of Seafields and Sol stares, hopelessly, into every side street, but there's no sign of his van and there's no sign of her. As they reach the main road, the big wheel, from which Sol caught a glimpse of a quite different future only two days ago, towers over the village, and he feels sick, so he opens the window.

Last Saturday, Sol had no notion of Addie's existence.

A week later, look at the pain of being without her.

How does this happen?

Does anybody know?

Saturday 13th May

When Star arrives at the hospital, Addie can't open her mouth to say hello. Her teeth have been wired together to set her broken jaw. The nurse gives Star a pair of pliers, and, pulling back Addie's upper lip, shows her how to undo the wires, should Addie need to vomit.

Star says, 'Got it,' in her loud, enthusiastic voice, and Addie wonders if she should have gone to Robyn's instead, but she can't resist seeing where Sol grew up. Not that Sol will want to know her any more. He'd had the van a week. One week. He'll be furious. She would be.

'The plaster will come off in six weeks,' says the nurse, 'and we'll undo the wires a week after that.'

They leave the hospital, Addie trailing after Star up the path between beds of dead shrubs, with only one living flower, a huge hydrangea head.

• • •

While Tim is at work, Sol walks in circles around his grey flat. Tim has bought a number of house plants in white plastic pots, but he doesn't appear to have watered them. Their large leaves droop hopelessly from the windowsill. He can't find out much about the crash on the A1, other than people moaning about the congestion, which was cleared after two hours. There have been a lot of crashes on the A1 since the internet was invented.

'Can't you see it?' Tim said after Sol had given a brief summary of what had happened. 'You always have this naive belief in people's goodness. I mean, why the hell would you leave a stranger in your van with your keys and your phone?'

'She wasn't a stranger.'

Sol leaves the flat and walks in circles around the park, trying to avoid treading in dog shit. He could contact her mother, but her mother won't know where she is because she was determined not to tell her. And if she did know, he'd have broken his promise to Addie, and even if he found her, she'd never forgive him. He goes into a small dark café and sits and drinks a not very hot cappuccino, pausing to write a letter to Brother Andrew, which he will email to the monk in Durham. He types, deletes, types, deletes and ends up with: 'All going as well as can be expected,' which he convinces himself is true. Then, crucially, he enquires after life on the islands, in general terms, asking casually if the *daughter* (who, he understood from the *mother*, had disappeared) has returned to Rokesby.

He should never have left Seafields. He should have stayed and tried to find her.

He skims through teaching jobs and applies to the one with the least demanding application process, though it's a long way away on a Scottish island, and it's a primary school, but as he probably won't get it, he isn't sure it matters. At least he feels productive.

'I applied for a job,' he tells Tim when he gets back from school. 'It's on Fair Isle.'

'You mean the Scottish island?'

Sol nods.

'When will you know?' says Tim.

'Fast,' says Sol. 'The headmaster's dropped down dead.'

'Good,' says Tim.

'Not for the headmaster,' says Sol.

He tries to stay humorous around Tim, although he's dying inside. Tim will never understand how much he's dying.

'This Addie,' says Tim.

Sol nods.

'Did you sleep with her?'

Sol shakes his head.

'But I think I love her,' says Sol, surprising himself.

'Can you love someone you hardly know?' says Tim. 'Someone you weren't even in a relationship with?'

'I was in a relationship with her,' says Sol.

'Well, only so far as we are all in a relationship with anyone we meet. I mean you were in a relationship briefly with the taxi driver.'

'Don't say that,' says Sol.

'I'm trying to help you,' says Tim. 'Women can be very manipulative. I've had my fair share of nightmares. I know what I'm talking about. And you do too. Look what Bee's done to you.'

'Addie gave every sign of liking me too.'

'And what were these signs, Sol? Run me through the detail. How it all started. What exactly happened between you.'

'Well,' says Sol. 'We ran into each other, and we basically waved at each other. That's how it started.'

He feels a fool, but he keeps going.

'Then we talked briefly over the fence. She was in her garden.'

'And then?'

'I phoned her because there was this huge storm and—'

'Did she sound pleased to hear from you?'

'I wasn't sure.'

'So?'

'We talked again. I was lying in the grass. I should have got up. I don't know why I didn't. I apologised for phoning.'

'And?'

'She had to rush off.'

'So what then?'

'I left her some feathers on a window sill.'

'You did what?'

Sol feels awkward: 'I know it sounds—'

'Very odd,' says Tim. 'Did she like them?'

'Well, come to think of it, she never mentioned them.'

Tim smiles nervously.

'But she brought me chicken eggs.'

'Chicken eggs?' says Tim, frowning.

'She keeps chickens,' says Sol, as if this might make the eggs more acceptable to Tim.

'People with chickens often have too many eggs. My mum's always giving them away.'

'She came over, though, and left the eggs on the table outside.'

'I mean, I'm not feeling that's a massive signal.'

'But then she came again. She said she wanted to say hello. Why would she have done that?'

'I really hate to say this but did she maybe see you just as someone who'd help her get away. Like was she coming on to you for a reason?'

'She didn't really come on to me. I'm not sure if anyone's ever really come on to me.'

'Well, then, what made you think she—'

'Hold on,' says Sol. 'She nearly died trying to get over to Ora.'

'Because she wanted to escape. Because it sounds like something weird was going on with her mum.'

'But you weren't there. You didn't see us together. I made her food. I read to her.'

'You read to her?' says Tim. 'Did you kiss or anything?'

'No,' says Sol. 'But her mouth was bleeding.'

'Hold hands?'

173

'No.'

'And the next thing you paid for the boat, and gave her your van and your keys and loads of money?'

'We went to the fair before that.'

'And?'

Sol wonders if he won't mention the merry-go-round now he thinks about it. It sounds a bit wet. Or the candy floss. Or the goldfinches. Perhaps Tim is right. She saw him as a useful means to escape, and that was that. Women aren't to be trusted.

'We went on the big wheel, and stayed the night in the van.'

'And what happened that night? A bit of passion? Anything?'

'I slept on the bench seat, and she slept in the bed.'

Tim laughs.

'She shafted you,' he says. 'Totally bloody shafted you. You got her to the mainland and she nicked your van. Boom! She was off.'

'No, but she'd left a rucksack she needed and I said I'd get it for her.'

'But when you got back with it, she'd gone?'

'Well, actually, I forgot to get it but—'

'I don't want to be brutal, but I think this might be in your head. I really think you need to move on.'

'I don't think I can move on,' says Sol. 'Also I'm really worried she's not OK. I mean, what if she's dead?'

'I don't think that's likely. There'd be something online. There always is if there's a fatality.'

He clears his throat.

'You've been here a week,' he says, handing Sol a bottle of beer.

Sol takes it.

'I haven't liked to say,' says Tim, rocking back and forth on the balls of his feet.

Sol looks at him, still unable to decide if he likes his beard, and wishing he'd kept his story to himself.

'Say what?' says Sol.

'I don't want to be uncharitable,' says Tim. 'What with everything.'

'You've been extremely charitable,' says Sol. 'I turned up out of the blue and you've been nothing but kind.'

'The thing is this,' says Tim. 'I'm going to just come out with it. You can't stay any longer. You'll easily find a job. I mean, you've got no ties. You can go anywhere.'

Sol gets up.

'Can we talk about this another time?' he says, and he takes a gulp of beer.

Sunday 14th May

'Closure is important,' says Star as she and Addie make their way through the sitting room doors to the outdoor sofas on the terrace, manoeuvring through clusters of olive trees in enormous terracotta pots, looking out at the swimming platform and the private broad. The house has huge glass windows, stone floors, exposed copper piping. There's nothing on any of the surfaces, except books piled in size order.

That van meant everything to him and I can't face him, Addie writes on her spiral notepad as her wired jaw makes speaking impossible. *He was planning to go travelling in it. I've ruined his life.*

'You should get in touch with him, or you'll be forever running and never peaceful,' says Star, who likes to give advice.

Maybe he's rich and has already bought a new van, Addie writes, though she knows he isn't rich enough to buy another van. He's a teacher. She sees his wistful eyes and his open face, and her body contracts with regret – if only she could go back to the coach park again and take a different path.

'Still, you should get in touch with him.'

He'll have left Ora, and I have no idea where in the world he is.

• • •

'We need to go back to our conversation,' says Tim to Sol as they walk back from The White Horse, where Tim has drunk four pints of beer in quick succession.

'The one about me leaving? Can I just wait and see if I get this job?' says Sol.

'Well, not really,' says Tim. 'Because you know Harriet.'

'Well, I don't.'

'Because she's been away.'

'Harriet's the Hinge date?'

'Well, that's a little reductive,' says Tim.

'But she is?'

'Yes. I've asked her to move in with me. You've got to jump when you find the right one. I haven't had much luck with women.'

'How long have you known her?' says Sol.

'Three months. Just over.'

'Isn't that a bit quick?' says Sol.

'You can talk,' says Tim.

Friday 26th May

Star has said she will pay Addie's fine. She's also given her an old phone she didn't need, and she's bought the raw silk (again), and Addie has started the dress for her sister (again) and the bolero jacket (again). Star makes tasty meals in her liquidiser, which Addie ingests through a straw in the gap made by her extracted tooth.

Addie's guilty, and grateful, and embarrassed.

'You didn't think about your lack of licence or insurance?' Star asks her.

Addie shakes her head.

'Oh Mowgli,' she says. 'Your mother didn't do you any favours, did she?'

What do you mean, Addie writes.

'By cutting you off from real life.'

Addie flinches: she's Weirdo at Weirdo House again, though she can see Star is busy unweirding her. Organising a bank account. Sorting a passport. Turning her into an administratively valid human being.

I'll pay you back for all of this once I'm earning, Addie writes.

'I've booked you onto a special driving course,' says Star. 'It ends with your test. You might as well get on with your year's ban.'

Addie writes, *I don't know if I want to pass my driving test.*

Though she wants to write, *Please stop calling me Mowgli.*

'When something goes wrong, you have to face your fears. That's what I say to my mermaids,' says Star.

Addie doesn't like the way she says *my* mermaids.

'Life will be totally impossible if you don't learn to drive,' says Star. 'Particularly as a mermaid. How would you get to competitions?'

Addie writes, *I don't know if I want to be a mermaid.*

'You're made for it,' says Star. 'I'm happy to be your agent. The sky's your limit.'

Addie runs and reruns what happened with Sol. She sees he really had no choice but to help her. She invaded his retreat and said she had to get away, so he paid for the boat, lent her his van, stocked the fridge and left as soon as he could.

He asked only one thing of her: to look after his van.

•   •   •

As Sol waits at the departure gate, he tries to imagine the island, the stone schoolhouse, his dark little cottage, the new life he didn't want. Everything's happened so fast it's hard to assimilate it. He's sent his new address to Brother Andrew via the Durham monks. He's not totally sure why.

He received an email from the police, and he called the number and found that Addie was alive. It was hard to hear the policeman through the joy of it.

She's alive!

That's all he could think.

She'd be punished, said the policeman, for taking the campervan without his consent and for driving it without a licence or insurance: a fine and a twelve-month driving ban, so he said, didn't he, he found it hard to concentrate. The policeman seemed to expect Sol to be pleased by her punishment. He made it clear that, like

Tim, he considered Sol to be a gullible fool for lending his van to a stranger, which probably he was. Sol asked if she'd been badly hurt, and the man said, a few broken bones, but when Sol asked which broken bones in particular, he said he didn't know or at least he couldn't remember. Sol asked him if he had any contact details for her, and the policeman said she lived on an island in the middle of the North Sea, which might explain her driving ability. And then the policeman laughed. Hahaha.

Sol pictures her in a wheelchair with her limbs in plaster, unable to move, and he wonders if her accident was his fault for leaving her alone, or at least partly his fault, as well as partly hers. It wasn't her fault the fair arrived, of course, but it was her fault to drive the van.

If he wasn't flying to Fair Isle, would he be touring hospitals trying to find her? And would she want him to? And would he want to?

Addie's illegal act of driving without licence or insurance will preclude any pay-out from his insurance company, so Sol spent almost all of Aunty Peggy's money on a van he owned for one week, a van that no longer exists. The van is gone, the money is gone, she is gone, and he has absolutely nothing to show for any of it, except a broken heart. If it wasn't a tragedy, it would be a farce. Another farce on the back of the farce of Bee and his father.

As Sol flies, he's seized with a horrible pointless anger, which will change nothing, because Addie's robbed him of what he most wanted, to be free, to not have to teach, to travel the world in memory of his mother.

Also, the money.

That hurts too.

It seems absurd that the course of our lives should be changed by such utterly inconsequential things.

Things like Zippo's Fair coming to the coach park in Seafields.

If the fair hadn't come, this would be quite a different story.

Or if it hadn't rained on the A1.

Our own choices count too of course.

Addie called Star, and not Robyn.

Sol applied for a job on Fair Isle.

Other people, often strangers, intervene and change our lives.

Like the Chair of Governors at Fair Isle School.

Sol was his second choice (of two).

The first choice, a woman called Vera Bates who Sol would never meet, pulled out after looking at the annual weather patterns online.

So Sol went to Fair Isle.

There are now 800 miles between him and Addie.

Monday 5th June

Addie negotiates the path across the lawn on crutches. She's become strangely accustomed to her tightly wired mouth, though her teeth ache with the pressure of being jammed together. She sits, leaning her crutches against the bench on the jetty looking over the shimmering River Bure and the swaying reeds, thinking of Sol who lived here on the Broads nearly all his life, wondering if he ever thinks of her, and if he does, what exactly he thinks. That he hates her, she supposes.

Who wouldn't?

She didn't think for a moment about her lack of licence and insurance because these things are outside the limits of her experience, though she doesn't want to excuse her bad decision. Some days she thinks of different ways she might be able to get in touch with him in the absence of any sign of him online and his phone having been crushed in the crash. If she could get her address to him, it would be up to him if he wanted to respond. The only people who might help are some monks in Durham who organise the retreats on behalf of Brother Andrew, so her mother told her.

Addie emailed her mother on Star's computer, speaking being impossible with a wired jaw, telling her that she was safe and well.

Her mother responded with questions: why did she leave, how did she leave, how dare she leave, and where was she now, and when would she be back? Addie replied saying that she'd tried to explain why she needed to leave before she left and that she wouldn't be coming back to live on Rokesby. She said she would like to visit her mother at some point, but she didn't say where she was. Her mother didn't reply, and Addie is therefore not contacting her again. She has to take a stand, in order to be well, in order to become an adult. On this, Star is right.

Midges swarm above the rowing boat in a shaft of sunlight, dabchicks paddle under tree roots, and here's a tiny moorhen, all alone, picking her awkward juddery path through a fleet of paired mallards, her head bobbing back and forth, back and forth, because, Addie reads on her phone, she's *the only duck without webbed feet.*

Little Hen, she thinks, *you are me, and I am you: a moorhen in a world of mallards, without the right feet to glide through life.* Little Hen inclines her head and looks at her.

We'll be OK. You and me. Alone together.

Her phone pings. It's Star saying it's lunchtime, which is kind, but also tiring. The moorhen climbs over the tree roots and swims off. Addie can't wait for her plaster to be off so that she can swim, although Star will be lurking with tails and training regimes.

'You could be something big,' Star tells her repeatedly.

But Addie would prefer to stay small.

However grateful she feels, she isn't going to be *contingent on her* (those powerful words, Star's gift to her) or moulded into a shape she hasn't chosen. She gets up and heads for Mermaid Cottage, passing The Boathouse on her right, a clapboard building which accommodates a vintage river boat underneath, with a guest flat above. She meets Star coming across the garden saying, 'Where were you? I couldn't find you.'

Addie points at the river.

• • •

Sol is up early for his first day with the children.

Over Half-Term, he met the long-serving staff: Miss Gunn, the teacher (short but fearsome) and Miss Fay, the teaching assistant (self-effacing and willowy) and Mrs Inkster, the administrator, cleaner and dinner lady (verbose and cheerful).

He saw Miss Gunn on three separate occasions, and she wore a different kilt on each, with a white blouse and what his mother called stout shoes. He also met the Chair of Governors – a loud, shaggy man, who lives on the island.

'We were slightly desperate,' he says.

Sol nods.

'I'm sure my skills are transferable,' says Sol.

'Let's hope so,' says the Chair of Governors.

There are only sixteen children, who must be taught in a mixed-age class.

'Next year, there will be more,' he says. 'And, to be clear, the February Half-Term trip is part of the contract. No extra pay, I'm afraid.'

As Sol watches the sun rise over the sea from his sitting room window, the anticipation of his first day, and the second, third and fourth, in fact all his days, makes him feel trapped. The sky glows pink. Pink sky in the morning, shepherd's warning. There are shepherds here, and sheep, and birds, and birdwatchers visiting in pursuit of the elusive Fair Isle wren.

The sun rises and the sun sets at the pencil-line horizon, and whatever time of day it is, he can't forget Addie. He tries, he fails, he writes poems and puts them in numbered envelopes. He loves her. He hates her. She's either in Alnwick with Robyn or on the Broads with Star. She could be anywhere, he supposes. Mac flashes into his mind. Is she with him? She said it had ended. Was she lying? Is Tim right? Did she use him? The pain of that. The shame of it. The disappointment. The fury of going back to work when he should be halfway to Tromso.

He gets up, picks up the keys to the schoolhouse, walking along the path parallel to the cliffs past the nesting puffin pair, who are taking it in turns to incubate their egg or head to sea, returning with impossible rows of silver sand eels drooping from their resplendent bills.

He lets himself into the schoolhouse, opens his computer and stares at the children's names on the list, readying himself. Ah, and here's Miss Gunn, taking off her tweed coat, revealing the colour of today's kilt, which is – ta-da! – purple and grey! Miss Fay arrives soon after.

'I need to print out the photosynthesis worksheets,' says Miss Gunn.

'I'll do them for you,' says Sol.

As he takes her worksheets off the printer tray, he reminds himself that his mother told him to look out for the *good things* in every day. He thinks hard. He breathes. *Ah yes*, he thinks, *breath. That's a good thing. You couldn't argue with that.*

'Amazing the way plants produce oxygen, isn't it?' he says to Miss Gunn.

She nods a little uncertainly.

'It's so easy to take breathing for granted, isn't it?' says Sol. 'But we mustn't. Breathing is a gift.'

'If you say so,' says Miss Gunn, tucking in her white blouse, running her hand through her short grey hair.

Miss Gunn opens the door, and there's a boy with red curls standing by the slide. *Red curls.* Sol walks out and shakes his hand. The boy has freckles, which, if you look carefully, run in lines and swirls, like hairline cracks under his skin.

'I'm Mr Blake.'

'I'm Barry Forfitt.'

'Nice to meet you.'

'Have you met the puffins, Mr Blake?' he says. 'They've been nesting on the Jut for years.'

'The Jut?'

'That bit of cliff that sticks out. I'm worried that it's going to erode.'

Erode, Sol notes.

'Anyhow, I've named them Puer and Puella, from the Latin,' he says.

Latin, Sol notes.

'Great names, Barry,' says Sol.

'I estimate that the egg will hatch in the middle of June,' says Barry Forfitt.

Estimate.

'We could all take bets,' says Sol. 'On the hatching date. What do you think?'

'I think the egg will hatch on the 15th of June,' says Barry Forfitt. 'Also, just so you know, my mum is ill.'

'I'm sad to hear that, Barry,' says Sol.

'Everybody's sad to hear it,' says Barry. 'But I'm sad all the time.'

'Sometimes we don't have enough space for our sadness,' says Sol. 'And that's the moment to let some of it out. I'm always here if you want to do that. But I also understand if you don't.'

'Thank you, Mr Blake,' says Barry.

Thursday 15th June

The plastercast is off, and, as Star drives, Addie can't stop looking at her dry, white, hairy shin. Her jaw will be unwired in one week's time, which she longs for, from the point of view of eating, but slightly dreads, from the point of view of talking. Star runs through the importance of exercise and her swimming plan for the week ahead.

When they get home, Addie presents Star with the letter she has written, deleted and rewritten five times.

I can't tell you how grateful I am to you for, basically, saving my life.

That's how it begins.

I want you to know that I will pay back every single penny you've spent on me.

Addie gets to her main point.

This is going to be hard to say, but I've decided that I don't want to be a professional mermaid. I don't like people looking at me, that's the first thing. And the second, I'm anti competition. That's what I hated about school.

'We can work on all of this,' says Star.

I don't think I want to, writes Addie.

'I don't understand you,' says Star.

I possibly don't understand me either, writes Addie. I think my next job is to try to understand me. Before I do anything else.

. . .

Barry Forfitt arrives at school wearing a striped silk scarf, which is against school rules. Sol watches Miss Gunn give him a mark on the points chart and confiscate the scarf.

'You are in Year 5, Barry,' she says. 'You know the uniform rules.'

'It's my mum's,' says Barry. 'She's gone into hospital and it smells of her.'

'We can't make exceptions,' says Miss Gunn.

At breaktime, Sol urges her to rethink. He says that he will not undermine her by taking off the mark, but that he will subtly return the scarf to Barry's father. She disagrees, but he overrules her. She's furious.

'June the 15th, Barry!' says Sol to take his mind off his uniform mark, but just before the school day ends, Sol checks, and the puffin egg hasn't hatched.

'It could still hatch before midnight,' says Barry.

When Sol gets home, there's a letter on the mat. Sol stares at it as if it's alive. He doesn't get letters. He has a strange feeling that it's from Addie, although it can't be because she doesn't know where he is, unless somehow she's found out.

He opens it.

It's Brother Andrew, via the monks, reminding him that grief is a long journey, that death and loss are part of the pattern, that there will always be a return to life, so we should look for this and expect it. He reports on the craziness of the breeding season, the abundance of chicks, the antics of the seal babies and says that the *daughter* has been in touch with her mother saying that she is safe and well. All shall be well and all shall be well and all manner of thing shall be well, he ends, quoting Julian of Norwich.

That's it.

No further information.

Sol looks at his photos of Ora and Rokesby, and berates himself again for not taking one of her before his film ran out. Why would you want one, he asks himself, she's caused you nothing but pain and loss. He should look out for a return to life. So said Brother Andrew.

Ah, here's the photo he took in the garden of The Retreat, when he heard the monks' voices on the air. A burst of sunlight emerges from the left-hand flint stump and reaches over towards the right-hand stump, seeming to follow the shape of the original arch. He still doesn't remember seeing this. It comes to him that when the arch was whole, the left side and the right side curved over and touched each other, at the top, in the centre. And then, over time, the two sides crumbled, ending up some distance apart.

There is a time when our lives touch, he writes, and it's his next poem.

He writes and crosses out and writes, and rips up the paper, and starts again, and when he's finished, he puts the poem in an envelope and numbers it. *Number 7.* The holy number, round and complete and perfect, though the poem isn't. He always disappoints himself when he writes. It's the next poem that will always be perfect, the one he hasn't written yet. Like the bit of life we haven't lived yet, the one where we get things right.

It's nine o'clock and he hasn't eaten. He boils some pasta, which he eats with pesto, in silence, in the kitchen. He watches the ten o'clock news, has a shower and goes upstairs. When he looks out of his bedroom window at twenty past eleven, Barry is on the Jut, peering inside the burrow. Sol puts a jumper over his pyjamas and heads out to the cliffs.

'Barry,' he says. 'Do be careful out here! It's so dark and you're very near the edge. Does your dad know you're here?'

'He's at the pub,' says Barry.

189

'I think you should go home,' says Sol. 'I'll walk with you until I can see you go in.'

'The egg didn't hatch,' says Barry, and tears stream down his face.

'I'm not crying about the egg,' he says.

'I know,' says Sol. 'I know.'

Will it be Addie who goes to Fair Isle?

It seems unlikely.

Or will it be Sol who finds a way to forgive his father and return to Norfolk?

Or will it be something else entirely that shrinks the 800 miles between them?

So that they can see each other again.

Which of course they will, and they must.

Friday 30th June

Addie's getting used to her voice again.

It was painful to remove the wires because her gums had grown over them, but once they were off, she took herself to an Italian restaurant and ate fried courgettes and crunchy garlic bread mixed up with blood, moving her unfamiliar jaw up and down, up and down. She called in at a charity shop and bought herself a smart green coat with a swingy shape and gold buttons.

The next day, Star's sister came to try on the wedding dress with the upside-down-tulip skirt and the fitted bolero jacket with pearl buttons up its sleeves, gasping at her reflection in the mirror.

'You're a genius,' she said.

I could do that again, thought Addie, because she'd done it, on her own, without Grandma Flora. Twice!

Addie's finally alone. Star was offered the central role in a new film coming out in the States, with a famous Spanish film director whose name Addie can't remember. It's some sort of adult fairy tale based around a timeless mer-creature. And it was wonderful news because Star no longer cared that Addie would not be coming with her for mermaid-training.

'I'm going to need to be away for at least a year,' Star said to her. 'I've put Mermaid Cottage on Airbnb and been totally inundated with bookings all through the summer. So why don't you run it, do the changeovers and the cleaning for me? And you can live in The Boathouse in return. Win-win, don't you think?'

After so much losing, Addie knows she's won, but the losses still hurt. She makes a rule that she may only think of Sol for ten minutes a day. She has to find a way to live happily alone, which was always her plan. She walks and she feeds the ducks and she talks to Little Hen and she swims in the broad, and she decides, whilst swimming, to put Sol's suggestion into action.

At the local printer, she has cream leaflets and posters printed with a gold feather in the top right corner. *Goldfinch Wedding Dresses.* She cycles around the local villages, her leg now strengthened and almost back to normal, dropping leaflets through letterboxes, sticking posters in newsagent windows, calling at churches to ask them to advertise her services to would-be brides.

Surely Sol's father's church must be around here somewhere. The first church is squat and ancient, with no tower, but the door's locked; the second is prettier, with a rose garden and a cheerful lady who calls herself the warden and takes a poster and some leaflets; next, a modern box, all bright stained abstracts, with friendly staff who are pleased to help; and now, as she cycles down a quiet lane, a tower looms above the trees, and, as she approaches, there's a wooden gate and a large free-standing crucifix, which she imagines might illuminate at night.

She leaves her bike and walks down the path to what looks like the office, which has a tidy noticeboard with lists of courses and events for every day of the week and large posters for SUMMER YOUTH CAMP, with photos of attractive teenagers, playing frisbee and guitar. There's a tasteful wooden board with a list of names, headed by *Reverend S Blake.*

Her skin prickles.

Reverend S.

Is he also called Sol, Sol's father who he doesn't see anymore?

His father who, like her, has no idea where Sol is. His childhood bedroom must be over there in the vicarage, she supposes. His mother's grave in the graveyard.

A woman comes to the door, admires her poster and invites her to come along one Sunday. Addie panics and leaves quickly, wondering if Sol might change his mind about his father, if he might be drawn back here one day. Then she wonders if she might ever go back to Rokesby and see her mother. She doesn't think so.

Will they both stay estranged from their families forever?

And, unbearably, estranged from each other?

As she cycles, she sees him walking down the lane, coming out of the baker, crossing the high street and finally, back at The Boathouse, there he is in his boat rowing along the river.

That's more than ten minutes, she tells herself.

So stop.

. . .

Before Sol leaves for school, the postman arrives with a box. He cuts open the packing tape to find that it contains his salvaged possessions from the van: a kettle, two towels, a duvet, a pillow and a bag of damaged books. *Murder in the Cathedral* and *Blood Wedding* are missing. He's already bought two new copies which he reads and rereads, in a desperate bid to bring Addie back, to be together again. He cherishes a fantasy that Addie hung onto his two favourite plays to remind herself of him, but they were probably lost in the crash.

When he arrives at school, Miss Fay makes him a cup of tea, and then Miss Gunn appears, taking off her coat, revealing – ta-da! – a dark green kilt, with a faint stripe of turquoise. Mrs Inkster brings in a cream envelope to Sol's office, saying, 'You're probably expecting this.'

He's not expecting anything.

He tries to live without expectation, looking for his mother's *good things* in every day. Perhaps the smallish cream envelope is *a good thing*. Perhaps not. His name and address are in typed italics. Might it be from his sister, Rachel? He gave her the school address and phone number. Whatever is inside feels stiff. He opens the envelope and takes out a cream card:

Please save the date for our wedding.

Saturday 24th March, 2018.

It's really happening. His father is marrying Bee.

Wednesday 26th July

Addie sits sewing, a hum of satisfaction inside her, as she shapes the ivory silk to life: a puffed shoulder narrowing into a long sleeve, which is split open, waiting for its buttons. Yesterday, she finally dared to look for the website of the Durham monks, through which she might contact Brother Andrew.

She goes upstairs and makes coffee icing for the cake, which she puts in a tin. She picks a bunch of white roses from the garden, and takes the cake and the roses to Mermaid Cottage, leaving them on the kitchen table for the new guests. She checks that the key is in the lockbox. Then she goes out on the river in the rowing boat, allowing herself her daily allocation of Sol as she turns into the creek.

Ah, here comes Little Hen, swimming jauntily towards her. Addie moors by the bank.

'So here we are, you and me,' says Addie, reaching out her hand.

Little Hen leans up towards her and takes the birdseed from her hand. Addie gives her some more. Then she takes out her two plays. She knows the first five pages, and the last three, of *Murder in the Cathedral* off by heart already. She says them aloud to the wind, hoping to build courage. When she gets back, she sits at the computer, looks up Brother Andrew's Prayer Retreats, finds the email for the Durham monks and prepares to email.

I have a strange request. A man called Sol Blake went on retreat to Ora this year, on—

She checks the date on her phone.

Saturday 29th April.

He is a friend of mine, but we have lost touch. I was wondering if you would be able to pass his email address/phone number to me, or send mine (below) to him.

Quite quickly a monk responds.

Dear Addie

I am afraid we are not at liberty to give out the details of our retreat guests, nor to send unsolicited communications. I pray that you will find another way to find your friend.

Best wishes.

· · ·

It's the last day of the Summer Term.

The school is empty.

Sol's last email is sent.

He finds himself googling *Star Norfolk, Star Broads,* because with a name like Star, surely he might find her, and if he finds her, what then? He works his way through astronomers and dark skies and star-gazing trips in East Anglia. Then he googles possible cottage names: Star Cottage, Starwater, Star Barn, Mermaid Cottage. Boom! Mermaid Cottage, on Airbnb. The whole cottage – he checks out the photos, and there it is with the private broad Addie mentioned. He checks the reviews, all raving about the place. Different guests through July.

So Star can't be there. And if she isn't, where is she?

How about trying *Star, mermaid*? Star mermaid! Yes! There's an agency in the UK, in Cornwall, called Heads & Tails. Ah look at this, Star Sykes, heading the list. That'll be her. Location. International. *Norfolk, UK.*

Star Sykes: Not currently available for UK work.

He has her name now, so he can search more effectively. Star Sykes is making a film in the States. So she's clearly let out her cottage and Addie can't be with her. How sad. He liked thinking of her there. She must be in Alnwick with Robyn the birdwatcher. He starts googling Robyn. It's getting dark when he locates her on Twitter, where she posts bird updates. He gets in touch. She doesn't reply.

Look at the time!

Tomorrow he's off to Crete for a holiday, so he must go home and pack his case. He will fly into Heraklion and catch a bus to Aghios Nikolaos, where he's rented an apartment. It's apparently a short ride to Elounda, from where he can walk to the peninsula, to his mother's thin place.

Barry Forfitt's mother is dying. Sol hates to leave him here on Fair Isle, with his father who comes home drunk from the pub every night, poor man. Poor Barry. Poor everyone.

Robyn replies just before midnight:

I haven't heard a word from Addie since last Christmas.

2018

The providence of God?

Their own free will?

The power of desire?

Or of forgiveness?

*It's strange to think that abstract things – desire
and forgiveness – which seem so flimsy, might
have the strength to change concrete things.*

*Or, if not abstract things, small things like a poster
which measures only 21 by 30 centimetres.*

*You wouldn't think it would have
the weight to change a life.*

What happens next probably isn't a coincidence.

Unless we make our own.

*You decide what it is that brings Addie
and Sol back into each other's lives.*

~

Here they are.

The second spring.

Wednesday 21st March

Sol walks his familiar path to school, finding *good things* to be grateful for: the sea and the big sky and a job that demands little and pays OK. There's no sign yet of Puer and Puella on the Jut, but it can't be long until they fly in again and reunite for the breeding season after six months apart at sea.

Sol is flying out soon. Easter is early this year, and he has special dispensation to close the school even earlier because of *the wedding*.

Ah yes, the wedding, which he'd had no intention of attending, until Archbishop Thomas spoke to him from his horribly new copy of *Murder in the Cathedral*, encouraging him towards a decision taken by a bigger person through a bigger principle than revenge and hurt. We overcome by suffering, he told him. This is life's pattern. Didn't Brother Andrew also say that? His mother came to him in dreams reminding him of the primacy of love, and Barry Forfitt spoke too by going on loving his father who let him down every day.

Sol asked the Chair of Governors if the term date could be altered to accommodate his departure, knowing that the answer would be no. The Chair said yes.

Sol hasn't left the island since the summer. Crete was hot and sunny, and he ate fresh fish and king prawns and watched people dancing in circles in the square, but the tiny beach on his mother's list of thin places now has a café with loud music and sunbeds and a glass-bottomed boat which arrived every afternoon. He had no sense of her on the peninsula, no sense of God either.

In the autumn, there were repeated invitations from Sol's sister Leah and her husband Alan to join the family on Christmas Day. He didn't. Barry Forfitt's mother died on Boxing Day.

Sol turns away from the cliff as he heads right towards the school house.

He still writes his pain into poems. He has twenty-one in total, which seems quite enough, or far too many. From time to time, inspired by his success with Star Sykes, he googles Addie Lemming. Nothing. Addie Finch. Nothing either. Addie Lemming Wedding Dresses. Addie Finch Wedding Dresses. Nothing. Robyn in Alnwich continues to assure him she hasn't heard a word. When Brother Andrew was in touch again via the monks, he said in passing that two previous guests were helping Addie's mother at The Retreat, as the daughter never returned.

He opens the school gate, and he walks through the peace of the empty playground, unlocking the door and going into his office, anxiety like a clamp around his temples. He takes off his black anorak, identical to the one he lent Addie a year ago. He doesn't have much imagination when it comes to buying clothes.

• • •

In the early morning, Addie has breakfast wearing her (Sol's) black anorak on the balcony of her flat at The Boathouse, looking out for marsh harriers gliding above the reeds. She doesn't see any. She goes downstairs to what Star designed as a changing room for boaters and swimmers, which Addie's converted into a sewing workshop, with a vintage tailor's dummy, a French cheval mirror and a Victorian four-panel room divider, made with mahogany and glass.

She has money. She has clients. She keeps herself to herself, attending carefully to each dress, not asking too many questions, people still being risky to her. She has found that the less you ask, the more they want to tell.

She's gaining a reputation, and the phone often rings.

She takes up her lace, wooden bobbins dangling in clusters over her knees, four of the five lace doves complete, one still headless. The doves are a last-minute addition to the dress. The groom's daughter saw them in a vision, apparently. The bride explained that it was the gold feather at the top right of Addie's poster that drew her, because of the gold-feathered doves of Psalm 68, which was, she said, the psalm of the fatherless.

Addie had no idea what she was talking about, but the doves are beautiful, and beauty consoles her.

She still badly needs consolation.

Every day.

• • •

Sol tries to picture himself tomorrow evening, at the family dinner, sitting at the vicarage table again, with his father at the head and Bee beside him, *Bee beside his father*, Bee who was his fiancée two years ago.

It still feels wrong to him. Not that he has any right to feel proprietorial. His engagement to Bee ended, and it would never have worked, and both of them are free to do what they like. No, it's not that. He finds it hard to articulate what it is.

He thinks of the three-tiered plate with sandwiches at the bottom and scones in the middle and brownies and butterfly cakes on top, and the champagne leaning against the hamper. He sees himself lying on his back beside Bee, propped by both elbows, which meant he had to collapse and turn on his front and reassemble on all fours like a dog, absurdly, before going *up* on one knee. The memory still turns his face hot.

He hears Bee's voice: 'Yes, Sol, yes, of course. I've always wanted to be a vicar's wife.'

He knew that was the wrong answer, but by then, he was forcing the ring onto her finger, and as it wouldn't fit, she took a tube of hand-cream from her bag to ease it on, and it made him think of the jelly stuff that can apparently be useful for lubrication when both are virgins and tense on the wedding night.

He sits at his desk and stares out of the window at the sea, and he wonders how his father proposed to Bee. If it went better. It could hardly have gone worse. Why Sol proposed to Bee he really can't fathom. He can't find it in himself to want anyone but Addie, but he must believe in *fish in the sea*. Plenty more, so people say.

Maud Hamilton (who lives here on Fair Isle) is not one of those fish, *oh dear*, though she's pleasant enough company. Bee is not one of those fish either.

It would have been a total disaster for him to marry Bee, but that doesn't mean his father should be marrying her.

• • •

Addie has discovered that wedding dresses turn into money, and this magic never ceases to amaze and delight her. She did it! She made a wedding dress business. She'd like to tell Sol that.

Her bank account is full. She has proved her mother wrong. She'd like to tell her too, but her mother still hasn't been in touch. She knows that her mother's waiting for her to come crawling back to her, apologising. But she won't.

This dress, the most intricate she's ever made, a web of intertwined lace images over silk, is finished, and Grandma Flora would be proud.

Addie walks across the garden, admiring the new daffodils: the jetfires with orange trumpets growing in the borders, the fragrant little minnows in pots by the water – she crouches to smell them

– and the traditional yellows around the blossom trees, the Jack Snipes, white and yellow, bursting in lacy clumps over the lawn.

• • •

Sol looks up from Miss Gunn's reports to see a goldfinch land on the gorse bush outside his window. There were goldfinches outside the Rokesby chapel, and goldfinches at the fair where he ate candy floss with Addie – stop it, he reprimands himself, you have work to do.

He's reading through the final, final version of Miss Gunn's reports, her harsher comments now softened by Sol's alternatives. He's told her repeatedly that it's no good saying that *Joel* (or anyone else) *should be more confident in Maths* because that's the teacher's job, building the children's confidence.

'Course it is,' said Miss Gunn crossly. 'Everything's our fault these days.'

'It's not that,' said Sol. 'It's just that no human being can generate his or her own confidence. Other people have to give it to them.'

He wishes he were feeling more confident. He imagines himself in his father's church being stared at by the hundreds of people who were expecting *him* to be putting the ring on Bee's finger.

By the time the bell rings for morning break, the reports are checked and printed and the envelopes ready for distribution, all communication on paper here and not online, as voted for in Sol's parent survey.

Sol heads for the jumper shop (because Rachel wants a Fair Isle jumper), thinking that if he's buying for Rachel, he'd better buy for Leah, and if Leah, perhaps Bee? And if Bee, what about his father? His father would look awful in a Fair Isle jumper, especially with the paunch he was growing when Sol last saw him, but who knows, perhaps his young fiancée has brought about what Sol understands is called a *glow-up*.

Could jumpers be a wedding present for the happy couple?

He supposes they're happy.
He wishes he was.
He remembers being happy briefly.
Last spring.

. . .

The doorbell rings, and Addie opens the door to Barbara, who takes off her large puffer coat. She's wearing a clingy sweater dress, and she's looking very thin. She's pulled back her fair hair into a clip, with some strands hanging around her ears.

Addie lays the dress on the table.

'The doves!' says Barbara, smiling.

'Such a great addition,' says Addie.

'A masterpiece!' says Barbara.

'A mistresspiece!' says Addie, laughing.

Barbara says quietly, but firmly, 'You know I'm not a feminist. Quite the reverse.'

Addie wonders what a reverse-feminist is – somebody who wants women to be treated unequally?

'It's beautiful,' says Barbara.

'Well, let's get you into it,' says Addie, summoning up some professional energy. 'So exciting. Three days to go!'

'*One* day until the whole *merry-go-round* starts,' says Barbara, and there's something almost defiant underneath her voice.

Oh, not merry-go-rounds, thinks Addie. The taste of candy floss and the citrus smell of him. She shakes the memories out of her. She must concentrate.

'We're having a family dinner tomorrow evening,' says Barbara, giving away much more than usual.

'How lovely,' says Addie.

'Except that it isn't lovely,' says Barbara.

Addie nods.

'I'm making myself ill with the stress of it,' says Barbara.

Addie nods again, not wanting to be drawn in.

'Will you come?' says Barbara.

Oh dear.

'Come where?'

'To the dinner.'

'Me?'

'If you can't come to the wedding, please say yes to the dinner. For me,' says Barbara.

For her?

Addie says, 'Of course. I'd love to.'

Which is the right (but not the true) answer.

'Would you like to put the dress on?' says Addie, gesturing towards the changing cubicle.

• • •

Sol returns to the schoolhouse with two bags of jumpers, and this means that the wedding is real, that these jumpers will be put on the bodies of the people he has chosen not to see, and now will see.

His phone pings.

It's his sister, Rachel, texting him the final schedule for the wedding arrangements.

Gloom descends on him. Or is it panic?

It was Rachel who rang the school beseeching him to come, then rang again, and again, and again, demolishing every argument, destroying his defences, invoking his mother, who said that love never failed, that love was a verb – it meant you did things, things you didn't necessarily want to do, that love was a sacrifice, that he should honour his father.

'I'm sure Dad will pay for your flights,' Rachel said conclusively. 'And I'm happy to book them for you.'

'I wouldn't hear of it,' said Sol.

Money isn't his problem. When he has supper with Maud

Hamilton, he sees Addie's face. This *is* his problem, or one of them. He's promised Maud nothing, except pudding. Maud likes pudding, and Sol likes to bake.

But there is only Addie: she made him feel like he'd never felt before, and even though he had that buzzy electrified feeling so briefly, he wouldn't give it up for the world.

Or, practically speaking, for £25,000, which was the cost of the van.

That's what it cost him for forty-two hours with Addie.

£595 per hour.

He thinks (though this may be bewildering to others) that it was worth it, that it was better to have had the feeling and lost it, and lost the van with it, than never to have had it at all.

He takes his rucksack and goes out to the playground to meet Miss Fay. Miss Gunn is staying behind with the youngest ones.

'Well, come on then,' he says to the line of paired children. 'Let's go for our last-day-treat!'

. . .

'I'm going to get undressed in front of you,' says Barbara to Addie. 'Like a kind of practice run for the wedding night.'

'An *undress rehearsal*!' says Addie, smiling.

Barbara pulls her sweater dress over her head, and Addie looks at her large beige pants and her rather empty beige bra, and feels an unexpected burst of compassion for her, but she also realises that her breasts have shrunk to such a degree that the dress is going to be problematic.

Addie crouches below Barbara's buttocks, and starts to do up the tiny pearl buttons, one at a time.

. . .

At the beach, Sol asks the children to help him make a fire, and as they do so, he tells them that he once saw a mermaid.

'She had a tail and long ringlets and I saw her bobbing up and down in the waves as if she was drowning. And I have a question for you. Do mermaids drown?'

There are various shouts of *no they don't*, but Barry Forfitt is looking thoughtful.

'Fish are incapable of drowning,' he says. 'Because they don't have lungs. They have gills. They suffocate when their gills collapse but they don't drown. Mermaids do have lungs and therefore could feasibly drown.'

Feasibly!

The other pupils look at Barry Forfitt like the other pupils used to look at Sol.

Sol gives the children two options. They can stay with Sol by the fire to play *Lie Me Some Truth* and find out if the mermaid he claims to have seen is true, or they can make sand sculptures, and there will be prizes. Sol won a lot of academic prizes: all of them were disappointing.

'Can't we play football?' says Joel.

Sol sometimes wishes he was a man who liked football because although men who like football can be disappointed in their team or the referee's decision, they never seem to be disappointed in football per se, the concept of it.

'I didn't bring the ball,' says Sol.

Nine children scuttle over the beach with Miss Fay to make sand sculptures, but Barry Forfitt stays by the fire.

'We could just talk,' says Sol to Barry.

'I'd prefer that,' says Barry, putting his hand through his curls. 'Are you excited about your trip, Mr Blake?'

'Oh not really,' says Sol because he finds he can never be dishonest with Barry. 'Families are complicated.'

'They are,' says Barry. 'My brothers try really hard to like me, but it's not easy for them.'

'I don't know how anybody wouldn't like you,' says Sol.

211

'I think sometimes we don't get on with our brothers and sisters because we define ourselves *against* them,' says Barry.

'You could be right,' says Sol.

This child!

'When will you be back, Mr Blake?'

'A week today, in the afternoon.'

'That's good,' says Barry. 'Not long then.'

Sol nods.

'You know you told us your mother died,' says Barry. 'Were you still missing her when you saw the mermaid?'

'Yes I was,' says Sol.

'I find that sadness can make you see things that aren't there,' says Barry. 'I sometimes see Mum walking over the beach.'

'How are you doing?' says Sol. 'Is it getting any easier?'

'I'm a bit lonely,' says Barry. 'But maybe things will be better at secondary school.'

They won't, thinks Sol, *and you'll be boarding and I worry for you.*

'Or university?' says Barry.

'Maybe,' says Sol.

'Do you talk to your dad about being lonely?' says Sol.

'I don't want to make him sad,' says Barry.

'I felt the same when I was your age,' says Sol.

'Is it better now?' says Barry.

Sol manages, for the first time, to lie to Barry.

'Oh yes,' he says to Barry Forfitt. 'It's much better once you're an adult.'

• • •

'I have to tell you something,' says Barbara still facing away from Addie.

Addie waits.

'Addie,' she says, her voice trembling slightly. 'I was once engaged to the son.'

212

'Oh,' says Addie, buttoning upwards.

Then, 'Ohhhh' again.

'As in, your future husband's son?'

Addie makes her way, one button at a time, towards her neck. Barbara has little moles on her upper back like a dot to dot. Of . . . Of a harp?

'The first engagement ended six months before the second one began.'

Addie can't think what to say, but Barbara waits for her response.

'Serial monogamy is what everyone does,' says Addie.

'But not normally with the son, then the father?' says Barbara.

'There is no normal life,' says Addie.

'So you think it's OK?' says Barbara.

'Fine,' says Addie, thinking that it is in fact quite strange. 'Absolutely fine. Nothing to worry about.'

How old is this man of hers, Addie wonders, bearing in mind that she was once engaged to his son? Or how old is the son? She won't ask. She doesn't ask questions. She doesn't want to be involved.

'I wanted you to know,' says Barbara.

'All done,' says Addie, but Barbara stays where she is and doesn't turn around.

'Let me finish,' she says to the wall. 'You see, the son hasn't spoken to us since we got engaged, which is over a year ago. We had a long engagement hoping he'd come round. But he's never answered our calls or texts or emails. He once rang me but he didn't say anything.'

'Oh well,' says Addie to Barbara's back. 'These things take time.'

Barbara nods.

'Now turn around,' says Addie.

'It's worse than that,' says Barbara, not turning around. 'One of the sisters has persuaded him to come back for the wedding because it would look very odd if he wasn't there, wouldn't it? So the son's coming to the family dinner tomorrow. That'll be the first time either of us have seen him since he found out. Last time I saw him, I was *engaged to him.*'

Wow, thinks Addie.

This is quite intense.

Barbara turns around, looks in the mirror and points at the bagginess of the lace around her diminished bust.

'What's happened here?' she says, her face crumpling. 'It's all wrong.'

'I'm wondering if the dress might need to be altered a little,' says Addie.

If she altered the dress to fit her, Barbara's chest would be flat as a board, and this is not something she feels she can say.

'But it's this Saturday,' says Barbara.

'That's why we have the final fitting so near the wedding.'

'I can't believe this is happening to me,' says Barbara.

'What would help,' says Addie, and her voice has turned very slow and soft, 'would be a different sort of bra.'

'You think I've got time to go bra-shopping?' says Barbara, with a tone of rising panic.

'I keep some bras here,' says Addie. 'Would you like to try one?'

She brings a pink one out, with padded cups as plump as chicken breasts.

'But when I get undressed on the wedding night, won't I take off my breasts with my bra?'

There is that, thinks Addie.

'Won't that be off-putting for him?' says Barbara.

'He won't notice. He'll be too excited!'

'Won't he be disappointed?'

'He's not marrying your breasts,' says Addie.

'Or theologically speaking,' says Barbara, 'he is. *The wife's body does not belong to her alone but also to her husband.*'

'What about the husband's body then?' says Addie. 'What does God say about that?'

'The same,' says Barbara.

'Well, I guess that's fair of him,' says Addie. 'Or her?'

'Him,' says Barbara firmly.

• • •

Sol eats his packed lunch (a sausage roll and an apple, both disappointing) and gets ready for the Easter egg hunt. He waits as Miss Gunn and Miss Fay line up the children, and as they walk to the designated spot, he feels tension humming so powerfully inside him that he wonders if other people can hear it.

He accompanies Miss Fay to hide the eggs. Miss Gunn is in a bad mood because she doesn't like Easter eggs being hunted early. She stands at the bottom of the slope with her hands in the pockets of her tweed coat, shouting if a child moves one foot out of line. This bothers Sol, and he will have to speak to her about it next term.

As the children start hunting, Sol sees Maud Hamilton on the path, now walking towards him. This is not good news. She appears at his side, with her rosy cheeks and mousy hair, and she says, 'I used to do this here when I was a child.'

'Lovely,' says Sol, feeling self-conscious because he doesn't want the children to ask if Maud's his girlfriend.

Maud, one of the few younger people on the island, leads services in the chapel and doubles as the curator of the museum, which relates the story of her ancestors. Her *ancestory*, she likes to say, which is a word that irritates Sol, and which he has not, and will not, put on his word list.

'Are you excited about the wedding?' says Maud.

'Well, it's a bit of a mix with these family occasions,' says Sol.

'Do you like your father's new wife?' says Maud.

Sol could tell her.

But he won't.

'She's much younger than him,' he says. 'I'm still acclimatising.'

'Midlife crisis?' says Maud.

Sol doesn't answer.

'Have you seen *American Beauty*?' says Maud. 'You know, with Kevin Spacey. Before all the hoo-ha.'

'I have actually.'

'It won some Oscars I think.'

That's it, thinks Sol, or at least it's part of it. It was weird when the middle-aged dad fell for his daughter's friend in the film, like it feels weird that his own father (and in particular *his* father with all his *views*) should have fallen for the much younger woman *he* was going to marry. Or is Sol wrong? Is it all OK?

'I always think it's weirder if the woman is older,' says Maud.

'I think that's probably cultural conditioning,' says Sol.

'I knew you'd say that,' says Maud.

Then she pauses, and the children's delighted shrieks blow in on the wind, and Easter will come, and the year will turn.

'Do you think you'll ever get married?' says Maud.

Barry Forfitt comes and places an egg in each of their hands.

He goes back to the group, sitting down a little apart from the others, which hurts Sol, as he and Maud eat their chocolate eggs in silence.

'Do you?' says Maud, her mouth full of chocolate egg.

'It's hard to say, isn't it?' says Sol.

'It's something I've always wanted,' says Maud. 'Marriage. My father told me not to get ordained. He said it would put men off marrying me.'

'Nonsense,' says Sol.

Maud opens her mouth, and her tongue is brown with chocolate.

'I'd better go and round up the kids,' says Sol.

'See you later,' says Maud. 'What time shall I come?'

'Maybe seven,' says Sol, wondering if there is anything he can do to put her off.

He takes the children back to school for the final dismissal of the term, and he hands out their end-of-term packs to their parents and wishes them all a Happy Easter, when it comes.

'I'm leaving now,' says Miss Gunn, coming into his office.

'Thank you for everything you've done this term,' says Sol.

She clears her throat and does up the first button on her tweed coat, then says, 'Hope it all goes well,' before leaving.

Sol locks his filing cabinets and locks the schoolhouse door, then goes back to check it's locked.

• • •

Addie crosses the gravel drive and goes into Mermaid Cottage, which smells of cabbage and dirty bins. There are cup rings on the dining table despite Addie leaving out mats and coasters and aggressive notes in capital letters, as Star requires. Whenever the cottage is mistreated like this, Addie feels as if it's her fault, as if Star will be cross.

She makes her way around the bedrooms and the bathrooms, plucking condoms from bins and hair from plugholes.

She feels tired.

She needs to work on Barbara's dress, but she must also change the beds, hoover and dust and clean, pick flowers, make a cake – the new guests are due late tonight.

• • •

Sol chops carrots and mushrooms and tomatoes, fries onion and minced lamb, and then goes upstairs for a shower. When he's showered and dressed, he takes his blue trousers and blue cord jacket downstairs on a hanger and hooks it over the door of the hall cupboard, trying to convince himself that this will be the perfect combination for his father's wedding.

Maud Hamilton arrives with her thin hair up in a pony tail, which makes her ears stick out. She is wearing a checked coat and perfume which smells of roses.

217

'I'm wearing these,' he says, pointing to the hanger. 'To the wedding.'

'That's not really wedding-smart,' says Maud. 'Also they don't go. The two blues.'

'I could buy something when I get to the mainland,' he says.

'You're probably quite difficult to buy for,' says Maud. 'Your body isn't exactly mainstream.'

Don't say that to me, he thinks, *just days before the whole family and the whole congregation watch my father marry the girl who dumped me. What I need right now is confidence.* And you can't build your own, as he has failed to persuade Miss Gunn.

'Let me put the food in,' says Sol.

He does so, returning to the sitting room, where Maud is standing by his book shelves. He notices that her ears are small and veiny and circular-shaped. A pair of whorls. He's not sure how your pronounce whorls. He's never said it aloud.

He sits on the sofa.

'What are those twenty-one envelopes?' says Maud. 'On the bottom shelf?'

She has clearly picked them up and seen the numbers, but he really hopes she hasn't opened any of them because that would be excruciating.

'Oh, just scribblings of mine.'

'Why've they got numbers on them?' she says, walking over to him.

Sol sits on the sofa.

Maud sits very close to him.

'Are they letters to your father?'

'Musings.'

'When are you going to tell me your whole story?'

Sol panics.

'Well, my mother died four years—'

'Which I know,' says Maud.

'My father and I never quite hit it off. He wanted me to be a vicar. So I started training, and then stopped.'

'And why was that exactly? You never really said.'

'I wasn't sure what I believed. I tried acting like I believed, hoping this would morph into believing. It was my mentor's idea.'

'*Credo ut intelligam*,' says Maud, moving even closer to him. 'I believe so that I understand. Anselm of Canterbury.'

'Yes, exactly,' says Sol, as she takes hold of his hand.

'I prefer it the other way round, you see,' he says, as Maud starts to stroke his palm. 'I want to understand so that I believe.'

He wishes Maud would stop stroking his palm.

'Maud,' he says. 'It's no fun for you spending time with a man like me.'

Could he just end the (sort-of) relationship tonight? He'd feel so much better if he did. Perhaps he should deliberately start a row with her. No, that feels uncharitable and underhand.

'Sol,' says Maud, as she lets go of his hand. 'There's nobody here I'd rather spend time with.'

'Which isn't saying much,' says Sol. 'Bearing in mind that most people here are under eleven or over eighty!'

He laughs tensely.

She doesn't laugh.

'You're my best hope of staying on Fair Isle,' she says.

There we go again: women wanting him for his job, or his van, or for just being male and alive and local.

'Perhaps you only want me because I'm here and nobody else is,' he says. 'I wouldn't blame you if that was the case.'

'Well,' says Maud. 'The same could be said for you.'

'You're right,' says Sol.

'Romantic love is probably an illusion,' says Maud.

Sol knows it isn't.

If you'd ever experienced it, he thinks, *you'd pay £595 an hour to experience it again.*

219

He says to Maud, 'I'd better go and check if the shepherd's pie is burning.'

. . .

Addie washes her hands and threads her needle, knowing that she has a long evening of alterations ahead of her. The phone rings, so she lays the dress on the table and answers.

'Addie!'

'Dad!'

He never phones.

'Is everyone OK?'

He says: 'I wanted you to know that Pattie has died.'

'I'm sorry.'

He doesn't reply.

'The world must feel very odd without her in it. You've been a good husband to Pattie. The best.'

Her father makes an indeterminate noise.

'You're good at seeing things from all sides. Your mother always said that.'

'Does she still? Does Mum see anything good in me at all now I've left?'

'I don't know why you won't go back and see her,' says her father.

This is what he says every time they speak, and why she doesn't phone him. So far, he seems to have kept his promise not to tell her mother where she is, or maybe he's told her and she doesn't care.

'I've explained! She doesn't answer my emails or my texts or my calls. If she wanted me to visit, she would.'

'If you came with me and Sydney, we could work it out together. We'd persuade her.'

'I don't want you to *persuade* her to love me. She was never like this with you and Sydney when you left.'

Her father doesn't reply.

She swallows.

'I know this is very, very late notice,' says her father, 'but I'm going to spend my first weekend ever with your mother. Because weekends were always Pattie's.'

'I know,' says Addie. 'I was there.'

'Well,' he says. 'I'll be driving past your house, sort of, on Friday. That's in two days' time.'

'Yes. Well, do call. I'm actually having a few days off and—'

'Perfect!' says her father.

'What's perfect?'

'Is there any chance you could sew something for me?'

'Like what?' says Addie, suspiciously.

'She only wants something very simple, do you remember?'

'What are you talking about?'

'A simple dress,' says her father. 'I want to surprise her with it.'

'What kind of dress?'

'A wedding dress. You said you had a few days off.'

'This is all weirdly rushed. Perhaps you should pause a little.'

'We won't have the wedding this weekend! I just want to surprise her with the ring and the dress. She's waited so long for me, and she's been so patient.'

'You do still like each other, do you?' says Addie. 'I'm never sure.'

Her father laughs.

'I'd be so grateful to you,' says her father.

And that's that.

Addie feels like screaming as she says goodbye to her father, but she goes downstairs and she finds that she is unfolding the ivory silk and unrolling the netting. She knows exactly what her mother wants. *I'll just do it*, she thinks, *and then it's done.*

She can do Barbara's alterations in the morning, she tells herself, and Barbara can come and get the dress later than planned, in the afternoon. Her shoulders ache. She puts her arms above her head and stretches.

Her mother's the same size as she is, a bit larger around the waist – she assumes she hasn't shrunk or expanded in the year since she left – so Addie measures herself, and she chalks the material, and she draws the simple bodice, and she begins. A single tear rolls down her cheek. She angrily wipes it away.

She texts her father.

Am doing it.

She sends it with no kiss.

It's still so surprising that her mother should want a ballerina skirt.

She rips the first piece of netting.

She wipes away another tear.

Grandma Flora never cried, even when Grandpa Fred hurt her, even when he hit her.

'I won't give him the pleasure,' she once said to Addie.

Addie's not crying about her mother's dress. She's crying about everything she's never cried about. Her front and her hands and her face are drenched with the whole of her life. As she cries, she can't stop herself wondering what she's always stopped herself wondering. The way her mother treated her, was it eccentric, or selfish, or blind or misguided, or was it something much scarier? When she thinks of her past, it's as if she's blindfolded, feeling for it with her fingertips, which are always slightly numb.

Her phone pings.

It's her father.

Thanks, Ads. x

· · ·

Sol walks Maud to the door, takes her checked coat off the banister and holds it out to her. She slips in her left arm, then her right, after which she turns and moves her face towards his.

'Oh no,' he says, as the tip of her nose touches his. 'I don't think—'

'Relax, Sol,' she says. 'Relax!'

'I am relaxed.'

'I don't think you are,' she says.

She gives up on the kiss and steps back.

'If you could just relax, it would all be fine,' she says.

'Well,' says Sol. 'I'll do my best to relax whilst I'm away. How does that sound?'

'That sounds good,' says Maud.

'Well,' says Sol, sweating. 'If you'll excuse me, I need to go and finish my packing.'

'Thank you for the shepherd's pie,' says Maud. 'And the tart.'

Sol sits quietly on the sofa, breathing deeply. He's got her out, which is good, but he's left her hanging, which is bad. He'll worry about that when he's back, but for now, silence. Wonderful. And also terrible. The wedding is about to pounce on him.

He picks up books from his shelves and puts them down. He turns off the light and opens the window. He likes to watch the moon, thinking of it pulling the earth's tides, tracking its months and seasons. In his entirely dark house, he stares through the window, and then he bends over and unlaces his shoes, and takes off his black socks, and he heads for the back door. In his tiny walled garden, he stands barefoot under the moonlit sky, and the feeling comes, the feeling he first had on Ora when he connected with the grass and the ant and the eider duck, when life lit up.

Sol supposes that the feeling the moon bestows on him barefoot in the garden is awe, and he's found that it's the best way of washing away his circling worries, his regrets and his losses, and it also helps him to sleep. Sometimes Addie comes and stands beside him under the moon. He waits and he waits because he very badly wants her tonight, but she doesn't come.

He goes back inside and climbs the stairs to his bedroom, where he goes through his hand luggage, checking for his passport, money, bank cards, phone charger. He gets into bed and carefully sets his alarm.

Then he stares at the ceiling for several hours.

· · ·

Addie stands with a strong coffee on her balcony looking at the moon in the ripples of the river. She feels emptied out, and penetratingly, deeply alone, as if she were the only person on earth tonight.

Grandma Flora.

Eureka.

Sol Blake.

The best of them, and all gone.

If only he hadn't gone back. If only she hadn't crashed his van. If only they'd driven to Tromso together to see his mother's thin place.

She forces herself to keep working on her mother's dress, stopping to jog on the spot, slapping her cheeks to stay awake. She hears the guests' car crunching down the drive. She looks out of the window: a black Range Rover. It often is. She wonders if her mother will say yes to her father. If they'll be different with each other. She wonders what they say to each other about her.

She knows Barbara will find it hard to cope with a changed appointment time, so perhaps she should get her alterations done now and forget about sleeping tonight. She sits at the sewing machine, but she's too tired and risks making a mistake on the best dress she's ever made.

She really wishes Barbara hadn't shrunk her tits.

Sol will be drawn through the sky towards the vicarage.

As Addie was drawn to Norfolk.

As Barbara was drawn to the feather at the corner of the poster, the feather of the goldfinch which carries the thorn in its beak.

Sol and Addie carry their thorns with them.

We all do.

Perhaps that's why to know each other is inevitably to hurt each other.

Though we wish this wasn't so.

Thursday 22nd March

Sol looks out of the window of the plane in the dawn light, and there's the little white hut (the terminal) in the drizzly early morning and there's the schoolhouse and his cottage, getting smaller and smaller and smaller, and vanishing, Fair Isle with them, and there is only sea, until the Orkney Islands appear below him.

Soon after, the pilot points out John O'Groats, a town which he says is named after one Jan de Groot who in the reign of James IV ran the ferry from the mainland to Orkney – a potential quiz-winner, that, Sol thinks. The pilot says that Jan de Groot built an octagonal house and an eight-sided table so that there would be no arguing amongst him and his seven sons over who should sit at the head.

Sol's father will be sitting at the head of the table, and Bee, he supposes, will be beside him. Tonight. It makes him feel slightly sick.

He'll land in Lerwick in under half an hour, and from there fly to Glasgow, and from Glasgow to Stansted, where he'll hire a car and drive straight to the vicarage.

He's not sure he can.

He's not sure he will.

He hopes that the plane doesn't land, although that wouldn't necessarily be a good thing either.

· · ·

When Addie phones Barbara to say that she will have to make her final dress-fitting appointment a little later in the day, Barbara says, 'Please don't do this to me! Not before my *massage!*'

'Or perhaps it's the ideal moment to be stressed – before a massage?' says Addie, regretting it, regathering herself and saying, 'Any time from three thirty onwards should be fine.'

She picks up Barbara's dress.

Then the new guests ring on the doorbell, asking for pub recommendations.

· · ·

At Glasgow Airport, Sol sits with his coffee. His rucksack is full of Fair Isle jumpers wrapped in now-ripped tissue paper with the Number 7 envelope down one side.

The Arch.

There was a moment for him and Addie, but they fell away from each other. His poem foresees another moment in another shaft of sunlight. But how could that possibly happen? Neither of them has the first idea where the other is.

He stuffs the poem back in his rucksack and rushes to the gate.

· · ·

Barbara's dress is finished, and Addie too is finished.

She needs to find a way to get out of tonight's dinner, she thinks, as she takes a scone to the jetty, where she sits watching the river. An otter paddles fast along the side of the bank and disappears. Then a cormorant lands on the post opposite and puts out its wings to dry, and there is Sol on the bank, with the wind in his hair, his blue jumper pulled up to his elbows, with his tanned forearms, and his smile, and his intensity and his goodness.

Enough, Addie tells herself.

Here comes Little Hen, cheerily alone, calling *kup kup kup.*

'Ah there you are!' she says.

It's OK.

Everything's OK.

Oh help, a car's arriving. Addie rushes over the lawn to The Boathouse.

'I've hardly slept worrying about the dress,' says Barbara.

Addie considers mentioning that she hasn't slept much either.

'The dress will be beautiful,' she says.

'I bought one of those bras,' says Barbara, taking it out of her bag and showing Addie. 'I hate the word bras. Do you?'

'I've never really thought about it,' says Addie.

'I still find it embarrassing, all that padding,' says Barbara. 'I think I'll try and hide it under the bed or something.'

Barbara has never been so talkative – it must be nerves.

'When you're pregnant, your breasts grow, don't they?' she says.

'I think so.'

'I want to make a family as soon as we can. I'm not using contraception. Do you think his sperm will be OK? He's forty-eight.'

'Oh, men can make babies any time.'

Barbara nods.

'Well, let's get you into the dress,' says Addie, hoping to close this rather over-intimate conversation.

Barbara goes into the cubicle.

Forty-eight, thinks Addie, *that is actually quite old* – older than her mother. She's not sure how old Barbara is. Thirtyish?

'Are you ready, Barbara?'

'Yes.'

'It must be strange going to bed and not going to sleep,' says Barbara to the wall as Addie crouches to do up the buttons. 'I keep thinking that. How I'm going to keep my energy up for bedtime. It sounds a bit tiring. Do you think I should try to do less in the day once I'm married?'

Could you do less, Addie wonders.

'Well, that's one way of looking at it,' says Addie, laughing, and again trying to close the conversation.

But Barbara says, 'I'm not joking. I'm actually quite worried about it.'

Addie goes on buttoning.

'You can always *not do it* at bedtime,' says Addie. 'And do it another time.'

'Is that right?' says Barbara. 'Really? In the vicarage? Would that be OK?'

Addie wonders if perhaps daytime sex in the vicarage wouldn't be such a good idea.

'I know it's not normal to keep sex for marriage these days,' says Barbara. 'But it's something I feel strongly about.'

'That's not a bad thing,' says Addie. 'I think it's a good thing. I admire you for not following the crowd.'

She does.

'I'm sure I'll be exhausted on the wedding night,' says Barbara. 'After all that smiling.'

Smiling, thinks Addie, laughing to herself – who else would be exhausted by smiling?

'But I still want to do it. It wouldn't be right to wait until the morning.'

'I agree,' says Addie. 'Quite right. You must definitely do it on your wedding night. After all, you've waited your whole life.'

'I wasn't waiting for sex when I was a baby,' says Barbara.

Addie laughs – did Barbara mean to be funny?

'What's it like?' says Barbara. 'Sex?'

'It's quite hard to describe,' says Addie. 'You know a bit like coffee's only really like coffee.'

'I don't know if it appeals to me that much,' says Barbara. 'Sex, not coffee. I like coffee.'

Oh dear, thinks Addie.

'All done,' she says. 'Turn around.'

Barbara turns.

Addie feels a wave of exhaustion, but she pastes a radiant smile on her lips as her eyes burn.

'Stunning.'

'So here goes,' says Barbara. 'The great reunion dinner!'

'I was thinking,' says Addie.

'You absolutely have to come,' says Barbara.

Oh shit.

'Of course I'm coming,' says Addie.

. . .

Here is Stansted, and here is Sol's return to the vicarage, now only two hours away. Sol races through the terminal to collect his car, a Fiat 500 (why did he hire a Fiat 500?) into which his non-mainstream body almost doesn't fit (he hired it because it was the cheapest category), and he puts his case on the backseat and his rucksack on the front, and he punches the postcode of the vicarage into Maps, and he feels as if his knees are under his chin as he drives off, and he is going, or he supposes that he is, and the blue line thrusts him forward, helpless, and anxious, counting down the minutes like his father's sermon timer, to moment zero, when his tyres will crunch over the drive.

. . .

Barbara's dress has *gone* and is out of Addie's life for good. She lies on the floor with her eyes closed. *Right,* she says to herself, *I'll go to the dinner tonight, finish Mum's dress tomorrow – no fiddly bits, no lace, no embroidery, plain as plain – and get Barbara into her dress on Saturday morning, and that is it.* Her next appointment is on Wednesday. She can get out on the river, go swimming, do whatever she likes for a few days.

She walks across the lawn, following the bank to the soft place under the willow tree, where she sits among the curly ferns and the liverworts, moving her hand back and forward over the velvet moss, trying not to think about Sol, trying not to think about her mother who doesn't want her and her father who only wants her when she's useful, trying not to start crying again. She really doesn't like crying, it turns out.

Addie goes back to her workshop and restarts the first layer of netting for her mother's dress, but her eyes are closing. She takes a strong cup of coffee to the balcony and she watches Little Hen, swimming jerkily the way she does. Along come the paired-up mallards, sliding effortlessly over the water, little webbed buggers. She goes inside for a tin of sweetcorn, which she directs forcefully at Little Hen. The mallards snap around her. But Little Hen holds her own, determinedly seeing them off, snaffling the sweetcorn, cool as anything.

Addie feels cheered. She looks at her watch. She mustn't be late. She stares into her wardrobe, and grabs her denim pinafore and a white blouse with lace cuffs onto which she's embroidered a bee, a ladybird and a butterfly. She puts on enormous gold hoop earrings which almost reach her chin, and pulls her hair up with a clip, ringlets falling each side of her face.

In the mirror, her face is grey with exhaustion – she looks ill. In the drawer, she has mascara and lipstick and blusher that she never wears, but perhaps she should. She takes the mascara out of the box and flicks the wand over her long eyelashes, brushes her cheeks pinkish and paints her lips the colour of coral.

She takes the cherry clogs from her wardrobe and carries them downstairs where she puts them in a carrier bag. She pulls on her swingy green coat and wellies, locks the door, picks a bunch of jetfire daffodils from the garden, puts them in the bike basket with her clogs, and she cycles out of the gate.

. . .

Sol is back on roads he knows, leaning into familiar bends, noticing a new house here, some metal gates there, a Union Jack flag on a flagpole, and then it comes to him that he needs to get changed. His father will expect a shirt and a jacket. He pulls into the car park of The Heron and drags out his creased linen shirt and the cord jacket he intends to wear to the wedding. Then he thinks he'd better take off his jeans and wear the creased blue Chinos. He stands in his boxers behind the very small driver's door and pulls them on.

If he's wearing his wedding outfit for the dinner, what will he wear to the wedding? He'll worry about that another time.

He feels nauseous.

Why on earth is he here?

He's here to be a big man, he reminds himself, and maybe it will be cathartic for him.

Breathe!

He turns into his childhood road, seeing himself as a toddler, a little boy, a teenager, traipsing sadly along on his growing feet, getting taller, like those evolution diagrams his father hates so much.

He passes the church and the oak tree by the vicarage gate, but his hands won't turn the steering wheel. They seem to have gained a power of their own, and they're keeping on straight and driving him to the end of the lane, a dead end, with nothing but the entrance to the farm and the fields, where there's a sign with two red hearts saying PARKING FOR WEDDING.

. . .

Addie puts the address into Maps.

Hold on, she thinks. *Am I going mad? Isn't that Reverend S Blake's church?* And therefore Reverend S Blake's vicarage? And therefore . . . Surely not. Her mind is trying to compute the possibilities as she cycles faster than ever, powered by her own bewilderment, being rain-sprayed by lorry tyres on the main road.

Can Barbara possibly be marrying Reverend S Blake, who is Sol Blake's father, meaning, no this can't be right, that she, Barbara, was once engaged to him. To Sol! How did she catch no sense of this before now? And how can it possibly be? She must be wrong. She re-computes. Re-computes. Re-computes.

She keeps going, puddles splashing the back of her wellies and the top of her socks, the cogs of her mind turning faster as she flies down the lane – and there's the church, and the crucifix, illuminated white.

She wheels her bike across the gravel, her hands shaking, and she changes into her cherry clogs and rings on the doorbell, holding the wellies and the daffodils in carrier bags.

. . .

Sol turns the Fiat around and makes his way slowly back up the lane. Outside the next-door neighbours' house, he stops, and his heart lurches, and he hears his own breathing, and his fingers tremble, because he's watching the silhouette of his father in his gold-lit study, his father he hasn't spoken to for over a year and a half. The curtains are open as always, visible over the low hedge, as he sits, hunched, at his desk.

He remembers the silhouettes in the glass pyramid on the roof his first night on Ora.

Addie.

He wonders where she is and what she's doing.

His father's head is in his hands. Sol wonders what he's thinking, or what he's praying, or what he's feeling, and whether he's happy in his relationship with Bee, who Sol always found, even in their engagement, strangely distant.

But perhaps real love (if real love it is, which seems unlikely) has changed her.

He dismisses the scene in *American Beauty* with the naked girl and the rose petals.

I can't do it, he thinks, and he turns the car engine off.

I don't have to.

I could go somewhere else.

He gets out of the car and hides behind the oak tree to get a better view of the drive, and he sees the back of a woman with a bike who's wearing a green coat, with two gold buttons on a little strap in the centre below her shoulder blades, with her hair up in a kind of clipped bun. She's very short, and makes Rachel look huge when she answers the door, wearing a long blue dress, looking slightly Amish.

Rachel closes the door, and Sol gets into his car and drives away from the vicarage back to the end of the lane.

• • •

The woman who opens the door to Addie says, 'I'm Rachel. I assume you're Bee's dress lady?'

Bee?

Bee's dress lady?

'I suppose I am,' says Addie smiling at her round face, her pale hair pulled tightly back.

'Well, come on in!'

Addie gives her the daffodils and takes a step forward, her clogs clopping on the hall tiles. Rachel stares at Addie's clogs, puts her hand to her heart, blushes, looks up, looks down, says, 'Gosh! Sorry!'

Her mind starts computing again.

Oh no, the clogs, the clogs.

Maybe, Perhaps, Possibly

The woman called Rachel takes Addie into the conservatory – clop clop clop – where silent people stand holding glasses of champagne like cardboard cut-outs.

• • •

Sol sits in the Fiat at the end of the lane, wondering if he really will go in.

He must.

He's come all this way.

It's 7.40.

He tells himself that he'll drive back up to the vicarage at 7.45.

But 7.45 passes and he doesn't.

He'll drive back up at eight o'clock, definitely.

Eight o'clock comes, and he starts the car.

He parks beyond the drive, beside the church, and he gets out.

• • •

A man with a beard says to Addie, 'We're the cousins. I'm Matt, and this is Martin.'

'Pleased to meet you.'

Can Sol really be coming here, thinks Addie.

It feels impossible.

Two women in long dresses and boots say, 'We're the wives.'

'And this is Mike, and this is Max,' says possibly Matt or Martin.

Addie shakes hands with the quartet of bearded Ms, who are all wearing slightly ill-fitting suits and nylon ties, and she looks around for Barbara, who she can't see.

'I'm the brother of the groom,' says a bald man wearing a dog collar with a vivid blue shirt. 'And the father of this lot. My wife's got a cold and can't be here.'

He's so bald. So old. Quite startling.

Both brothers, vicars.

'I'm Leah!' says someone who is tall and fair like Rachel, but

235

slightly more imposing. She looks down at Addie's feet, and freezes for a second, before grasping her hand and leading her towards a small woman, sitting alone at the extreme left-hand end of a sofa, surrounded by cushions.

'This is Bee's mother, Pamela,' says Leah, again looking at the clogs.

So many names.

Should Addie take the clogs off?

Is he really going to come?

Addie moves three bird cushions out of the way and sits next to Pamela, who is folded in on herself, one arm across the waist of her pink dress, with a dripping nose that she periodically dabs with a pink tissue.

'How lovely to see your daughter getting married,' says Addie, scrunching her wet toes and trying to stay in the present.

'She always had her eye on a vicar,' says Pamela. 'I don't know where we'd be without the church, you see.'

Addie leans forward.

'She'll have told you,' whispers Pamela.

Addie smiles, and Pamela dabs her nose again.

'It was a terrible business,' she says. 'But he's dead now.'

Addie smiles again.

'To think I married the man,' she says.

'We all make mistakes,' says Addie, doing her best to fill in the gaps of the story she doesn't know, and definitely shouldn't ask about, not here, not now, not with her head spinning like this.

'It's so much better now he's dead,' says Barbara's mother. 'But Barb and I wouldn't have made it without the church. They scooped us up, and that's how we got through.'

'Well, that's wonderful,' says Addie. 'And now your daughter's marrying a vicar.'

A disastrous father, Addie guesses (poor Barbara), which

explains Psalm 68, psalm to the fatherless, and also the older husband, who is presumably some kind of replacement father figure as well as the personification of the church who looked after them.

'Don't say anything to anyone,' whispers Pamela to Addie. 'But the son was more handsome. Though look where handsome got me!'

The son!

Handsome, yes.

'And the son is definitely coming?' says Addie.

'I think so,' says Pamela.

Addie might throw up.

•   •   •

'Is that Sol?' says a voice, and the voice comes from a fat version of Ricko the youth leader, pushing a bike. Sol and Ricko stand, illuminated, each side of the Fiat 500 (which Sol intensely wishes wasn't a Fiat 500) staring at each other.

'Ricko!' says Ricko.

Sol always wondered why he couldn't call himself Rick, dispense with the attention-seeking *o*, but there we are. He reminds himself that to judge the judgmental is a particular irony.

'Long time no see, Buddy.'

He comes round to Sol's side, grasping his upper arm with one hand and shaking his hand with the other, in that over-friendly way he always had.

'No need for you to park out here. There's plenty of space for a *small one.*'

Ricko is waving his arms around, as if Sol doesn't know how to park a car, and Sol wonders if his father posted him behind the oak tree to escort him through the door to the table like he used to bring him round for *spontaneous* conversations about drug-taking and masturbation.

'You've done the right thing, Sol, in honouring your father,' says Ricko.

Patronising sod.

· · ·

The more dominant sister, Leah, hushes them all, and the door opens, and in comes Barbara in a pale beige silk dress, hand in hand with Reverend S Blake. Addie's eyes take time to acclimatise. Barbara waves, self-consciously, and Addie smiles and waves back.

Barbara has had her hair curled and it hangs in separate undulations over her pale dress, which buttons to a shallow *V*, with a tiny gold cross and a pearl hanging from a chain around her neck, which is caught on a small mole. She's not wearing her padded bra.

Reverend S is wide and well-built. He has a mop of fair hair on his head, and blondish tufts at the neck of his open shirt (no dog collar) and he appears at ease, rather pleased with himself. He opens his arms wide in a slightly forced gesture of welcome and invites them all into the dining room.

Addie tries to balance on the toes of her clogs to avoid them clopping, but she catches one of the Ms staring at her oddly, so she reverts to normal walking.

Reverend S sits down at the head of the table, with Barbara beside him. She seems nervous. She turns her head to look at him when he speaks, and Addie thinks she looks pretty, and she also looks proud, which is a good omen, no, not an omen, we don't think about omens in a vicarage, do we? We think about something else: blessings, yes, probably blessings. And here's the first blessing, hallelujah etcetera: it looks as if Barbara loves Reverend S, and he loves her.

What a relief, after the hours she's invested in the dress. But also, help, what on earth happens next? There's an empty chair opposite Addie, and an empty chair beside her.

238

Sol.

Plus?

Who's he bringing? Oh no, please not a girlfriend. What a terrible thought. She'd have to leave if he brought a girlfriend, although of course she couldn't, and she wouldn't.

A woman brings in a starter of king prawns and smoked salmon, with a blob of caviar on the left of each plate. Addie takes hold of her knife and fork, notices nobody else has and replaces them with a clink.

. . .

'Do you still lead the youth club?' says Sol, getting his rucksack out of the car.

Ricko nods.

'I wouldn't do anything else with my life.'

'Just so you know,' says Sol, smiling and summoning his new self. 'Not everyone likes Twister.'

. . .

'Uncle Peter will say grace,' says Reverend S Blake.

Bald Uncle Peter closes his eyes. He looks like a billiard ball. Everybody closes their eyes, except Addie, who watches, fascinated, as Uncle Peter says a long and loud prayer, and Reverend S (who the prayer makes clear is *Stephen, not Sol*) grunts, 'Mmm, mmm,' to encourage him along.

'Amen,' says everybody.

Addie wonders when Sol might arrive, and who with, and if she will keel over before he does.

. . .

Although Sol has a key to the front door, it no longer feels right to use it, so he lets Ricko ring the bell.

Ricko says, 'Just so you know, I'm the best man on Saturday.'

239

Course you are, thinks Sol.

'Bravo,' says Sol. 'Brav*o* Rick*o!*'

• • •

Addie jumps when the doorbell rings. Both sisters' heads flick to the door of the dining room. Leah leaps up and leaves the room. Rachel picks up her napkin and wrings it.

Addie sees that Barbara's left hand is now under the table. Oh dear. She looks as if she is hyper-ventilating. Addie thinks she's hyper-ventilating too. Perhaps she and Barbara will both collapse. She feels her own nails pressing into her palms. All the colour has left Barbara's face, and her nipples are pointing through the beige silk.

• • •

Sol is approaching the dining room door. He can't hear anyone speaking, but he assumes his family is in there, probably his uncle and aunt and the cousins. He tries to imagine Bee sitting next to his father.

'Our special guest,' says Leah as they enter.

But what he sees isn't what he was expecting to see.

Is he losing his mind?

Addie.

Seated at far side of the table, looking up at him.

This is so arresting that Sol is unable to feel the full shock of Bee, his former fiancée sitting, now standing, looking thin, yes very thin, beside his father. His head turns to the left and to the right, as if he's at a tennis match.

Leah seats Ricko beside Addie.

What can Addie possibly be doing here?

His father opens his arms and holds him for perhaps the first time in his life, his breath smelling slightly stale. Then he ejects him.

'The prodigal son!' says his father in his theatrical-sermon-voice into the hushed room.

'Hold on a second,' says Sol.

But before he can say any more, his father is pushing him towards Bee, who is holding out her long pale arm to him, and his uncle starts clapping, and his aunt doesn't seem to be here, and his cousins are clapping, and Bee and Bee's mother are clapping, and so are his sisters, but not Addie, who has frozen. Sol notices that Bee has patches of dark sweat spreading from each armpit, and these are turning the beige silk brown.

How can Addie possibly be here? Perhaps she is living with Star, although she can't be because Star is in the States and Mermaid Cottage is permanently rented out to guests leaving five-star reviews. Perhaps she's living somewhere else. Perhaps she's something to do with the wedding dress. In fact, that would make sense.

Sol looks again at Bee, and he feels nothing at all. In fact, he feels like laughing. Or perhaps this is the shock of seeing Addie. He flicks his head at Addie and he smiles. She smiles back, and then she puts her hand over her mouth as if to suppress a laugh.

Uncle Peter, balder than he remembers, stands up, and now one by one, everyone stands up, and they seem to be giving Sol a standing ovation. Addie is also standing up, and also clapping. A woman Sol doesn't recognise brings in two starters. He feels like laughing, but he mustn't laugh.

The four annoying Blake cousins leap to their feet and grab four champagne bottles, which were lined up along the window sill, and the corks go off – bang bang bang bang – hitting the ceiling and ricocheting into the flower arrangements along the centre of the table.

Leah seats Sol in the chair opposite Addie. He sees that Ricko is watching suspiciously.

'Well let's say grace again!' says Uncle Peter.

Sol catches Addie's eye, and she again covers her mouth with her hand, as Sol's father grunts, 'Mmm, mmm.'

He mustn't laugh at his father's prayer-grunting. He must think serious things. He mustn't look at Addie. Sol's father knocks his fork against his champagne glass and stands.

'The prodigal son!' he says again.

The room is silent.

'In this case,' says his father very loudly, 'it was the oldest who left.'

Sol thinks: *bearing in mind that my sisters are twins, am I the old*er *or the old*est?

The silence grows. A bubble of laughter rises up Sol's throat. He must not look at Addie. He clears his throat.

'But he came to his senses, like the prodigal son, Luke 15, verse 17,' says his father, in his loud sermon voice, gesticulating with his arms, becoming unstoppable, 'and he came home. And his father saw him and was filled with compassion. He ran to his son and threw his arms around him—'

'Hold on,' says Sol firmly, swallowing his laugh.

But his father doesn't fancy holding on.

'His father said, bring the best robe, put sandals on his feet, bring the fattened calf—'

'Hold on,' says Sol again.

He finds himself standing up. He and his father are both standing up now, and Sol is taller, looking down at his father, with Bee beside him *holding his hand*. The silence deepens around the table.

'This isn't right,' says Sol, and he turns and looks at Addie, who is staring at his father.

'With all due respect, Dad,' says Sol, 'I haven't squandered your inheritance on wild living like the prodigal son did. You haven't given me any inheritance, for starters, and I've definitely not been living wildly. If only!'

Matt the cousin laughs loudly.

Such a relief: Sol lets out a bit of laughter and so does Addie.

'Unless you mean in the other sense of wild,' says Sol. 'As in, the *wilderness*! I'm a teacher on a remote Scottish island! My nearest neighbours are *puffins*!'

Addie smiles.

'It's hard to go that wild with *puffins*.'

His father breathes deeply, fills his lungs with air and says, wrinkling his nose, 'What about the Greek islands? Tim said you gave up your job.'

Sol's uncle and his cousins and their wives and his twin sisters and Ricko the youth leader and Bee's mother are still and silent, their faces inclined towards him.

'That story was a cover-up,' says Sol, smiling.

'What did you have to cover up?' says his father.

'I went on a retreat to the island of Ora, where Mum went before she married you. She said it was a thin place.'

This is not the moment to mention his mother, and not the moment to mention thin places, of which his father disapproves – but it's too late, the words are out.

'Why would you need to cover that up?' says his father.

Sol mustn't be cowed. He must keep going.

'I didn't want to admit where I was going. Tim wouldn't have understood, you see.'

'Are you telling me the truth?' says his father.

Sol nods.

'This is a total coincidence,' says Addie.

Bee's head spins around to look at Addie.

Sol looks at her too.

She spoke.

'I actually met Sol when he was on Ora. I was on the next-door island when he came for the retreat. My mother lives there. This is just so weird. So weird!'

He has an alibi!

He has this alibi!

This alibi who simply couldn't be better, either as an alibi or as anything else.

She is unimprovable.

'You never said!' says Bee to Addie.

'Said what?' says Addie. 'I had no idea that Sol or Ora were anything to do with you.'

'Well, how exactly did you meet?' says Bee. 'In what circumstances?'

'In a storm,' says Addie.

'She was wearing a tail,' says Sol.

'A tail?' says his father in the voice he reserves for the darkest of sins. 'What kind of a tail?'

'Urethane and latex,' says Addie.

• • •

Addie watches as Reverend Stephen Blake inhales deeply. Barbara slips her arm through his arm, and encourages him to sit down. Sol sits down too. Nobody speaks. It comes to Addie, slowly, like a blurry image sharpening, a fragment at a time, on a screen.

B on Sol's mobile was *Barbara*! Of course she was. When Addie rang B from Sol's van a year ago in the coach park, she was in fact ringing Barbara, and B, who was Barbara, answered in her clipped voice.

Her clipped voice!

She never made the connection, and why would she have done? She could never have imagined their paths would cross as intimately and intricately as this. And also. How could Sol possibly have been engaged to Barbara?

'I wonder,' says Stephen, 'if Sol and I should have a moment in my study. Do carry on, all of you. We will be right back.'

'And me?' says Barbara.

'And Bee too,' says Stephen.

The three of them leave the room.

• • •

Once in the study, Sol's father says, 'You shamed me publicly.'

'My public shaming happens on Saturday,' says Sol, surprising himself. 'With a rather wider audience.'

'You said you were going to be a vicar, Sol,' says Bee. 'That was part of the deal. Part of my yes. It's not your father's fault. We fell in love.'

'Did you?' says Sol. 'Is it real?'

Bee nods.

His father nods.

Perhaps it isn't weird, Sol wonders, perhaps it's OK, perhaps it's not like *American Beauty*.

'Well, that can only be a good thing,' says Sol, and he attempts to smile. 'But can you see how bad Saturday's going to be, with everyone looking awkward and trying to say the right thing to me.'

'We weren't right together,' says Bee, still holding his father's arm, which Sol finds to be transfixing. 'We probably both knew that. Perhaps you should be thanking me for getting you out of an unhappy marriage.'

'I totally agree with you,' says Sol. 'One hundred per cent.'

Bee blushes.

Perhaps one hundred per cent sounds uncharitable, it comes to him, but it's also true.

'All that being so,' says Sol. 'Do you think either of you could have made this easier for me? Found a better way of telling me? Explained how it came about so soon after? Or said sorry at the start? Or something?'

As he says this, he loses confidence in his own point of view. This is what happens to him when he's with his father.

Bee says, 'Do people have to apologise for falling in love?'

245

Then there's the sound of clopping in the hall – the clogs, they must all have noticed. Sol's father wipes his upper lip with his handkerchief and puts it back in his pocket. The clopping stops, and there's a knock on the door. Addie opens the door a little and stands half inside the study and half in the hall.

Sol stares at the tiny embroidered bee and ladybird and butterfly on the lace cuff of her one puffed sleeve and at her one clog and at her one enormous hoop earring and at the auburn ringlets hanging around her left cheek, and even the sight of half of her gives him courage. She has nice ears. Not like Maud Hamilton. He would prefer to have half of her than all of Maud Hamilton or anyone else, that's what comes to him. Perhaps even a third. A quarter. An eighth. Her left arm with the embroidered bee on it might even do. Or her ear.

'I just wanted to say that I think I should probably go,' she says. 'This feels like a moment for family. So I came to check you were all OK, you know . . .'

Sol's father does not require people to check if he's OK. It's other people who aren't OK, and he's here to help them get OK again. That's basically his life. Spreading his sainted OKness around, like in other churches they spread incense from thuribles.

'Is there anything I can do to help?' says Addie.

'Help?' says Sol's father as if he is unfamiliar with the word.

'Come in,' says Bee, to Sol's surprise. 'Come and tell us what you make of it all.'

'Oh no,' says Addie. 'I came to say goodbye, and thank you. Delicious food. So nice to meet the family.'

'Who's in the wrong here, Addie?' says Bee. 'I can't think straight.'

Sol's father says, 'I hardly think your dressmaker will have the answer!'

Your dressmaker!

Only his father would say that.

'I think the whole prodigal son thing was a bit hard, Stephen, if I'm being honest, if you don't mind me saying. I mean, it's nothing to do with me,' says Addie to his father.

Sol loves her, he knows he does, he loved her from the first moment that he saw her, when she was sitting on a rock, and then he loved her every single moment after that, even when she crashed his campervan and ruined every single one of his dreams. He doesn't love Bee, he never did, and he doesn't love Maud Hamilton, and never will. There are no other fish. In the sea. Or indeed anywhere else.

There is only one fish.

Bee stares at Addie, who says, quietly, 'I really ought to go.'

Sol rises to his feet, and he follows her into the hall.

'Don't ever go,' he says. 'Please don't ever go again.'

It comes to him that he couldn't give a toss that his father is marrying Bee on Saturday.

. . .

As Addie turns to walk down the hall, Sol follows her.

'I'm coming with you,' he says.

'Speak quietly,' she says. 'They'll all be listening.'

'Why are you walking like that?'

'Because of these bloody clogs,' she whispers. 'I'm wearing your mother's clogs in your mother's house. Everyone kept looking at them.'

'Yes, that will take some explaining,' says Sol quietly, suppressing a smile.

'Anyhow, I'm leaving now.'

'And if you're leaving, I'm leaving too,' says Sol.

'You need to stay here and see out the dinner,' whispers Addie. 'And I've spent nearly a year on that dress. So please don't bugger up the wedding.'

Sol laughs.

'Shhh!' says Addie.

247

'I tried to find you online,' whispers Sol. 'And I wrote to Brother Andrew through the monks to see if you were back on Rokesby. I was glad you weren't. I found Star but she's in the States, I think. And Robyn hadn't heard from you. Then I found Mermaid Cottage, which has to be Star's place.'

Addie nods.

'But I didn't think you could possibly be there because it's on Airbnb and rented out all the time.'

'I live next to it in a flat on the river,' says Addie. 'I can show you. I tried to find you too. But the monks in Durham wouldn't give me your email, or send you mine. And there's no sign of you online. Obviously, I was terrified of what you might say. How angry you'd be with me.'

'Never mind that. When can I see you?'

'You can come to my workshop tomorrow. I'm in Horning. Goldfinch Wedding Dresses.'

'Ah! I didn't think of that.'

'I'm making my mother's wedding dress. My father's wife's died—'

'Your father's wife isn't – wasn't – your mother?'

'That's right,' says Addie.

'I still can't believe you're here.'

'I'm not here. I'm going.'

'*Blood Wedding* and *Murder in the Cathedral*?'

'I stole them from you. I know them almost off by heart.'

'Oh good. Keep them.'

'I already have.'

'True.'

'Sol,' whispers Addie, taking his hand. 'I really am so, so sorry. I did a terrible thing, but I honestly didn't mean to.'

'I forgive you,' he says.

'Did I ruin your life?'

'Kind of, yes.'

'I thought so. It's just that this policewoman came and told me to move, and I couldn't get hold of you. But obviously it was totally the wrong thing to do. I should have explained to her. But I just didn't think—'

'It's happened,' says Sol.

'Also, were you really with Barbara?' whispers Addie. 'I just can't really imagine—'

'Please don't try to imagine us together. And neither will I. And then we'll both feel a lot better.'

'Don't take any shit from your father, will you, Sol? Be truthful with him. He needs to hear the truth. But also, give the marriage a chance, won't you? Barbara's vulnerable.'

'Do you think so?'

'Honestly,' whispers Addie. 'In a way, I think they're both vulnerable.'

'My father?' Sol says, creasing his brow. 'Vulnerable? Are you mad? He's a tyrant!'

'He can be vulnerable and a tyrant,' says Addie. 'People have lots of selves. We're all like Russian dolls. Don't you think?'

• • •

Sol wonders if that's true. Perhaps he shed his outer doll on Ora, and he's working his way down to the real him. He watches Addie take off her clogs, put on her wellies and her coat.

'Let's give each other our numbers,' he says, taking out his phone. 'I'm terrified of losing you again.'

She takes out her phone, and they exchange numbers. He opens the front door, and gusts of rain come slanting on the diagonal and splattering the striped toucan wallpaper.

'You can't possibly cycle in this,' he calls to Addie. 'It's not safe.'

'Watch me!' says Addie.

'No, let me drive you home,' says Sol.

'You must get back to the dinner,' says Addie, and she's gone, and it seems she might never have been here.

Sol pokes his head into the dining room. His father and Bee aren't there. Everyone is eating in silence. Ricko has that saintly disappointed look on his face. But Sol feels different, as if Addie, present here so briefly, has given him confidence. Whatever Miss Gunn thinks, this is how it works. He walks back to the study, worrying about Addie on her bike with the rain and the lorries on the main road. Not another crash, please God, not now, when they've found each other.

'There was no need to cross me publicly,' says his father as Sol re-enters the study.

'Dad, I'm twenty-seven,' says Sol. 'And I've had enough of being made to feel bad for things I don't need to feel bad about. You've done this to me my whole life.'

Bee reaches out for his father's hand, but his father doesn't take it.

'I was forgiving you with grace,' says his father.

'But I don't need forgiving. It's like you deliberately poured dirt all over the carpet just so you could hoover it up. Which is what you also do in sermons. It's just come to me. You never start with what's good. You never ever told me what was good about me.'

Sol breathes, looks at the door, thinks of Addie.

'The thing is', say Sol, and he prepares to tell his father the truth for the first time, 'I never felt you loved me from the beginning.'

Bee winces.

His father stares.

'And you never loved me either,' says his father slowly and deliberately.

'You didn't treat Mum right,' says Sol, finding that now he's started, he can't stop. 'That made it hard for me to love you. Because of how much I loved her.'

'Bee, would you rather join your mother?' says Sol's father.

'No, she says. 'I need to be here.'

'You didn't let Mum be who she was,' says Sol to his father. 'She was clever and had things to say and dreams that she couldn't—'

'Your mother wasn't perfect,' says his father.

Bee opens her mouth, but his father raises his hand, as if he's stopping the traffic, and she closes it.

'No human being is perfect,' says Sol. 'And after she'd gone, I had no one.'

'I tried,' says his father.

'You didn't,' says Sol.

His father looks shocked.

'I was suffering,' says Sol.

'I was suffering too,' says his father.

Sol looks at his father, and his father looks back, and the texture of his skin changes – his pores seem to enlarge, and his cheeks colour.

'Now it's my chance to try again,' says his father. 'Do you see that? Might you be able to be pleased for me, Sol?'

His father's face looks almost tender as he turns his gaze to Bee, and Sol feels himself softening with it.

'I want your marriage to start happily, Dad,' he says, surprising himself. 'For both your sakes. I want you to be kind to Bee, Dad. Because you weren't always kind to me.'

Bee reaches for his father's hand and this time his father takes it.

'That's an awful thing to say, Sol,' says Bee.

'It's not my fault if the truth is awful,' says Sol.

Sol looks at his father's hand, freckled with age, and Bee's, pale and smooth and young, and he thinks that perhaps their relationship has a chance. Perhaps they really do love each other, which he hadn't believed to be a possibility until now.

'You tried to make yourself look big by making me look small,' says Sol. 'Which has been a habit of yours. For you to present yourself as a gracious, forgiving father, you had to paint me as a shit of a son.'

He has sworn in front of his father. This is a big moment.

'I was always frightened of you,' says Sol, 'and frightened of God. And perhaps the two things are linked.'

His father and Bee sit, hands joined, staring at him.

'It was hard to believe God loved me without believing you loved me,' says Sol.

Is it a terrible thing to tell somebody the truth when the truth is as stark as this? Should we only tell the sort of truth that doesn't hurt?

His father looks down at his knees, then up at the ceiling, and he purses his lips, but no words come out, so he tries again.

'Perhaps I've got things wrong,' says his father.

He said it with *perhaps* but it will do.

'Thank you for saying that, Dad,' says Sol. 'It really helps.'

Sol wonders if his father will say he's sorry, but he doesn't.

'I want you both to know that I give your marriage my blessing,' says Sol. 'I want you to be happy, both of you.'

'Thank you,' says his father.

'Thank you,' says Bee.

'Shall we go and have dinner?' says Sol.

'Another thing,' says his father. 'You look a right mess. Can you get hold of an iron before Saturday?'

• • •

Addie takes off her coat in the bathroom and hangs it on the radiator.

Though the weather was terrible, and the roads slippery and wet, how wonderful it was to escape in the rain and the wind, letting her thoughts free on the breeze, shouting *wooooohoooooo* to the air, glorying in the reunion, the unlikelihood, the marvel of it, the miracle of him being here.

She will sew her mother as many layers of netting as she wants, and she will turn her into a ballerina bride, and she doesn't care if her parents are a total pain in the arse, and she doesn't care if

Sydney's even worse, because Sol will be coming tomorrow, and his family is even weirder than hers.

'I need wine,' says Addie to the air, and with her wine, she descends to the sewing room, on a burst of adrenaline, hysteria, glee, joy, who knows what the bloody hell it is, let's get this dress done tonight and I will be free.

$\cdot$ $\cdot$ $\cdot$

After pudding, the party moves to the garden room, the slightly awkward hiatus now airbrushed out, along with the unexpected connection between Sol and the dressmaker, and her early departure.

Leah approaches Sol with that predatory look.

'Why was the dressmaker wearing Mum's clogs?'

'Was she?' says Sol.

'Don't lie to me,' says Leah.

As Rachel joins them, it comes to him that he has ruined the evening, yet he can't suppress his elation at finding Addie.

'We need to do the coffee,' says Rachel. 'Everyone's looking tired.'

'Sol won't come clean about the clogs,' says Leah.

Leah and Rachel serve coffee with home-made *petits fours*, and Sol fears he might fall asleep where he is on the sofa. Uncle Peter starts making his excuses, which unleashes everyone to make their excuses, so Sol gets up too. He rushes to his rucksack in the hall and grabs his parcels of Fair Isle jumpers, keen to distribute them and get out before he is left alone here with his father and sisters.

'Just a little something,' he says, throwing the ripped parcels at Leah and Rachel and Bee and his father. 'And I must be on my way.'

'You aren't staying?' says his father.

Sol shakes his head.

'I'm sure Rachel said you were staying.'

'A slight change of plan,' says Sol smiling.

'I see,' says his father.

'I made up a bed for you,' says Rachel.

'Where are you then?' says Leah. 'With the dressmaker?'

'Course I'm not with the dressmaker,' says Sol, and he walks through the front door, and he climbs into the Fiat 500, and he waves, and he breathes.

He finds that he's driving to The Amusements, which is an odd choice. He's no idea what he's going to do when he gets there. Go on the big wheel on his own? See if he can win a teddy bear? But look, he's arriving. The arched sign isn't flashing red. It's *shut*, as in *shut down*, he realises, no longer operating.

He parks the car at the side of the road, two wheels up on the pavement, and he gets out, turns on the torch on his phone and sees that someone's forced open the metal gate and then pushed it back in place. The rotting helter-skelter is surrounded by wire fencing and red signs saying DANGER KEEP OUT. The merry-go-round stands halted, encircled by a barbed wire fence.

He pulls back the vandalised wire gate and drives his Fiat into the old fairground, then he puts the gate back into place, and he keeps driving over the grass, turning his lights to full-beam over the graffitied toilets and the boarded-up building where he used to spend his 2p's and 10p's, where the grabber never grabbed the toy he wanted.

The story of my life, he thinks: *the grabber never grabs the thing I want, or it grabs it and then it drops it.* It dropped his mother, the van, Addie, his nomadding tour, Tromso, and gave him Fair Isle and Miss Gunn and Maud Hamilton instead, which is a bad, bad exchange. He feels terrible about Maud.

But the grabber's picked up Addie again.

The joy of it!

He drives over the grass – which probably isn't allowed – towards the dream bank where he first saw a mandarin duck, and there's a brand-new caravan where Tommie's old one used to be. He wonders if the new caravan is Tommie's, or someone else's, and then he wonders if whoever lives there will come out with a dog and chase him away, but he parks anyway, with his headlights on the ripples of the river.

Somebody is opening the door of the caravan. Somebody with a familiar shape. Sol stays inside his Fiat. Tommie the bird warden (it's definitely him) is wearing shorts and a big jumper and a cap, and he's carrying a torch, and Sol finds that he's getting out of the car, unfolding himself, holding out his hand to Tommie.

'I don't suppose you recognise me?' says Sol. 'Especially in the dark! We hardly spoke at the funeral.'

'Of course I recognise you,' says Tommie the bird warden, and he ignores Sol's outstretched hand, and draws him towards his chest, which is a surprise, but also rather nice.

It's a long time since anyone embraced Sol like this, and he feels himself relaxing into Tommie's chest, as if he's been holding his breath for a long time – not minutes, or hours, but more like a whole year, since he lost Addie and his van overnight, and of course he was holding his breath long before that. But now he breathes out.

'I guess I was always expecting you,' says Tommie.

'I don't suppose I could spend the night here with you. I mean, I know that this is probably quite a surprise. And rather forward. Only the place I was going to stay isn't suitable.'

'Isn't suitable?' says Tommie.

'It *is* suitable actually,' says Sol. 'It's more that *I'm* not suitable for *it*.'

'You'd be more than welcome,' says Tommie. 'Come on in.'

He shows him into a room with mallard curtains, where he dumps his bags.

'Tea?'

Sol nods: 'Milk, no sugar.'

Back in the main room, Tommie reaches for a mug from a hook. Sol feels a pang: he had mug hooks in the campervan.

'Have you ever lived anywhere other than here?' says Sol.

'I don't need any more world than this.'

'That's interesting. Because I'm dying to be everywhere. I was going to go off on a nomadding tour last year, but I wrote off my van and couldn't afford to buy another one.'

'You didn't have insurance?'

Sol shakes his head: 'It's quite complicated.'

'Why don't you catch me up on your life?' says Tommie.

• • •

It's four o'clock in the morning when Addie closes her eyes.

She sees his dark eyes, his wavy hair that he has to keep brushing back, his creased linen shirt and his cord jacket which doesn't quite match his trousers, like he doesn't match anyone or anything, like she doesn't match anyone or anything either.

Neither of them match anyone or anything.

Except perhaps, dare she think it, each other.

*You'd think that the possibility of love would
have been crushed by all that has happened.*

But it seems that love can grow in a void.

Can grow for a person who may not exist.

*A person who, if she exists, has wronged you
and let you down.*

If life were logical, that would be impossible.

But here they are, only three miles away from each other.

There is still so much that can blow them off course.

There always is.

Friday 23rd March

When Sol wakes, after a disturbed night, he can't work out where he is.

Ah yes.

The mallard curtains!

He swings his legs over the bed, creeps to the shower, dresses and wonders if Tommie is up. He pushes open the front door, trying not to make any noise. What a sight in the sun: a table laid with his mother's sort of breakfast, with a big coffee pot, and a bowl of yoghurt and heaped granola and cut-up fruit – mango and kiwi and orange and strawberries – and one of those plaited challah loaves, and butter in a butter dish and several pots of jam and a big glass jug of juice, and Tommie sitting in a deck chair, with the river behind him glistening, and look, there are the mandarin ducks, calling *akk akk, akk akk.*

Sol feels strangely choked. The next time he's with somebody he loves, he will make them a breakfast like this.

'How are you doing this morning?' says Tommie.

'I slept well, but I'm dreading the wedding tomorrow.'

'I take it you have no feelings left for Bee?'

'I'm not sure I ever had any feelings for Bee. Also, I don't have a suit.'

'Do you want to borrow mine?' I think we're about the same size. You can try it on while I have a quick swim.'

It fits him well, but he's pretty sure it's a crap suit: a little shiny, the trouser legs too wide. He thinks people wear them quite narrow these days. He'll have to wear it though, to protect Tommie's feelings, and also, because he can't face either driving to the shops or spending money on something he'll never wear again.

That's when the thought resurfaces.

Perhaps I won't go to the wedding.

• • •

Addie holds up the ballerina dress.

It's done!

She puts it into its protective cover, along with any thoughts about her mother, and closes the zip.

When the doorbell rings, she taps her app and peers at her phone – it's so good to see Sol standing by the gate. She wants to go on savouring him before she lets him in. Because there's nothing so lovely as anticipation, as long as you know it will be fulfilled.

With Mac, there was never any anticipation. She wonders why she did it. Was she expressing some unexpressed part of herself, escaping before she could escape? Or was it something else?

Sol rings again, and this time, she lets him in. He drives towards The Boathouse in his ridiculously small car and gets out, and as he does so, they look at each other and start laughing.

'Why are we laughing?' says Sol.

'Because your family's so strange,' says Addie. 'I thought mine were bad.'

'I've been thinking. I'm not sure I'm going to go to the wedding tomorrow after all.'

'Oh no! Did it all go wrong after I left?'

'Not really.'

'Was it very weird staying in the vicarage again?'

'I didn't stay in the end.'

Addie nods, and she wonders if she could invite him to stay here with her. It's really very tempting, especially now he's rolling up his sleeves and she can see his tanned forearms.

What's the matter with me?

'Are *you* going to the wedding? Because that would make all the difference.'

'Just to button Barbara into her dress.'

'Is it that complicated?' says Sol. 'How will my father rip it off later?'

They catch each other's eyes, and she thinks, briefly, of ripping *his* clothes off later.

'So they didn't invite you to the wedding?'

'They did, but I said no,' says Addie. 'I don't go to weddings.'

'That seems like quite a big professional hindrance?' says Sol, laughing.

'Once the dress is on the bride, it's their story, not mine,' says Addie.

'Fair enough.'

Addie looks at Sol, and Sol looks at her.

'So here I am and here are you,' says Sol.

'Yes, exactly,' says Addie.

'I have to say this one word to you,' says Sol.

Addie wonders which word it will be.

'Mac?' says Sol. 'Just for the sake of tying up ends.'

Oh, not that word.

'No idea. I never saw him again.'

'I imagine he came looking for you—'

'Well,' says Addie. 'Every cloud has a silver lining. I wasn't there. I was smashing up your van.'

Sol smiles.

'Is there anyone in your life?' says Addie, dreading the answer.

'Someone who might want to be,' says Sol. 'But I'm not interested. She's a vicar, and I'm kind of done with vicars. And you?'

'No,' says Addie. 'I've never wanted my life to be contingent on another person, you see. Not after my mother! That's been my guiding principle.'

Addie wonders, for a moment, whether she simply likes saying the word *contingent* because it makes her sound intelligent and Cambridgey like Sol, and then she wonders if it's a good idea to repeat the same line again and again without checking if it is still what she means, or if she's grown bigger than her opinion, like a snake shedding a skin that's too small for it. In fact, she wishes she could rewind the conversation and not say the sentence at all.

'Shall we take a picnic on the boat?' she says, by way of changing the subject.

• • •

Sol and Addie get into the rowing boat and Addie rows them upstream. It's all so reassuringly familiar: tiny dabchicks fussing in and out of the reeds, coots skittering across the water, a grebe diving, geese squabbling, gulls flapping over a crust in the water.

Home.

Bliss.

But for the fact that Sol can't stop rolling Addie's words around his mind.

She heads for the bank and he jumps off to moor the boat.

Should he push her to explain? Or should he let it go?

He can't.

'Addie,' he says, 'why don't you want your life to be contingent on another person?'

'I loved my grandmother with everything I had,' says Addie. 'Then she died. And I was broken. Love is too dangerous.'

She blushes and hesitates, and looks as if she might say something else, but she doesn't.

'I hate it that Mum died so early,' says Sol. 'But I'm glad I had her love.'

'Perhaps I'm not strong enough for love,' says Addie. 'It's wonderful when it's happening but I can't handle losing it.'

'What happens if you don't lose it?'

'You always lose it in the end.'

Sol tries to process her words as they eat the picnic inside the boat, and as he rows them home.

'Might you really not go to the wedding tomorrow?' says Addie.

'Really. But it's not an angry decision. I want the best for them. I honestly think it will be easier for them too. Perhaps especially Bee.'

After all his lofty decisions to be the big man, is he making empty justifications in order to spend more time with Addie?

'So what are you going to do now? You came here for the wedding?'

'Ostensibly. But this isn't bad either.'

She smiles: 'This?'

'Us. Here. The river.'

'How long have you got?

'I'm flying back to Fair Isle on Wednesday. I have five days. I'm running a little birdwatching camp before term starts. I'm really doing it for a boy called Barry Forfitt. I must tell you about him.'

Then it comes to Sol that you can do things, all kinds of things, in five days. If he didn't go to the wedding, he could go to Tromso. Addie could come too. He could recover some fragment of his nomadding dream before he goes back. If he goes back. He has to go back. He has the birdwatching camp. He has a contract. He has the school. He has Barry Forfitt.

But what he also has is now.

This moment.

And he will give himself to it.

Forget about her guiding principles: we all say things we don't mean.

'You look pensive,' says Addie.

'Oh, it's probably just last night,' he says.

It isn't. It's *now*. It's how much he wants to go to Tromso with her. It's whether she really doesn't want her life to be contingent on another person, and what that really means. Addie inclines her head towards him with her auburn ringlets falling across her cheeks, and the sun comes out, and her freckles glint.

'Perhaps', says Sol, 'we shouldn't resist what can't be resisted.'

'That's Lorca, isn't it? You said that to me before.'

And then.

Sol doesn't invite her to Tromso.

Bugger it.

(He finds bugger to be especially liberating now he's started swearing.)

The right moment will come for him to mention Tromso, he assures himself.

They row back along the river, and the screeching of geese is overlaid with the quack of mallards and the chattering whistles of tufted ducks.

. . .

As they reach the jetty, Addie see her father's car in the drive. Her father waves as they approach, and grabs her hand. His nails are chewed as usual. Sol shakes his hand. Sydney keeps his hood up and nods at Sol.

'We're off to Rokesby, and we're hoping you'll come with us,' says her father. 'Did you manage to get the dress done? I want to give you something for it. To thank you for messing up your days off.'

'No, really, that's not—'

'I won't take no for an answer,' says her father.

263

'I'll leave you all in peace,' says Sol.

Addie stares at her father and her brother, standing in her drive, and, as she shows them into her workshop, she has the strange feeling that she doesn't know them at all.

. . .

Sol walks back across the garden. Her father's invited her to Rokesby before he plucked up the courage to invite her to Tromso. Why didn't he spit it out when they were eating lunch in the creek? What's the matter with him? This was his moment.

He missed it, so now he'll crumble.

Like the arch.

He sits on the bench on the jetty, and he searches *flights to Tromso*, but there's no Wi-Fi, so he puts his phone away, and watches the water and the birds, and he remembers googling hotels in Tromso *without* a swimming pool for his honeymoon with Bee, which produced a list of hotels in Tromso *with* a swimming pool because Google isn't quite the genius he thinks he is – or she, or it, no, Google is definitely he. All those testosteroney facts.

Perhaps Addie won't go to Rokesby. Or perhaps she will. Perhaps she'll say no to her father. Or perhaps she'll say yes, which would be too terrible. He thinks he'll go for a walk and look at ducks. Looking at ducks always makes him feel better, or at least helps him not feel worse.

. . .

'I'm afraid there's been no time to embroider or make lace,' says Addie, showing her father the dress.

'Though there was time for a romantic rowing trip?' says her father, smiling.

How dare he say that?

'I haven't had a day off for weeks. I had to work through two nights to get this done.'

'Only joking!' says her father, maddeningly. 'Now all I need to make my joy complete is for you to say yes, and for the three of us to go and surprise Mum tomorrow.'

'I'm not sure about that,' says Addie, wondering if he should be quite so joyful so soon after Pattie's death.

'Oh come on, Ads,' says Sydney, sounding bored.

'Does she want me?' says Addie.

Sydney hums *Don't You Want Me Baby.*

Addie wants to murder him.

'We're surprising her,' says her father. 'Picture her face when she sees the three of us walking up from the harbour—'

'I'm afraid I would have to speak to her first,' says Addie, and she feels a swell of tears in her eyes. Not more tears. She swallows them, and takes a deep breath.

'She's ignored all my attempts to be in touch with her. So I'd need to take the temperature, if you see what I mean.'

'I'm starving,' says Sydney.

'Have you eaten?' Addie's father asks her.

She nods, deciding not to offer to make them lunch, which is what they will expect.

'Is there a take-away?' says Sydney.

'Fish and chips or Chinese,' says Addie. 'Turn left and you'll get to the high street.'

'Come with me, Syd,' says her father. 'We'll get some food and make a plan.'

'I'm not going unless she wants me, OK?' says Addie.

Sydney hums the song again.

'You could maybe embroider a little something while we're gone?' says her father. 'That might be really nice. A finishing touch.'

Her father and Sydney pull out of the drive, and she feels the tears swelling again. She refuses them. She takes a piece of antique rose silk, and thinks it would do as a simple sash. She threads her sewing machine and hems it. Tries it on herself. Adds three popper positions. She has a tiny rose left over from another client. She attaches it to the sash. Done.

When her father and Sydney still don't come back, she goes out into the garden to try to find Sol, but though his car is (promisingly) still in the drive, she can't see him. She goes back inside and stares at her mother's dress, and the tears bubble again. She's humming that bloody song.

Her father and Sydney return.

'We've rung Mum to say we're coming with surprises.'

'I hope you didn't say I was coming.'

'We didn't mention you.'

'I'm not going without speaking to her first.'

'Well, phone her,' says her father.

It sounds so easy.

'She's your mother.'

'I can't do it with you listening. You go for a walk and I'll call.'

Addie wonders if she'll just pretend. She's not sure she can do it. She stares at the phone. She's shaking as she calls.

'Mum!'

'Addie!'

Does she sound pleased?

'Would you want me to come and see you, in theory?'

'That's entirely a matter for you,' says her mother.

'But would you like it?'

Her mother doesn't reply.

'Well, that all depends if *you*'d like to see *me*,' says her mother.

Addie feels the tears again, and she again refuses them.

Her mother says, 'It was very cruel of you to leave as you did, and that kind of cruelty leaves wounds – wounds that don't heal overnight.'

'It's been a year,' says Addie.

'Mac told me that the man on Ora took you away. Why did he do that?'

'I asked him to because you remember I had no money. But I do have money now. I've set up my own business.'

'You talk about money, but I gave up everything for you! My home. My partner. My son. And look how you repaid me.'

'Is it all OK at The Retreat?' says Addie.

'Do you remember Dee?' says her mother. 'The one who couldn't stop eating cake?'

'Yes.'

'She came over with a friend of hers to help me,' says her mother. 'They were brilliant, but they couldn't take the isolation.'

'Do you understand that?' says Addie.

'Of course I do,' says her mother.

'Except not for me?'

'It's different for you,' says her mother. 'You don't like people.'

'I do like people.'

Her mother doesn't respond.

'You didn't answer my emails or texts,' says Addie, feeling her voice quietening. 'I phoned and left messages but—'

'I've had enough of this.'

Addie hears her mother put down the phone, and she feels one warm tear rolling down her cheek, catching the outer edge of her top lip, where it tastes salty, like the sea. She wipes it away. She mustn't cry in front of her father and Sydney. She washes her hands carefully and puts her mother's wedding dress back in its carrier. They're ringing at the gate.

'I can't come with you,' she says, swallowing. 'I'm so sorry.'

'I think you'll regret this,' says her father, laying the dress on the back seat, and looking at her as if she's guilty.

'Can you understand why?'

'Whatever,' says her father.

The dress lies on the seat like a corpse.

• • •

Sol sees Addie's father and brother getting into the car.

He finally found Wi-Fi at the back of The Boathouse, and, standing up against a wooden pole, next to a spectacular vintage river boat, leaning slightly left, he was able to identify glass igloos in Tromso which you can stay in.

He sees Addie go back inside, and he waits ten minutes. Come on Sol, he says, *you can do it.* He scrolls through the photos: the sauna, the open fire, the bed with ninety-five pillows, the attractive couple lying in bed with tanned shoulders looking at the northern lights through the domed glass.

He gets up, walks to The Boathouse and tentatively knocks on her door. Addie lets him in and he sits on the linen armchair where the brides sit for consultations, and he wishes he had tanned shoulders.

'Everything OK?' he says.

'Not really,' she says. 'Dad wants all of us to turn up with the ring and the dress *tomorrow.*'

Sol's heart sinks and his tongue tastes of copper.

'And are you going?'

He asks the question in what he hopes is a casual voice.

'My mother doesn't want me,' says Addie.

What a relief.

Sol remembers Brother Andrew's words, and he thinks: *if you're asking, ask.* He gets ready to put all his feelings into his question because *this, and only this, is his life at this moment.*

He says: 'Addie, please will you come with me to Tromso tomorrow?'

• • •

'Tromso?' Addie says. 'In Norway?'

Sol nods.

'Tomorrow? Are you serious?'

'You're answering my questions with questions. But what I want is an answer.'

'Tomorrow? Saturday? I have to put Bee into her dress.'

'We can go afterwards. There are afternoon flights.'

My mother hates me, thinks Addie, *yet she loves Sydney, whatever he does. She says she sacrificed everything for me, but in fact I had to sacrifice everything for her. Our relationship was unhealthy, and it was dysfunctional, and other words I'd rather not think.*

'How long would we stay?' says Addie. 'I'd need to be back on Wednesday to sort out Mermaid Cottage. And I've also got two brides.'

'We'll fly back on Tuesday. I'm leaving for Fair Isle on Wednesday. So that works.'

'I don't have anything to wear in the snow,' says Addie.

'You can hire it all out there,' says Sol. 'I just need your shoe size.'

'Let me have a think,' says Addie.

'Let's neither of us think, or we'll think ourselves out of it,' says Sol.

'I'll come,' says Addie. 'I'm size 38.'

She is hot, she is cold, she can't believe she said yes.

Sol is fiddling with his phone.

'I'm going to book before you say no,' he says.

She nods.

He takes out his wallet.

• • •

As Sol and Addie head back to The Boathouse after a walk along the river bank, Sol feels something most unfamiliar. He feels happy. He feels as if he is walking to The Amusements with his mother, and the lights are flashing red, and he will be allowed to eat candy floss, and the grabber will grab the toy he wants.

'I can't believe we're going,' says Addie. 'Is it a bit scary? We hardly know each other.'

'Very scary,' says Sol.

'What are *you* scared of?'

'I don't know if I want to say.'

'Try,' says Addie.

'It's embarrassing.'

'It doesn't matter. We're friends.'

Friends?

Is that a bad sign?

Should he have booked another bedroom?

Oh help, bedrooms!

'Um,' says Sol.

And does he dare?

He never admitted to Bee that he couldn't swim. Calamitously, there's a spa with a swimming pool in the main building of the hotel, and he knows Addie loves swimming. And then there's the other thing. *Only one bedroom.* So clearly. That. And he does not have tanned shoulders, or anything else that might be necessary.

'Tell me,' says Addie.

'I'm not sure I can.'

He must, he must, he knows he must, but what if his admissions put her off him?

'Addie, I don't know how to tell you this. Bearing in mind that—'

'Just say the words.'

'The thing I'm most scared of is you finding out something about me.'

'You're married?'

'No.'

'You're a vampire?'

'No.'

'I give up.'

'Addie, this is incredibly embarrassing, and I think there are reasons for it, that go back to my childhood. I think I mentioned a boy at school called Carl Turlington, but there's no reason you should have remembered something so incidental—'

'Say it any way it comes,' says Addie.

'There's a pool at the hotel and I can't swim,' says Sol.

He stops walking.

She stops walking.

He feels as if he is naked.

'Is that it?'

Addie is looking at him with her full attention.

'Well, he used to try to drown me in the school pool when I was a small boy. The teachers turned a blind eye. And it happened every week. And, sorry, I know this all sounds quite ridiculous at my age, but it had quite an effect on me.'

'Do you want to learn to swim?'

'It's no good. I've tried everything.'

'Have you tried flippers?'

'*Flippers?*'

Addie nods, smiling.

'No.'

'I think they might help. Shall we try now?'

'I'd rather not.'

'We should do,' says Addie. 'Come on.'

'I hate getting wet. I can't stand the feel of the water.'

'I said yes to Tromso. So I think you should say yes to flippers. And there's no time like the present. Star's should fit you. She has big feet. Anyway, your toes are out so it should be fine.'

They walk through the door of The Boathouse and go upstairs. Addie changes into her swimsuit in the bathroom and puts on Sol's black anorak that she never gave back to him, and they go downstairs with towels, and out of the door, and to the shed, where Addie disappears and reappears with a pair of orange flippers.

'Those are very bright orange!' says Sol. 'Quite alarming.'

'The colour won't make any difference.'

Sol feels stress rising up his legs.

'I don't have any swimming shorts,' he says as they reach what she calls the swimming platform.

'Boxers are fine.'

Is this really happening, thinks Sol. *I'm getting undressed in front of a woman.* As she gets in, he pulls off his jeans, and he wonders if his legs look unacceptably thin or hairy.

'What's your advice?' he says, sitting down with his feet over the water, electrified by her being so close to him – his toes are almost grazing her shoulder, and *she isn't moving out of the way.*

'Just move your legs like this,' she says, and she holds the wooden edge of the platform and kicks.

He takes off his jumper and his shirt and she is looking at him, and he gives his chest hair a quick brush with his hand to spread out the fronds.

'Is it cold?'

'Freezing.'

'Do I put the flippers on?'

'No, that comes later.'

He lowers himself in, gasping.

'Very dramatic!'

'You don't have balls.'

'I'd quite like to know what it feels like to have balls. Do they get in the way when you walk?'

Sol laughs.

'First let's get you underwater. Keep your feet on the ground and bob down.'

He does.

'And again.'

He does.

'Now hold on to the edge.'

'I feel like a prat.'

'We all feel like a prat when we're learning things.'

He holds the wooden platform.

'Let your legs go out behind you.'

'They don't float. Look, they actually don't float.'

'Let me help.'

Addie takes hold of his legs, and pulls them out behind him, and the skin of her hands on his legs sends shockwaves through his body – it's so lovely to feel her, skin against skin.

'You're distracting me!' he says, laughing. 'I can't think about swimming.'

'Solomon Blake!' she says. 'Concentrate!'

He's laughing.

'Now when I let go of your legs—'

'Please don't let go of my legs! I don't care if I don't learn to swim. I just like you holding my legs!'

'Behave yourself!' says Addie. 'Now kick!'

He kicks.

'Keep going!' says Addie. 'Keep going!'

He does.

He kicks and kicks and kicks.

'Now we need to get the flippers on.'

Sol raises himself onto the swimming platform to pull them on.

'I look ridiculous.'

'Who cares? Nobody's watching.'

'You are.'

'I don't count. Get back in.'

He does.

'Now try kicking and see how much easier it is,' says Addie.

He does.

It is.

'In no time, you'll be learning to swim.'

In no time.

He believes her.

For a moment.

'Someone's walking over the lawn,' says Addie. 'I'm afraid it's your favourite bride!'

'Surely not,' says Sol.

He leaps out and pulls off the flippers, and Bee's looking at him, and he feels awkward because she never saw his body, and bodies aren't really her thing, and he's standing shivering in his underwear. He panics and gets back in the water.

'What on earth are you two doing?' says Bee, looking down at them.

'I'm trying to teach him to swim,' says Addie cheerfully.

The mud is very slimy against Sol's feet.

'You can't swim?' says Bee, creasing her brow at Sol. 'I can't believe I didn't know you couldn't swim.'

'Well,' says Sol. 'There we are.'

He feels less bad about it with Addie beside him, like it isn't the most shameful thing in the world.

Bee starts laughing, saying, 'I can't believe you can't swim.'

The she stops laughing and says, 'I came to say that I'm sorry it all went so wrong last night.'

'No need to apologise,' he says, trying to stop his teeth chattering. 'And I meant what I said. I give your marriage my blessing. I wish you both every happiness.'

'Thank you, Sol. That means a lot to me.'

'I'm wound up like a spring,' says Bee to Addie.

I might freeze to death, thinks Sol.

'It's all going to be absolutely wonderful,' says Addie in a voice Sol doesn't recognise. 'Don't worry about a thing. I'll be there in the morning to get you into your dress and it's going to be the most perfect sunny day for you both.'

'You know what, Bee,' says Sol, trying to unlock his jaw, 'I do have something to say to you and Dad. So perhaps I'll get out and come with you to the vicarage.'

'I'm not seeing him today. It's tradition. Not the day before the wedding.'

'I'll tell you separately then,' says Sol, looking up at Bee, his voice (and his balls) tight with cold. 'I think it's best I don't come tomorrow. I'm not saying that angrily. I think it will be best for everyone. And maybe especially for you.'

'I think I might feel more comfortable,' says Bee. 'But don't tell your father.'

'Exactly,' says Sol. 'You can get on and enjoy your wedding and know that I'll be wishing you both the best possible day and the best possible life.'

'Can you really not swim?' says Bee. 'I just can't imagine a man not being able to swim.'

As she walks across the lawn, Sol leaps out and pulls a towel around him, rubbing himself dry and pulling on his jeans which squeak up his legs.

. . .

Addie can't believe Barbara's reaction.

These reverse-feminists really are quite callous!

Imagine having to be the sort of man a reverse-feminist requires: one hundred per cent strong and unbreakable and capable at everything, not able to show the slightest sign of weakness lest it detract from one's masculinity. Addie seriously hopes Stephen is up to it! She thinks he is. She thinks he likes this view of himself, though whether he can pull it off full-time, who knows? He did seem rather tense. Perhaps it makes a man tense trying not to have any weaknesses. Perhaps that's why husbands in old films seem so uptight all the time.

'That was strange,' says Addie.

'I felt like I was doing something really wrong.'

'Me too! Interesting reaction about the wedding, didn't you think?'

'I'd better get to the vicarage and tell Dad I'm not coming,' he says, 'though she may already have phoned him. Or is that also against the rules, calling each other the day before the wedding?'

'No idea,' says Addie.

'The great thing is that I can't change my mind because I've booked our flights. And nothing's going to stop me getting on that plane.'

Sol disappears across the lawn.

I'm going to Tromso, thinks Addie, a little startled. She'll have to hope that the guests have no issues while she's away, or Star will never forgive her.

. . .

As Sol and his father walk down the hall, Sol realises that not only does he truly believe that he might learn to swim (and also possibly the second thing, maybe, maybe, don't think about that, and definitely not here in his father's study), but he also feels that he might be able to tell his father that he will not be coming to his wedding. This new confidence is unnerving.

He's anxious, obviously, but here he goes, aiming to persuade his father that it will be better for everyone, and especially for Bee.

His father says, 'I see all that, but what will people think? What will God think?'

'God isn't like an interview panel,' Sol says to his father. 'I didn't know that until I went to Ora. There's a hermit there called Brother Andrew. And this is what he said. He said that if we want to know God, we have to welcome what he brings into our lives with all we have. He said that who we are and where we are right now is where God is. If you're walking, walk. If you're eating, eat. Then all of life's a prayer. So, I think you should give all of yourself, everything you've got, to your wedding tomorrow, and then to your marriage. And then it will become a kind of prayer.'

His father looks shell-shocked at this about-turn in roles.

'I also wanted to tell you what happened to me on Ora,' says Sol.

'You know I don't believe in thin places,' says his father.

'I know,' says Sol. 'But I decided to believe in them, like Mum. I thought God would perhaps come bursting out of the sky or something. But in fact, I came bursting out of myself. Like a new person. And that felt like a divine thing.'

'I'm not following you,' says his father. 'It all sounds rather outlandish.'

'Let's leave it right there,' says Sol. 'My God doesn't have to meet your approval any more than your God has to meet mine. It's OK. I'm going to leave now, Dad. And I really hope you have the best day tomorrow and the best marriage.'

His father turns to him, and his face looks different: there is, for a fraction of a second, a quiver under his skin on the left side, and his mouth opens and he hesitates and doesn't speak, and perhaps Sol could believe that he is both vulnerable and a tyrant, like Addie said.

His father pulls himself together.

'I'm worried that this isn't the right decision,' he says to Sol. 'That people will see it as wrong.'

Sol wonders if perhaps it isn't the right decision to miss his own father's wedding. But it's too late. He's going to Tromso with Addie. And that is definitely the right decision. Even if missing the wedding is in some ways the wrong one. Perhaps both those things really can be true at once, like his mother used to say.

'I understand that our views differ on this,' says Sol. 'I pray it's a very special day for you both.'

'I meant to ask you why the dressmaker was wearing your mother's clogs.'

'She didn't have any shoes. So I lent them to her.'

He strides through the tiled hall towards the front door, which he walks through, feeling that he may well fly away over the river, over the reeds and never come back to earth.

• • •

Addie takes Sol onto the balcony of The Boathouse and gives him a glass of wine and a bowl of crisps, and she says she must pack her case.

When she joins him, Sol says he's booked husky-sledding, Ski-Doo riding, a boat trip to see eagles and, most importantly, a night out with an astronomer and a group of six others hoping to see the northern lights. He thinks the reindeer farm might be awkward so he hasn't bothered with it. They sit watching the sky in their identical black anoraks as the light drains from the day.

'Are you staying tonight?' she says.

'I need to go and see Tommie before we head off tomorrow. And also—'

'I can't believe we're really going.'

Addie pauses.

'Sol?'

'Yes.'

'Did you book us one bedroom or two?'

'One. Is that OK?'

'That's good,' says Addie.

'Also,' says Sol. 'You never told me what you're scared of.'

'I don't want to.'

'But I told you, and I didn't want to either. I felt a prat.'

'You told me one thing. Is there anything else you're scared of?'

'Let's go for one thing each. That's enough to get us started.'

Addie hesitates.

'I could make something up. That feels easier.'

'I'd rather you didn't. And it should be easier to confess in the dark. We don't have to look at each other.'

'Sol, I'm scared of falling in love with you.'

Saturday 24th March

Sol wakes beneath the mallard curtains in the caravan.

She's scared of falling in love with me.

When she said it, it felt huge, and rousing, like an aria spreading from the balcony over the water, and the first thing he felt was elated, so elated that he couldn't find any words that were big enough to respond, so he looked at her and he smiled and he took her hand, and it came to him that being scared of things can stop them happening, like fear had stopped swimming happening for him, so perhaps, in the same way, love wouldn't happen for her, and that's when his own fear set in. There was elation bubbling on one side of his brain and fear bubbling on the other, and there was her hand in his, and there was his mouth saying nothing, until his mouth said, finally, 'Then that makes me scared of you *not* falling in love with me.'

He's now looking at the half-mallard with the half-beak observing him over the hem and he's trying to work out if that was a terrible answer. His father is getting married today and *he's not going to the wedding.* He sends a warm text to him. Job done.

Also, will being scared of the second thing stop *the second thing* happening? Or will *the second thing* perhaps feel like a normal thing to do in the bed with ninety-five pillows in the igloo beneath the northern lights? Even if he doesn't have tanned shoulders?

What if he doesn't measure up, so to speak?

I am a man who hates going to urinals.

Will I ever be brave enough to be naked with someone else?

He has at least tried taking his jeans off in front of her when he got in the water. That went OK. Perhaps he will offer his self-control, as a gift, and say, We can wait. He doesn't think anybody (except his father and Bee) would want that gift these days. It's fallen massively out of fashion. He doesn't want to wait now either. All he wants is to hold her in his arms. To feel her skin against his skin like when she held his legs in the water, except obviously not quite like that.

'One man and one woman,' says his father, and Sol has always seen the beauty in that.

It's been something to aspire to, but to wait so long in an era that doesn't wait has also made him feel odd and misshapen. It's been something to aspire to, but it's also been something to hide behind because he's shy and self-conscious and not confident around bodies.

'One man and one woman,' he hears his father say again, and he thinks that today there will be one man and two women standing by the altar. It all seems less straightforward than Ricko made out at youth club.

But he can hear Tommie getting up.

Sol goes into the kitchen.

'Can I make you tea, Tommie?'

'Lovely.'

'I'm not going to the wedding,' says Sol. 'But I'm taking Addie to Tromso for a few days. It's a secret, though. Don't tell anyone.'

'That sounds wonderful. I was thinking I could give you a key to the caravan and you can come and go as you please?'

· · ·

Maybe, Perhaps, Possibly

Addie knocks on the door of a small terraced house, and Barbara's mother, Pamela, opens the door, dressed in salmon pink, with a small salmon pink hat pinned precariously to the side of her head, and she shows Addie to the bridal bedroom, where Barbara sits in a pale silk dressing gown, her long white waxed legs goose-pimpled, her face perhaps a little too made-up, her lips a little too shiny, her hair pulled into a bun, with corkscrew ringlets bouncing like springs each side of her face.

'You live miles away,' says Addie. 'How did you ever meet Sol and Stephen?'

Oh dear, not both of them in one sentence.

'We had a church away day,' says Barbara.

'You're looking lovely,' says Addie.

'Sorry about interrupting you and Sol yesterday,' says Barbara, in a strange, taut voice.

Her teeth are chattering and her skin is bumpy with cold. Addie takes a fake fur throw from the bed and puts it round Barbara's shoulders.

'I really am sorry. I acted strangely.'

'That's fine,' says Addie.

'And I'm sorry about Thursday night.'

'Oh no worries. We all have families!'

'Nobody speaks to Stephen like you spoke to him. Everyone's a bit in awe of him at the church.'

Addie smiles: 'That's not good for anyone, Barbara.'

'Is Sol OK?' says Barbara.

'He's fine,' says Addie. 'Now today is about you and about Stephen. So Sol will be fine and let's—'

'You're sure he's OK?' says Barbara.

'Absolutely,' says Addie.

'I wonder what he'll do today,' says Barbara.

'I'm sure he'll think of something,' says Addie. 'Now let's get you into this dress.'

Barbara takes off her silk robe, and she's wearing the padded bra. What a relief: the dress will work.

'What I most want to be,' says Barbara, 'is the best wife ever. That's always been my dream.'

Odd, thinks Addie, and also maybe beautiful, but perhaps only if you're a reverse-feminist, or who knows? Who knows? Let's get this bloody show on the road and go to Tromso.

Barbara is holding out a pair of lacy pink pants.

'Are these OK?' she says.

'Perfect.'

'Is sex easy?'

'Very.'

'Have you had a lot of sex? I mean sex with a lot of people?'

'No, not really,' says Addie, trying to stop her mind flickering to tonight.

'It's nice, is it?'

Addie nods, smiling a little too eagerly she thinks, and stopping smiling.

Barbara's mother comes in with the wedding photographer, a woman with a beehive hairdo and small Sindy feet. She takes some photos of Barbara in the silk robe, and Barbara with her mother, and Barbara with Addie – Addie hates photos.

'Some sexy ones!' says the photographer. 'Slip your thigh out of your robe!'

Sexy isn't that, thinks Addie, *it's something else.*

'Do you want a photo in your underwear?' says the woman.

'No thank you,' says Barbara, looking panic-stricken.

Barbara's mother escorts the photographer out, and Addie notices that her hat is slipping down the side of her head.

'Step in,' says Addie, holding out the dress, wondering what Barbara would think if she knew where she was going today, and with whom.

· · ·

Sol waits in his car in Addie's drive, and he hopes she's being careful on her bike. He's sure she should be back by now. How long does it take to button up a dress? Girls' clothes, a total mystery. Girls' body parts, terrifying.

He remembers the diagram at school: all those strange names. How on earth is he going to find his way around?

If he is.

If he is.

· · ·

Addie gets onto her bike, turns left out of Barbara's white painted gate, and cycles along the road. Her phone rings, so she stops at the side of the road and pulls her phone from her pocket.

'Addie,' says her mother's voice. 'I said yes! I said yes! I said yes!'

She sounds odd: giddy, teenage, slightly manic.

· · ·

Sol imagines that Bee might be begging her to go to the wedding. Perhaps that's why she's not back. Then he imagines that Star has called her and said she's unexpectedly in Norfolk, and can they meet up? Or what if her mother or father or Sydney have some major emergency on Rokesby? Or what if one of them has persuaded her to change her mind about the surprise family visit? Or what if she changed her own mind?

There are no guarantees.

Will they really go to Tromso?

He finds himself praying: 'Please don't take her away from me.'

Then he remembers that this was the last prayer he prayed for his mother.

· · ·

'Mum,' says Addie. 'I'm standing at the edge of the road. I'm not sure this is the best place—'

'I don't care where you're standing.'

'It's quite a main road,' says Addie.

'You made me the dress I always dreamt of,' says her mother. 'How did you know? Did I ever say? Thank you so much. It's so beautiful. That lace rose!'

'You told us on my eighteenth birthday,' says Addie. 'When Dad told me about Pattie and—'

'Oh let's not talk about her. Please come over and celebrate with us, Ads.'

She sounds, almost, as if she would like that.

'I can't, Mum. I have plans.'

'Cancel your plans. What could be more important than this?'

Going to Tromso with Sol could be more important than this, thinks Addie, or is she wrong? Is going to Rokesby more important?

'I'll pay,' says her mother, which is most unexpected.

Her father's voice: 'Ads, go for it!'

Does he sound a bit drunk? Is her mother a bit drunk? Are they all a bit drunk?

'I need to go, Dad. I'm standing at the edge of quite a main road.'

• • •

Sol sits in the Fiat and he runs through his emails: their flight numbers, flight times, transfer details. Then he scrolls through photos of husky dogs and Ski-Doos and sea eagles and snow and snow and snow and starlit fjords, and the northern lights, swirling electric green through the domed glass curve of the igloo.

He decides to get out of the car to see if that might help her appear, if his presence might magnetise her down the drive. He laughs to himself at the thought of him magnetising anyone anywhere. Minutes pass slowly, and the drive remains empty, the gate closed. Something terrible has happened. He tells God, *I will*

never ever ask you for anything again, which, it comes to him, is
untrue, always, whenever people pray it.

• • •

'Don't go before you've said yes,' says Addie's father.
  'And *alsho*,' says her father – he is definitely drunk. 'I was driving.'
  'What do you mean you were driving?'
  'When we had the accident. It was me who killed Pattie.'
  'Oh dear,' says Addie. 'Oh no.'
  Her mother comes back on the phone.
  'All expenses paid!' she says.
  'I need to get off this road,' says Addie, looking at her watch.

• • •

Sol waits and he waits and he waits, and it becomes less and less
likely to him that she will come. He's losing faith in Tromso. The
gate to the drive will never open. He can't even imagine it being
open.

• • •

Addie gets off her bike to open the gate, and walks down the
drive.
  'Sorry, Sol. My mum rang. She loves the dress and she's pres-
surising me to go and join them on Rokesby.'

• • •

'You must do what feels right,' says Sol. 'We don't have to go.'

• • •

As Sol drives towards Stansted Airport, Addie processes the fact
that her father was driving: she knows how bad she felt about
destroying Sol's van, but imagine destroying your wife's life.
Also, that's surely why he's such a nervous driver, a nervous

person, chewing at his cuticles until they bleed, never settling to anything.

'Are you getting cold feet about missing the wedding? You look tense.'

He looks a bit tenser when she says he looks tense.

'I'm serious,' says Addie. 'If it feels like a mistake, we really don't have to go.'

. . .

Sol's body is taut with anxiety as he gets out of the car, as he unloads their luggage. Addie doesn't want to come to Tromso with him, he can tell. She wants to go to Rokesby to reconcile with her family. They make their way to the terminal in silence.

Although they're now inside the terminal, which is a going-on-a-plane type of place, he isn't at all sure if they are going on a plane. There are queues at all the counters, and his heart is racing because what if she can't make up her mind and they miss the plane? And also, what if she decides not to come and he doesn't miss the plane? What if he ends up going alone? Would he go alone? Or would he go to the wedding?

'Addie,' says Sol, and he digs deep to find words that a man like him finds very difficult to say.

'Addie,' he says again.

She nods.

'I have never ever wanted anything more in my life than I want you to come to Tromso with me.'

'Me too. I mean, with you, obviously.'

. . .

Addie sits staring out of the porthole as the plane rises into the sky, and she knows her mother will hate her now, possibly forever, and she feels scared. She squeezes Sol's hand, because she's terrified of flying. She can't stop thinking about the combined weight of people and cases and metal, and the way the air is basically nothing.

Sol holds her hand tightly.

Little shocks of joy pass between them.

. . .

At Tromso airport, while Addie's in the loo, Sol runs into a café and picks up pots of yoghurt and granola and stuffs them in his rucksack. Then they both get on the minibus. They drive out of the dark city, and they cross a bridge, where fjords glimmer in the glare of the headlights, and they climb higher, higher, flatter, through snowy woods and past iced houses with orange-lit windows and Ski-Doos parked outside, until the road narrows and they arrive.

The light above the door of their igloo gilds the deep snow, and the sky is heavy with cloud. They go into the wooden cube, which has a tiny kitchen and a sitting room with the fire lit, and a bathroom, and a wooden sauna, and a lobby with a floor-to-ceiling cupboard full of snowsuits and enormous boots and snowshoes with their names attached on labels. The air smells of burning wood and pine needles. They take off their identical black anoraks and eat the cold meats and cheeses that have been left out for them.

Sol grounds himself by going into the kitchen to check there's a tray.

'Tray tray tray,' he says to himself to stop his euphoria overtaking him.

'What?' calls Addie from the bathroom.

'Tray tray tray,' he says, speaking aloud to his body, which is alert and aroused and uncontainable.

He comes back out, and he sees, through the lobby, the glass-domed bedroom, and a double bed with the white duvet puffed up like a cloud, and the ninety-five pillows. He feels he might collapse.

'Wow!' says Addie. 'Wow wow wow!'

She throws herself onto the bed and stares through the glass dome at the cloudy sky.

'No northern lights yet,' she says.

'Lie down next to me,' she says.

Sol lies down next to her.

'Here we are,' he says, through his breathing, holding her hand. 'We made it. Let's just stay here for a minute. Drink it in.'

They don't speak.

Is he having a heart attack?

Sol has never heard his breathing so loud.

The more he tries to quieten it, the louder it gets.

'I forgot how terrified I am of flying,' says Addie.

'I'm terrified of this. And now. And what happens next. It's my second thing.'

He feels a fool.

Addie looks up at the sky.

'You know the flippers?' says Sol. 'Do you have something up your sleeve for this?'

Addie starts laughing.

Sol starts laughing.

And that's how it begins.

With laughing.

Laughing and undressing.

Sol's mind fills with years of his father's advice, and Ricko's advice, and long-ago lectures about sexual urges, and difficult questions, and he looks for answers, and he looks and looks and looks until he finds his only answer, *the answer*, which becomes the only thought in his head, a thought so weighty that it squashes the rest, a thought so light that he is able to fly out of his own mind inside it.

I only ever want to be with Addie, nobody else, ever, and if I can't have her, I'll have nobody, by which he means, if I can have her, I have everything, always – and everything gains a terrifying clarity when he feels Addie's skin against his. When he lets himself. Finally. Go.

They wrap themselves up in each other, and time stops, and in the end, no flippers or diagrams are needed, none at all, laughs Sol, laughs Addie, laugh both of them, and they are lost inside each other, and they curl up together, and Sol dreams of tree roots.

. . .

Addie wakes with a fright in the night, groping around for her lamp on the left that isn't there and finding, instead, Sol.

Sol is here instead of a lamp.

He is finally here.

The moon lights his peaceful sleeping face.

She didn't disappear like she used to on Bird Beach.

She's here too.

The herest she's ever been.

Sunday 25th March

Sol wakes with the sun at five thirty, and in the dawn silence beyond the glass, the snow comes so casually, falling around him, beside him, on top of him, beneath him, snow stacking up against the rounded glass igloo walls, catching the leaves of the birch forest beyond the igloo, and should he wake her?

What's the best way to wake a person, he wonders – there are so many things he doesn't know. He looks at Addie's sleeping face, her snub nose, her smattered freckles, her mouth, half-smiling, surrounded by her hair on the pillow. When he looks at her, he feels more human than he's felt before. Is that it?

'Addie,' he whispers.

She opens her eyes.

'I thought you'd want to see,' he says.

She looks through the glass at the snow falling, and he looks at his watch, and the second hand is ticking, and even though this holiday is only just beginning, he's already scared about it ending.

• • •

When Addie next stirs, Sol isn't in bed, but she can hear noises coming from the kitchen.

'Breakfast in bed,' says Sol, coming into the bedroom.

He's put a red and white gingham tablecloth on the tray like Grandma Flora used to. There's a jug of juice, two frothy coffees, yoghurt, granola, a bowl of fruit, toast in a rack and butter and jam.

'Where did you get all this?'

'At the airport.'

Addie helps herself to fruit and yoghurt and granola.

'Did you think about the wedding yesterday?'

'Hardly at all. Did you think about Rokesby?

'Hardly at all either. I know I've probably missed my one chance with Mum. And if I have, it's worth it to be here with you.'

'Shall we make a rule while we're here? Let's think today's the only day. That's what Brother Andrew told me to do. To give myself to the moment. Are you up for that?'

'I am.'

She is.

• • •

At the husky farm, as Sol and Addie meet the wheel dogs and the team dogs and the elite leader dogs, which form the partnered teams of six, Sol checks himself. He's really here. In Tromso. With Addie. He squeezes her hand.

The dogs jump and whine for attention, and they are blue-eyed, grey-furred and beautiful, and Sol wills himself to stay now, stay here, not to fear that soon this will all slip from his grasp. Even if it does, he tells himself, you have it now.

Today is the only day.

They have a brief training session, and the dogs are harnessed into three pairs, and they're all barking and jumping, mad with anticipation.

Sol stands at the back of the sled, with Addie wrapped in furs in front of him. With his foot on the brake, he waits for the guide up ahead to give the signal, feeling entranced by the dogs and the bright-white view and the acute sensation of being alive. The signal is given, the sled in front starts, and he slowly lets the brake off, allowing the dogs to rush forward in a great surge of joy into the snow, which stretches for miles around them, untrodden and vast. As the dogs run on, snuffling and barking with pleasure, Sol follows the sled in front, hurtling into the infinite white, and the present is his, is hers, is theirs.

· · ·

Back at the igloo, Addie drags Sol outside in the dark to build a snowman, which, once formed, she decorates with a tangerine for the nose and Minstrels for the eyes and mouth. Then she lies on her back, and scissors her arms and legs, and feels elated. Sol watches with a slightly confused expression.

'You must know about snow angels. Come and do one!'

'I'm too self-conscious,' says Sol.

'You seem to be in the mood for doing things you never do.'

'Yes, well that's one thing! But snow angels?'

'Well, how about that crab thing you did on Rokesby?'

'I can't think what came over me that day, but whatever it is, it's still coming over me. And I think perhaps I like it.'

'I told you we're Russian dolls,' says Addie. 'And we're heading down a layer. Who knows what we might find?'

The minibus arrives.

'I've never done all these strange things with anyone else,' says Sol. 'I never would.'

The way he's only hers, the way everything's only theirs – it makes her heady.

· · ·

Sol stares out of the minibus window. He's wanted to see the northern lights since he was a young boy. His mother wanted to, but she ran out of time.

They're off with the guide and six other people, chasing along roads beside fjords, up starlit mountains, down starlit valleys, over the border into Sweden, and it's midnight, he notices, looking at his watch, and he seems to have become a night-time person since he came here. Most surprising. They make a fire by the side of the water on the snowy night-time beach, and it's minus ten degrees, and they sit in their snowsuits and put feet-warmers into their boots and hand-warmers into their gloves, and at two thirty, a greenish waft of cloud slithers above them, and the guide points, but everyone admits it's rather disappointing compared to the photos on the website.

It's a long journey back, and they arrive at their igloo in the first light of dawn.

Sol says, 'It's Monday already. Saturday and Sunday are gone. And now we'll sleep and half of Monday will be gone.'

He feels time running forward without him.

• • •

'Well, let's not sleep then,' says Addie. 'Let's have a sauna.'

After the sauna, they set out, in snowshoes, with poles, sleepless, trying to cheat time. The snow glistens as the sun rises, but clouds come over as they walk through the birch trees somewhere, anywhere, in order to stop Monday using itself up.

Monday 26th March

After snowshoeing, Sol and Addie collapse into bed under the glass dome, and the joy of it, the utter bliss of it. Inside her arms, he finds himself able to silence his inner narrative, to refuse its questions, to escape its demands. As he pushes past himself, as he surrenders, time bursts open and, curiously, vanishes.

When later they hire a Ski-Doo, Addie drives him at terrifying speed through the pine forest, and Sol puts his arms around her waist and closes his eyes, pressing himself to escape into the rush of the chill wind and the heat of her body. But when they get off, he hears his boots in the snow, crunch crunch crunch, and there is time again marked by his footsteps, and there is the inner narrative, restarting, wanting answers.

'I think the cloud might be clearing,' says Addie.

'Tomorrow is Tuesday and–'

'And we're going out in the boat.'

'Tuesday is our last day.'

'Let's not think about it.'

Sol is thinking about it. He feels the gloom hovering over his head, and he tells it to leave, but he knows it's still there.

'We have one more chance to see the northern lights,' says Sol.

'I bet we will.'

'I bet we won't.'

He pauses.

'I wish I wasn't Eeyore,' he says.

'Who would you like to be?'

'Anyone but Eeyore. Or Tigger. Tigger gets on my nerves.'

'I always thought Eeyore was cute.'

After the quickest day of his life, Sol lies down with Addie under the glass dome, and then it happens. It bursts out of nowhere, a green, gelatinous shape forming and re-forming against the dark sky.

Sol can't speak.

Addie can't seem to speak either.

Words are again obliterated, time cancelled, as tentacles of luminous green light spread longer longer longer over the sky above their bed, unfurling across the roof of the world, iridescent green undulating in waves to the palest hint of pink-purple. The great illuminated octopus above them stretches and reshapes herself until she becomes a huge shimmering magic carpet, emerald shot with violet thread – and here they are beneath, tiny and speechless and full of joy.

'Wow!' says Sol.

'Wow!' says Addie.

Again and again and again, wow, because what else?

'I think it's Eureka,' whispers Addie.

'I've absolutely no idea what you're talking about,' whispers Sol. 'And why are we whispering?'

Addie smiles.

'Haven't I told you about Eureka?'

Sol shakes his head, and Addie explains all that is explainable.

• • •

'What is actually happening?' says Addie, incredulous that such a thing should be possible in the normal order of things.

'It's solar wind blowing through space carrying protons, and when it runs into our atmosphere, it bashes into the particles and makes energy, which we see as light.'

Addie shakes her head.

'No, that isn't it,' she says.

'I don't think it's compatible with words.'

'Do you think it felt like this when the world started?'

'I wasn't there,' says Sol.

'But what was it?' says Addie. 'The force that wanted it all into being? I guess it must have been like human desire times a billion, if it was going to generate so much world.'

'Not just *so much*,' says Sol. 'As in quantity. But as in variety. I mean, who would ever have thought of all the things that ended up being here? I don't just mean dugongs and narwhals. I mean, the abstract stuff.'

'Like?'

'Well, I don't know, illogical things? I mean, how would love and hate have appeared out of nowhere?'

'Oh not love,' says Addie, and she thinks of Eureka, and she wonders, was it love that made her die for her babies to live, or was it, as suggested in the 1977 experiment at Brandeis University, her optic gland secreting a hormone? Which do you choose? Logic, which feels cleverer and more palatable, or mystery?

'My mother thinks mystery's below her,' she says.

The luminous emerald octopus dances and sparkles and stretches and billows and unfurls and curls and expands and contracts through the night, on and on, until she creeps away, leaving the sky exhausted and depleted.

. . .

'I miss Eureka,' says Addie.

Sol is starting to miss Addie. As he holds her in his arms, he misses not holding her in his arms.

'I never want to leave,' says Sol. 'I don't want tomorrow to come.'

'Time is weird. When I was on Rokesby, every hour went on forever.'

'Yes. Double English with Year 9 on Friday afternoon.'

They both stare at the empty sky.

'Oh well,' says Addie. 'We've still got the boat trip.'

'And when the boat trip ends,' says Sol. 'Then what happens to us, Addie?'

'I guess real life happens again.'

'But real life is you in Norfolk and me on Fair Isle.'

'Do you remember the thing I was scared of?'

'I do,' says Sol. 'And it felt so unlikely, yet the thought that it could conceivably happen changed my life, I suppose. Or changed my view of myself. I couldn't believe anyone would consider falling in love with me. I'd just never imagined that would be possible.'

'Well, it's worse than *possible*,' says Addie.

'Worse?' he says, holding her close.

'It's happened. Despite all my best intentions, all my principles, I *have* fallen in love with you. And so quickly. But remember I said I didn't want my life to be contingent on another person?'

'I decided to ignore it and hope for the best,' says Sol.

'I'm still really, really scared of that,' says Addie. 'Becoming dependent on you. Because if I lost you, for whatever reason, I couldn't possibly deal with it. I know I couldn't. It's nearly ten years since Grandma Flora died. I know I can't go through it again.'

'What if I promise that you won't lose me?'

'Nobody can promise that,' says Addie. 'That's why love's so dangerous.'

Sol looks at her troubled green eyes, eyes he loves more than

297

any other eyes anywhere in the world, strange and inexplicable and illogical though that is, and as he looks at those eyes, he knows that she's right – nobody can promise that.

· · ·

Addie stares through the glass-domed ceiling at the empty sky, and then she props herself on one elbow and looks at Sol.

'What I feel for you is basically too much for me,' she says. 'It's like I don't dare give in to it. Like I have to keep a bit of myself back, to be sure that there's part of me that can function without you. Then if I lost you, that bit would be able to survive.'

Sol says nothing for a while, until he says, 'I'm not sure it works like that.'

Addie lies down on her side, closing her eyes and drawing up her knees, and she feels him reach for her hand. She opens her eyes. He looks smaller suddenly, and she hopes he will re-inflate, but he doesn't seem to, and she can feel herself shrinking too – and this is the danger with love. It can make you smaller, as well as make you bigger. Whereas, if you stick in the middle without it, loveless, you stay the same size – middling.

She should never have come to Tromso.

She should have stayed middling without him.

She was OK on her own.

Not great, but OK.

Tears are rolling down her cheeks, and it feels as if her mouth is full of sea again, like when she blew over to him in a storm.

Tuesday 27th March

Sol and Addie pack their bags in silence.

'If only today was still the only day,' says Sol.

'I ruined the thing we had.'

'The thing we *have*,' says Sol.

'No. The thing we had. Before I said what I said, the thing we had was different. Kind of pure and unstained. Then my words ruined it.'

Sol can't think what to say.

'Words are such a liability,' says Addie. 'Yet people are so casual about talking.'

'What we have is unruinable,' says Sol firmly, wondering if this is true.

'So can we take it with us then?'

'Let's try.'

They carry their bags outside, and Sol takes a photo of the igloo, and he imagines himself looking at the photo as an old man, and he wants to ask that old man whether they did manage to take the thing they had with them, or whether it was left behind, or whether it changed into something else. He wants to ask the old man if life ever felt as good as it has felt here.

They climb onto the minibus for the drive to Tromso, and Sol looks back at the igloo, which soon won't exist, or will exist only as dreams exist, dismembered and faded.

Soon, Tromso won't exist, or Norway. They'll go on the boat trip, and they'll be off to Stansted, and who knows what will happen next? The minibus stops at two different hotels to pick up passengers. Nobody speaks to each other. The wind is beating the sides of the minibus, and Sol wonders if the boat trip will be cancelled. When they arrive, the driver takes out snowsuits and snow-boots and they all jostle against each other as they put them on, sheltering under the raised up-and-over door. Then they wait in the harbour, being lashed by sleet. A large man appears wearing a fake fur hat dripping rain down his face.

'So sorry,' he says. 'So sorry. Bad weather.'

Addie and Sol stand disconsolately with the small group of strangers looking at the man, and the sleet, and the water, and each other. Then they get on the boat.

· · ·

Addie takes Sol's arm, and they leave the other passengers in the cabin and go out onto the deck, where they stand close together in the freezing cold, peering at snowy peaks through the sleet which is now turning to snow.

'What might we see?' says Addie.

'Pilot whales and dolphins. Hopefully sea eagles. But the orcas and hump-backs will have moved on by now.'

Sol puts his arm around her, and she leans into the warmth of him, and she feels both the deep agony and the deep comfort of his presence, and she wonders if her parents ever felt like she feels now, or whether they always hated each other a little bit inside their love.

· · ·

Sol swallows his nausea and stares at the sea eagle as it flies past, broad-winged, yellow-beaked, yellow-clawed, fearsome and majestic, and he wonders whether somewhere out here in nature – in the sea eagle, or in the sea, or the sky, or the snow – he can find an answer which will assuage Addie's fears, or his own. He assumes the sea eagle knows nothing about love, and he thinks that would be easier.

The boat moors in a sheltered cove and they hang their fishing rods over the side, and Addie catches a cod, and so does a man with a beard and a young girl with plaits sticking out of her hat. A woman appears on the deck, and she takes the flapping fish back to the kitchen in a purple bucket, and Sol wonders if the plural of cod is cod or cods.

Sol stays on deck as the others go inside to eat cod stew. A pod of pilot whales come ponderously by, passing under the boat and re-appearing – and Addie and the others run onto the deck to see them.

Sol looks for an answer in the pilot whales, disappearing.

As they head for the harbour, the sky clears, and for a few minutes dolphins swim with the boat, arching and diving, and Addie takes Sol's gloved hand in her gloved hand and squeezes it until the dolphins speed off left, shrinking smaller and smaller until they are dots and spray and nothing. Sol looks for an answer in the dolphins, but he's no longer sure what the question is.

Addie says, 'I wish we could live in the present like they do. I see dolphins and I think of all the other dolphins I've seen. And especially Sydney and Dad leaving, with the dolphins round the boat.'

'That's being human,' says Sol. 'Having past, present and future all at once.'

The boat moors in the harbour, and Sol and Addie climb off, and they take off their snowsuits and go to the loo and find their luggage and get on another minibus to the airport, and they're shunted through security and passport control, and they're flying, and Sol takes Addie's hand and feels it flinching when the plane bumps, or the engine noise changes, and she falls asleep on his shoulder, and he wishes he could stop time, and they would always be here, suspended above real life, her head nestled into his neck.

．　．　．

Addie looks at the now-familiar shape of Sol's hands as they change gear under the motorway lights. Then she falls asleep, waking as they reach Mermaid Cottage. She presses the button to open the gate, and the automatic light turns on. The Fiat crunches down the gravel. Mermaid Cottage is still there, looking, miraculously to Addie, just as it did when they left, with the guests' black Range Rover outside it. And there's The Boathouse, curiously unchanged as well, and the lawn and the river beyond.

They get out of the car.

'Let's go and look at the river,' says Addie.

．　．　．

Sol puts his arm around her, and they stand under the moon looking at the wind rippling through the reeds, and it seems possible that Tromso never happened, and he remembers when he fused with the grass and the ant and the eider on Ora, when he was unseparate from everything, like he's unseparate now from Addie, like he's even unseparate momentarily from God.

．　．　．

'You'll stay until the morning, won't you ?' says Addie.

Wednesday 28th March

Sol and Addie take their coffee to the balcony to watch the sun rise.

'There's nothing I want to go back for,' he says, wishing he hadn't, because if she doesn't want her life to be contingent on another person, presumably she doesn't want another person's life to be contingent on her.

'Except Barry Forfitt,' he adds.

He wishes he hadn't signed a contract with a two-term notice period, and he thinks how unfree it feels to be alive.

'I need to go now,' he says.

'I can't stand it. Stay a bit longer.'

'However long I stay, I think it will feel the same.'

'I wanted to swim with you again before you left. I'm sure you'd have the confidence to float with one more session.'

'I'll take your confidence with me. I must see Tommie briefly before I fly.'

'But can I just get you those flippers? I want you to take them with you.'

'Don't they belong to Star?'

'I'll buy her some new ones. I want you to keep practising with them back on Fair Isle, OK?'

'I never know what to do with my arms.'

'I love your arms,' says Addie.

Sol looks at his arms, and finds it hard to process this thought.

'Honestly,' says Addie. 'But anyhow, keep your arms by your side, as if you don't have arms. Forget about them, and kick your legs. And the flippers will do the rest. OK? Keep at it, and you'll be swimming in no time. Let me know.'

They go outside.

'The guests left early,' says Addie as she walks across the lawn to the shed, coming out with the orange flippers, which start to change shape, in his mind, as she comes towards him.

'Puffins!' he says. 'That's it!'

'What's *it*?' says Addie. 'What's puffins? What are you talking about?'

The flippers are becoming huge puffin feet in his mind, orange and webbed and ridged.

'We need to be *more puffin*,' says Sol.

'I'm really not following you.'

'Puffin pairs are monogamous and faithful, but they spend half the year apart and half together,' he says. 'Do you see? We could do that, and your life wouldn't be contingent on another person. Half the year you'd be alone.'

She looks up at him.

'We can come together for the breeding season,' says Sol, smiling.

'Now that does sound good,' she says. 'The breeding season. As long as I don't have to lay an egg. Do you know Mac thought women's eggs had shells on them. He actually thought that.'

Sol laughs.

'We'll just adjust the puffin dates,' he says, feeling a little dart of optimism. 'To fit in with school terms! So let's make a puffin pact. Here and now.'

'Meaning?'

'I fly off,' says Sol. 'We're apart. Then I fly back and we're together.'

'And then?'

'Let's not complicate it,' says Sol.

. . .

'I've never really done goodbyes,' says Addie. 'Grandma Flora never said goodbye. Come to think of it, nor did Dad or Sydney. And nor did I. When I left Rokesby. So I've no idea how this works.'

'Like this,' says Sol, and he takes her in his arms and he kisses her, and she kisses him, but it ends, of course, and it's not enough, she wants more, like we always want more, like nothing is ever enough, because everything ends. Everything.

'Do you think the world will eventually come to an end?' she says.

'Hopefully not before I see you next,' says Sol, laughing.

'Or would something stop it coming to an end?'

'Maybe.'

'I don't understand anything,' says Addie.

'Nobody understands anything. Even the people who say they do.'

Addie smiles.

'I suppose I get in the car now,' says Sol.

'Which means I open the gate.'

He puts his luggage in the Fiat, and he drives to the gate, and she walks behind him, and he stops and opens the car window, and she looks at the orange flippers on the passenger seat.

'There aren't any words for Tromso,' she says.

'I used to think there were words for everything,' he says. 'Before we went.'

'I've just thought. Let me pay for Tromso. I have money now.'

'You owe me nothing,' says Sol.

'I possibly owe you everything,' says Addie.

'I'll fly back in. The puffin pact!'

'The puffin pact! Let's shake on it.'

They shake hands, laughing, though their laughing sounds fragile to her, as everything feels fragile, and breakable, like glass, and Sol closes the window and drives the Fiat through the open gate, and she watches him vanish around the corner, and she's not laughing because she's crying.

She walks up and down inside the tracks the car has left – proof that he was once here.

• • •

As Sol drives, his peace starts eroding because they didn't exactly clarify the meaning of the puffin pact. What are the rules for getting in touch with Addie when it's out of season, he wonders, and are they out of season from today, and not to contact each other at all?

Puffins definitely wouldn't, but puffins don't have mobile phones.

No analogy is perfect, he reminds himself, as he used to tell his students.

He parks outside The Amusements and dashes in to give Tommie his keys, but Tommie says that he should keep them, and he hugs him goodbye, says, 'Come back soon!'

• • •

The sheets are in the washing machine and the two halves of the coffee sponge are out of the oven, on a cooling tray, and Addie's busyness is a welcome reprieve and a distraction and a relief, as in pain relief, as in something much stronger than paracetamol or ibuprofen – no, more like codeine or morphine.

Because the pain of him not being here is so big, his absence so much bigger than she expected. Whereas his actual body took up, what, six-foot three of height and however wide he is, say three feet, longer with his arms out – an area of about twenty square feet – now he's not here, his absence is everywhere.

Here's the new client, parking an old red car. She has a ruler-straight black fringe and dark tattoos reaching out of her T-shirt up her neck, and a ring in her nose.

'I'm Chang,' she says.

'Come on in, Chang,' says Addie, taking her into her workshop. 'And tell me your dream dress.'

'I'm thinking kind of medieval,' says Chang. 'Dark red.'

Addie thinks of the red thread in *Blood Wedding* unfurling, as her own fate unfurls ahead of her, like a kind of ancient sat nav – and she wonders where it will take her and what the obstacles will be and where it will end. The future terrifies her, the way it crouches in the dark.

'I'd like a stiff corset and flarey sleeves to cover my hands,' says Chang. 'I've got awful eczema. But Bill doesn't mind.'

'Love's like that,' says Addie, surprising herself. 'Don't you think?'

Sol never seems to mind the way she talks to ducks and wears tails and funny clothes and doesn't know about normal things. Driving licences, say, and car insurance.

'Bill says he *likes* my eczema, but of course I don't believe him!'

'I'd love to make that dress for you.'

'Epic,' says Chang.

'So we'll agree this basic drawing, and then I'll go away and cost it and get back to you with a quote.'

'Epic,' says Chang again, standing at the open door on the deck. 'So easy. Thank you!'

Chang kisses her on the cheek, gets into her car and drives away.

• • •

Sol goes through security and buys himself a cheese and ham roll with a coffee for about a million pounds, and he takes out Poem 7 and wonders if he should have given it to her. He catches a plane, and another plane, and another plane, and when he lands, he goes into the tiny terminal on Fair Isle, grabs his luggage and heads out into the dark.

'Mr Blake,' says a voice from the shadows. 'I was waiting for you. Welcome home.' It's Barry Forfitt.

'Have you been waiting all day?'

'You said afternoon.'

'I'm sorry, Barry, I must have got the time a bit wrong.'

'Don't worry. There's nothing to do anyway. It's the holidays.'

'So?'

'I hope the wedding was OK,' says Barry.

'It's a long story,' says Sol.

'Well, I thought it would be nice to be here to welcome you back.'

'It is nice, Barry.'

'Puella's back,' says Barry. 'Very early.'

'That's wonderful.'

'It is,' says Barry. 'It always is. Every year.'

'See you at birdwatching camp!' says Sol.

'Also,' says Barry. 'You can tell it's Puella because she's much smaller than Puer. With a much smaller bill.'

· · ·

Addie is in bed at The Boathouse, unable to believe that she was ever lying with Sol beside her, beneath a domed glass roof with the sky illuminated green, billowing in folds above them.

Thursday 29th March

In the early morning, after a restless night, Sol puts on his swimming shorts and his navy sweater. He takes the orange flippers, lets himself out of the front door and makes his way down to the beach. He puts the flippers on and he walks backwards into the water. It's so cold, so freezing, freezing cold, but he's under, and he keeps his arms by his side, as if he doesn't have arms, and he kicks his flippered feet, and it happens, it happens, it happens, he's crossing a boundary, as he finds himself propelled through the water by her confidence in him, or by the flippers, or both.

Sol Blake is swimming!

He swims and he swims and he swims.

Then he heads back, elated, dresses and walks to the schoolhouse to meet his birdwatchers, and they set off on their walk, armed with binoculars and notebooks and a picnic, which they eat on the cliff.

Sol walks home in the early afternoon, his head full of her.

• • •

Addie is eating a late lunch on the balcony when the phone rings. Sol? Did she ever give him her landline number? Or perhaps he looked up her website? But why would he when he has her mobile number?

She answers.

'My name's Tiffany.'

Not Sol.

He's flown to sea, like she told him to.

'I saw that you make wedding dresses,' says Tiffany.

'I do,' says Addie.

'I'm a shepherd.'

'My first,' says Addie.

'The thing is, I don't really wear dresses. I don't know where to start. My mother died last year. So she can't help.'

'I'm so sorry. I'd love to help. Would you like to come and see me? I have a little workshop in Horning, by the river. It's very private. It would be just you and me. Nothing scary.'

'Could I come later today?' she says.

'How about four o'clock?' says Addie.

'Perfect,' says Tiffany.

As Addie puts down the phone, her mobile pings.

I'm not sure if I'm allowed to text out of the breeding season, but I wanted you to know that I put on the flippers. AND I SWAM. Thank you for everything. Xx

She texts back.

So delighted. Congratulations to you and the flippers.

She can't bear to be without him – and this is exactly the feeling she didn't want.

She adds:

Perhaps we shouldn't text out of the breeding season, Sol. Shall we specify when the next breeding season begins? Xx

She presses send.

She feels sick.

• • •

Sol reads her text, and feels sick.

He checks his calendar.

Half-Term is from 27th May to 4th June, he texts.

He counts: that's over eight weeks. Eight weeks without seeing her face, without hearing her voice, without feeling her skin.

Would you like to come to Fair Isle for the week?

She doesn't reply. He tells himself he may only check his phone once an hour. He checks at two thirty, and then again at ten to three, because he can't wait.

He puts his phone face down on the kitchen counter. He goes to the food shop, and he comes back and makes fish pie. She still hasn't replied. He puts his phone in the cutlery drawer. He makes brownies and flapjacks. He goes for a walk to the Jut. Puella is looking out to sea.

• • •

Addie can't decide if she's brave enough to fly to Fair Isle alone in May. Stansted to Glasgow, didn't he say, then to Lerwick, then a tiny plane to the island. Also, she should look at her diary. She has brides with weddings on Thursday 1st June and Saturday 3rd June, with final fittings that week. So she can't go to Fair Isle at Half-Term – whether she's brave enough or not, it doesn't work.

Perhaps he could come to The Boathouse.

The bell rings, and she lets in a battered Land Rover.

Tiffany the shepherd, who doesn't have a mother.

311

Alone in Tromso, love was simple, uninterrupted,
uncluttered by dates and times and jobs and families
and logistics and arrangements.

But love so easily finds itself squeezed
between the gaps of two lives.

Where there isn't space for it.

Where it can't quite breathe.

Thursday 5th April

Sol is walking along the cliffs alone, breathing in the dusk air.

He's agreed to go to The Boathouse for May Half-Term, the whole glorious week, and he wishes he could speed through the stretching tedium of every day until then. He hopes it will be the same between them. But look, as he walks towards the Jut, there they are, Puer reunited with Puella, rubbing their bills together in the frenzied joy of their reunion.

Sol sits down to watch, and he knows he must have the same faith Puella had as she waited for Puer to return.

He will find Addie again, and she will find him.

Like they did in Tromso.

Puer and Puella head into their burrow.

Sol heads home.

• • •

Addie's out on the jetty in the dusk when a text comes through from her father.

Her parents' wedding date has been set for Saturday 26th May, and *they both hope* she will come early to help get things ready and be there to celebrate and stay on for the following week on Rokesby.

Addie looks at her calendar. Sol was supposed to arrive in Norfolk that day.

Tiffany the shepherd doesn't have a mother, so however crap her mother is, perhaps, having not gone to Rokesby for the engagement, she should go for the wedding. Is that right? She has no one to ask.

She knows it's against the rules of the puffin pact, but she phones Sol.

• • •

'Addie!'

'Sol!'

'Addie!'

'Sol!'

'Your voice!' he says. 'It's your voice!'

'Yes. My voice that's about to tell you something you don't want to hear.'

The thing he's been dreading. Sol feels it coming. The grabber always lets go of the thing he wants, but please not Addie, he'll do anything, anything, to keep her. She explains the problem.

'They want me to come a few days before the wedding and stay for the whole week after, which I obviously can't do. Because of those dresses.'

'And also because I'm coming?'

'Exactly.'

'Why didn't you say that first?'

'Because we both knew you were coming.'

'So how long would you be on Rokesby?'

'I guess until the Monday.'

'There aren't any boats on Mondays.'

'There are on Bank Holidays.'

'No doubt they're expecting you to organise the whole wedding?' says Sol.

314

'I met this bride who doesn't have a mother, and it made me think that I do have a mother. So despite everything, despite how awful she's been, perhaps I shouldn't give up on her completely. Or what do you think?'

Sol feels his jaw tightening.

'We'd have Tuesday onwards together,' says Addie. 'I just have a few appointments. Thinking about it, you couldn't take a different week off?'

'Obviously not,' says Sol. 'I can't go away in term time.'

'I don't know anything about schools.'

'Clearly.'

Sol hears himself.

He hates himself.

'This doesn't make me feel much of a priority,' he says, and he regrets it because he thinks if you love people, you should say only nice things to them.

. . .

'You missed your father's wedding for me,' says Addie. 'So you probably don't think this is very fair.'

. . .

'I'm not always in favour of fairness,' says Sol. 'It can be too inflexible.'

'What do you mean?'

'You remember I told you about Barry's scarf? The one he wore because it smelled of his mother. And Miss Gunn and I violently disagreed because I thought any other child should have got a uniform point for wearing a stripy scarf that day, but not him.'

'Which isn't, strictly speaking, fair?'

'Precisely. I don't especially see fairness in the essential patterns of life. Do you?'

. . .

315

'What *do* you see?' says Addie. 'If not fairness?'

'There's order, then disorder, then reorder. On repeat.'

'Which bit are we in?'

'Disorder, I think.'

'Oh,' says Addie. 'Is the reorder guaranteed?'

'That might be up to us.'

When she puts down the phone, she goes down to her sewing workshop, and she feels a bit wobbly because she didn't know life had essential patterns, and she has to hold the hand rail.

Sunday 27th May

It's Half-Term, and Sol wakes in an unfamiliar bedroom, the bedroom of a flat belonging to a man called Hamish, who bears a slight resemblance to a highland bull.

Hamish – and this is why Sol's here – is dating his sister, Rachel.

Sol's father requires Hamish to put in an appearance at church today, and at dinner last night, Rachel begged Sol to come too as Hamish is not familiar with churches. Regrettably, Sol said yes. He'd drunk too much wine, and he felt sorry for Hamish.

They'll meet Rachel at the service, but first they are eating bacon and sausage and fried eggs and Hamish's speciality black pudding.

'I don't think your father approves of me,' says Hamish.

'My father doesn't approve of anyone,' says Sol.

•   •   •

Addie's in the kitchen at The Retreat eating breakfast alone, exhausted, her feet aching, her head aching. She cooked for seventy-six people: long-lost Lemmings and Mimmses, Rokesby islanders, selected Retreat guests, a bunch of Sydney's strange friends who made up the wedding band. She'd made long tables from wooden planks and barrels and laid them out on the lawn with folding chairs that came across in the ferry alongside white tablecloths and white napkins and pouches of sugared almonds and boxes of fat cream candles.

Addie filled all the bottles and jars from the pantry with wild flowers, and she arranged them in mismatching rows down the centre of the table, with candle flames gleaming into the night, as the guests danced.

She didn't dance. She's never danced. She doesn't think she ever would. She drank instead, watching from the kitchen window as she washed up.

'Ah, Cinderella,' said Sydney through the window. 'Get us a glass of water, will you?'

'Get your own,' she said, rejecting Cinderella, as she rejected Mowgli, determined to move forward.

She drank a bottle of champagne as she washed up, straight from the bottle, glug by glug. Her mother found her in the kitchen, glugging.

'You've been marvellous,' she said, grabbing the champagne bottle and knocking some back.

'Thank you,' said Addie.

Her mother handed the bottle back to her.

Addie glugged.

They both glugged.

'We should have got drunk together more often,' said her mother. 'We'd have got on better.'

Then her father came in and picked her mother up and said something about going over the threshold, and then they were gone, and Addie didn't like to think what happened next.

It was strange to be back in her bedroom again. She looked around, wondering what she could take back with her on the train. She took her Russian dolls, her jar of buttons, a bag of lace, a photograph of Grandma Flora in the garden of Stone House. Then she hesitated and took one of her mother and father and Sydney standing on the beach at Holy Island. She squeezed all these things into her rucksack. Then she folded her second favourite tail into a Spanish basket that used to belong to Grandma Flora, and filled the spaces with clothes and fabric offcuts.

Addie's mother and father haven't appeared this morning. She feels a bit used and very hungover, as she waits to make them breakfast.

She checks her emails. Star's written saying she's decided to stay on in the States, where she's become a bit of a celebrity.

'Men and mermaids!' she writes. 'I'm not going anywhere! Are you happy to keep going with Mermaid Cottage?'

Addie replies saying she'd love to. The situation suits her very well.

Sol has arrived in Norfolk. He's staying with his sister's new man.

She can't wait to get to him.

Can't wait.

Perhaps she shouldn't have come.

But that wouldn't have felt right either.

Monday 28th May

Sol is at Tommie's caravan, when he gets a text from Addie saying she's half an hour away.

'All these goodbyes and hellos,' he says. 'I don't think I can stand it.'

Tommie smiles.

'I'm feeling nervous,' says Sol, as he gets up to leave.

Sol waits outside her gate, listening to a professor on the radio talking about the death of the semi-colon.

There she is. *There she is.* On her bike, with a big rucksack on her back and something bulky in her basket. He waves at her through the car window, which is steaming up. He should have leapt out and kissed her, but he didn't. He feels a bit sad about semi-colons, and also terrified. What if what if what if what if? She gets off her bike and leans it against the fence. He parks and gets out. He opens his arms and she folds herself inside them, and he thinks he may well die of desire, or is it happiness, or is it both, who knows? He must think of semi-colons to calm himself down.

He says, 'They think the semi-colon is dying out.'

Addie stands back and laughs.

'Who does?'

'This professor on Radio 4.'

She holds out her hand, and he takes it.

Sol says, 'I love semi-colons.'

Then he really wishes he hadn't.

'You?' he says.

'Me what?'

'Punctuation marks. Do you have a favourite?'

• • •

Addie stares up at his dark eyes, and she loves them as much as she did, maybe more.

She isn't sure whether she has a favourite punctuation mark.

'How was the wedding?' he says.

'Let's go in,' she says, and the relief of being here, not on Rokesby, seeps into a deep and delicious longing for him, a rush of blood so powerful that she can't seem to get her extremely familiar key into the extremely familiar lock of her extremely familiar front door.

Friday 1st June

Sol wakes, feeling frustrated.

'It feels like we've had no time together,' he says, as they eat breakfast. 'And now it's our last day.'

After her arrival on Monday night, there were dress appointments on Tuesday and Wednesday, a last-minute dress mishap which wrecked Thursday morning and a protracted visit from Leah in the afternoon to criticise Rachel's relationship with Hamish.

'It's all just life. I've had such a wonderful time.'

Sol tries to dislodge his grumpiness.

He can't.

His mother used to say that if you pretend for long enough, you forget you're pretending.

. . .

Addie and Sol row with one oar each, in time, playing the bird game, whereby the last letter of one bird must form the first of the next. They are excellent at it, leaving hardly a millisecond between birds.

'Teal.'

'Linnet.'

'Tufted duck.'
'Kite'
'Eagle.'
'Egret.'
'Twite.'
'Eider'
'Robin.'
'Nuthatch.'
'Heron.'
It starts to rain.
'Nightingale,' says Sol.
'Egyptian goose,' says Addie.
'Eagle owl.'
'Lapwing.'
'Goldcrest.'
'Treecreeper.'
'We could go on forever.'
'We could,' she says.
It's now pouring.
Addie turns her face to the sky as the rain soaks her.
'Isn't it wonderful?' she says. 'Being alive?'

• • •

When they return to The Boathouse, Sol climbs, at Addie's instruction, into a very full bath. He's never had a bath with anyone else before. Even as a child. His sisters had baths together, but not with him. He feels a titillating mix of awkward and excited, and can't help wanting to cup his genitals in his hand, which is something he used to do in the communal showers after PE.

• • •

Addie watches him and laughs.
'Are you feeling shy?'

'Always.'

He leans back in the bath.

'I can't leave you tomorrow,' he says.

She can't bear him to leave either.

'Could the puffin pact allow more communication between visits?' he says.

'I wonder if it could.'

'This trip has had too many interruptions.'

'I agree.'

'Puffins don't have to put up with all this shit.'

'What shit?'

'Wedding dresses, impossible sisters, Scottish boyfriends, term dates. Do you really want to go on like this?'

'You don't?'

'I want to go on,' says Sol. 'Obviously. But not like this. I want to stay within bathing distance of you. I don't want to be apart.'

She laughs, but she doesn't think he's being funny underneath.

Absence, famed for making the heart grow fonder,
can also make the heart grow colder.

Especially if the absence seems, to one party,
unreasonable, or avoidable.

Sometimes we hate what we're doing to
each other, but do it anyway.

Thursday 9th August

As Sol heads to the terminal, he wonders if his heart has grown sick in over two months of being apart. He feels resentment like a drone following him above his head because he wanted Addie to come here, to his home, to Fair Isle, to see his life this summer, in late July or early August, but then Hamish proposed to Rachel, so Addie said, what's the point? If they were flying to Palma for the wedding, why would she fly first to Fair Isle, only to fly back to Stansted? Much better to extend their time in Mallorca after the wedding.

She's probably right, but it isn't about that, but about the fact that he can't help feeling he's the one who makes the effort in their relationship. If it qualifies as a relationship. Or maybe it's not about that either. Maybe it's the fact that Hamish and Rachel, though they haven't known each other long, are getting married.

The wedding will take place, surprisingly, in Deia, in Mallorca, because, surprisingly, Hamish's parents live out there and, surprisingly, Rachel has agreed to it. It's been a very quick engagement, which his sister Leah approves of, because she, like her father, has opinions, although she doesn't especially approve of Hamish. Sol's father and Bee are coming although they are unhappy about the civil ceremony. Hamish was briefly married for a couple of years. No doubt they are unhappy about this too.

• • •

Addie wakes having dreamt of a bride standing by a river next to a huge black horse that wouldn't drink. She waits anxiously at Stansted Airport. Ever since he left in June, the horse has been there when they've texted or called. But she hasn't mentioned it.

There's Sol, with a slight frown, leaning forwards. She walks towards him, and he walks towards her, but when they meet, he doesn't put down his holdall or his suit-carrier, so she can't hug him. Instead of hugging him, she points to his suit-carrier and says, 'Did you buy a suit?'

He says he did, and it's blue, and he hopes it's OK, and they should probably go straight to bag-drop. They're not very good at the self-service machine, and the woman has to come over and press the buttons and sort the sticky labels out, and then they're walking to security, and it's too late to hug, but if they don't hug now, when will they?

So she says, 'We never hugged.'

And he says, 'Oh, sorry.'

And they hug.

• • •

After the hug, Sol says, 'Would you like a coffee?'

• • •

On the plane, Addie takes Sol's hand.

He takes his hand out of her hand to adjust his seat belt.

She doesn't take it again.

She tries leaning her head on his shoulder, and she can hear his stomach rumbling.

She says, 'Are you looking forward to the wedding?'

327

He says, 'I really haven't had time to think about it.'

She's not sure what to say next.

She feels panic rising up from the soles of her feet, reaching her belly and cramping.

. . .

Hamish wants to marry Rachel and be with her all the time, thinks Sol. Nobody else has a puffin pact, and he doesn't want one either.

Addie says, 'You don't think Rachel's pregnant, do you?'

'Pregnant?' says Sol.

'And that's why they're getting married so fast?'

'I guess they might just want to get married.'

It's not that he has to marry Addie now, or next year, or even the next. It's that she might be open to the concept of permanence. Being properly together.

He takes Addie's hand and he says, 'I'm sorry.'

'What are you sorry for?'

'I'm not sure,' he says. 'Perhaps for loving you too much.'

The air steward offers him a drink.

He says, 'No, thank you.'

. . .

Addie says, 'No, I'm the one who's sorry.'

'What are you sorry for?'

Where would she even start?

'Everything,' she says.

. . .

Sol could ask her what's included in everything, but he knows that he should change tack, that this conversation is taking them where they definitely shouldn't be going. He searches inside himself for a different mood.

328

'If she is pregnant,' he says, finding a smile, 'that will go down very badly.'

He emits a strained laugh.

'Although,' he continues in his light, humorous, fake voice. 'Rachel says Dad and Bee are *trying*.'

'I hate that expression. It sounds—'

'Like you're constipated,' says Sol, repeating his strained laugh.

Addie laughs and stops, very quickly.

'Barbara said they weren't going to use any contraception,' says Addie.

'No, Addie, no,' says Sol. 'He's my father. I can't take it.'

They sit silently after that.

Then Addie goes to the loo.

• • •

'Did you know?' says Addie, when she gets back. 'My parents' wedding was the first wedding I've ever been to.'

'What?' says Sol.

'I know that sounds odd with the job I do.'

'I could never really tell if you enjoyed it or not. You were cagey about it.'

'I wasn't cagey. I chose not to talk about it.'

'Because?'

'Sydney called me Cinderella. I hated it.'

'Cinderella *wanted* to go to the ball,' says Sol.

'What do you mean?' says Addie.

'If you want to go to the ball, I'd love to take you.'

'What ball?'

'Any ball.'

'What are we talking about?'

'I'm not sure.'

Addie still finds metaphors unnerving.

• • •

It's like there's some obstacle between them that makes understanding each other, even understanding himself, feel impossible. Sol's brain feels foggy, his insides twisted.

He remembers their first night in Tromso, the night he dreamt of tree roots. He sees the roots growing and growing, breaking through the soil, turning into a stem, turning into a trunk, thickening and thickening like a great oak tree, and he's on one side and she's on the other, and if he hadn't given up writing poems, he would write one, and it would be Number 22, and it would be called *The Tree of Unsaid Things*, and it would almost definitely be crap.

There are so many unsaid things growing on its branches that he can't see her.

• • •

'I can't quite find you, Sol.'

'I can't find you either.'

Addie closes her eyes and pretends to be asleep, and hopes everything feels better when they land.

Wednesday 15th August

At the hotel in Deia, Rachel requires Sol to be a host, so that rather than spending time with Addie, he has had to spend time with Hamish's family, and his friends from Scotland, and from his accountancy firm, as well as his father and Bee. His father hasn't forgiven him for missing his wedding, but he is obliged to talk to him because the other wedding guests don't appeal to him, or don't admire him, which comes to the same thing.

'Hamish's family are not our type,' Bee confirms, making a strange face.

'When are you going to get a ring on her finger, Sol?' says his father.

Sol can't stand it.

Addie definitely can't stand it, the preponderance of people, and the infinity of chat, so she mainly escapes to the balcony of their bedroom.

There are constant explosions of tension downstairs in what Rachel, annoyingly, calls *the engine room*. The day before the wedding, when the Blake side of the family arrives, the chef appears in the courtyard to say that the avocadoes have come and they're hard as rocks, and Rachel seems to lose control of everything, her bodily movements, her muscles, her words, her emotions, sending the chef rushing back inside shaking. Sol tells the chef it will be OK. Then he tells Rachel it will be OK. He says the wedding guests can sit in the courtyard and squeeze one avocado ripe at a time.

'No,' says Bee. 'That won't work. Just lay them out in the sun.'

Sol rushes inside and comes back with the crates, and he lays the avocadoes in rows, moving them with the sun, until he tires and escapes.

Addie is sketching the mountains on the balcony, and she doesn't turn around when he comes in, which bothers him.

'What's the matter?' he says.

'I don't like there being so many people,' she says.

'Nor do I.'

'But right now,' she says. 'It's you and me and the door is shut, so why don't we feel like we normally feel?'

He can't say what he wants to say.

He can't say, We're here for a wedding which is making me want to marry you, not now, but some time, at a time that would suit you, to be sure that we really are going to be together. That's what I want every minute of every day, to know that we can always be together, but I can't tell you that, and this makes it impossible to talk to you about other things, because between me and all the other things is *the thing I can't say*, like one of those coloured overlays that I use for pupils with dyslexia which turns everything green or red and yellow, and everything for me is permanence-coloured, and what stands out for me, when I'm looking through the overlay of you not wanting me properly, is me wanting you so much it's making me horrible.

'Oh it's probably all the pre-wedding tension,' says Sol. 'We've just had a slight avocado drama.'

· · ·

'Avocado drama?'

'They're not ripe for tomorrow's giant tricolore salad.'

'You can't squeeze fruit ripe.'

'I now know that.'

'By the end of tomorrow,' says Addie, 'it will all be over, and we'll be off to your mother's thin place.'

'I hope it's not too crowded.'

Thursday 16th August

The wedding eventually happens, the officiator a beautiful Spanish woman with curves and luxuriant hair, wearing a cream linen suit, to match the canopy, which is surrounded by palm trees and huge terracotta urns. Sol looks at his father sweating in his dog collar, which Rachel advised him not to wear.

• • •

As Rachel and Hamish start to say their vows, Addie puts her hand into the sun beyond the canopy, and she feels the heat on the slightly rough surface of the curved terracotta urn, and it's lovely. She wishes she were a cat, and that she could curl herself around it and be hot and quiet and sleepy all afternoon, and not have to make conversation the way humans do.

She puts out her other hand, and she feels Sol's hand squeezing hers with the syllables of the vows, like a kind of morse code, and she thinks, *oh yes, oh I see, that's the problem, yes, if only, could I ever, I wonder, how terrifying, how beautiful, that's it, that's what the issue is, me again, always me, maybe not always. After all, I've already changed a bit, and these things take time.*

Human beings are like avocadoes.

They can't be squeezed ripe.
They must ripen.
In their time.

2019

If love were a tadpole, it would effortlessly become a frog.

*If love were a year, it would make its way
calmly through the seasons.*

But love doesn't work in a linear fashion.

Its progression can never be guaranteed

It's pulled in a thousand directions.

It rises and falls, sputters and fades, lights and relights.

Dies and lives.

Again and again.

~

*Meet Addie and Sol, as they enter their
third and most significant spring.*

Monday 1st April

As Addie sits at the elbow bend of the river to observe the frog spawn, the black dots have turned to a mass of black commas. Commas, she should have said when Sol asked which was her favourite punctuation mark last May.

She's been working on his secret present since September. She saw the old ambulance sitting on a garage forecourt along the A11, and she bought it on the spot. She panelled the inside of it with rustic wood through the autumn.

Sol didn't come in December: his plane couldn't leave Fair Isle because of the snow. She checked the weather forecast on her phone to be sure, and felt sick that she'd doubted him. They badly needed to be together after their unsettling summer. They'd stayed in Mallorca for another three weeks, finding his mother's thin place up in Cap de Formentor, but it was packed with tourists, and Addie got sunburned and couldn't be touched. She covered herself in Sudacrem, and laughed, but underneath their laughter, they were stinging. They didn't speak of Rachel and Hamish's wedding.

As the taxi approached Palma airport, Sol said, 'Hope deferred makes the heart grow sick.'

341

Addie said, 'On the day we left England, I dreamt about a great black horse standing by the river, not drinking.'

The taxi driver said, '*Estamos aquí.*'

On the plane, they were given seats four rows apart from each other, and Sol sat watching her spiralling curls hanging to the left of her seat.

They hugged each other, unsolved and panic-stricken, at Stansted Airport, and Addie froze with sadness on the train, and Sol ached on the plane, both berating themselves for wasting the time they'd had together.

Soon it was autumn, and separately they read *Murder in the Cathedral*, and felt the year passing, and avoided thinking that they were only partly living. Throughout December, Addie tried to befriend a nervous robin on her bedroom balcony, but by the time the advent candle was burnt to twenty-four, he was still flying away every time she opened the glass doors, and on Christmas Day, unseasonably, he didn't appear at all, so she fed Little Hen bits of roast potato and watched the guests at Mermaid Cottage, silhouettes in paper crowns. On Boxing Day, she built lockers with antique brass latches for the ambulance in the barn.

'Couldn't you take the children away some other time?' she asked Sol in January, but he said he couldn't – the February Half-Term trip was in his contract. Addie made work surfaces for the tiny kitchen and built the wooden frames for the seating and the extra-large bed, and she wondered if they would ever sleep in it together.

One of the dark commas starts to move, to wiggle its tail, perhaps the first of the batch to emerge.

'In three months,' Addie says to the tadpole, smiling, 'you will be *a frog.*'

She laughs to herself: *You have no idea what a frog is, but you are one.*

Will he really come this time? Will it be OK? Will they find each other again, like they did in Tromso? She stares at the comma-tadpoles, thinking of the tiny cells inside them which will read their own DNA, causing their tails to be absorbed, their legs to grow, their gills to be covered, their lungs to be built, their intestines to adapt for digesting bugs instead of algae, their eyes to creep over their heads.

Imagine if human beings could change so drastically.

Imagine if she could.

. . .

Monday morning, the last of the term, and Sol is walking to school. After the Easter holiday, he will have one term left here. In December, he dug his way out of the cottage and took himself, wrapped and booted, to the airfield, and he watched the snow layering itself onto the wings of the plane. He felt trapped. He thought of Addie's seven years on Rokesby, and he understood her a little more.

As the snowbound days became a snowbound week, Sol sat, helplessly, and he wrote to the Chair of Governors, giving two terms' notice, and he hand-delivered the letter, thigh deep in drifts.

The Chair rang him, said, 'So what are your plans after the summer?'

'I'm going to travel,' said Sol, as the snow battered the window panes. 'I'm sorry to let you down.'

Sol feels bad for the children – he should have stayed longer – but pleased that Barry Forfitt will be leaving on the same day as he does. Barry knocked on his door on Christmas Day with a mince pie. He took Sol outside and blew a huge bubble with a new contraption he'd got from his aunt, and they stood together watching the bubble freezing into gold feathery shards, which closed over to make a hard glistening sphere, like a bauble.

'Happy Christmas, Mr Blake,' said Barry, turning down the path.

Sol stood staring at the frozen bubble.

'Happy Christmas, Barry.'

The bubble looked fragile, but it didn't break.

It comforted him.

When Sol sees Addie, if he's brave enough, he will tell her he's handed in his notice and he will ask her to travel with him and she will say no, he tells himself, though she might say yes. Until she says no, there is always that possibility. If she says no, he will go without her, and who knows what will happen?

Enough: he will not hypothesise. Except to think that he might die without her, but that he is also dying with her. If *with her* counts as mainly *without her*.

Sol loves the quiet emptiness of the early morning, the time of day when dinosaurs roam over hilltops and medieval burghers come past in horse-drawn carts. He takes his phone out of his pocket because he lives hoping that Addie will send a message. She doesn't. Except once a week. As they agreed.

Without seeing her, he loses faith in her existence, like he easily loses faith in God (who remains invisible), or his mother's long dark curls and throaty laugh (which are gone) or in the igloo in Tromso or the islands of Rokesby and Ora (which only exist as dreams exist in the morning).

Philosophically, he supposes this is solipsism, which holds that only one's own mind is certain to exist. Everything else cannot be known. *I think, therefore I am.* Yes, he does think, far too much, but thinking is not enough to make an existence, not a fulfilling one anyway. With Addie, he found himself reaching beyond his mind into his heart and his spirit and his body, which is probably what it means to be whole.

He might be fracturing again without her. He hasn't swum for months, which is a bad sign, a sign of his retreat into the mind. He wonders what Addie's thinking these days. He stares at his phone. There's no message from her.

1 April, says his phone.

April Fools' Day, which is hell, obviously, for a serious person. Puella walks beside Sol, and he talks to her, reassuring her that soon Puer will return from the sea and they will rub and tap each other's beaks and she will lay her egg, and everything will be well in the world.

Sol opens the door to the schoolhouse, follows the corridor to the kitchen, puts on the kettle, makes himself a cup of tea and sits at his desk. He looks out of the window at the goldfinches, and he says, aloud, 'April bloody Fools' Day.'

He googles *April Fool jokes for primary schools*. Give out O-shaped cereal, such as Cheerios, and tell your pupils to plant them to grow doughnuts. Absolutely not. Rearrange desks to face backwards? He supposes that would be possible, but whether it's funny, he's no idea. Remove all the chairs? Also possible. But excruciating.

Ah here's Miss Gunn taking off her coat, revealing – ta-da – the red tartan kilt, Royal Stewart.

'What do you think about facing all the chairs backwards?' he says.

'Backwards?' she says, grimacing as she flattens her hair into the helmet shape she favours. 'What? Away from the board?'

'Or we could remove the chairs all together?'

'Remove the chairs?' she says. 'Why on earth would we remove the chairs?'

'It's April Fools' Day,' says Sol gloomily.

'The children will think we've gone mad,' says Miss Gunn.

'Ah right. So leave well alone?'

He goes to the school door to greet the children.

'There's still time, isn't there, Mr Blake?' says Barry.

'Plenty, Barry. Plenty. Puer turned up some time after Puella last year.'

'One week and a day,' says Barry. 'I have my notes.'

Sol nods.

'I'm getting worried,' says Barry.

'Me too, Barry,' says Sol. 'Me too.'

Friday 5th April

In the early morning, Addie finds herself heading back to the elbow turn of the creek again, and there, she is rewarded by a mass of tadpoles. The commas have now grown tails, and are floating, free of the jelly, motionless, breathing through their gills, busy absorbing the remaining yolk from the egg.

Sol will be here later today, and she's hired a crappy little dayboat with a motor for his week with her. This time, there will be no obstacle between them, and she will throw herself into his arms, and she'll perhaps say, because she likes to rehearse the first line, 'What's the meaning of a single tadpole?'

Another comma emerges from the jelly.

'You are metamorphosing,' she tells the tadpole, a little unsure which syllable to stress.

• • •

As Sol flies away from Fair Isle in the early morning, he sees that Barry Forfitt is on the Jut, sitting by Puella's burrow. He waves at the plane with what looks like his striped scarf which probably doesn't smell of his mother any longer. Sol waves back through the porthole, though of course Barry can't see him. One more term, and in September he'll be off to boarding school on the mainland, and Sol can't think of any way to prevent this.

Sol finds himself thinking about his father's baby. He hopes it's a girl because his father can't love boys. Or couldn't love him.

Sol sent a postcard to his father and Bee a week ago to say that he would be in Norfolk with Addie, and would love to come and see the baby, *whenever he or she emerges.* He now rather regrets using the verb *emerges.* The more he thinks about it the more graphic it becomes.

Sol decides (again) to give Addie Poem Number 7.

•   •   •

Addie walks past the barn, and she thrills to the thought of her secret, which will be ready by the summer. Ah look, Tiffany, her favourite bride, is climbing out of her Land Rover.

Be more Land Rover – is there something in her mother's irritating metaphor? Could she *get off road* for him, she wonders. Go somewhere dangerous with him? As in, not necessarily a location.

Tiffany's hair is pulled back and she has mud on her nose, mud all over her in fact. She goes to the back of the Land Rover and takes out a tiny lamb.

'I had to bring her,' she says sadly. 'She's so little and a fox got her mother last night.'

Addie strokes the lamb's little dark face.

'Can I bring her in? She might shit.'

'Let's put her on this rug,' says Addie. 'Keep her away from the fabrics.'

Addie takes the wedding dress off the rail and unzips the protective cover, holding it high because Tiffany's tall and the dress is long. The lamb watches.

'I'm very dirty,' says Tiffany. 'I didn't think of that.'

'Would you like a shower?'

347

As Tiffany showers, Addie strokes the lamb, which shits on the rug.

'I never wear make-up. Do you think I should?' says Tiffany coming back out in a towel.

'I've got a few bits you could try. Though I don't really wear it either. We'll put it on once you're in the dress.'

She runs upstairs for her bag of make-up that she used when she went to the vicarage for the pre-wedding supper, and comes back down with it. Tiffany pulls her fair hair out of its elastic and turns her head upside down and shakes it. When she flicks her face up, her beauty is a shock – her strong cheekbones and her wide smile. She steps into her dress. Addie's cut it from guipure lace and lined it in silk, with a hand-crocheted *V* falling to a cut-out crocheted waistline and a scalloped front split and long lace sleeves tight over her lovely muscular arms.

The lamb bleats.

Addie brushes a little blusher onto Tiffany's cheeks.

'This really isn't me.'

'Or me.'

She hands Tiffany the coral lipstick and the mascara, and she thinks of girls she's seen in films doing this kind of thing with friends, and she feels, what is it, *normal,* and a little giddy, and not Mowgli or Cinderella at all. She can change. She has changed, even if her eyes haven't moved over the top of her head like the tadpoles. Not all change is drastic. Or fast. Look at avocadoes.

Tiffany says, 'Sean won't recognise me.'

And cries.

Addie finds that she's crying too.

The first time she's cried over a bride, though she probably isn't crying over a bride – her tears have simply been waiting to find something safe to attach themselves to.

'I know you said you don't normally go to weddings,' says Tiffany. 'But will you make an exception for me, Addie?'

'Possibly in exchange for a lamb!'

Tiffany puts her strong shepherding arms around her so tightly that Addie feels her feet leaving the ground.

．　．　．

By the time Sol boards the plane at Glasgow, he's flying into the powerful headwinds of unanswerable questions: will we find each other like we didn't in the summer? Will absence have made us bigger or smaller? Will this be the time that she says it's run its course? Please God, no. Or will this be the time that I say I can't do the puffin pact anymore? When I ask her to come travelling with me, will she say no? Of course she'll say no. And the thing is this: you can't love someone who isn't with you, who *refuses* to be with you. He hates to feel angry, but he is angry by the time he arrives at Stansted Airport.

As he drives down the familiar Norfolk lanes, though, his windows open to the damp reedy air, he finds his anger changing into a glorious hope that everything will be different, that she'll say yes, and it is this hope which powers him down the drive, through the gate, and there she is, there she is, there she is. He takes her into his arms, and they're a chemical reaction, he thinks, and he may well explode.

Addie stands back and looks at him the way you might look at something inanimate, say a painting, or a sculpture in a gallery. Sol folds his arms across his front.

'I did something very odd,' she says. 'I agreed to go to Tiffany's wedding.'

'When is it?'

'Saturday 13th. Just over a week.'

'Same day as the baby's due,' says Sol. 'I could come with you.'

'Will you see the baby if it comes while you're here?'

'If I'm invited to. Which I probably won't be. What about Tiffany's wedding? Would you like me to come?'

'I want to take you to see the tadpoles,' says Addie. 'Leave everything here. The sun's going down.'

As they walk across the lawn, Sol takes her hand in his, and their fingers interlock, finding their familiar spaces between each other, but her hand isn't quite a comfort to him because he's asked her twice and she hasn't said if she wants to take him to Tiffany's wedding.

'Look at the jetty!' says Addie. 'I've hired us a little dayboat with an engine.'

'Perfect,' says Sol.

'Oh look there's Little Hen,' says Addie. 'She's always on her own, and always so chirpy.'

'Puella's still waiting for Puer on the Jut,' says Sol, 'She's not chirpy. I guess it's harder to have had and lost than never to have had.'

'What do you mean?' says Addie, quick as anything. 'Little Hen *has* lots of things.'

Sol feels his stomach contract.

'Sorry,' says Addie. 'I didn't mean—'

'Don't worry,' says Sol.

'Can we start again?' says Addie.

He nods.

He watches Little Hen juddering her way forwards along the river, her neck moving back and forth, back and forth, and he's not sure if she does look chirpy. Birds probably don't look anything because they don't feel. Except, what about Puella? She seems to. Francis of Assisi and his mother would say that animals do feel. He walks with Addie between the last of the browning primroses, overtaken now by daffodils.

'You remember the primroses around those old arch stumps on Rokesby?' says Sol, determined to lift the mood.

Addie nods.

'You didn't tread on them so I knew you were a poet. Are you still writing poetry?'

He nods.

'Why do you never show me?'

'You said you don't like metaphors, which is tricky with poems. I wrote one for you called *The Arch*.'

'I'd like to read it,' she says.

She takes his arm to show him the tadpoles, and he doesn't care about the tadpoles.

'This is the question I have for you,' she says 'What's the meaning of a single tadpole? What's the point of it?'

'Tricky one,' says Sol.

She looks up at him.

'Maybe *becoming*,' he says. 'You know, fulfilling its potential.'

She nods.

'I mean, it wouldn't if it stayed a tadpole,' says Sol. 'I guess that's the thing we all dread. Stasis.'

'I don't know that word,' says Addie.

'Being stuck,' says Sol.

'Oh,' says Addie. 'And also, yes I'd love you to come with me to Tiffany's wedding.'

Sol smiles, lets desire run through him, feels it prickling the pores in his skin.

The moon has appeared in the still-light sky, perfectly spherical. It hangs in the silence of the breezeless evening, motionless, and, in his mind, not quite real, the way things aren't that you can't touch.

'But before that,' says Addie, smiling, 'let's definitely go inside.'

· · ·

'You remember the moon in *Blood Wedding*,' says Addie when they're in bed, languorous with the taste of each other. 'The bride's escaping from her wedding with Leonardo, and they don't want the moon to be so bright because it'll light them up and they'll be found.'

'I love it how you love my plays,' says Sol.

'I love it too,' says Addie. 'Pretending to be clever!'

'Anyhow?'

'I feel the opposite. I've got this strange new feeling. That I want to be completely found.'

Addie gets up and she opens the curtains wide, and the moon hangs, a great silver orb, over the reeds, against a dark screen of night, pin-pricked with light.

. . .

'What's that noise?' says Sol.

'Someone's bought the field over there and put two black horses in it. We can go and see them tomorrow. They do that every night. That mad whinnying.'

Sunday 7th April

On Sunday, Addie is woken by the sun, the curtains open to the glory of morning. She creeps to the glass doors, and the robin, frustratingly, flies away.

She yawns, hibernatory with their Saturdaying, when they didn't go and see the two black horses, when they hardly left the bedroom, when they only had energy for each other, caught in that Tromso time that is no time, the clocks stopped, the door locked, the clouds low, making an ethereal mist over the river, a permission to hide away.

But today, she feels the water calling.

· · ·

Sol wakes and leaps up to make them tea, and soon they're packing up provisions and heading for the crappy dayboat moored at the jetty, and they set off along the River Bure, passing the whinnying black horses, which gallop in a pair, mane and tails unleashed, and Sol says, 'Very Lloyds Bank,' and Addie says, 'Very *Blood Wedding*. He got on his horse and his horse went to her door. He couldn't stop it, and it wasn't up to him. I love that.'

Sol laughs and says, 'Precisely.'

He recalls the old meaning of *precision*, the shearing away of the extraneous, and he feels himself into that freedom from all that is inessential, which is all that is not here in the boat. The way he felt in Tromso, it comes again, as they make their way along the river.

• • •

At South Walsham Broad, Addie turns the boat towards a bank and moors, and she leads Sol down country lanes to an old barn, which has a sign saying ARCHITECTURAL SALVAGE, ODDS & ENDS, VINTAGE PAINTINGS, THEATRICAL MEMORABILIA. And here in the courtyard there are stone pillars and stone grey-hounds in sombre lines, and rusty garden furniture, and crumbling statues, and inside the first barn, Addie pores through old costumes, hung mustily on rails, recalling the smell of *Clara's Costumiers* in Braxham, and inside the second, there are trestle tables full of every manner of curiosity, from tiny porcelain animals to ancient potties to bald teddy bears, and then to the art barn, hung with paintings, crammed together in no sort of order, frames crumbling, paint flaking.

'Let's choose each other one thing,' says Addie. 'One thing for under twenty pounds. You start in this barn. Set your phone for five minutes and then we swap. Put it in a bag and we'll give them to each other over lunch.'

• • •

They prepare to eat their picnic on the open deck at the stern of the boat: sandwiches and crisps and cakes and strawberries and two glasses of wine – and two brown paper bags, one large, one small.

'You open first,' says Sol, hoping to get the experience over with. His normal routine when buying presents is to spend hours looking, and just as he approaches the till, to be overcome with a great wave of inadequacy, staring at said item in hand and thinking of a hundred different reasons why nobody in the world would possibly want or need it. This time, the deadline helped, though now he feels panic-stricken.

Addie grabs the small bag, feeling the shape of it, child-like in her excitement.

'It's very knobbly,' she says.

'Yes, I mean, you probably won't—'

'I'm going in!' says Addie, and she takes out a tiny metal octopus, perfectly formed, darkened with age.

'I wonder if it's silver, under the grime,' says Sol.

'Eureka!' says Addie. 'I didn't spot her. This couldn't be better.' She kisses him.

He feels her easy joy and he loves her.

His turn: the receiving nearly as nerve-wracking as the giving. The shape of a painting, no doubt about it. He reaches in without looking, pulls it out, and there it is, a flaking painting of a man on an ancient wooden sleigh being pulled across the snow by a team of dogs, tiny houses and fir trees behind weighted with snow, the gold frame cracked.

Sol says, 'Tromso!'

Addie hands him his wine, and takes hers: 'Today's the only day again!'

Saturday 13th April

Addie wakes to hear her robin trilling on the balcony, trembly, a little squeaky, even wistful, in the bright light of the morning.

The sun has been unusually present through the week; the mallard ducklings soft and golden in a line behind their mother as she and Sol trundled down rivers, across broads, into bluebell woods, to a wood-carving festival where a woman made story-telling chairs, the air, warm and desirous as they too have been warm and desirous, easy with each other in the spring air. They've spent their days on the river, picnicking on deck, lazing together on a rug on the lawn, their conversations light and playful, unburdened by the future, happily present, until yesterday afternoon, when Sol asked her what time they were leaving for Tiffany's wedding.

'Why did you say wedding like that?' she said, and she so wishes she could take it back.

'Like what?'

'Loudly, like you were making a point.'

Weddings really set something off in him, she reflects, before wondering if it is in fact that weddings really set something off in her. She was antsy for the rest of the day, and has been restive all night, turning over and over.

She gets out of bed, puts on her big white shirt and tiptoes to the window, drawing back the curtain. The robin doesn't fly away. Encouraged, she creeps to the kitchen for seed, and she returns, pushing her flattened palm through the opening in the glass doors.

The robin lands – she feels the sharpness of its feet on her palm – and starts to feed from her hand!

. . .

Sol wakes to see Addie facing away from him, the curtains pulled back on the right-hand side, the door open, her arm stretched through it, and the robin, finally, on her palm.

He was climbing up a rocky staircase with no railings and a sheer drop on each side, holding a baby in his arms, and the baby bounced out of his hands down the steps and crashed off the edge of the mountain. Is this a terrible sign? A warning? The baby is due today. His brother or sister. Half. And half Bee's, which is still quite odd.

Today is the wedding, and he's woken without peace, dream-addled and over-sensitive. His phone pings, and the robin flies away.

Addie turns round.

'I'm sorry,' he says. 'That was Rachel. Bee has contractions.'

'Only Barbara would have her baby on the actual due date. That was the first time he's fed from my hand! I thought our relationship was never going to progress.'

Sol chooses not to say anything, or at least not to say anything about relationships never progressing, because as she fed the robin in her white shirt, with her red curls around her shoulders and her bare muscular legs and her perfectly compact feet with her toenails painted different colours, she was more beautiful to him than she'd ever been.

But the wedding hangs over the day.

The wedding and now the dream.

He texts back a thumbs-up emoji to Rachel.

357

Then the baby bounces off the rockface again.
He closes his eyes, then opens them.

. . .

Addie puts on a flouncy dress she's made in red silk with black
dots on, like a flamenco dancer.

'Do I look too odd?'

'You look oddly lovely.'

'Is that your Deia suit?'

'Is it too smart?' he says.

'No idea,' says Addie. 'I think they're all farmers.'

'I feel inadequate around manly men,' says Sol.

'You need to change your definition of manly.'

She stands on the toes of her clogs and kisses his cheek.

As they climb into the blue Ford Fiesta, the new guests are
arriving at Mermaid Cottage, and Addie says, 'This car smells like
bad perfume.'

. . .

When they sit down on the hard wooden pew of the church, Sol
takes Addie's hand, and tries not to think about weddings, which
is quite hard at a wedding. Weddings don't matter, he tells himself.
What matters is the chemical reaction. When an atom of oxygen
meets an atom of carbon, it makes carbon monoxide, life oddly
becoming death, which is what life always does. Is that a poem?
Quite a depressing one. The organ is striking up.

As Tiffany comes into the church on her father's arm, Sol feels
tears in his eyes, and he wonders what he could possibly be crying
for or about. He doesn't know the bride or the bridegroom. But,
as he watches the bridegroom turn to see his bride approaching,
he sees in his utterly unmasked face the perfect meeting of hope
and hope, and he feels his own hope rising, and he tells it not to.

He hasn't told Addie that he handed in his notice, and he hasn't asked her to go travelling with him because they agreed to stay in the day. If he asks her, she'll have to answer, and he can't bear to hear. His phone pings, and he quickly turns it to silent.

As the wedding proceeds, as Tiffany and Sean make their highly risky vows, Sol panics about the silenced ping, worrying that there's something wrong with the baby, as the dream foretold, but he doesn't take his phone out because that would look rude, or as if he didn't respect the sacredness of the service.

He does respect the sacredness of the service, which is what he tells the woman sitting next to him at the wedding breakfast when she tells him that she thinks it's all a load of pointless crap.

'I disagree,' he says to her long, disappointed face. 'There's such power in saying I will love you forever. Nobody ever wanted their partner to say, I will love you for the next five minutes, or the next year, or the next five years, or as long as I feel like it, or as long as you don't piss me off.'

After saying this, he feels a little off-balance.

· · ·

The man to the right of Addie is called John. The seat to her left is empty, although there's a place card on the table saying Ellen. John is telling Addie in detail about every gig he's ever been to in his entire life. Occasionally Addie looks over at Sol, but he seems very involved with the woman who looks like a horse. She wonders why anybody would enjoy this kind of thing.

· · ·

'It's ridiculously risky to promise to love someone forever,' says the woman to Sol.

'The risk is what makes it beautiful.'

'Fifty per cent of all marriages end in divorce.'

'I don't think this one will.'

'How do you know Sean and Tiffany?'

359

'I don't.'

'Well, how do you know it won't end in divorce then?'

Sol hesitates.

'And also, why are you here if you don't know Sean and Tiffany?'

'Oh,' says Sol. 'I was invited by my . . .'

He stops.

My who?

Who is Addie exactly?

'Your . . .'

My *chemical reaction*?

He nods across the table at Addie, and says, 'The one with the red hair.'

As he does so, he remembers his phone pinging in the service.

'Excuse me,' he says, and he gets up and leaves the marquee, sitting down on a hay bale to take out his phone.

'Baby Blake in the world!' Rachel has written.

Sol texts, 'Boy or girl?'

'Boy.'

Oh dear, thinks Sol.

The speeches are about to begin. He loves a bridegroom's speech, or a bride's – the least cynical thing you'll ever hear in a cynical world. The best man's speech he dreads. The forced humour, the awkward vulgarity, men so pathetically trying to be men.

• • •

Addie laughs and cries through the speeches, including the best man's, which majors on what a great friend Sean is – this crying, so much crying, what is she crying for – and the band is now arriving: a man brings in his drums; another, an electric guitar; a girl brings in speakers; and a man in a trilby, microphones; and there are things in Addie's veins, tadpoles perhaps, little wiggling commas, or are they not tadpoles, are they perhaps mayflies, dragon-flies, fluttering things?

John has moved on to Live Aid in Hyde Park in 1985, which he went to when he was fifteen, and he's running through the relative merits of every act, worst to best, crescendoing to a peak with Freddy Mercury who was apparently wearing a white leotard. It was very hot. Addie can't quite remember who Freddy Mercury is.

'He was quite a character,' says the man.

Addie smiles.

'Tell me about your favourite gig,' he says.

Sean the bridegroom has a big blond beard and honest eyes, and he's big and burly and Tiffany is in his arms, and without meaning to, Addie has transposed her own head onto Tiffany's head and Sol's head onto Sean's and they are dancing, they are dancing, though she never intended them to.

'Do you dance?' says the man.

He doesn't know that she has never in her life danced, never been to a gig either. She hasn't been to any place where people might dance apart from her parents' wedding where people swayed about the garden of The Retreat with hens around their feet, and Sydney's band played songs that had no beat. She watched through the kitchen window as she loaded the dishwasher.

'Dance?' Addie replies. 'Oh, not much.'

Then she wonders if the man was asking her to dance with him, so she leaps to her feet, finding her feet to be less stable than when she sat down, and she rushes to the ladies, and inside her cubicle, as she wees several glasses of champagne into the bowl, she thinks that she must leave before the dancing gets going, but she remembers she's not here on her own, so it's only partly up to her.

She picks her way carefully back to the table and says to Sol, 'I think—'

But before she says what she thinks, he says, 'Yes, so do I. Shall we?'

'Shall we what?' she says, a little slurry from the champagne.

'Or maybe not?' says Sol. 'I really don't dance, in the normal run of things. I mean, at school, we had these dances where they bussed in girls. The other boys used to mark them out of ten. I always—'

'Or shall we go?' says Addie. 'I mean, make a move.'

Sol hesitates.

'I think,' he says, 'that maybe we should try dancing.'

'You know you and swimming?' says Addie.

'Yes,' says Sol.

'That's me and dancing.'

'OK. I'm afraid I don't have any flippers.'

Addie laughs.

She says, 'I think I'm a tiny bit drunk.'

'That might help. My mother used to say being drunk helps lots of things, including dancing.'

'What else?' says Addie.

'Writing poems. And talking to boring bastards at weddings.'

Addie laughs.

John who went to Live Aid when he was fifteen is staring at her.

Addie says, 'Who's Freddie Mercury again?'

Sol says, 'You know, the lead singer of Queen. He died in 1991.'

'Did he wear a white leotard?'

'I can't remember.'

Addie can see that Sol's nervous as he rises out of his chair and takes her hand.

'Becoming,' she says. 'That's what you said about the tadpoles, do you remember?

'What?'

The band starts playing a song that Addie remembers from Grandma Flora's Roberts radio.

'Freddie Mercury,' Sol whispers in Addie's ear. *'Crazy Little Thing Called Love.'*

They stand nervously at the edge of the dance floor, like two people about to dive off a cliff. Next to them is a girl wearing a silver dress with her hair in the highest longest pony tail Addie's ever seen, singing very loudly every word, and every echo. As she sings, she bounces and twirls on her silver-platformed feet, and her long pony-tail bobs and sways like the tails of the whinnying black horses when they gallop. She sings that this thing called love cries like a baby – *yes*, Addie thinks slightly hazily, *yes* – and that this thing called love swings and jives and shakes. *Maybe*, thinks Addie, perhaps, *possibly*.

Sol takes the plunge, pulling Addie with him, keeping hold of her hand, and he starts to move, he sways a bit, bounces about on his feet, and he can dance, he really can, he has flexible hips, he has rhythm, it must be those school dances, and he twists Addie around, and she lets herself twirl under his arms, and he pulls her to his warm chest, his chest which is hers, and nobody else's, and in she comes, and out she flies, and in again, and they are in the flow of it now, turning, turning, and she closes her eyes, and the girl in silver is bellowing take a long ride on my motorbike, and then there's a change of tempo and there ain't no mountain high enough, and the girl yells that no matter how far, call my name, and her pony tail lashes a woman's face so hard she has to leave the dance floor and pour water in her eyes, and it's hard now for Addie to know where she begins and where Sol ends because their bodies seem to have taken leave of their minds, and their minds are no longer in charge, and here in the marquee with the swirling green-purple-white lights, she is in Tromso, she isn't here, she is nowhere, or everywhere, or she is, perhaps, if only she could remember which syllable to stress, metamorphosing.

• • •

Sol is shocked to discover that they are still dancing when the guy in the trilby says it's the final dance. They are still dancing when the guy in the trilby says it really is the final, final dance, no kidding.

Sol finds he rather agrees with whoever the singer is, that though he has no idea what road exactly they are on, he doesn't want this night to end.

It will, of course.

Wednesday 17th April

Neither Addie nor Sol have talked about Tiffany's wedding, as if they're in some way embarrassed by the version of themselves that was there, that danced, that came home drunk, that made love in the sewing workshop and the sitting room and the kitchen like they were crazy.

Sol is out for the day, first seeing Tommie, then catching the train to London to see Tim because Addie needs to make some progress on her current wedding dress. She finds herself distracted by an unsettling thought, the thought that Sol's waiting for something to conclude.

She keeps looking at her phone.

She walks over to the broad for a swim to see if it might help her focus.

• • •

Sol is on his way back from seeing Tim in Aldgate when he finds himself going down the up escalator, his feet tangling with a large woman's feet and a wheelie case crashing into his shins. He mutters and turns around and bolts to the nearest gents toilet to recover his equilibrium and set out again as someone else.

Why would anyone go down the up escalator?

Once he's on the train, he thinks that maybe he's going down the up escalator *IRL*, as Tim would say. (Oh dear.)

His phone pings.

Addie: What's that word you told me when we were talking about tadpoles?

Sol: What word?

Addie: You know, being stuck?

Sol: Stasis.

Addie: What's the opposite?

Sol thinks for a second.

Sol: Dynamicity?

Addie: We have dynamicity!

That's what her text says.

He reads it, rereads it, rereads it.

The most promising sentence he has ever seen. Has their stasis finally turned to movement in the intense loveliness of this week on the river? Have they finally broken through the puffin pact? Are they no longer going down the up escalator? Have they ripened like avocadoes? *Too many metaphors, Sol, calm down.* Can he now ask her to travel with him this summer? He closes his eyes and remembers the dancing and the picnicking and the everything else.

He wants to tell her how much he's loved this week, but he realises that, despite his extensive vocabulary, he's actually terrible at talking about things. He has so many words inside his head, but never the right ones for what he wants to say.

He read in the paper, as Saturday's wedding synchrony crept away into Sunday's newspapered daylight, that in successful relationships you were supposed to talk about making love, ask awkward things about what exactly, precisely, anatomically, felt good and what didn't and whether, picture it, she'd ever like to use a vibrator. He couldn't imagine anyone actually doing this, or he certainly couldn't imagine himself doing it. He wasn't totally clear about vibrators.

When he and Tim went out for lunch, the tables were very close together in the small Italian restaurant and this gave him an excellent excuse not to bother to ask Tim whether he and Harriet had done this kind of talking. He suspected that Tim might not know about vibrators either.

Tim had run out of hope that he would ever find a woman as lovely as Harriet again. He told Sol that he didn't know how lucky he was to meet someone IRL. He actually said IRL, rather than in real life, and Sol thought of saying that this didn't suit him, talking in acronyms, and also, that in the same Sunday magazine, he'd read about something called the ick. Apparently, some women found that men talking in acronyms gave them the ick. Sol found that the word ick gave him the ick. He didn't bring any of this up. They talked about nothing and then Sol left.

He remembers saying FYI to Addie when he left her in his van in the car park in Seafields. He blushes. He stares at his phone.

We have dynamicity!

He tries out a few responses, his heart seeming to bob like a buoy in his chest. He settles on: By which you mean?

Addie replies: There are thousands of froglets at the edge of the broad. I never even saw the spawn here. They're going crazy!

You fool, Sol, you fool. The woman opposite him on the bench seat who's wearing a bright orange mac looks up, and Sol realises he has said *you fool* aloud. He clears his throat. It's the bloody froglets that have dynamicity, not him, not them. His phone pings. It's Bee.

Your father and I are wondering if you'd like to come and meet Baby Joseph.

For some reason, he reads this as Baby Jesus.

Thursday 18th April

'I won't wear the clogs to the vicarage this time,' says Addie, taking her green boots out of the wardrobe.

'I *will* wear the blue Chinos,' says Sol. 'Because I only ever wear blue Chinos.'

'They suit you,' says Addie, pulling on a black jumper onto which she has crocheted yellow stars, with sparkles.

It feels lovely getting dressed together, so ordinary.

'I could crochet stars onto your Chinos,' says Addie.

'And then I'd never leave the house,' says Sol, laughing.

When he laughs, his face changes.

'My clothes are a tribute to my grandmother. I wish you could have met her.'

'I wish you could have met my mother.'

• • •

Sol looks at his watch, panics and says, 'We should leave. We're going to be late. Prepare for a short speech on Maundy Thursday.'

'What does Maundy mean?'

'There are various theories. All dull. Do you really want to know?'

'Give me two theories.'

'I'll tell you on the way.'

They go downstairs and out into the drive, waving at the holidayers at Mermaid Cottage, who are taking photos of each other feeding mallards on the lawn. People always do this, without exception.

'How are you feeling?' says Addie, as he drives through the gate in the highly fragranced Fiesta.

'Tense,' says Sol.

'So, Maundy Thursday?'

'Well, it could be Maundy from *mandare*, Latin for command. Because at the Last Supper, Jesus gave a new commandment – love each other as I have loved you – and he washed their dirty feet.'

'I love that,' says Addie. 'God washing dirty feet.'

'But I always think if *mandare* was the root of it, why wouldn't it be Mandy not Maundy?' says Sol. 'Am I boring you? Because I'm boring myself.'

'What's option two?'

'Maundy from *mendicare* in Latin, to beg. This is more about the maundy purses of alms, traditionally given to the poor.'

'But then wouldn't it be Mendy Thursday?'

'Let's make it Mendy Thursday.'

'I crocheted a blanket for the baby,' says Addie. 'It's not blue.'

'It isn't pink, is it?' says Sol. 'I don't think I can take Dad's reaction.'

'Primrose yellow,' says Addie.

'Highly risky,' says Sol, and he turns into his father's road, and as he crunches over the vicarage drive, he feels the fear he's always felt approaching his own front door. His father painted it dark grey, over his mother's red. He'd never liked the red, he said.

'I hate that grey front door,' says Sol.

'Grandma Flora painted the front door every year,' says Addie.

'Different colours?'

'Yes, but she also painted things on it.'

'Things?'

'Like, I don't know, bees. She put bees on everything. I do too.'

And this is why I love you, Sol doesn't say.

Sol says, 'I want bees on my front door,' surprising himself.

As Sol pulls up the hand brake, he says, 'I had a dream about cliffs. I dropped a baby. Do you think it means something terrible about Joseph?'

'I imagine it means you feel a bit weird about him.'

'Not that I'm going to kill him?'

'Don't be ridiculous.'

There's his father, opening the door, looking at his watch. There's nothing discernibly different about him since he married Bee, impregnated her, made a baby, became a new father at the age of nearly fifty.

Sol opens the door of the car, and Addie opens hers, at exactly the same moment. He wants to say to his father, You should have seen us dancing – he's no idea why.

'Well, well, well,' says his father, and Sol, as usual, can't think what sort of response he might make.

His father stares around him.

'So here you are,' he comes up with.

'Yes,' says Sol, approaching, thinking what will it be? Obviously not a hug, possibly a handshake, possibly nothing.

Ah yes, nothing.

Just a little awkward linger on the doorstep before his father turns into the dark hall. His mother liked to leave lights on. His father likes to say he's good with money. He remembers his mother saying, 'You're good at saving it and I'm good at spending it.' And his father replying, 'Anyone can be good at spending it. The skill is in the saving.' Then his mother going on, boldly, 'You wouldn't know where to start on a big splurge. You just don't have the skills.'

His mother always seemed as if she was flying up above their arguments, and was never cowed by his explosions. Sol wonders if his father explodes at Bee as he did at his mother. He hopes not. He sees the baby bouncing off the cliff face and falling into the abyss. He should tell his father not to explode at Joseph.

'Mother and baby doing well,' says his father, still walking ahead of Sol.

Sol wonders why he says it like that with no articles and no auxiliary verb, as he and Addie follow his father upstairs, and up again.

As the door opens into Sol's bedroom, which is clearly no longer Sol's bedroom, it reveals Bee in a pale blue dressing gown, looking faintly Virgin Mary, sitting holding Baby Joseph, in a low chair Sol doesn't recognise. Or is it a dressing gown? Or possibly some kind of wrap-around dress? He thinks new mothers have to wear specially designed clothes to keep their breasts accessible. He definitely doesn't want to think about Bee's breasts.

More importantly, he thinks, *this is my bedroom, where did you put all my stuff? And should you have told me or am I being unreasonable?*

. . .

'Oh look at you, Joseph!' says Addie, moving towards Barbara.

Barbara says, 'Would you like to hold him? You know about holding the neck, don't you?'

'Yes,' says Addie. 'I was six when my brother was born. I know all about the neck.'

She takes the baby, and as she does so, she has the strangest feeling. The feeling of *being* the baby. For a second. The feeling of her mother taking her and immediately handing her away.

'Do you know about the neck?' says Barbara to Sol. 'You have to support it. It's still at the floppy stage.'

. . .

Sol can't stop looking at Addie holding Baby Joseph, supporting his neck. He dismisses and re-dismisses the dream.

He remembers Tiffany's bridegroom, Sean, the turn of his head as Tiffany walked down the aisle, hope meeting hope, love pledging love, in a surge of wanting so big that you could almost feel it making something that didn't previously exist. He looks at Addie, and she looks back, and he doesn't know if she will ever find the means to join her hope to his to make something new out of it.

She says, 'Sol, do you want to hold your baby brother?'

Sol finds that he has tears in his eyes as he says, 'No, I don't think I dare. Not with the neck.'

He mustn't cry in front of his father.

Why on earth does he want to cry?

This is most unexpected.

. . .

Addie stares at the tear running down Sol's cheek.

'When you held me,' he says to his father, wiping away the tear. 'I mean when I was a baby, did you worry about my neck?'

'Well,' his father says. 'I can't say that I exactly remember. You know, it's some time ago.'

His father laughs nervously and his left hand plays the piano on his corduroy thigh.

Addie watches Sol saying, 'Were we always odd with each other, Dad?'

Baby Joseph is asleep in her arms, and his warmth feels good against her chest.

'Or was there a bit I can't remember?' Sol says, turning, his face open and hopeful, to his father. 'I always hope there's a bit I can't remember.'

Addie can't bear to hear his father's answer. She can't stand the look of vulnerability on Sol's face. She wonders, to distract herself from Sol's hopeful face, if there's a bit she can't remember with her mother.

'I hope you'll be able to give Joseph what you couldn't give me,' says Sol because his father, unbearably, still hasn't answered.

Addie doesn't move.

Nobody moves.

'I really mean that, Dad. And I hope you'll be able to give Bee what you couldn't give Mum.'

. . .

Sol knows he shouldn't have said that, yet he can't quite bring himself to regret it.

'Your mother,' says Bee in a loud, firm voice.

Sol and Sol's father and Addie are all looking at Bee, and Sol is wondering what on earth Bee will say about his mother. He thinks, *you may have married my father but that doesn't give you any right to speak about my mother.*

'Your mother,' Bee begins again, in the same loud, firm voice, 'didn't love your father, Sol.'

'I don't blame her,' says Sol.

Then he says, 'I'm sorry. I shouldn't have said that. And definitely not now. You've just had a baby. It's a vulnerable moment.'

But Bee continues.

'You must stop putting your mother on a pedestal, Sol.'

'This isn't the moment,' says his father. 'Perhaps there are things it's better not to know. You know, Genesis 2. The tree.'

'It needs to come out,' says Bee. 'There will never be a right time. And I'm feeling strong.'

'Ah good,' says Sol, wanting the conversation to end. 'We actually brought Joseph a present.'

He nods anxiously at Addie, hoping that the yellow blanket might divert the conversation elsewhere.

'I haven't finished,' says Bee. 'Stephen, I think you need to take

373

Sol out and have that conversation. Like we agreed. There's been too much hidden in this family.'

Sol's father stutters, 'I'm not—'

'Darling,' says Bee.

Bee has just called his father darling, and the air seems to crackle with the dazzling unexpectedness of this.

'Darling,' she begins again, yes again she dares, with such confidence. 'Tomorrow is Good Friday. It might be the perfect day for it.'

Sol's father smiles at Bee in a way that seems to approve of her more totally, Sol thinks, than he has ever approved of a human being before.

'In that case,' says his father. 'Let's go to my study.'

· · ·

Joseph has fallen asleep in Addie's arms.

'You were probably a bit surprised by my outburst,' says Barbara. 'But I've felt for a long time that Sol should know. It's time for everyone to grow up, don't you think?'

Barbara is no longer the uncertain bride who came for dress fittings.

'You see, Stephen's marriage to Sol's mother was very difficult, and Sol always blamed Stephen for that.'

Addie remembers that Sol and Barbara were once together. Perhaps his chest was once hers too. Horrible thought. Perhaps they danced.

'There are always two sides to a story,' Addie begins, wishing she'd thought of something that wasn't a cliché, something that supported Sol better, or proved her own superior knowledge of Sol's emotional life.

'There is sometimes one side,' says Barbara. 'Or one important side.'

Addie searches for something to say, but too late, Barbara is speaking again.

'His mother had another man, you see,' says Barbara. 'And I don't think Sol ever knew. But it changes so much.'

'Oh,' says Addie. 'Oh dear.'

'Yes, I thought if Sol knew that, it might help him see things more clearly, and stop blaming his father for everything. You know, it might give their relationship a chance. Do you agree?'

'You know,' says Addie, 'I don't want to speak for Sol.'

Barbara peers at her.

Joseph wakes up and makes a mewling cry, so Barbara gets to her feet, lifts him from Addie's arms, sits back down, opens the button of her light blue wrap dress, and offers him a breast. This is not the breast Addie knows. It is spherical and veiny and swollen, and would have been perfect for filling out her wedding dress. Her nipple protrudes like a small cork. Her breast has metamorphosed. Joseph clasps his mouth around it. Addie tries not to stare.

'The feeding's come so easily,' says Barbara.

Addie worries what might be happening in the study.

'What's going on with you and Sol?' says Barbara over the sucking noises. 'I mean, you hardly ever see each other, but then—'

Addie interjects, 'We both have our separate lives.'

'Yes, but do you also have a together life?'

'Whatever that means,' says Addie.

'You sound like Prince Charles,' says Barbara. 'You know in that terrible engagement interview with Diana when they asked him if he was in love. Are you in love with Sol?'

Addie stutters.

'Forgive me for being bold,' she says. 'But, you know, we're family.'

Addie thinks, *no we're not, no we're not family, whatever makes you think we're family?*

She says, 'I crocheted a blanket for Joseph. It's actually yellow like the room.'

'We were hedging our bets,' says Barbara.

She pauses.

'Addie,' she says. 'Are you hedging your bets with Sol? Are you with him, or half with him, until something better comes along?'

Addie hates this question.

'How about you, Barbara?' says Addie. 'Did the sex work out in the end? Did you like it more than coffee?'

•   •   •

Sol finds it odd that his father is sitting with him on the sofa, when he normally looks down on him from his leather swivel desk chair. His father updates him on various worthy things his worthy cousins have done. Then he stares out of the window before twisting his head around towards Sol and saying, 'Bee thinks I need to treat you like a grown-up.'

This feels both true and deeply patronising.

'The thing is this,' says his father, breathing in and out, head turned away.

Sol waits.

'There was a complication,' says his father, twisting his head back. 'With your mother.'

'What sort of a complication?'

'A human one.'

'What sort of a human complication?'

'It was the bird warden over on Miss Turner's Island,' says his father.

'Tommie,' says Sol. 'What do you mean? What was him?'

His father is staring through the bay window beyond his desk to the dark hedge and the neighbours' high window, their fat tabby cat sitting on the window sill, face on.

'Your mother wanted a divorce. But I said no,' says his father. 'She said she wouldn't give him up. Whatever I did or said.'

'Tommie?' says Sol, and his voice comes out slightly higher than he would have liked.

His father nods.

'I said she could see him but not commit adultery.'

'Tommie?'

Voice lower this time, getting a grip.

'Yes. I told your mother she should keep it quiet. For your sake, Sol, and your sisters. Though it pains me to say it, she felt for him what she couldn't feel for me.'

Sol can't think of one thing to say. Wouldn't his mother have told him? She told him everything. His father always said they were *in cahoots*. When he looked up its roots (because he always liked etymology), it came from the French *cahute*, hut. They were in *the hut* together. They often *were* in the hut with Tommie on Miss Turner's Island, or in the bird hide, huddled together with binoculars and hot chocolate and cake. Tommie was the only man Sol knew who baked cakes.

They were always, apparently, looking for the bittern, a bittern, any bittern, which was never there, so they had to go back and back and back. He now sees that a bittern makes a rather useful accomplice to a love affair. He was a boy, and he would never have guessed that bitterns and cakes were anything but bitterns and cakes. He ate the cake and sketched the birds with Tommie and was happy to be away from his father.

'Why didn't you let her divorce you?' says Sol quietly, feeling the cogs of his mind turning.

'In my position,' says his father. 'I mean, how could I possibly have credibility with the congregation?'

'So it wasn't to do with us, Leah and Rachel and me, it was to do with your reputation?'

'Well, it was such an awful thing being a vicar and—'

'It's nothing to do with being a vicar.'

'It's everything to do with being a vicar. Look at the position she put me in. My whole life and career would have imploded if people had found out.'

'Do Leah and Rachel know?'

'Bee says I should tell all of you,' says his father. 'But I'll see how I go. I don't want them to think less of me.'

He hesitates.

Sol stares at him, and his father adds, 'Or her. Of course.'

'Is that it then?' says Sol, feeling a powerful desire to get out of the dark study.

'Please, Sol, please never tell anyone else,' says his father. 'Bee said I could trust you not to. And you won't tell . . .'

Can he not remember Addie's name?

'I don't like the way she looks at me,' says his father.

Sol gets up.

'Bee felt it would help us, you know, you and me, if you knew,' says his father, and his face looks different, as if a layer has been peeled off. 'She thought it might stop you blaming me for everything.'

'We should leave you in peace,' says Sol, and he reaches out and puts his hand on his father's shoulder.

His father stands rigid, and the top layer returns to his face.

• • •

Addie gets into the car, examining Sol carefully.

When the doors are shut, he says, 'My mother was apparently having some kind of a thing with Tommie.'

'Tommie? Barbara told me she had another man.'

'My father said he didn't allow her a divorce. Allow her!'

'Because?'

'Because he was a vicar. So he apparently told Mum she could still see Tommie but not commit adultery. Which is a very Dad thing to say.'

'No sex?'

'I guess that's what he meant. He was never very keen on too much sex.'

Addie laughs, and adds, 'Though apparently it's all going well in that department with him and Barbara.'

'I don't want to know,' says Sol.

'Seriously though, how are you feeling?'

'No idea,' says Sol.

'Is it possibly good that it's out in the open? Is there a chance it could even be *Mendy Thursday*?'

'If there's any chance of it being Mendy Thursday, I think I should go and see Tommie.'

'Yes, of course you must. Drop me here. I'll walk back.'

'I'll take you home first,' says Sol. 'It was so much better with you there. The whole thing, you know, being alive, would be unthinkable without you.'

Being alive would be unthinkable without you.

His words hit her at the bottom of her back, the sacroiliac, the joint that supports the entire weight of the upper body. She feels her ligaments contracting, and she grasps for something she might say. Being alive would be unthinkable without him too. She mustn't, mustn't, feel this. She must be strong and chirpy on her own like Little Hen.

'All good on the yellow blanket by the way,' she says in a breathy kind of voice. 'What with the matching yellow room.'

'I couldn't believe it wasn't blue.'

They both appear to be holding their breath.

'Barbara said they were hedging their bets with yellow as they didn't want to find out the sex of the baby beforehand.'

Still holding their breath.

'Fair enough.'

'She asked if I was hedging my bets with you.'

As the words come out of her mouth, Addie knows she shouldn't have said them, and the ligaments tighten again around the base of her spine. Not everything bears repeating.

'I obviously said I wasn't,' says Addie, as fast as she can. 'I'm sorry. I shouldn't have told you that.'

'It's OK,' says Sol, meaning that it really isn't OK, and then he says, 'I'd better get going to Tommie's. I won't be long.'

'Don't be, will you?' says Addie, as she climbs out of the car. 'We have so little time left, and I want us to get out on the river this afternoon.'

• • •

Is she hedging her bets, Sol asks the air of the Fiesta. The smiley-face air freshener swings in response, and he realises how much he hates its sweet vanilla and orange smell.

Was his mother really having an affair with Tommie?

The air freshener swings again, releasing its cloying smell up Sol's nose. He tries to take it off the rear-view mirror, but it won't come, and he nearly veers into an approaching car, and he thinks of Addie's father, the way he killed his wife, slowly.

It's awful to learn something new about his mother when there are no new conversations to be had, no questions to be answered, no way of re-sculpting the past together. No, she is forever unknowable, and he misses her, the mother he knew completely. How much do we know of anyone? How much will he ever know of Addie? *Is* she hedging her bets?

He reaches The Amusements, parks the car on the kerb, gets out, moves the metal fence, drives in, gets out, moves the fence back into position, gets back in, unties the air freshener and puts it in the glove box, from where it still emits its cloying smell as he heads for the caravan.

And there's Tommie, except it isn't Tommie, or not the Tommie he's known until now. He parks the car and Tommie rushes out to greet him.

'Let me make you some lunch,' says Tommie.

Sol sits on the deckchair, tapping his feet as he prepares to ask him about his mother, but he isn't able to, it turns out, not at lunch, nor when they go for a walk along the river, nor when they stand and watch the grebe on her nest, no, the wordsmith can't find the words again, not over tea and lemon cake, ah lemon cake, he remembers, but he still isn't ready.

'You don't think we could go over to Miss Turner's Island?' says Sol.

• • •

As the afternoon wears on, Addie's anger intensifies. *Why would he waste one of their precious days together?* She absolutely understands that he needed to see Tommie, but he doesn't need to stay all bloody day. She told him she wanted to get out on the river this afternoon, and the afternoon's nearly over.

She texts, more and more curtly, but he doesn't reply, so she takes her tail to the broad, stopping off to see the dynamic froglets, but they've leaped away. Because nothing stays the same.

Dynamicity or decline, but never stasis.

What a statement! So clever and bookish! But is it true, she wonders as she puts on her tail and swims through the weed.

• • •

As Tommie guides the boat expertly to the jetty on Miss Turner's Island, Sol prepares himself again. They both get out.

'I think my mother used to escape to be with you here,' says Sol to the top of Tommie's head as he ties the painter to the post. 'In fact, Tommie, let me come straight out with it. This morning, I found out that my mother wasn't only coming to Miss Turner's Island for the bitterns . . .'

381

Tommie stands up.

'I found out she was coming for you,' says Sol. 'My father told me, on the advice of his new wife, so I understand.'

They are standing on the jetty, close together, face to face, looking straight into each other's eyes.

'Told you what exactly?'

'That's what I'm not so sure about,' says Sol. 'My father said he knew you were seeing each other, but he didn't *permit* her to commit adultery. Which was a very Dad thing to say though didn't strictly speaking make much sense.'

Tommie puts his hand through his thinning hair.

'I can't really see my mother holding back,' says Sol. 'She wasn't a very holding back sort of person.'

'You probably don't want to get involved in the technicalities,' says Tommie.

'I think I do need to know,' says Sol. 'I think you were lovers, weren't you?'

'I'm afraid we were,' says Tommie, and he looks anxious and not very loverish at all, though of course, Sol reminds himself, anybody can be a lover, even him. This week. Still dizzying.

'When did the whole thing start?' says Sol. 'If you don't mind me asking.'

'Shamefully, it started before she got married, but for lots of reasons, your mother didn't feel she could get out of the engage-ment. So it went ahead. We kept trying to break it off. And we did manage for a couple of years but then we gave in again. Is this a terrible thing to find out?'

'Surprising,' says Sol. 'But not terrible. It helps that I like you. I always did. You were nice to me when I was little. You made good cakes.'

Tommie's face creases into an anguished smile.

'And, though it's awful to say this, it probably also helps that my father wasn't nice to me at all. He never has been.'

'Your mother and I both carried terrible guilt. I still do. He wasn't an easy man, but perhaps nobody's easy when their wife's in love with someone else.'

'I think he would have been difficult anyhow,' says Sol.

'Let me make hot chocolate,' says Tommie, and they sit on the bench outside the hide, slurping, and Sol feels he might like to stay here and be a child again.

A barn owl swoops towards them.

The owl's white face – dark eyeslits, hooked nose-beak – splits the grey air, and Tommie puts his arm around Sol's shoulder and says, 'What a gift.'

• • •

As Addie walks back from the broad in the near-dark, hair wet, anorak on, she sees Sol's car, and it infuriates her, he infuriates her, everything infuriates her.

'I've been so worried,' she says as he gets out of the car. 'I can't believe you didn't answer my messages.'

'We were over at Miss Turner's Island,' says Sol. 'The messages only came through when we got back. And then I answered, but you must have been swimming. Let's get inside. You must be freezing.'

'I'm not freezing,' Addie finds that she is saying. 'I'm furious.'

'Furious?'

'Because I never thought you'd be gone so long. And also, we have so little time before you leave—'

'And whose fault is that?' says Sol, his eyes flashing like she's never seen before. 'I'd give you all my time. All of it. Forever. You know that. Don't you? Here it is – the whole of my life. The whole of me. You can have it. But you don't want it.'

'I do want it,' yells Addie, surprising herself because she isn't a person who yells, and also what is she saying?

'Well then, have it!' he yells back. 'Stop hedging your bets!'

'Don't you dare say that,' Addie shouts. 'You know I'm not hedging my bets. I've only ever wanted you. Nobody else. Hedging your bets is choosing, isn't it? Between two people?'

'You *are* choosing between two people!' Sol shouts.

'And who is this second person?' shouts Addie, finding that she is starting to shiver, cold water dripping down her neck from her hair.

'You!' says Sol. 'You're choosing between yourself, relying on yourself, taking a bet on yourself, forever. Or choosing us. Do you see that? And also, you need to go inside and get warm. You're shaking.'

Addie walks inside without looking at him and closes the door behind her.

• • •

Sol doesn't have any keys, that's what comes to him, and he isn't sure he dares to ring on the door. He hears a voice behind him, and he turns and a long-haired woman, one of the guests, is walking down the drive preceded by a strong smell of Chinese take-away. Sol finds himself coming over all Hugh Grant, hopping from foot to foot as he assures her that everything is totally fine, it's just he's mislaid his key, and although he doesn't have, and has never had, a key, he is searching through his pockets to find it.

'You'd better get inside,' he says. 'Your food will go cold.'

'Oh look!' says the long-haired girl, pointing at a light going on in the upstairs window of The Boathouse. 'I think she's in. You can ring on the door.'

'Wonderful,' says Sol, as the girl heads for the front door of Mermaid Cottage.

He acts as if he's walking towards the front door, but when he's sure the girl and her Chinese take-away are inside, he shuts himself in his car to try to get over the fact that he has shouted at Addie. *He has shouted at Addie.* Yelled at her. He doesn't shout at anyone, so why would he shout at her? He hates himself. He always promised himself that he wouldn't be like his father, that he would be a person who never shouted, and more specifically, never shouted at someone he loved.

He sits in his car suffocating in the vanilla-orange scent of the air freshener wafting from the glove box, wondering what Tommie meant, what was *the gift*: the barn owl, the island, the moment, his mother, or feasibly himself. Himself, a gift? Hardly. He opens the glove box, takes out the air freshener and gets out of the car. The guests at Mermaid Cottage are staring at him through the sitting room, so he has to look confident as he approaches the door.

He rings. He waits. He does not turn to see if the guests are still watching from the window. He hears, or at least he thinks he hears, Addie's footsteps on the stairs, and he hears, or at least he thinks he hears, the thump-thump of her slippered feet on the wooden floor of her workshop, and she opens the door.

She says, 'What's that?'

He realises that he has the smiley-face air freshener dangling from his left forefinger on a string.

'Ah yes,' he says. 'I wondered if I could throw this in the bin.'

She starts laughing.

'Who else would try to make up an argument with that on their finger?' she says.

'I've no idea how to make up. I've only really argued with people in my head until now.'

'What about your dad?' says Addie.

'I'm getting bolder since I met you, but not bold enough to properly let go and yell,' says Sol. 'You know, like just now. So I've never had any need for making up.'

'We did rather let go,' says Addie. 'Like the dancing.'

'Well not much like the dancing.'

'It's all part of the same thing, isn't it?'

The orange and vanilla smell wafts up Sol's nose.

The night is very still.

Very silent.

'I was just wondering if I could come in. Or—'

'Or?' says Addie, smiling, tilting her head at him.

'If only to throw this in the bin?' says Sol, nodding at the dangling smiley-face.

'If we throw it in the bin, the whole place will stink.'

'So?'

'Chuck it in the outside bin,' says Addie, gesturing over the drive.

'You won't lock me out when I turn my back?' says Sol.

As he turns, the guests are watching out of the window, standing in a row, putting food in their mouths.

Probably prawn crackers, Sol thinks.

Friday 19th April

'Happy Good Friday!' says Addie tentatively when she wakes.

'Um,' says Sol. 'We don't normally say that.'

'Why not?'

'Well, it's, you know, not that happy, the crucifixion.'

'So why's it good then?'

'There are so many views on this,' says Sol. 'And I'm just waking up.'

'But what's your view?'

Sol rubs his eyes.

'It's good because Jesus lived his principles of love and non-violence so seriously that he allowed himself to be killed by the people who hated him, rather than retaliate.'

'I need time to think about that. Why don't people ever mention that?'

'I'm not sure.'

'How do you feel about your mum and Tommie this morning?'

'I'm glad she found happiness, but I hate it that she didn't tell me. She was so against lying, and it turns out she lied to me her whole life.'

387

'I'm not sure it's a thing a mother would, or should, tell a child,' says Addie.

Then she pauses.

'It makes me feel a bit hopeful in a way,' she says. 'The way they managed to love each other part-time. You know, they had their own puffin pact. And it worked.'

'We have no way of knowing if it worked.'

Addie feels herself shrink.

'Maybe you should ask Tommie,' she says. 'See if he's got any tips.'

'I guess he chose to make a huge sacrifice,' he says.

'Is that the same as compromise? Brides always go on about how you have to compromise in a marriage.'

'I think sacrifice is giving up things you have whereas compromise is giving up things you might have,' says Sol.

'Like Eureka giving up her actual life for her babies?'

'Yes, isn't it giving up something really valuable for something else really valuable? Or at least, that's how I see it.'

• • •

'What are you supposed to do on Good Friday?' says Addie.

'Think about the way Jesus laid down his life,' says Sol. 'Even killing God oddly couldn't put him off us, so he—'

'Jumped back up like a divine jack-in-a-box?'

Sol laughs: 'Kind of.'

'But what do you actually *do* on Good Friday?'

'Immerse yourself in the suffering in the world.'

'Are there any other options?' she says, smiling.

He loves her, and perhaps that is enough, he needs to keep jumping back up, whatever happens, like a jack-in-a-box.

'Perhaps we needed the argument to appreciate coming back together,' says Addie, moving towards him. 'Are we allowed to touch each other on Good Friday? Or is that not very respectful of the suffering?'

Saturday 20th April

'Of course you must go and say goodbye to Tommie,' says Addie over breakfast on the balcony. 'But promise not to be too long. We can't possibly have another argument. It's our last day together.'

'I promise,' says Sol. 'What are you going to do while I'm gone?'

'It's a secret.'

•   •   •

In the car, Sol wonders if he should be optimistic about Addie's secret. He wonders if he will tell her today that he's resigned, and that he's going travelling. If he will ask her to come too. He imagines he might need to have a second breakfast with Tommie, and yes, as he draws up outside the caravan, the table is set.

'Our farewell banquet,' says Tommie.

'Tommie,' says Sol. 'There's this one thing I've been wondering.'

'Which is?'

'How you coped being with Mum part-time.'

'I'm not entirely sure I did cope,' says Tommie.

'I'm not sure I'm coping either,' says Sol.

'Coping with what?'

'Coming and going. Like a puffin. It's what Addie and I agreed

389

last spring because it's all she can handle. Possibly all she will ever be able to handle. She's had a hard time with love before, you see. She lost someone very close to her and never really got over it. But I'm not sure I can cope with all the goodbyes. All the hope. Maybe it's the hope I can't stand.'

Tommie nods.

'Did you ever give Mum an ultimatum? Say it's all or nothing?'

'I didn't,' says Tommie. 'She couldn't manage *all*. So it would have been *nothing*. I didn't want nothing, and I knew she didn't either.'

• • •

Addie opens the door of the barn and stares at the ambulance.

The long-haired guest comes over.

'What's that in the barn?' she says.

'Nothing,' says Addie, pulling the doors shut.

'Please don't say anything to my . . .' she says, hesitating.

My what, Addie wonders.

'Oh why?' says the long-haired girl.

'Just if you don't mind, don't mention it if you see him,' says Addie.

'Did you have a row the other night?' says the girl.

Addie doesn't answer.

'I think he's gorgeous,' says the girl. 'You know, in that posh English sort of way. He's definitely a keeper, that one.'

Addie can't think of one thing to say to her.

'Well, thank you for everything,' says the girl. 'We're off now.'

'Thank you for coming,' says Addie.

The guests head off.

He's definitely a keeper.

Funny expression.

Like a zoo-keeper.

Do people keep people?

Is that the thing?

That she doesn't want to be kept?

Or, if she does want Sol to keep her, as in hang onto her, and if she does want to keep him, as in hang onto him, she's frightened of wanting it, or frightened of what it might mean. The giving up of her autonomy. Is that the sacrifice? She opens the barn doors again and climbs into the ambulance. She picks up the bag of Easter eggs, and she stares about, feeling a shiver of satisfaction at the work she's done so far. He will love it. She wonders if she should show him this afternoon or wait until it's finished this summer.

Addie takes the bag, locks the ambulance, closes the barn doors and starts to make her way around the garden, like Grandma Flora, along the path to the creek, hiding eggs as she goes, back across the garden, over to the broad.

· · ·

When Sol gets back, earlier than he said, Addie is waiting for him, wearing her big black anorak.

'Shall we get in the water?' she says.

'I didn't bring my flippers,' says Sol.

'I can't believe it,' says Addie.

'They're quite big to fit in hand luggage,' he says. 'Also I kind of lost the desire.'

He wishes he hadn't put it like that.

'Will you come to Fair Isle for Half-Term this year?' he says.

'It's such a busy time for dresses,' says Addie. 'Perhaps if you come to me again in May, I'll come to you in July.'

'So much coming and going,' he says. 'It's so exhausting.'

'Did Tommie have any tips?'

'He never gave Mum an ultimatum,' says Sol. '*I guess he just let her make him unhappy.*'

He knows he shouldn't have said that.

'I'm going swimming,' says Addie.

He watches her put on her tail, and she is again the mystery girl he saw on the rocks, the mermaid who blew over to Ora in a storm, and he wonders who he was before he met her, and who he'd be if he moved on from her, and he wonders how unhappy he's willing to be for her.

• • •

Addie swims half-heartedly, and she's not sure she's ever swum half-heartedly.

Tommie let his mother make him unhappy.

That's a terrible thing to say.

Don't ruin the last day, she says to herself, not after a week like this. She gets out and she dries and gets dressed, but she can't see him anywhere. She goes into the garden, and there he is, sitting on the jetty, looking over the river.

'I have a surprise,' she says.

She looks into his eyes and sees, for the first time, uncertainty, or if not uncertainty, then perhaps distance, as if he's already moving away from her, although they have all of today, a whole night before he leaves.

'I've hidden Easter eggs,' says Addie, but she feels he's only half listening. 'Here's a basket to put them in.'

• • •

Sol takes the basket but he feels self-conscious as he lifts stones and looks into bushes. If the children could see Mr Blake on his own Easter egg hunt!

Is this the secret she promised? He clearly over-anticipated.

He feels a fool doing this.

When they reach the elbow bend of the creek, there's a dead froglet on the bank, which neither of them mentions. Little Hen is dabbling in the reeds, alone, surrounded by the mallard pairs, as usual. Sol wonders if she looks chirpy or not chirpy, but he won't bring this up. They go back past Mermaid Cottage towards the broad, where Sol finds a few eggs beside the reeds, and they walk up to the terrace, where he finds more eggs between the terracotta pots. They sit on the cushionless sofas and they eat the chocolate eggs, one after another, too quickly, saying, exaggeratedly, 'Mmmm', and, 'Delicious'.

'I hate our last days,' says Sol, finally. 'I think I hate the puffin pact. Do you think there's any chance we can have a normal relationship? I don't necessarily mean now. But you know, perhaps by this summer. Or ever.'

Addie feels her body tense.

'I'll think,' she says.

'Can I think too?' says Sol. 'Because if only you think, it feels imbalanced. Like I have no power. No say in anything. No voice. I imagine Tommie must have felt that too. But at least she had a reason. You know, a marriage and children.'

'Are you saying that I don't have a good enough reason?'

'Shall we stop this conversation?'

'Yes, I think so.'

Sunday 21st April

Addie wakes early but the robin isn't there.

'No robin!' she says. 'But Happy Easter!'

• • •

Sol opens one eye: 'What time is it?'

'Ten past'

'Did I forget the alarm? Oh shit.'

'It's OK to say Happy Easter isn't it?' says Addie, sounding nervous. 'It's the good bit.'

'I'm late. I need to get going.'

She moves towards him, and he puts his arm around her.

'I've got a special breakfast,' she says.

Sol looks at his watch.

'I don't think there's time,' he says.

'For what?'

'For anything.'

• • •

Addie climbs out of bed, and her legs feel heavy and her heart feels heavy as she goes into the kitchen, where she has a challah loaf and

yoghurt and granola and fruit and all the things that were supposed
to make a perfect farewell breakfast. She wraps what is wrappable
in foil, and it isn't a happy Easter, the pattern's gone wrong.

. . .

Sol still hasn't told her that he's handed in his notice, that he wants
to go travelling in July, that he wants her to come too. He doesn't
dare. She hands him his packed breakfast, and he pulls an envelope
out of his rucksack.

He says, 'I have something to give you. But don't read it until
I'm gone.'

Addie takes it and slips it into the pocket of her big white shirt.

Sol says, 'Are we still on *once a week* texts?'

'Does that sound OK?'

'Anything's OK as long as I know,' says Sol. 'I need to go.'

'The last kiss?' says Addie.

. . .

His car disappears through the gate. She doesn't walk inside his
tyre tracks. She makes her way to Mermaid Cottage to start the
cleaning. The envelope crunches in her pocket, but she doesn't
take it out. She's not brave enough to open it. Also, there's a lot
to do. There are new guests coming later.

. . .

Sol doesn't look back. He fills the car with petrol, and he puts
Stansted Airport into Maps. He follows the blue line. He hands
back the Fiesta, and he flies to Glasgow, and from Glasgow to
Lerwick, and onto Fair Isle, where he walks out into the dark,
wondering if Puer has come back. He can't bear Puella's loneliness,
or more particularly, he can't bear her hope, as each day, she looks
out from the cliff edge to the sea.

A voice says, 'Mr Blake.'

'Barry!'

'I knew the timings this year,' says Barry.

'Should you be out here so late?' says Sol.

'They're all at the pub. I saved you one of my Easter eggs.'

He hands Sol a creme egg.

'My favourite,' says Sol.

'I know you went to see your special friend. You know, the mermaid.'

'How did you know she was the mermaid?'

'I worked it out.'

Sol smiles at him.

'So anyway,' says Barry. 'I thought you might be sad.'

'Yes, I am a bit sad.'

'The creme egg will help,' says Barry. 'Also, Mr Blake. Puer hasn't come back. I thought you'd like a warning. Before you see Puella. She's getting very desperate out there on the Jut on her own. It's not nice to see.'

'Thank you, Barry,' says Sol. 'That was thoughtful of you.'

'I have a new baby brother,' says Sol.

'A *baby brother*?' says Barry, creasing his brow. 'You're too old to have a baby brother.'

'Turns out I'm not.'

'He's probably a mistake,' says Barry. 'Like me.'

'That's not true,' says Sol. 'No baby is a mistake.'

'My dad says.'

'Don't believe him,' says Sol. 'Grown-ups say a lot of things.'

'Dad bought me two creme eggs though,' says Barry.

'And you're giving me one of them?' says Sol. 'You should keep it.'

'I want you to have it.'

'OK,' says Sol.

'You look worried, Mr Blake.'

'I have a lot of thinking to do.'

'Sometimes I wish I could think without words,' says Barry Forfitt. 'But I can't. Can you?'

Sol pauses.

'I don't think so.'

'I love words,' says Barry Forfitt. 'But sometimes I feel like my thoughts get tangled up in them. The grief counsellor told me that pictures can help. I just thought I'd mention that. She told me to draw a picture or take a photo and think that way.'

'Thank you,' says Sol. 'I didn't know you were seeing a grief counsellor.'

'I saw her while you were away.'

'Oh that's good, Barry. I never did that.'

Barry turns.

He says, 'I hope you sleep well, Mr Blake. Happy Easter!'

'Happy Easter, Barry!'

Sol unwraps the creme egg and takes a huge bite, and as it explodes in his mouth, he watches Barry walking towards an entirely dark house.

· · ·

Addie sits on the balcony in the dark, watching the moon. She holds the envelope in her hand, but she still can't make herself open it. Number 7. Where are numbers one to six?

What might it say? Might it say that it's over? That he can't do puffin love any longer? Although hopefully not because he mentioned once-a-week texts before he left. Might she wait until tomorrow and open it then? She gets up, turns on the balcony lights and opens the envelope.

The Arch.

Here's a photo of the old arch stumps, the entrance to the monks' chapel, at once so familiar and so far away. There are primroses growing in the grass and a strange burst of light which appears to emerge from one side and curve into the next, like an echo, or a mirage, of what once was.

Except once she reads the poem, she realises that it's what she and Sol once were, or once had the potential to be, meeting so perfectly and seamlessly, arching over towards each other, and now they're a mirage too. Is that what he's saying in the poem? That her choices caused them to crumble into their separate spaces, no longer able to touch – they didn't properly touch for the last two days.

She stands up.

Surely they could meet in the middle.

That's the whole point of arches, after all.

Terrifying – she's started thinking in metaphors.

• • •

Sol, sitting on his sofa in the dark, exhausted but not sleepy, isn't sure if he should contact Addie. The cottage smells of mildew. He turns on the heating. Ping.

Help! I've started thinking in metaphors. I'm wondering if we could meet in the middle.

What does that mean?

He's already meeting her in the middle.

There's no way he's going to sleep now.

Was that her once-a-week text, and had he better reply to it now? Because if he waited, it might count as twice-a-week. He taps out possible sentences and deletes them, tap, delete, tap, delete. He won't respond. He feels angry. He has nothing further to say.

He makes his way to the Jut, which is gradually eroding – one day, the old burrow-nest will fall in the sea. The dark is very dark on Fair Isle, so he turns on the torch on his phone, and it lights up his large feet. Large feet like Tommie. Large feet like Puer who doesn't come, large feet like Puella who waits. He keeps walking. The edge of the cliff is very near. He shines his torch on it.

There is no moonlight. There is only the torchlight and his feet and the edge of the cliff, and Puella, he supposes, deep inside her burrow, not coming out, hoping and trusting and not knowing.

He sits and he stays and he tries out sentences which he deletes, and the dark lightens, long hour by long hour, into the dawn. Puella comes out from the depths of her burrow and she stands at the entrance.

And what can he do and what can he say?

He says, 'I know, I know, I know.'

He says, 'He'll come, he'll come.'

And then he says, 'I can't promise that, Puella.'

Then Barry Forfitt comes by.

'Did you sleep well?' says Barry.

'I was here. I didn't sleep. My thoughts were tangling up in words, like you said.'

'Bad luck.'

'Thanks.'

'She's not going out to sea to fish,' says Barry. 'Do you think she'll die of loneliness?'

'I don't think you can die of loneliness,' say Sol.

'I do,' says Barry.

Maybe you can, thinks Sol, and he watches Barry, with his striped silk scarf wrapped around his neck, heading down the path and standing looking out to sea.

Saturday 25th May

Sol is coming today for Half-Term.

Addie has Mermaid Cottage ready for the new guests.

The plumber came yesterday and installed the toilet and the sink and the shower in the ambulance, but it's not quite ready to show him. She wants it completely finished.

Her phone rings.

• • •

At Glasgow Airport, Sol sees that Addie has texted.

You're not going to believe this, but I have to head to Durham. I am so so sorry. Sydney's in hospital. I hope you understand. I'll be back as soon as I can. xx

He puts his head in his hands over the plastic table and he knocks his coffee over. He gathers himself, dries his thighs with a wad of napkins and tells himself to be reasonable.

He replies: Of course. What's happened?

But she doesn't reply.

He boards the plane, and when he arrives in Stansted, his phone pings.

He was found unconscious. He has a drink problem. Has done

for a while. They've all been hiding this from me. Will keep you posted. I'm so sorry. I left the keys under the rock. xx

Sol keeps going, and she doesn't keep him posted. He arrives at Stansted, picks up a white Ford Fiesta, throws away the air freshener and stops at The New Inn where he eats chicken and chips on his own, not knowing what to do with his disappointment. Here he is in Horning and she's not here because Sydney has a drink problem, which he would mind about if he was a nice person.

When he gets to the gate of Mermaid Cottage, he can't go in, no, he can't stay if she's not there, so he keeps driving to The Amusements, where he pulls back the metal fence and lets himself in. He knocks at the door, before putting his key in the door.

'Tommie, it's me,' he calls.

Tommie comes out, blearily, in his pyjamas and hugs him.

'Go back to bed,' he says.

'Everything OK?' says Tommie.

'Addie's had to go to Durham. Her brother's in hospital.'

'Is it serious?'

'I'm not sure. We'll know more in the morning.'

. . .

Addie picks up the phone, whispering to Sol from her sofabed so as not to wake her parents.

'My parents assumed I knew about his problems, that's what Dad said. He's going to be OK, though. He just overdid it.'

'You've seen him?'

'No, he doesn't want to see me, but I'm making food for them to take him. The food is shit at the hospital apparently.'

. . .

'That doesn't sound very grateful,' says Sol.

She doesn't answer.

'Is it worth being there if he won't see you?'

401

'I'm supporting my parents.'
'Could they support each other just while I'm here?'
'I'm sure I can come soon.'
'Am I being selfish?' says Sol. 'I probably am.'

Sunday 26th May

Addie wakes, wanting Sol so badly it hurts her stomach. She packs the cool bag with food for the day, before making a cup of tea for her mother and father, which she takes to them in bed. They don't say thank you.

• • •

Sol wakes early, checks his watch – seven o'clock – and he thinks it's too early to text her. He lets himself out of the door of the caravan, and there's Tommie, standing in his swimming shorts, dripping. Sol can't stop looking at the grey hair which runs in a line from the top of his faded old swimming shorts, spreading into fronds around his nipples – there really is no mistaking the palm tree shape of it.

Now he finds that he's looking at the long trunk of Tommie's body, his long narrow feet, his long arms, his long legs, his concave stomach – and his brain is struggling to catch up with his eyes.

'Are you OK?' says Tommie, peering at him. 'Do we have news from the hospital?'

'He's going to be OK,' says Sol. 'No, it's not that. It's just *your body.*'

'My *body*?' says Tommie looking down, confused.

'I mean let's start with your chest.'

'My *chest*?'

'I mean, perhaps it's better if I show you mine,' says Sol.

'Your what?'

'My chest,' says Sol.

'I'm not quite sure where you're going with this.'

'You will be,' says Sol. 'You will be.'

Sol holds his T-shirt up.

Tommie stares at Sol's chest.

'Chest-wise,' says Sol. 'It looks like there's *something going on* here, Tommie. We have the same palm trees.'

'Palm trees?'

'Look!'

Sol traces his chest hair.

'We have the same bodies, Tommie. Your suit fits me. Am I on the right track here?'

'Your mother and I—'

'She's not here any more, Tommie,' says Sol. 'But we are.'

Tommie looks up at the sky, as if maybe she is here, listening, but she can't be, that couldn't be heaven – eavesdropping on other people's conversations about you. No, that would be hell. Tommie opens his arms the way he did when Sol first met him, and they stay there embracing, as if this is something both of them have wanted for a very long time, perhaps twenty-eight years even.

'Tommie,' says Sol. 'Is this really true? Is it real, what I'm seeing? Are you—'

'We decided not to say for the sake of your father, but whether that was the right decision, I—'

'Not my sisters though?' says Sol.

Tommie shakes his head.

'They came along in the two years we broke it off. Look at them. They're the image of your father.'

'Do you have any other—'
Tommie shakes his head.
'I'm your only one? *Your only child?*'
Tommie nods.
'So I'm, unequivocally, your favourite?' says Sol.
'You are,' says Tommie.
It feels so good.
Even now.
So late in the day.

Tuesday 28th May

'Do you think Sydney will ever let me visit?' Addie asks her mother
and father, all sitting in a line on the large sofa of her father's small
terraced house.

'He loves your food,' says her father.

'Yes, he said thank you for the food,' says her mother.

'Did he really?' says Addie.

'I'm sure he did,' says her mother.

Which means she isn't.

'You know what,' says Addie. 'I'll stock the freezer, and then I
think I should head back, in the next day or so.'

'What? Leave us?' says her mother.

'You have each other,' says Addie. 'And he's going to be OK.
But like I said, he needs proper help. There's not much point me
being here if he doesn't want to—'

'He will eventually,' says her mother.

'And if he does, I'll come back,' says Addie. 'It would be good
for us to spend some time together. We don't really know each
other, do we? We haven't lived together since he was nine. But
that's up to him.'

Her mother opens her mouth, and Addie expects her to start

blaming her father for leaving the island, but she doesn't. She closes her mouth, which is startling.

'The thing is', says Addie, 'someone's come to visit me at The Boathouse. He's been waiting for me since Saturday.'

'Oooh,' says her mother. 'Do we have a love interest?'

'Was he the man I met?' says her father.

'Well, you didn't exactly meet him,' says Addie.

'I can't believe you didn't tell me, Peter,' says her mother. She looks at Addie.

'What's he like?' she says.

'He's lovely,' says Addie. 'A bit too lovely.'

'Is it going to last?'

'I'm not sure.'

'Why aren't you sure?'

'I don't know if I'm brave enough for love.'

'I never thought you'd meet anyone,' says her mother. 'But you're definitely much less odd these days.'

She still doesn't hear her.

'I'll take that as a compliment,' says Addie.

'I think your mother meant it nicely,' says her father.

'I thought you must have met someone,' says her mother. 'You look different.'

Addie smiles at her mother.

'You look pretty, Addie,' she says.

Her mother has said she looks pretty.

● ● ●

Sol sits in his socks in Leah and Alan's sitting room, his long feet surrounded by small Lego bricks and children, with Rachel and Hamish, because Leah has called a family summit.

'It's about Tommie the bird warden,' says Leah. 'Dad has now told all of us about the *affair*.'

Nobody speaks.

407

Leah says, 'I can't believe Tommie did that to us as a family.'

'It was Mum's choice too,' says Sol.

'And she made a vow,' says Leah.

'So did Dad,' says Sol. 'He vowed not to treat her horribly.'

'I mean,' says Rachel. 'Perhaps it was a Charles and Diana situation. Mum and Dad just weren't meant for each other.'

Hamish puts his hand on Rachel's thigh and pats it.

'All done then?' he says.

Thursday 30th May

Addie lets Sol through the gate.

She gets off her bike.

He gets out of the car.

She feels the strange nerves of their first hug.

He opens his arms, and she falls into them.

It feels good.

• • •

'I have so much to tell you,' says Sol. 'Let's go to the pub.'

'We never go to the pub.'

'Let's start.'

• • •

At the pub, Addie tells Sol that Sydney is going to be OK, but he won't go on being OK without help.

'Oddly, Mum, Dad, and I all agreed on that. It's the first thing we've agreed on in a long time. Possibly ever.'

'But Sydney still didn't want to see you?'

'I realise that we don't know each other,' says Addie. 'I want to change that, but he needs to want to too. How was everyone?'

'Alan was more bearable today, and Rachel feels different somehow, with Hamish,' says Sol.

'Mum said I was much less odd these days. And I decided to take it as a compliment,' says Addie, laughing.

'Then you're a saint,' says Sol.

'Then she really pushed the boat out and said I looked pretty.'

'How did it feel?'

'Unnerving.'

• • •

Sol returns with a second beer for him, and a second glass of wine for Addie.

'I feel a bit bad about drinking now I see the mess Sydney's in,' says Addie.

'I don't think you need to take on his issue,' says Sol.

'I've always had enough of my own.'

'You look beautiful tonight,' says Sol.

They hold out their glasses to each other.

'To Poem 7!' says Addie.

Sol feels shy.

He wants to ask her lots of questions about Poem 7, but he doesn't.

'Let's agree not to crumble!' says Addie.

'I found something out when you were away.'

'Something big?'

'I found out that Dad isn't my father.'

'What?'

'I have a new one. A much better one. One I love already.'

Addie takes a sip of wine and says, 'Can I guess who?'

Sol nods.

'I'm really hoping it's Tommie. Am I right?'

He nods.

'Can I meet him while you're here?'

'I'd love you to.'

Friday 31st May

'Take off your flippers,' says Addie, and Sol casts them onto the
swimming platform. 'Now go!'

He goes.

He floats.

Without flippers.

'You did it!'

. . .

Sol leaps out of the water with his arms in the air, and for a moment
he feels like one of the enthusiastic teenagers on his father's summer
camps, which is most, most out of character.

But he did it.

He did it!

She did it.

Obviously.

'You taught me to swim!' he says.

'You taught me to dance!' she says.

. . .

'It really is the most heavenly day,' says Addie. 'If only it wasn't your last.'

'Let's do a Tromso,' says Sol. 'Today is the only day. Let's walk along the river.'

They walk to the elbow bend where there are no longer tadpoles and no sign of frogs, alive or dead. The mallards are smug and coupley and hungry. They walk for miles. There are boats out on the river: families on cruisers for Half-Term, yachts tacking into their path. They lie in the sun and take their shoes off. They buy ice creams with flakes in from a van and walk back past the creek to the garden.

'Let's sit on the jetty for the last time,' says Addie.

'Don't say the last time,' says Sol.

'Let's see if Little Hen is about.'

Then she gasps.

It's Little Hen, but she's not alone.

She's sailing along beside a mate.

In a pair.

'Oh my word!' says Addie, and she feels strangely discombobulated, as if this change of circumstances is an affront, or a question, or a challenge to her.

'Man Hen!' says Addie, a little crossly. 'Where've you appeared from?'

• • •

Little Hen looks chirpy, arguably *chirpier than when she was alone.*

But Sol won't say this.

He'll think of something less controversial.

Addie is staring at the moorhen pair with her forehead crumpled

'The only male to be called a hen, the male moorhen. I never noticed,' says Sol.

Addie doesn't reply.

They sit together and watch Little Hen and Man Hen dabbling

at the edge of the river, a passing cruiser washing over the tree roots, to which they cling, very effectively, with their super-power feet. Then they settle on the bank together, huddled up.

Sol decides to take a risk.

He takes Addie's hand.

'Look at them,' he says. 'Just look at them.'

Saturday 1st June

The alarm goes off at five o'clock because Addie knew she couldn't take another rushed departure. She feels mortified by how little time they've had together. She isn't sure she needed to go to Durham at all. It's yet another wrong decision. She thinks of Little Hen with her *partner*. It still feels wrong. She feels wrong inside.

• • •

Sol puts his rucksack in the car and goes back upstairs. He hasn't told Addie that this is his last half-term at school, and he still hasn't invited her to come nomadding with him.

'I'll come to Fair Isle in July,' says Addie, looking at her diary. 'It's my turn, and I promise to come this time. It will have to be late July as I've got a load of weddings, and then there's a gap. After the 27th July, and before the 17th August . . .'

All these dates.

All these numbers.

He can't be bothered with them.

'Actually, I think I should be back for the final fitting on say the 13th, and then there'll be bookings at Mermaid Cottage to think about too.'

414

More numbers!

'This doesn't work,' says Sol.

He sees her face whiten.

'We work, but this doesn't work,' he clarifies. 'I don't think I can keep recovering.'

. . .

'Don't say that,' says Addie.

'It's just true,' says Sol. 'We aren't puffins. Or I'm not.'

'I'm sure it can work,' says Addie, taking his cold hand. 'It's just I don't think I could come and live on Fair Isle. I hate islands, for a start, and there'd be no brides wanting dresses, and I've just got this business started.'

'I get that,' says Sol. 'But I'm not going to live on Fair Isle either. I've never found the right moment to tell you. I resigned at Christmas when I got snowed in.'

'So when do you leave?'

'At the end of term.'

'And then?'

. . .

'I'm hoping to get around to that nomadding tour,' says Sol.

He wants to say, Come with me. Drop everything and come with me.

But he doesn't.

'I can't believe it.'

'I didn't tell you because I didn't want to scare you by being so free and available.'

'There's been a lot against us.'

'I suppose the thing we need to decide is whether *we're* against us. Or for us.'

'I sent you a text about meeting in the middle, but you never answered.'

'I'm already meeting you in the middle, aren't I?' says Sol. 'I have been since we met.'

Sol looks at his watch.

'Forgive me,' he says. 'This is the worst possible moment for this conversation.'

'I think you leaving the school will be good for the puffin pact,' says Addie. 'It'll give us more flexibility if you don't have term dates.'

He can't help himself.

He says, 'Do you think there's anything you could do that would be good for us?'

Then he has to leave.

. . .

Addie throws open the windows at Mermaid Cottage to the dewy morning, trying to hold herself together. She unbuttons the white duvet cover in the green room and pulls it off, throwing it into the corner. She removes the first white pillowcase, the second, and the third, and the fourth, gritting her teeth. She sees that the green cushion covers have been spattered with coffee – which is irritating – so she takes them off too. She moves to the blue room, where the guests seem to have had a fight with a Times newspaper: double pages are spread all around the room and over the bed, where the newsprint has blackened the white Egyptian cotton.

Addie picks up the first double-page spread, still gritting her teeth, feeling the threat of something in her belly, rising up her throat.

Notices of engagements.

Of marriages.

Of births.

Of deaths.

She sits on the floor and reads each one of them. Each announcement is so small, and so repetitive, and unoriginal, she thinks, and life's stories are, yes, so small and repetitive and unoriginal, yet when you're living your version, it comes to her, your version is enormous.

She wants to call Sol and tell him that. But no, not now. She never saw his life on Fair Isle, and now he's planning a new one without her. He didn't ask her to come with him. Of course he didn't. It's entirely her fault. She missed the moment. She must get on and finish the ambulance, which will be the perfect present at the perfect time, she tells herself.

His last question seemed so angry, but his anger doesn't need to affect her, that's the whole point. She's OK. She will regather herself. But instead of regathering herself, she gathers up the double-page spreads, and as she does so, she is shaken by sobs. She wipes her face with her hands, but the tears keep coming and don't seem to stop. When she goes into the bathroom, she sees that the newsprint has transferred itself onto the skin of her face: she is covered in engagements and marriages and births and deaths.

• • •

Sol pulls in at a garage and takes out his phone.

I'm heading for the airport and I'm thinking about you, Addie. I hate goodbyes and I miss you already. I'm very sorry about what I said and how I said it, but I know I can't be a puffin any longer. Maybe Tommie could. I want us to be moorhens, dabbling around at the edges together day in day out. What's it's to be, Addie? Puffin or moorhen? xx

He hesitates. He has to get to the airport. He presses send. What a risk he's taking, but he's done it now. He leaves the garage and heads for the airport.

If she opts for puffin, will he say it's over? Will he say, *it's moorhen or nothing*? He thinks he might have to, but it sounds quite ridiculous.

Everything ends, he thinks, *but even if it ends, you once had it.*
That's the thing to hold on to.
They once had it.
It was perfect.
Maybe if you hold it too long, it stops being perfect anyhow.

• • •

Addie walks by the river, where there are gold marsh marigolds, purple violets, pale yellow primroses and starry white-petalled wood anemones, their centres tiny suns. She goes back and sits on the balcony eating breadsticks, one after another, until she's finished the packet. She goes inside for more snacks. She eats two large bags of crisps. A glass of wine. Another and another. She keeps eating and she keeps drinking. She wonders if alcoholism is hereditary: if Sydney somehow caught it from Grandpa Fred, if she could catch it too.

She speaks T S Eliot's words – the first chorus – into the darkness. She finds the words come easily to her, as she strains to see the shape of her future. When the first chorus is done, she starts on the last, the great outburst of praise for the earth and all living things within it, and as she speaks the words, she hears *kup kup kup.* So late at night?

'Little Hen,' she says. 'What's up?'

She peers into the dark water.

'Where's Man Hen?' she says to her. 'You're on your own again!'

And she wonders if Little Hen's a metaphor, or would she be a symbol – Sol tried to explain the difference to her, but she can't quite remember what it is.

• • •

Sol walks out of the terminal, and he realises he's looking for Barry Forfitt. But Barry isn't here. He takes the long route past Barry's cottage, and it's dark. He calls into the pub, which he never does. Barry's father isn't there. As he walks with his large rucksack on his back and his small rucksack on his front, he checks his phone.

He should never have reacted as he did, and he should never have given her such a binary choice. Puffins or moorhens. There's no way out of that. There's no half-puffin-half-moorhen. No middle ground. Tommie never gave his mother an ultimatum for that reason.

He lets himself into his dark cottage and climbs into bed, but he can't stop looking at his phone. The hours pass. It's two in the morning, and she hasn't answered. He wonders what he'd do if she never answered.

He puts his black anorak over his pyjamas and heads to the Jut. He shines his torch out over the sea but it only lights up the edge of the cliff. Beyond the lit edge, there is nothing. He feels the blackness hovering over the sea. He thinks it's about to swoop in on him again. He must think of all the good things that are waiting for him in the future.

She hasn't answered, so there are no good things. If there's no Addie in his future, how could the future in any way be good? The blackness is blowing towards him. There will be good things, he tells himself again and again, it's just you can't see them right now. Order, disorder, reorder. Love, death, rebirth. Round we go and round. Little deaths. Little resurrections.

He can't hear Puella in her burrow. Perhaps Puer came back and she finally laid her egg, although it's far too late in the year.

'Puella,' he whispers.

'Puer,' he whispers.

There's no sound.

If she's laid her egg, he doesn't want to disturb or discomfit her by shining his torch into the burrow, so he will sit here and hope.

· · ·

419

Addie can't sleep.

She takes out her phone again and again, staring at his message.

Puffin or moorhen?

Which is it to be?

He wants an answer.

It's very stressful.

He doesn't know that Little Hen's on her own again.

• • •

Sol sits in silence on the Jut beside the burrow.

Sunday 2nd June

As the sky starts to lighten, Addie still hasn't slept.

• • •

Sol is on the Jut when his phone pings.

He can't bear to look. If she says puffin, is it really over? He takes a deep breath and pulls his phone from his pocket.

Dearest Sol, The monks made me get a mobile phone, though nobody yet has my number. You're on my mind. I wonder if the grief's getting any easier, two years on.

Sol still feels bad about killing off his father. He has a vivid memory of the tiled vicarage hall: his father's looking into the mirror, adjusting his dog collar. He's clenching his jaw, as he always did. And Sol sees it for the first time: the man was only just holding himself together.

I've always wondered if dying is the peak of it all, odd though that sounds. If death is life spilling out into a fullness we can't quite imagine from here. I wonder if death, whether physical or psychological – our own or someone else's – makes us into a new shape. This can be true both for the one who dies (who gains a new form) and also for the one who grieves (who undergoes a transformation). Thomas Keating, the Trappist monk, said something along these lines. I hope you find this comforting. My love to you, A.

Sol would have done anything to stop his mother dying, but her death has shaped him, as her life did. His grief for her has shaped him, as his love for her did. We want to choose life over death, but there is no life without death – they're one – and we want to choose love over grief, but they too are one.

A continuum.

· · ·

Addie texts Sol.

Little Hen is on her own again.

· · ·

Sol won't reply.

He doesn't want to know what she means by that.

He looks inside the burrow.

Puella is lying on her side.

· · ·

Addie goes out to the balcony.

She thinks, *I'm not strong enough for love.*

Ping.

It's Sol.

Nothing saves you from grief except not being alive.

· · ·

Sol goes to the fish stall in the harbour, and returns to the Jut with a large hake.

Barry is sitting by the burrow.

He says, 'Is she dying, Mr Blake?'

'I don't know, Barry,' says Sol, though he does know.

'I left her fish when I went away,' says Barry. 'But she didn't eat any of it.'

Sol crouches down and puts the hake inside the burrow next to her bill, but Puella doesn't move. Sol puts his hand on her velvet feathers, and she's still warm, and her heart is still beating.

'Where did you go for your holiday, Barry?'

'It wasn't a holiday. I had to go to the mainland to see my new school.'

'How was it?'

'I didn't really like it.'

'I'm sorry,' says Sol.

'At least you're leaving too,' says Barry.

'Everything changes.'

'But will you come to see me when you don't live here anymore?'

'I will, Barry.'

'Will you take a photo of us,' says Barry. 'You and me together while you're still here and Puella's still alive. Shall we carry her out of the burrow?'

'I don't think so,' says Sol. 'Let's just know she's with us even if we can't see her.'

Sol takes a selfie: his long arm, his shoulder, his own face, and Barry's face, and the burrow behind them.

• • •

Ping!

Oh look, a photo from Sol: his long arm with the blue sleeve pulled up to the elbow. Addie enlarges the photo, zoning in on his lovely face, and there's a boy with him, she's pretty sure that's Barry Forfitt, who he often speaks of, oh look at him, with his curled auburn hair.

If I had a son, thinks Addie.

She stops herself.

If I had a son, she thinks, *I would love him, and I would suffer for him, and I wouldn't keep him, like a keeper.*

She gets dressed and heads for the jetty. As she crosses the lawn, she can see Little Hen, alone and chirpy, scratching at the edges of the river, happy as anything, bold and strong, with her *excellent long clawed non-webbed* feet keeping her balanced over the roots.

But look!

No, she isn't alone – isn't that Man Hen? There he is, a foot away, just behind the tree root. She hurries over to the river to get a closer look.

• • •

Sol sits beside the burrow and he prays for Puella. His father (who isn't his father) would say it's ridiculous to pray for a puffin, would say that there are no animals in heaven. His mother would disagree, and so would Francis of Assisi, and so would his father who is his father, he's pretty sure about that.

Ping!

Addie?

It's a photo of Addie on the jetty, and she's pointing to Little Hen and Man Hen and eight balls of black fluff with red bills, so small you could cup each one in the palm of your hand, and she's written underneath: *Weird gorgeous things.*

And then she's written: *Like us.*

With a laughing emoji.

Is this photo supposed to be her answer? Or is it simply a photo to show him that Man Hen is back with Little Hen and they've had babies?

What he sees is: *us.*

Such a small, humble word.

• • •

Addie reverses the ambulance out of the barn so that she can access her painting cupboard. She walks across the lawn holding her easel and a palette, with a rucksack of paints and brushes on her back. Her heart is racing.

There are crocuses growing through the grass: white and purple and yellow. She sets up the easel on the jetty, and goes back for a chair.

. . .

Sol wants to reply saying, 'What exactly does this mean?'

And then, ping.

A film of Addie.

She starts off on the jetty, with her easel set out, ready (he supposes) to paint the moorhens on the river, and behind her there are crocuses growing through the grass, and beyond in the drive is a large white van, and she is walking over the lawn towards the van, like the scene he imagined when he was lying in the grass on Rokesby two years ago because his mother told him that it's hard to have a life we can't imagine, that our future begins in our own mind.

The white van has bees painted on its doors.

Bees!

Addie's voice says, 'I made this for you. It's an old ambulance. I've been getting it prepared for the big nomadding tour. There's a map of Europe in the glovebox. I was planning to show you it when it was completely ready, but I've changed my mind. I want you to see what I've done so far.'

Sol looks at the rustic wood panelling, and the counter tops and the lockers made out of crates, and the blue and white Moroccan tiles behind the sink, and the taps made of antique brass, and the mugs on hooks, and the pans on hooks, and the hand-made wooden cupboards and drawers with tiny latches.

'I still need to get the oven and the hob and the fridge,' says Addie. 'They'll be coming soon.'

He looks at the shower room with a real stand-up shower and

Addie flushes the loo (a flushing loo!), and she pulls the fold-out table and shows him the bench seat and the huge frame of the bed.

'I haven't done the curtains or the bedcovers yet,' says Addie. 'There'll be lots of pillows. Like Tromso. I hope you like it.'

The film ends.

Even if it's over, look what she did for him. Even if he doesn't have her, he'll have the van as proof that she must have loved him. She must have really loved him to make him a van like this.

Sol can hardly breathe. He picks up his phone, and he says, 'Addie, you're a genius. It's beautiful. It's even better than Peggy.'

'I'm glad you like it.'

'Thank you feels inadequate.'

'Like sorry felt inadequate when I crashed the first one,' she says.

Then there's silence.

'What are you doing right now?' says Sol.

'I'm sketching the moorhens.'

He prepares his mouth to ask the question, but his mouth says, 'I'll leave you to it.'

Perhaps she's simply *sketching the moorhens*.

Perhaps it doesn't mean anything.

She doesn't like metaphors.

• • •

Addie sketches the moorhens in different groupings and positions, and her mind can't quite acclimatise to such an extraordinary change in Little Hen's circumstances. Little Hen walks over the roots towards the easel and she stands beside Addie's feet, and she looks up at her. Her ducklings follow and stand around her.

'Very good!' says Addie. 'Very good, Little Hen.'

Little Hen doesn't move.

She keeps looking up at her.

• • •

Barry comes back from the beach, and he sits beside Sol.

They both look out to sea, but neither of them speak.

Then Sol says, 'You know, a very wise man just wrote to me and he told me that death changes us, the person who dies and the person left behind. The person who dies gains a new form.'

'Do you really believe that? That my mum is somewhere?'

'I do.'

They are both quiet for a moment.

'But the person who grieves gains a new form too. I'm a very different shape now from the shape I was when my mother died. But the thing is this, Barry, though I'd have done anything to stop her dying, I like my new shape much more than my old one. Your loss will make you even more extraordinary.'

'I can't imagine being extraordinary,' says Barry.

'You are already,' says Sol.

Sol remembers his mother saying that God comes to us disguised as our life, and a great peace seems to descend on him.

Here is his life.

His life is a grieving boy called Barry Forfitt; and a puffin called Puella who's leaving behind her body; and a woman in heaven who believed in thin places; and a man in a caravan who turns out to be his father; and a man in a vicarage who turns out not to be; and an old ambulance made from love – very imperfect love, but powerful nonetheless – with blue and white Moroccan tiles behind the sink and bees on the door; and a young woman called Addie Finch who's sitting painting moorhens beside the river, which might mean everything, or might mean nothing at all.

And here and now, inside it all, the joy and the pain, the life and the death, the past and the future, the knowing and the not knowing, here, quite unmistakably, is God.

• • •

As Addie draws the moorhens, she feels a strange sensation, as if something is happening inside her aching belly, as if something is moving, something is giving, something that was hard and solid is *melting.*

She thinks of her antique Russian dolls, once again on her bedside table. It's that tiny doll who shrunk to the size of a kidney bean and sunk to the depths of her when Grandma Flora died, that tiny doll who lay fossilised in hardened love, unable to breathe or move.

She's waking up.

Addie puts down her pencil and she closes her eyes.

She feels the doll stretching out her toes and her fingers, shaking her hair, filling up with air as she pushes against the hard carapace around her, which strains as she grows bigger and bigger, much bigger now than the good doll or the bad doll or the sea doll. These doll-selves now crack and rupture to allow her through, and she's climbing out, blinking her eyes at the spring sunshine.

• • •

Sol hardly dares look at his phone.

Something is coming through.

Slowly, slowly, slowly, an image is revealing itself on his phone.

The pencil outlines of Little Hen and Man Hen and their duck-lings on Addie's canvas on the easel, waiting to be filled with colour and texture and depth.

I've chosen, Sol. xx

It must mean what he thinks it means.

Mustn't it?

Sol picks up his phone and starts to text her his reply.

• • •

Addie is mixing paint on the jetty when she hears her phone.

She smiles and keeps mixing the paint, and the reeds blow, and her phone pings again, and she doesn't look at Sol's answer, enjoying the anticipation in her bowels, the deep thrill of not knowing exactly what he's said yet, not knowing what's to come.

. . .

Sol takes his book from his pocket, and then his pen, and he writes on his word list: *Us.* It comes to him that this will be the final word on his list. His shortest and most powerful ever. No more lists. No more semi-colons.

Full stop.

The End.

Us.

Perhaps not full stop, but colon, the colon he saw through the glass window of the chapel on Rokesby two years ago, the colon being an open gate, an indicator of a whole series of elements that will amplify and illustrate what precedes it. The rest of his life, however long or short it is – none of us knows and we must live without guarantees – is coming, and it's coming with Addie inside it.

Us:

He closes his book on a colon, with a future beyond it.

He's broken the rules of grammar for the first time in his life.

Who knows what other rules he might now break?

Who knows what it is that will amplify and illustrate their joined existence?

But whatever will come beyond the colon, he's hungry for it.

Ravenous.

Grateful.

And utterly ready.

Saturday 31st August

Sol opens the back doors of the ambulance, on which there are four large painted bees, and he climbs onto the huge bed, propping himself up with Addie among the pillows.

They've been travelling for a month already. They made their way down through England, stopping off at Canterbury Cathedral, tourists trampling on holy ground, and they stood on the stone slabs where Archbishop Thomas was murdered in 1170, and whispered the last chorus under their breath, affirming, or at least accepting, the painful beauty of life's patterns.

They trundled happily through the length of France, and they drank wine and ate warm baguettes and cheese, and made up their route as they went along, passing through Lourdes, and into Spain, through Zaragoza to Lorca's Granada, to his birthplace in Fuente Vaqueros, to the house at number 4 Trinidad Street where the poplar trees spoke to each other in the wind. And on to Níjar, to recite *Blood Wedding* in the ruins of the dilapidated farmhouse from where the original bride eloped on her wedding day with her cousin, choosing, said Sol, to be true, though not necessarily right. Addie said that true turned out to be so much better in the end, whatever you have to give up.

'Being right', said Sol, 'is so tiring.'

And he thought of his father, and hoped he would become less right in time.

They drove along the coast, through Málaga, to Tarifa, the southernmost point of Europe, below which the world now hovers, unknown to them, waiting for them.

Addie doesn't mind that Star is cross with her because making someone cross is almost certainly the consequence of being true, and she doesn't mind that she won't be making wedding dresses for a while because she's given up something valuable for something else valuable.

Addie leans against Sol on the bed, watching the last kitesurfer of the day flying over the waves, beneath the revelatory moon. They stare out across the Straits of Gibraltar to the continent of Africa, to the lights coming on in clusters in dark villages under the hills.

Tomorrow they will catch the ferry to Tangiers:

They wait, as we must all wait, for tomorrow.

Tomorrow, they'll set sail beyond the colon.

ACKNOWLEDGEMENTS

To all those who have given their time, gifts and skills to Sol and Addie's story, my deep gratitude. To my exceptional agent, Susan Armstrong, by my side in unwavering support and partnership since 2017, championing both me and my books, and knowing the answers to all questions, on any subject. To two talented and insightful editors who are also deeply kind human beings: Carla Josephson, who set out with me, and Suzie Dooré, with whom I crossed the finishing line. All three of you are wonderful human beings and skilled professionals who draw out the best in me and my words.

My thanks to Ellie Game for designing a cover of quite extraordinary wonder. To Nicolette Caven for moving the islands of Rokesby and Ora from my imagination to the page in the gorgeous, evocative map. To Jabin Ali, for tending the novel with great love and attention to detail. To Vicky Joss and Maud Davies for sending it into the world, and into the hands of readers, with such skill and care. To the readers who make the book live again and again and again. To Eva Tarnok for taking my photo with her usual flair and patience. My sincere thanks also to Suzannah V. Evans, who gave her permission for me to use her beautiful poem, 'Puffin, The Little Hillyard', which inspired the book's title.

435

I've dedicated this book to my father and brother, who taught me to love birds. I was not an ideal pupil.

My first memories of birdwatching are on the Norfolk Broads, where my family used to go for a week each Easter, staying on a boat, mooring up in different broads each night. In cold springs, the condensation froze on the windows, so we slept in bobble hats. I have a photo, taken by my father, which shows my late mother, my brother and me sitting at the sunny stern of our favourite ever boat, *Gwendaline*. My brother is in full waterproofs and a lifejacket, just back from sailing. I have a pen in my hand and am writing a story in an exercise book. I must be seven years old.

'Marsh harrier!' shouts my father. Everyone looks up. I don't look up. I go on writing.

'I've seen one before,' I say, slightly bored. 'Last year.'

This is not the right attitude for a birdwatcher (though perhaps shows promise for a writer).

My long-suffering father let me be, and I came round to birds. Now the trees in my little garden are hung with sunflower hearts and suet balls, and I don't care how many times I see the gold-finches, they still make me look up.

To all the people in my life who've taught me to look up and see the beauty even when the world is ugly, thank you. There are too many of you to name, but I couldn't have written this story without you. My father taught me to love the natural world by loving it, himself. It was the gift he gave us as a family. Those who loved me first also loved birds and trees and streams and sky, so the two loves are forever bound together, as they are for Sol and Addie.

What is given to us we pass on. With Mark, I've watched thirty-five years of flaming sunsets and impossible stars from the same beach in El Palmar. When Charlie and Nina were born, we put them on a plane, and two became four. We're still on the beach watching, though four has now become six. I couldn't be more grateful to all of you for what you've taught me.

Author's Note

I feel a particular connection with the Norfolk Broads, the place of so many happy childhood holidays afloat. We called the little island on Hickling Broad 'Miss Turner's Island', though I see it is more properly known as Turner's Island. It always had a special but indefinable feeling about it and became one of the novel's thin places.

I love a pioneering woman. Emma Louise Turner, born in 1867, took up bird photography in 1901, giving illustrated talks for the Royal Photographic Society and becoming a professional lecturer by 1908. Her 1911 image of a bittern in Norfolk was the first evidence of the species' return to the UK as a breeding bird after its local extinction in the late nineteenth century. For twenty-five years, she spent part of the year at Hickling Broad, staying on her own houseboat. She also owned a hut with a photographic darkroom and a spare bedroom on her island, to which I've added a fictional hide and jetty.

I have taken such liberties throughout the novel, mixing real places with fictional ones from the start. This means that while we really can sit watching the northern lights beside an icy fjord in Tromso, we sadly can't cross the bridge from Rokesby to Ora with Addie, except in our imaginations.

The fictional Peggy is inspired by a real Peggy the campervan, Stone House by a real house, but neither bear any resemblance to their namesakes.